His heart quickened. He caught the light rush of her breathing and the musky scent of her perfume. She was so close, he could feel the electric press of air between them. But suddenly, she stopped.

Gallatin's breath snagged. He must not turn until she asked him to. What were a few seconds compared to the lifetime they would share together?

But what was she waiting for? A suffocating tension filled his chest. The trapped breath escaped him in a rush.

At last, she stepped closer. He felt the silken press of her lips at the back of his neck. Her voice was a breeze. "You can look now, Simon. Look. I want you to."

Simon Gallatin turned slowly, the smile forming on his lips. But it froze in a grotesque grimace as he saw what had been planned for him.

Her surprise was the shock of his life. And it was to be the last one.

Also by
JUDITH KELMAN

IF I SHOULD DIE
THE HOUSE ON THE HILL
SOMEONE'S WATCHING
HUSH LITTLE DARLINGS
WHILE ANGELS SLEEP
WHERE SHADOWS FALL
PRIME EVIL

Coming Soon:
MORE THAN YOU KNOW

ONE LAST KISS

JUDITH KELMAN

BANTAM BOOKS

NEW YORK • TORONTO • LONDON • SYDNEY • AUCKLAND

ONE LAST KISS
A Bantam Book/November 1994

All rights reserved.

ISBN 0-553-56272-X

Published simultaneously in the United States and Canada

Bantam Books are published by Bantam Books, a division of Bantam Doubleday Dell
Publishing Group, Inc. Its trademark, consisting of the words "Bantam Books" and the
portrayal of a rooster, is Registered in U.S. Patent and Trademark Office and in other
countries. Marca Registrada. Bantam Books, 1540 Broadway, New York, New York
10036.

PRINTED IN THE UNITED STATES OF AMERICA

OPM   0 9 8 7 6 5 4 3 2 1

For Matt and Josh Kelman, the new men in my life, with abundant love and abiding pride.

For their generous input, thanks to Dr. William Theodore of the National Institutes of Health, Assistant U.S. Attorney Peter A. Clark, and Brian Thompson of the Philip Kingsley Thrichological Center.

As always, I am grateful for the solid, splendid support of my agent, Peter Lampack, and my editor, Kate Miciak.

THE
FIRST

CHAPTER ONE

The front door was propped open. Simon Gallatin slipped inside and stole across the shadow-webbed foyer to the den.

Flaming embers crackled in the hearth. By the wavering firelight, he scanned the silent room. On the coffee table was a wineglass smudged with lipstick and a photo album laid open on its spine. A Navajo blanket nestled in the crook of the sofa's padded arm.

No sign of her.

Listening hard, Gallatin caught the clack of dripping water overhead and the drone of a radio announcer. He pictured her soaking upstairs in a bubble-capped tub, her skin flushed and glistening. He imagined shedding his clothes and slipping into the water beside her. Engulfing warmth, slippery flesh. There was an exquisite quickening in his groin.

Straightening his tie, Gallatin perched stiffly on the sofa, wove his fingers together, and stared at the dying fire. Soon, her face materialized in the flames. He envisioned the haunting copper-flecked eyes, the sculpted cheeks and stubborn chin, the rich spill of auburn curls that framed her face and dipped to caress her proud shoulders. His mind trailed the length of her body. Firm breasts, wisp of a waist. Long graceful limbs, fluid as a stream.

He saw her everywhere, thought of her constantly. She was the most remarkable woman: unassuming, unpredictable, pained and brittle over a core of quiet strength.

Gallatin had never known anyone like her. Heir to a

massive family fortune, he was accustomed to manufactured products of the privilege factory: well-turned ladies with lofted pinkies, studied manners, and firm itineraries. As the senior senator from Connecticut, he was accustomed to women viewing him as a stepping-stone, barrier, or ally, and treating (or mistreating) him accordingly. Given his pedigree and position, he'd had more than his fair share of attractive offers. But Simon Gallatin had never really connected with any of them, with *anyone*.

Until now.

From their first meeting at the midtown gallery a month ago, Gallatin had been her eager captive. She was like her paintings—deft, tantalizing strokes on an enigmatic ground. Each view offered a fresh discovery, each discovery a fresh delight. He was mesmerized; he was consumed.

For the past month, Simon Gallatin had suffered the obsessive attentions of a constituent. The woman was forever leaving bizarre messages at his office and turning up in the most unlikely places. Several times, he'd been forced to dodge her on his way to a critical vote or meeting. From time to time, vigilant neighbors had spotted the woman's car near the Gallatin estate. And once, the housekeeper had discovered her at the back door, rummaging through the trash. The police had warned that she might prove dangerous, that Gallatin would be wise to engage a bodyguard. But he had resisted. He would not allow some nut case to run his life.

Now, for the first time, he could empathize with the woman. In an odd sense, he'd become something of a nut case himself: single-minded, possessed. Gallatin knew he'd discovered the love of his life, the missing fragment of his soul. He knew that without her he could never be truly happy or fulfilled. However long it

took, he would persist until she arrived at the same realization.

Gallatin's family considered the entire business a
passing affliction, like the flu. Mother, never shy about
her opinions, made pointed remarks about sowing his
uncultured oats and advancing to more suitable pur-
suits. More than once, she'd outlined the crucial dis-
tinction between women one takes and women one
takes seriously.

His sister Marielle, who presented a fearsome combination of their mother's iron will and their late father's
stony silence, had expressed her displeasure in withering looks.

Last week, Gallatin's kid brother, now the junior senator from Michigan, scheduled a rare brotherly lunch at
the Colony Club to counsel Simon on the political inap-
propriateness of "a woman like that."

Little brother had sternly informed Gallatin of the irrelevant facts Simon already knew. "That woman" was
an artist of unimpressive lineage who'd been reared on
a shabby ranch in East Nowhere, Idaho. Her parents
were poor, poorly educated people, who would certainly
not play well at thousand-a-plate dinners or inaugural
balls. Her brother had followed in the family's manure-
soiled footsteps and now ran a heavily mortgaged cattle
farm and a brood of undistinguished offspring in North
Noplace, Montana.

Since Simon Gallatin had been deemed his party's
likely choice for standard bearer in the next presidential
election, his friends, colleagues, and family had treated
him to a ceaseless feast of unsolicited advice. And under
other circumstances, Simon might have listened.

Under other circumstances, his sole focus would be
on the capture of the presidency. From infancy, his parents had primed him for high office. Young Simon had
attended all the "right" schools, made all the essential

contacts. He'd cut his teeth on oratory and protocol and
the dizzying complex machinations of backroom politics.

From the first, he'd been schooled to believe that
public service was a Gallatin's right, duty, and destiny.
And his parents had assured him that politics could be
a noble profession, free of taint and compromise, if no-
bly approached and undertaken. The lifelong indoctri-
nation had been wholly successful. Never once had
Gallatin imagined an alternative future for himself. But
right now, all he cared about was being with this
woman, finding a way to penetrate the iron cocoon into
which she'd spun herself after her husband's death.

Flipping through the photo album, Gallatin saw her
posed in dozens of adoring clinches with a good-looking
young man. He felt a pinch of envy. He wanted all of
her, everything. Even her past.

Restless, he uncorked the half-finished bottle of merlot
on the sideboard and poured a measure of the scarlet liquid into the glass she'd already used. The wine was warm
and rich. He pressed his mouth to the stain of her lip
print and closed his eyes, tasting her. Wanting her so in-
tensely, it made him dizzy.

He must not put her off with his eagerness, especially
now, when she had finally taken the first affirmative step
in his direction.

Since the note arrived at his office early that morning,
Gallatin had been determined to play this exactly the way
she wished. Her tantalizing message reverberated in his
mind.

*Come tonight at seven. If I'm not ready, relax and enjoy
the fire. Please don't turn around when I enter. Don't spoil the
surprise. I've planned everything. I promise it will be perfect.*

Gallatin checked his watch. Only ten after seven, but
he felt as if he'd been waiting for hours. The silence had

intensified. The radio was off now, and the dripping overhead had been stilled.

Soon, she would be on her way downstairs.

Seconds later, a floorboard squealed overhead, and there was the low pulse of descending footfalls. Gallatin's heart squirmed. Nervously, he smoothed his thick, sandy hair and swiped the beaded sweat from his forehead.

It will be perfect, he thought. *Perfect.*

She was at the bottom of the stairs now. Gallatin heard her padding across the foyer. He pictured her barefoot and clad in something sheer. His imagination filled in the creamy swell of her breasts, the jutting nipples, the dark mound below. He ached to catch a glimpse of her, to get lost in her. But her warning echoed in his mind.

Don't turn around.

An electric thrill scaled his spine. Waiting was an agony.

She had planned everything. Mustn't spoil the surprise.

With the discipline he'd been taught all his life, he held himself stiffly in check. Not daring to blink, to move, he stared at the charred fragments in the hearth. The fire had died. A teasing tail of smoke wafted from the hill of powdery ash.

She was coming up behind him now. Gallatin was eclipsed by her shadow. His heart quickened. He caught the light rush of her breathing and the musky scent of her perfume. She was so close, he could feel the electric press of air between them. But suddenly, she stopped.

Gallatin's breath snagged. He must not turn until she asked him to. What were a few seconds compared to the lifetime they would share together?

But what was she waiting for? The seconds stretched to an excruciating mass. A suffocating tension filled his chest. The trapped breath escaped him in a rush.

At last, she stepped closer. He felt the silken press of her lips at the back of his neck. Her voice was a breeze. "You can look now, Simon. Look. I want you to."

Simon Gallatin turned slowly, the smile forming on his lips. But it froze in a grotesque grimace as he saw what had been planned for him.

Her surprise was the shock of his life. And it was to be the last one.

PERSONAL JOURNAL

7 March

They say I struck him seven times.

The trophy was a foot-high bronze figure teeing off between a pair of granite columns. By the time I'd finished, the golfer's head was dangling like a flower on a broken stem, and the columns had the crazed look of a cracked boiled egg.

Time slowed as I bent over his broken body. There was a rock stillness to the veins. And the eyes bulged with mute questions. His tie was angled like a noose; his petrified fingers clutched the starched bib of his shirt. I straightened the tie and unfastened the shirt's top button, believing against all logic that the collar must be pinching his neck. Of course, he was beyond pain or discomfort. I had put him there.

There was a torrent of blood. For days afterward, I scrubbed at stubborn droplets that seemed to have burrowed beneath my skin. For weeks, the stench of his final fear tainted my every breath. Even now, when I close my eyes I can see the mask of terror etched for all eternity on his face.

I can recall the hours before and the slow, hideous aftermath. What came between, however, is lost in the thickets of my subconscious. What came between is irretrievable. I have no grasp or control of it.

They say it took inhuman strength to kill him, reason consumed by a ravenous rage.

They say I cannot be held responsible.

CHAPTER TWO

Her journal had slipped behind the bed.

Thea Harper snapped open the suitcase latches and quickly slipped the pebbled notebook between the neat stacks of clothing inside. Her eyes narrowed as she scanned the room for other stray possessions. Crossing to the dresser, she opened and examined each barren drawer for the dozenth time. She checked behind the filmy curtains and shook out the tangle of bedclothes.

From outside came an impatient bleat from the taxi awaiting her in the hospital's circular drive. A familiar voice prodded her from the door.

"Go on, now, girlfriend. Get moving."

"I am, Billie."

"In reverse, maybe."

The dark-skinned nurse attempted a frown, but her sparkling eyes and sunny features prevailed. Billie's plump frame was swaddled in a crisp white uniform set off by massive aerobic shoes and paisley socks. "You need me to light a fire under you, or what?"

"Sure. You go chop the wood. I'll wait here."

The nurse nodded knowingly. "Feeling scared's perfectly normal, honey. You ask me, you always been way too normal for this place."

"What if the medicine fails? What if I—"

"Don't even be thinking such things. Doc Forman says you're fine, you are. Woman's never been wrong a single time in her life. It's just one of the many things I can't abide about her."

Thea sighed. "I don't know how I would have managed without you, Billie. Sure you don't want to hop in the suitcase and come home with me? I'd feel much better."

"Don't you worry. Old Billie'll be checking on you every now and again."

At that, Thea couldn't help but smile, too. As a little girl she'd had a habit of wandering off, losing track of time, place, and obligations. Her mother was forever asking Thea's brother Jimmy or one of the ranch hands to ride out and check her. Eventually, everyone had taken to calling her "Checker." Her folks still did.

"Bet that pretty little one of yours is itching to have you back," Billie said.

Magic words. For the last six months, while Thea was at Brook Hollow having her loose screws tightened, her nine-year-old daughter Gabrielle had been bunking with neighbors. No matter how difficult things were for Thea, she never forgot the far greater strain all this had to have been on her little girl.

Gabby was only three when her father died, but she'd felt and remembered the loss. His death had saddled the child with the terrible realization that anyone could be taken from her. Nothing was sure and permanent. No matter how solid a home Thea tried to provide, she hadn't been able to erase that dismal truth from her little girl's reality.

Thea flinched at imagining how the events of this past insane year had further bruised the little girl. There had been no way to shield Gabby from the horrors of the arrest, the dreadful headlines, or the interminable trial. No way to insulate her against the cruel condemnation of the town. No way to inoculate her against the plague of two-legged locusts bearing steno pads and handi-cams that had infested their quiet Westport, Connecticut, neighborhood.

With a shudder, Thea recalled the phone's incessant shrill and the dogged reporters who would lean on the doorbell in the middle of the night, hoping to goad her into saying or doing something worthy of another lurid headline. WESTPORT'S BLACK WIDOW CRIES FOUL.

They would trample any line to get the story. A few had tried to corner Gabby at school or while she was playing on the block with friends. One columnist for the *Post*, a rodent named Harlan Vernon, had even offered the child a lavish Barbie doll set. Thea wondered if that was the going rate these days for betraying your mother.

How is it living with a murderer, Gabby? Aren't you scared?

Through it all, Gabby had masked her pain and bewilderment. The child had squirmed away from each of Thea's attempts at talk or explanation. Gabby had asked no questions and reported none of the vicious fallout she had to be encountering from her peers as rumors and innuendo ripped through the town. The little girl had simply elected to slam the door on the subject. But Thea knew all too well that monsters as huge and determined as these would always find some way to muscle their way inside.

On her weekly visits to Brook Hollow, Gabby had remained awkward, distant, and reserved. Not surprising, given the nature of the place. The private hospital, for all its rolling lawns, stately plantings, and homey clapboard dwellings, was a funny farm, after all. While the bulk of Brook Hollow's patients had signed themselves in to shed trendy addictions or to wallow in their state-of-the-art neuroses, this was also a place of human wax figures and Jesus impersonators and one highly vocal resident who lived by the teachings of Chicken Little.

One Sunday, Thea had arranged for a picnic on the grounds, hoping the familiar activity might smooth the circumstances of her daughter's visit. But just as Gabby was beginning to unwind, Mrs. Argersinger had barreled through the grove under her ubiquitous gold umbrella screeching, "Freaking sky's falling in chunks. Run, damn it. *Get your sweet asses under cover!*"

Worse was Vita Negrone, a skulking presence who spewed grisly warnings under her fetid breath.

"Kill you, slice and chop, I will. Stew you 'til you're tender. Feed you to the pigs."

The staff swore that Vita was harmless. She'd been at Brook Hollow for a decade without incident. To be doubly sure, they held her on a firm chemical leash. Major tranquilizers. Regular tests to ensure that her runaway blood chemistries were kept in reasonable balance. But try convincing a literal little girl like Gabby that crazy Vita didn't really mean it when she said she'd liked to marinate and barbecue the child's ribs and serve them to a dog.

Thea shut the last suitcase. "Guess I'm ready as I'll ever be."

Billie wrapped her in a cushiony hug. "I'm here for you, honey. Anytime. You just holler."

"I will, and thanks, Billie. Thanks for everything. And if there's ever anything I can do for you—"

"You can get out of here. That's what you can do. Go on now, girlfriend. It's time."

The cab was scribbling smoke signals on the chill morning air. Eyeing her warily, the grizzled driver hefted Thea's luggage into the trunk and slammed the lid. She sat in the rear, cradling her purse in her lap.

Trailing the scent of exhaust fumes, the driver slid behind the wheel and trained his coal black eyes on her. A toothpick dangled from the corner of his mouth.

"Where to?"

"Twenty-one Linden Street. Westport."

"You work in this place?"

"No. Not anymore."

He puffed the vacant corner of his mouth. "Couldn't pay me enough. All those spooks and weirdos. Scare me just to look at them."

Thea smiled sweetly. "You'd be surprised. I'll bet you couldn't tell me from one of the patients."

"I'll take that bet, lady. No one'd mistake you for a crack-case. No way."

Funny how it didn't show, how the volcanic eruptions in her life had left the surface unscathed. Thea could still pass for a teenager with her headstrong mane of dark curls and lanky body. She still drew frequent comments about her Bambi eyes and her arguable resemblance to a youthful Audrey Hepburn.

After Simon's death, Thea had kept a wary eye on the mirror, expecting, almost hoping for some cataclysmic change. If her hair had turned white or her back gone suddenly stooped like a crane's, maybe she could have begun to accept the impossible fact.

She had killed someone.

Murder. The word was a rubber ball, manic, darting and elusive. She couldn't grasp it, couldn't find the way to place herself in that unimaginable moment.

The gruesome episode remained wholly incomprehensible. No matter how many times it had been explained, patiently set out as one would try to teach a painfully slow child, Thea could not connect with the bloodstained facts of it. They eluded her understanding like hieroglyphs or advanced concepts in astrophysics. Somehow, her rational self had been submerged, overwhelmed by brutal unconscious impulse. She had murdered Simon with her hands, but it wasn't her. She was guilty but innocent. The world had lurched momentarily out of control, bucking like a wild horse, and thrown her.

Get a grip, Thea. It was all the illness. You take the pills, you'll be fine.

Even without the pills, the chance of a problem was near zero, she'd been assured. Until that hideous night, Thea had never experienced a serious violent impulse in her life. The short circuit, as Dr. Forman blithely termed it, was a one-in-a-million occurrence. Countless people suffered from the same seizure disorder they'd diagnosed in Thea, and there were only two or three other documented cases in history of the kind of savage behavior she'd exhibited on that awful night.

Miraculously, after a grueling four-month trial, those slim precedents had gotten her acquitted. The law would not hold her accountable for her unconscious actions. By sidebar arrangement between the defense and the district attorney, Thea's sole consequence for taking a man's life would be a six-month stint at a local psychiatric hospital. There she would receive constant medical supervision and a welcome respite from the public eye and prying reporters.

Not guilty. So say you, so say you all?
We do, Your Honor.
This court stands adjourned.

As the cab drove through quiet streets sprinkled with autumn's first golden leaves, Thea recalled the jarring gavel *thwack* following the verdict. Flashbulbs erupted like a volley of gunfire. Questions pelted her, sharp and cruel as stones.

How's it feel to get off after killing someone, Miz Harper?
Gonna write a book, Thea?
Anything you care to say to Senator Gallatin's family?

Then, as now, she'd felt utterly lost. How could anything seem real or right when she, gentle Thea Harper, had smashed in the brains of the first man she'd allowed to get remotely close to her since Justin's death? She'd thought she knew herself. But somehow she had harbored a monstrous beast inside. And for a murderous moment, the beast had broken loose.

"You know? I keep thinking I know you from some-place." The cabbie's dark eyes were on her, framed in the rearview mirror.

"I don't think so."

"School maybe? You go to Bridgeport?"

"No."

"That toothpaste commercial? Was that you?"

"No." Occasionally, Thea had fantasized about fame, but she'd hoped for it to come through her art. She'd never imagined playing the continuing lead in *Lifestyles of the Sick and Heinous.*

He chewed on his toothpick. "It'll come to me. I never forget a face."

Thea shifted her purse and heard the crackle of the paper sack inside. She pictured the neat plastic disc with each pill settled beside the date it was to be taken. Foolproof. If she missed a day she'd still be protected by the remnants of the medicine in her system, Dr. Forman had assured her. The calendar dispenser would guard against any serious lapses. The medicine would keep her safe and sane. With the pills, there was no chance of an-other lethal seizure.

But nothing could change the hideous fact of Si-mon's death. No matter how the courts and the doctors and her few remaining friends absolved her of his mur-der, Thea felt the scorching guilt. She had taken the life of a beautiful, wonderful man. She had robbed Simon of his future. He would never see another sunset, never make love again, never have a child.

And she had stolen Simon from the world. Simon Gallatin was a fine, decent person, that rare—verging on endangered—breed of politician who had truly been in it out of a sense of hope and caring.

His earnestness and honesty had disarmed her thor-oughly. Before meeting Simon, Thea refused to consider letting another man into her life. Justin's death was too painful. Her grief remained a raw, throbbing wound. But Simon Gallatin moved her to muse about the formerly unthinkable: a fresh romance, a salve for her aching loneliness.

Nowhere in the fantasy was the murder trial or the stint in the booby hatch.

The driver was still staring at her. "I got it," he said with a snort. "You're the one who whacked the senator, right? The Black Widow."

Thea froze inside.

"Hey. It's okay by me. Never liked that guy in the first place. Rich, pretty boy type. I told my old lady he was way too good to be true, but she had a giant crush on the jerk. Thought he was the Second Coming or something. What happened? He try to force himself on you?"

The cab was veering along the curved spine of the Saugatuck River. When last she'd passed this way, the trees had been lush green, the gardens a shameless boast of early spring colors: lemon, lilac, and rose. Now, as the cab shot past, rusty leaves drifted lazily toward the ground. The lawns had faded to a dismal beige, and a sorry display of fading annuals filled the border beds. Lonely clumps of lawn furniture and empty kiddie pools awaited their overdue trips to storage. Squirrels were gathering their winter provisions, darting frantically about with their precious burdens like bargain hunters at a closeout sale.

So much could change in six months, Thea thought, feeling the greedy curiosity in the cabbie's eyes. Six months away, and a person could lose her place in the world.

CHAPTER THREE

Exiting the elementary school, Gabrielle Harper spotted the Greens Farms boys across the field. The gang, known by the name of the affluent Westport section in which they lived, were designer delinquents uniformed in the latest high-top sneakers, baseball caps, and baggy jeans. The dirt bikes they'd ridden over from the middle school were propped against a towering oak. The fledgling suburban terrorists were huddled in a mean circle, jabbing each other with cocked elbows and kicking up puffs of dirt. Rod Salvatore, Brian Carmody, Eddie Adelman. Bigmouth bully creeps. Gabby felt a squeeze of hatred and her neck prickled with fear.

In a desperate rush, she ducked back inside the school and dashed through the maze of corridors to her classroom. Those idiots wouldn't dare do or say anything if she came walking out with her teacher. But she found the door locked, the room shadowed and empty.

All the rooms were deserted. Her heart sank. Had to be a teachers' meeting or something. Gabby peered into the principal's office. But all she saw was nasty Miss Nardino with the squint eyes and tuba voice. No help there. All the principal's secretary cared about was sucking up to parents, especially the ones who were big shots on the PTA. Gabby ducked out of sight before the old witch caught sight of her and started yelling.

Outside, the Greens Farms geeks still waited. Walking stiffly, Gabby descended the stairs. She glued her gaze to the littered dirt path leading to the road. If she paid no attention to those rotten stinkers, maybe they'd disappear. Maybe they'd evaporate in a fat, ugly cloud, and the wind would blow them over a dangerous jungle in darkest Africa. They deserved to be eaten by a puma like the one she'd seen on last spring's field trip to the Bronx Zoo. Revolting thing smelled like an outhouse and had a temper on him like the principal's secretary.

Hugging her book bag, Gabby quickly made her way toward the number seven yellow bus idling at the distant curb. Only a trickle of kids were still waiting to climb aboard. If she didn't hurry, they'd leave without her. She couldn't allow that to happen.

Not today.

Today had to be perfect. Gabby had spent the past two weeks in fevered preparation for today. Ever since she'd heard that Mommy was finally coming home, her insides had felt like snapping rubber bands. Days, she kept going over every imaginable detail. Each night, she startled awake, heart hammering, terrified she'd overlooked something crucial that could make Mommy sick again.

Gabby had helped Mrs. Millport spiff up the house and stock the refrigerator. For tonight, they'd planned a special welcome home dinner, including all Mom's favorites and a giant cake shaped like an artist's palette. Gabby had dyed the frosting for the color blobs herself and set them in place with all the care she could muster.

This morning, Amber Millport had gotten up extra early to plait Gabby's dark mop into a neat French braid. The twins, Opal and Jasmine, had helped select Gabby's outfit: short denim skirt, ribbed tights, red blouse with pearl buttons, rainbow belt, strap shoes. The Millport girls had contributed the red bangle bracelet, bow-shaped earrings, and matching barrettes.

She would not let those idiot boys spoil *anything*.

Gabby walked faster. Fat Toby Blenheim was slogging up the bus steps now. Last one in line, as usual.

Ricky Dolan's head was lolling out the back window like a dog's. Ready to roll.

With a roar, the engine started. "Wait!" Gabby hollered and broke into a run. "Wait for me!"

The doors were closing. Gabby shouted again, but the motor's growl swallowed her cry. Racing full out, she yelled, "Hold it, Benny. I'm coming!"

Almost there. A few more steps and she'd be clearly in his sight. But suddenly, her foot caught, and she was sent sprawling onto the dirt path. As the hurt and humiliation pierced her shock, Gabby was assailed by the chorus of nasty voices around her.

Thea Harper took an ax,
Gave her boyfriend forty whacks.
When she saw what she had done,
Gave the guy another one.

Gabby lifted herself from the ground. She choked back a frustrated sob. Bloody bruises shone through the torn knees of her tights. Her palms were raked and stinging, her clothing splotched with dirt. Opal's red bracelet lay on the ground, cracked in ragged halves.

She turned to the sight of Eddie Adelman's smirk, a crooked, mocking wave in a sea of muddy freckles. With a flourish, Eddie raised a sneakered foot to demonstrate how he'd tripped her. The other Greens Farms boys clustered behind him. They cheered and slapped him on the back.

Before Gabby could retrieve the papers spewing from her fallen book bag, scrawny Brian Carmody scooped them up. He started crumpling the sheets into balls. All three boys gleefully joined the game, tossing and catching her best work to the rhythm of the chant.

Thea Harper took an ax—

Heedless of her aching knees and sore hands, Gabby chased the pages as they sailed over her head. She'd collected the papers to show Mom, to make her proud. Ev-

ery one bore a star or an A-plus. She railed in a frustrated stagger as each boy threw a paper, then darted
easily out of her reach. They were bigger, faster. Rotten
seventh graders. Gabby's rage exploded.

"Stupid jerks," she screamed. "I'll kill you! I swear
I will."

Rod bugged his eyes. "Gonna be a killer like your
old lady? Come on, little murder bird. Just try it."

Brian curled his upturned fingers, daring her to
come after him. Eddie pressed his palms to his mouth
and made a fake farting sound. Again, they started the
taunting refrain with which they'd been badgering her
for months.

Thea Harper took an ax,
Gave her boyfriend forty whacks.

"Shut up!" Gabby wailed. "Give me those! They're
mine!"

Eddie snickered. "You want your precious papers?
Hey, guys. Better give them to her before she sics her
old lady on us."

"Oh, no! Not *that*!" Rod clutched his head and stag-
gered backward. "Please, *no*, Mrs. Harper. Don't *hit* me
again!"

A wad of paper struck her cheek. Delighted with Eddie's example, the boys scooped up the crushed pages
and began pelting Gabby with them.

When she saw what she had done,
Gave the guy another one.

"Stop it!" she shrieked. "No!" Her fury erupted in a
torrent of tears. "Stop it, damn you! Stop!"

Suddenly, everything went still. Through her tears,
Gabby could read the fear in Rod Salvatore's eyes. Gabby
turned. An older kid in black jeans and a black leather
jacket had Eddie pinned from behind. One arm was
pressed across Eddie's throat. Eddie made a choking
sound, and his face turned the color of strawberry yogurt.

"Had enough, twerp?"

"Enough, Dill," Eddie croaked, squirming helplessly. "Lemme go!"

Cowardly Rod was about to run, but the older boy called Dill caught him easily by the scruff.

"Nobody moves 'til I say so. Got that?" Dill snapped. His voice was rumbly deep, like a grown man's.

Rod stood frozen in panic while the older boy gripped Brian's forearm with both hands and twisted the skin in opposing directions. Indian burn. Staring at Dill's hands, Gabby saw the dirty nails and the worm-like scars rimming his wrists.

"Enough . . ." Brian whimpered.

"I say what's enough, you little turd." Dill squeezed harder to prove the point.

He turned to Rod. "Now it's your turn, pencil dick. Last and definitely least."

Rod's face was the color of skimmed milk. "Hey, come on. . . . What'd we do to you?"

"I see you picking on a little girl like that, it spoils my appetite. I don't eat right, I get cranky. You see how it goes, scumbag? Or are you too dumb to get it?"

"We were just kidding around," Rod mewled. "Forget it, will you?"

The older boy swaggered over to Rod, his coal eyes slitted. "Sure I will. I'll forget all about it, soon as I make sure you're gonna remember but good." With the flat of his hand, Dill made a dusting motion across the surface of Rod's buzz cut. Then he raised his fist high overhead and hammered Rod's skull as if he were trying to sink a fence post.

Rod yipped like a wounded dog. Gabby bit back a giggle.

"Now, get the hell out of my sight, you little twerps," Dill snarled. The trio hastily scrambled away.

After they'd rounded the corner on their bikes, the older kid turned to Gabby. "You okay?"

Swiping an errant tear, she hitched her shoulders to pretend none of it had mattered. But everything was spoiled. The bus was gone. Home was a three-mile walk. By the time she got there, Mommy would be all worried and upset. Gabby imagined the fragile edges of her mother's health unraveling. The world coming apart again.

"Come on," the boy said decisively, his dark eyes fixed on her face. "I'll get you fixed up. Take you home."

"I'm not allowed to ride with strangers."

"You don't remember me?"

"No."

"Sure you do. Think." He lit a cigarette, cupping his hand over the flame.

Gabby squinted, trying to bring him into clearer focus.

"It's Dylan. Dylan Connable. You came to my mother's day care for a while when you were maybe three or four. I used to help her out there after school sometimes. I taught you to play Go Fish. Remember?"

Gabby remembered. She'd heard plenty about Dylan Connable from Amber Millport. At seventeen, Amber understood things Gabby could barely pronounce. From everything Amber said, avoiding Dylan Connable was simple common sense, like not licking a person's ice cream if she had a cold.

"So? You coming, or what?" He was watching her through his cigarette smoke.

Gabby searched the empty street for a better alternative, bit her lip, then nodded. No matter what, she had to get home to her mom. Hastily, she collected her fallen books and papers.

Dylan's car was parked at a strange angle. It was

painted a dull black with gold and crimson devil's claws
stenciled on the sides. The hind end was boosted so
high she could see the wire twisted around the rusted
muffler.

Through the open door, Gabby eyed the filthy interior. Cringing, she noticed the sprawl of crumpled food
wrappers, crushed beer cans, stained clothes, cigarette
butts, and paper scraps. With a sweep of his forearm,
Dylan cleared a space for her on the passenger seat. Reluctantly, she got in and searched for a safety belt.
There was none.

Dylan drove in angry bursts, his head swaddled in
the ghostlike haze from his dangling cigarette. Gabby
pressed hard against the cracked upholstery. She tried
not to breathe in the smoky air, tried to focus on the
dizzy rush of scenery. Power lines converged, crossed,
and scattered. Houses and trees whipped by. Her stomach lurched and dipped like knees on a falling elevator.

In minutes, they were at the river, barreling through
the familiar strings of curves. Gabby knew the route
from school to home by heart. Pass the ice cream place.
Get off the Post Road at the funeral parlor. Continue
past the Women's Club and the insurance company and
the doctors' building. Turn left at the third slow sign,
and her house was five down on the right.

They were beyond the second slow sign. Gabby
leaned forward, anticipating the turn. But Dylan barreled past her block without the slightest hesitation.

"Wait. You missed it."

"My place isn't far. You better get cleaned up first."

"But my mom's expecting me."

"Not expecting you to look like that, is she?"

Gabby couldn't argue. Seeing her all messed up was
sure to get Mommy upset. On balance, the few minutes
it would take to wash were probably a good idea. Not
that she had much choice. The black car was already

turning off a few blocks down on Juniper. He sped to the end of the street and bumped into a rutted stone driveway.

Gabby's legs were shaky from the ride. Stepping out, she started toward the front door. She tried to remember Mrs. Connable, but the woman's face wouldn't come.

As a little girl, she'd spent a sporadic few days here and there in day care while Mommy was busy with one of her shows or teaching art history at some college.

No matter. She'd just say a polite hello to Mrs. Connable, wash up real quickly, and Dylan could drive her home.

"Not that way," he said abruptly.

"I thought you wanted me to get cleaned up."

"My place is there." He pointed to the garage. A black drape blocked the tiny dormer window. A painted skeleton head stared out from the glass.

The place looked spooky. "I think I'd better just go home. . . ."

"Up to you." He shrugged. "You don't mind your mother getting a load of you like that, asking a lot of questions, it's nothing to me."

Thinking of the Greens Farms boys' taunts, all the months of teasing, Gabby flushed with shame. She could never tell her mother what had happened, what those big dopes kept saying.

Desperately, desperately, Gabby wanted all the bad times to be finished. If only she didn't mess up, maybe she and Mommy could get back to the way things used to be. All she had to do was wash away the dirt and pretend nothing had happened.

Slowly, she followed Dylan Connable up the shadowy stairs.

CHAPTER
FOUR

Three-fifteen. Gabby would be home any minute. Thea peered out the window, her throat parched with anxiety.

Somber clouds rimmed the tarnished steel sky. South-flying birds passed in a ragged wedge. Glenda Rossner's maroon Chevy wagon inched down the street, allowing the neighborhood nose ample snooping time. Thea hastily withdrew from the window. She was eager to postpone the inevitable encounter with Westport's one-woman wire service.

Glenda had always taken particular delight in meddling in Thea's affairs and disseminating dirt about her, real or invented. After Simon's death, the busybody had positively wallowed in the muck. While other neighbors declined to comment on Thea or the murder case, Glenda's moon face and monumental mouth were omnipresent on nightly newscasts.

"Sure, she's been a decent neighbor, but you never know what goes on behind closed doors, do you?" Glenda's snide voice still haunted Thea.

The phone rang, startling her. There had been so many jolting intrusions in the few hours since her release from Brook Hollow. At the hospital, incoming calls had sounded a tempered trill. Visitors were screened through scrupulous security procedures. Car horns and blasting radios were kept at a dimming distance. Thick acoustical ceilings and dense carpets blunted normal life sounds to a peaceful hum.

The phone rang again. Thea let the answering machine pick up. After Simon's death, she'd learned the hard way not to answer until she knew who or what was on the other end. She'd never forget the endless calls from the press, the hissing hate messages. The threats. The terse suggestions that she do the world a favor and drop dead.

This morning, she'd already had several calls from neighbors and salesmen, and one from Harlan Vernon, the reporter at the top of Thea's hate list. Vernon, whom Thea had privately dubbed "Vermin" during the trial, had somehow gotten immediate word of her release from Brook Hollow. Drawing a shaky breath, she let her anger go. If she allowed him to burrow under her skin, Mr. Vermin could single-handedly send her right back to the funny farm.

The final trio of messages were from her agent, Pru Whittaker. The same efficiency, dedication, and single-mindedness that made Pru a wonderful representative in the best of times made her nearly intolerable now that Thea was in no way ready to put her stalled career back in motion. Since the trial, Pru had been hounding her. Repeatedly, she suggested that Brook Hollow was a perfect place to paint. Think of the inspiration, after all. Thea could do a series of still lifes featuring nuts and fruitcakes.

But this time, after the beep, Thea was treated to her mother's drowsy drawl.

She picked up. "Hi, Mom. I'm here."

"Welcome home, Checker honey. Everything okay?"

"Fine. With you?"

"Same old same old," Ellie Sparks said, drawing on her extensive collection of stock phrases. "You sure you're okay, honey? I could come help out for a bit if you'd like."

Thea was sorely tempted to accept the offer. Her mother was a tonic, solid and unfailingly supportive. But with Thea's father seriously debilitated by Parkinson's disease, early Alzheimer's, and a host of other maladies, Ellie was indispensable at the ranch. "That's not necessary, Mom. Really."

There was a pause, and Thea sensed her mother's unspoken relief. Ellie had insisted on coming east for part of Thea's trial, but the visit had proved a trial in its own right. There had been daily calls from Idaho, a relentless barrage of issues and problems. Nothing like playing the rope in a cross-country tug-of-war.

"You're sure?" her mother asked.

"Positive. I'm fine. How's Dad?"

"Mean as a tick, so you know he must be feeling better."

An ugly memory pressed to the surface, a vivid reminder of the true extent of her father's "meanness." Her mother had never known the half of it, and, if Thea had her way, she never would. No point in dredging up old ugliness. Thea carefully emptied her tone of emotion. "Same old same old."

Ellie chuckled appreciatively. "Never did miss a nail and hit your thumb, did you, Checker honey?"

Thea managed a rueful smile. Ellie had a knack for keeping things light and level.

"Give my love to everyone, will you, Mom?" Thea's smile broadened as she caught the cowboy drawl creeping back into her voice. Talking to her mother was guaranteed to trigger an accent relapse.

"Sure will. Speak to you soon, honey."

Thea walked through the house, trying to reclaim the feel of the place. Caro Millport, world's best friend and neighbor, had made a valiant attempt to brighten the atmosphere. Welcoming posters and crepe paper streamers hung on the walls and ceilings. Everything was pin neat and redolent of lemon oil. But it would take much more than dust rags and decorations to bring things anywhere close to normal.

Nothing seemed wholly familiar. Skirting the den as

she had since the night Simon died there, Thea walked through the rest of her home with the unsettling sensation that she was visiting a museum. The images were familiar, the objects pleasing. But she could not bring herself to touch anything.

Upstairs, she unpacked her things, took a quick shower, and dressed in her standard work shirt and jeans. Somewhat fortified, she tackled the massive mail collection on the dining room table. Caro's husband, Drew, had culled the essentials during Thea's absence and taken care of the bills and other necessary business.

Fortunately, several well-timed commission checks from the gallery had kept her on decent financial footing during her time at Brook Hollow. According to Pru Whittaker, interest in her paintings remained strong. The gallery had reiterated its commitment to stage a one-woman show as soon as Thea was able to complete the appropriate body of work. For an artist, infamy was no handicap, Pru had assured her in a tone that suggested the agent wished all her clients would run right out and murder someone famous.

Thea couldn't complain about the opportunity. She loved her work. As soon as her unruly mind was sufficiently settled, she wanted to get on with it. But first, she had to set the rest of her life back on its pilings.

She made short work of the mess, dumping the stacks of circulars, announcements, and expired catalogues into a trash bag. No hate mail, Thea noticed with a trace of satisfaction, though it was entirely possible that Drew had taken care of that as well.

The barrage of vile letters had started arriving as soon as the news of Simon's murder hit the media. They'd continued throughout the trial. Most were anonymous, scrawled in angry script or kidnapper's block print. Somehow, the notes seemed worse than the phone calls, more poisonous and permanent.

Caro and Drew had urged her to ignore them, to rip them up and discard them unread. But that would be like trying to ignore a swarm of killer bees. The venom in them paralyzed Thea. She could not relate to the unspeakable turn her life had taken. In her heart and mind she was still the caring, sensitive soul she'd always been. Still her mother's prize. Still Gabby's doting mommy and Justin's grieving widow. No matter how others reminded her, no matter how many times an hour she reminded herself, she was brutally unprepared for what she had become.

On with it, Thea. Don't dwell!

All that remained were renewal notices for professional journals and organization memberships. Thea stuffed those in a drawer in the Shaker sideboard. First things first.

No sign of Gabby yet. Either the bus was running late, or the child was dawdling as she often did with the other neighborhood kids near the bus stop. Aching to see her little girl, Thea was tempted to walk to the corner. But she didn't want to appear anywhere near as anxious as she felt.

Instead, on an impulse she took the leather-bound photo album from the end table and settled against a pile of cushions on the living room couch. Since Justin's death, the family pictures had been a frequent source of wistful pain and comfort. They were her collection of perfect moments, real and vivid, better than frozen slices of wedding cake or faded corsages pressed between the pages of a book.

There were shots of her and Justin the winter they met in Manhattan. He'd been working as an intern at New York Hospital. She'd had the good fortune to break her wrist on a failed figure eight at the Rockefeller Center ice rink while he was on rotation in the emergency room. The incident had confirmed

Thea's belief in fate, though many would have termed it simple clumsiness.

Next came the page of photos from the year they lived in New Haven while Justin completed his residency at Yale and she wrote her thesis on visionary art in the Postimpressionist period.

Using the ancient Hasselblad camera he'd bought at a flea market, her father had immortalized the wedding. Everyone had agreed on a simple ceremony at the ranch followed by a small, homespun reception. Thea smiled at the memory of the parade of friends and relatives bearing casseroles, gifts, and good wishes. She could still conjure the heady mix of joy and trepidation. After the wedding, Justin confessed to downing a five-milligram Valium before the ceremony. Thea had gotten through with the aid of a generous slug from the brandy bottle her mother kept behind the row of kitchen canisters for emergencies.

Hard to believe how young and sturdy everyone looked eleven years ago. Harder still to accept how many firm dreams and solid expectations from that wonderful time had been leveled by a single stroke of the cosmic wrecking ball.

There were honeymoon pictures, pregnancy pictures, and the typical running record of the firstborn child: Gabby's first bath, first smile, first tooth, first step, first dance with Daddy, first world-class tantrum.

A picture of Gabby napping in her car seat reminded Thea of the long, lovely drives the three of them used to enjoy on weekends. A favorite route had taken them past Birch Hollow in the north woods of neighboring New Canaan. Riding by, she or Justin often made a crack about the hospital, locally known as a dry-out place for the julep-and-martini set.

Dried out didn't begin to cover it.

Finally, Thea turned to her favorite picture at the

rear of the album. It was a candid shot of Justin taken two months before his death. His pale green eyes seemed to be looking directly at Thea, offering her a direct line to his thoughts and sympathies.

"Why aren't you here to help me with this, you rat?" she said aloud. "I'm terrified that I'm going to foul everything up with Gabby. At least, if you were with me, we could screw up together."

She imagined the devilish smile glinting in his eyes. *You'll do fine, sweetheart. You've never needed me or anyone to help you make a mess of things.*

A board squealed overhead, and there was the whine of a door hinge. Heart thumping, Thea shut the album.

"Who's there?"

No answer.

"Gabby? Is that you?"

Silence.

Had she locked the front door behind her when she came in earlier? Thea had been away too long to rely on normal protective reflexes. If there were a burglar, she wasn't about to stick around and play host. She could call the police from the Millports' and head Gabby off from outside.

Starched with fear, Thea quickly crossed the foyer, turned the knob soundlessly, and opened the front door. She was halfway out when a voice from behind stalled her.

"Mommy, wait."

Trembling, she turned to the sight of her little girl lurking in the shadows near the stairs.

"Gabby? Why didn't you answer when I called? You scared me half to death."

The child dipped her doe eyes and went fidgety. Trademark fibbing posture. "Sorry. I didn't hear you."

"You must have *seen* me when you came in. I was right in the living room."

"Guess I was in a hurry to get to the bathroom. I didn't go all day.

The explanation made no sense. The child couldn't have gotten past her in the first place without sneaking like a cat burglar.

Forget it, Thea. This isn't anywhere near the right beginning.

Biting back the accusatory questions, Thea opened her arms. "A big hug and it's forgotten. Deal?"

Gabby's approach was shy and tentative. She was oddly dressed in clothes Thea didn't recognize: worn flannel shirt and oversized jeans cinched by a length of frayed rope. Strange outfit for the child, who'd always been meticulous and devoted to fashion. Stranger still was her choice of accessories: dress flats, elaborate barrettes, and mock ruby earrings set in plastic bows.

The child's slender frame felt cozy and familiar; then Thea recoiled.

"You smell of smoke, Gabby."

The eyes dipped again. "Must've been some kids smoking in the bathroom or something."

"I thought you said you didn't go to the bathroom."

"I didn't. Not today. Maybe it was from the last time I wore these. Amber had some friends over Saturday night. Lots of them smoke."

"Please, don't lie to me, Gabby. Whatever it is, I'd rather have the truth."

The child's eyes filled. "I would never smoke. Honest. Please don't be mad at me, Mommy."

Thea felt a pang of guilt. She pressed her daughter's face to her chest and smoothed the soft tendrils trailing from the high-pitched ponytail.

"I'm not, sweetheart. I'm so glad to be home with you again. Everything is going to be all right now. You'll see."

"I'm so sorry, Mommy. I ruined everything, didn't I?" A sob wracked Gabby's slender body.

Her heart pinched with regret, Thea held the little girl until the weeping stilled. "Ssh. It's okay. Everybody tries a puff once. I remember doing it behind the barn when I was ten or eleven. Pretty gross, huh?"

Gabby stiffened in her arms. "I told you, I didn't. Why won't you believe me?"

No sign she was lying now. But something was clearly wrong.

Careful, Thea. Cut the child some slack. She's probably just nervous about your coming home. Perfectly understandable.

Thea kissed her cheek and smiled. "How about something to eat? I'm starved," she suggested.

"Okay."

Thea rummaged through the provisions Caro Millport had set in the refrigerator and marshaled the fixings for a couple of monster sundaes. Rocky road ice cream, chocolate sauce, chopped nuts, whipped cream. Good old Caro. The woman hadn't overlooked any of the essentials.

She ferried the towering concoctions to the table. Fortunately, the child had inherited her blast furnace metabolism along with the sweet tooth. "Only thing missing is the diving boards. There's yours, sweetie. Dig in."

Thea attacked the treat with relish. Brook Hollow's fascist nutritionist had left no space on the menu for Thea's minimum daily requirement of empty calories. But her appetite evaporated as she saw her daughter picking listlessly at her sundae.

"What's wrong, Gabby?"

"Nothing."

"Whatever it is, you can tell me."

"There's nothing, I said."

The child refused to meet Thea's eyes. Her chin was quivering. "Can I be excused?"

"Sure. But—"

Bolting from the table, Gabby raced upstairs. Her bedroom door slammed with jarring finality.

Numb with regret, Thea relived every misstep in their dismal reunion. For months, she'd awaited this day, fretted over ways to make her homecoming a fresh, upbeat, new beginning for both of them. She'd spent hours mentally marshaling the necessary stores of patience, warmth, and understanding. And with all that, she'd managed in minutes what the most determined screw-up might have taken months to achieve.

Exactly what she'd been hoping to avoid.

Shaking her head, she went into the living room and once again opened the phone album to Justin's picture.

Her voice was a pained whisper. "Now what? How do I begin to make things right with Gabby?"

Don't push it, sweetheart. These things take time to sort themselves out.

She stared into his clear green eyes, passed a longing finger over the surface of his mouth. With Justin, everything had been so much simpler. Faced with a problem of any size, they'd sit together and talk it out. No matter if it took half the night. No matter if the other half was filled with lovemaking and no time was left for sleep. Being dull-headed and bleary-eyed seemed a paltry price to pay for such a dazzling collaboration.

In retrospect, the issues they'd agonized over back then seemed so tiny. Was it all right for Gabby to carry around her pacifier? Should they push the toilet training or simply plan to pack the Pampers when the child went off to college? And how would they ever afford to pay for that college education when they couldn't begin to see their way clear of Justin's medical school debts?

The ache in her heart grew heavier. Setting the album down, Thea listened for sounds from upstairs.

Silence.

She resolved to go upstairs and patch things up with Gabby. But when she peered through the child's bedroom door, she found her daughter facedown atop the covers, fast asleep.

Probably exhausted from the excitement, Thea thought with a swell of love. Fatigue was certainly a comforting explanation for Gabby's petulance and short fuse.

Quietly, Thea crossed to her sleeping child. Leaning down, she moved aside the mass of curly dark hair and planted a gossamer kiss on the back of Gabby's neck.

CHAPTER
FIVE

Thea had always felt completely at home at the Millport house. She suspected it was the sprawling ranchlike feel of the place. Despite the solid pack of people and pets, each Millport and every visitor—invited or otherwise—was granted a full ten acres of personal space. It never seemed to matter that multiple heads in the giant herd might lay claim to the same ten acres simultaneously. Nor was it relevant that the Millport spread was a cramped-to-bursting four-bedroom Colonial with an overstuffed garage and a post-stamp yard. Regardless of how crazy or chaotic things appeared on the surface, there was always an underlying aura of serenity.

Caro Millport's unflappable nature provided the storm's calming eye. The woman was a plump, blond Scarlett O'Hara, minus the angst and ego. Without a ripple of pique or frustration, Caro managed five kids, three dogs, two house cats, and a variety of strays who slipped in through the pet door or the front door, depending. Add to that one hyperamorous husband, a constant parade of repairpeople, and an astoundingly huge extended family with a penchant for surprise appearances. And, as if all that weren't sufficient, Caro's home-based party planning and decorating business, launched on a whim two years ago, had grown to necessitate a full-time assistant, a bookkeeper, and a platoon of part-time helpers.

When Thea and Gabby arrived at six o'clock, Caro was giving her assistant, Laurette, shopping instructions for a baby shower, a wedding shower, and three major

birthday bashes, all scheduled for the upcoming weekend. Opal and Jasmine immediately claimed Gabby and
spirited her upstairs for what sounded, moments later,
like a grape-trampling festival. Amber and a quartet of
her cheerleading friends were practicing cartwheels and
human pyramids among the delicate antiques and other
breakables in the living room. Ten-month-old Drake, a
sturdy towhead in the stock Millport mold, was creating a mashed-pea-and-carrot mural on the tray of his
high chair. Raleigh, his two-year-old brother, crouched
in the corner, red-faced and grunting.

Caro eyed the little boy with amusement. "You let
Momma know when you're done, darlin', and we'll get
you a nice, fresh diaper. You hear?" Spotting Thea, her
smile brightened.

"Now there's a sight for sore eyes."

"I can say the same for you, pal." Thea hugged her
friend hard and felt miles better. She lifted the large
wrapped package she'd bought and handed it to Caro.
"Not that there's any way I can ever begin to repay you."

Caro's moon face registered surprise. "For what?"

"Oh, nothing much. You just took care of Gabby
and all the rest of it. Saved my life. Little things like
that."

Caro flapped away the gratitude and untied the
package ribbon. "You see, Laurette? This plaid would
be just perfect for the sign-in board at Mr. Beasley's fif-
tieth." Laurette, a jittery mouse of a woman, scribbled
on a list as Caro continued. "Something in flowers for
the centerpieces at the Beller shower, I think. And get
a few yards more of that nice pink-and-blue stripe for
the Ongley party, will you? Two-inch, at least. The last
was too skinny."

Caro peeled back the wrapping paper and sucked a
breath. "You didn't. Oh, Thea . . ."

The painting was a vibrant oil of a girl on horseback.

Thea had finished the work before the trouble started,
and her agent had encouraged her to reserve it as the
centerpiece for the proposed individual show at the gallery. But Caro had admired the picture with rare ardor.
Now, she looked at Thea through the tears that had
puddled in her eyes.

"I don't know what to say—"

"That makes two of us."

Young Raleigh deftly changed the subject. "Peee-
ooo, Momma!" Holding his button nose, the two-year-
old toddled over with the broad gait of a soused sailor.
"New die-puh."

Caro propped the painting on a counter and hefted
her son on a hip. "All right, pumpkin. Be right back,
Thea. There's white wine in the fridge."

Thea helped herself to a club soda instead. Squeezing
in a lime wedge, she sat at the large oak table.

The baby had wearied of his finger-painting. Freshly
inspired, he raised his pudgy hands and smacked at the
mashed vegetables. The mess sprayed wildly, which was
Drake's notion of high comedy. Squealing in delight,
the infant escalated his attack. Familiar with Caro's
mothering methods, Thea scooted her chair out of firing range and gentled her tone.

"Food is not for ammunition, Drake honey. How
about you eat some of that yucky mush and let your
momma decorate the kitchen when she decides it needs
doing. Okay?"

Drake gurgled and dipped his face to the tray. A
sound like a constipated trumpet ensued.

The fanfare heralded Caro's reappearance. She was
toting a far less pungent Raleigh under her arm like a
rolled newspaper. After depositing the squirming toddler in his booster seat, she made short work of the baby's mess. That done, she cocked her head, turning to
the ominous silence that had settled overhead.

"Whatever you girls are doing up there, you'd best move on to something else, now," she called. A burst of giggles was followed by a comforting resumption of the noise over their heads. A beat later, a crash resounded from the living room. Caro sighed. "Amber, darlin'. Maybe it's time to move your practice down to the rec room like I suggested."

Thea laughed. "How the hell do you do it, Caro? I'll never understand."

"Do what?"

The kitchen door burst open. Drew Millport lumbered in, flanked by a rangy pair of golden retrievers and an arthritic Jack Russell terrier whose gait reminded Thea of a wind-up toy.

After tossing Thea a peck, Drew caught his wife in a bone-crushing embrace and buried his face in her neck. Sounded like feeding time at the trough. Drake crowed with delight.

Caro extricated herself with finesse and patted her husband's ruddy cheek. "There now, Drew darlin'. Have a beer and relax awhile, why don't you?"

Drew was a big man whose square jaw and linebacker physique had made their middle-aged compromises with the forces of gravity. His hairline was drifting south as well, and the remains had the sparse, patchy look of a burnt-out lawn. But age had not dimmed the man's cannonball personality. Drew was as loud, proud, and explosive as Caro was composed. The pair had met in sixth grade when Drew's idea of humor was playing slingshot with the rear of Caro's training bra. As Caro liked to tell it, she'd only hung around since trying to puzzle out the source of the attraction.

Drew settled at the table with a frosted can of Coors and a contented sigh. He lifted his two little boys and set them bouncing on the giant sequoias that were his thighs. Raleigh hummed to the jolting rhythm of the ride. Drake promptly offered back what little he'd downed of his dinner.

Home sweet home.

Caro cheerfully popped the baby into a fresh blue stretch suit, and settled him in the playpen with a bottle. Filling a pail in the sink with soapy water, she stripped Raleigh to his plump, pink flesh and set him to soak like a burnt pot. In the living room, the girls shrieked with delight.

Somehow, an hour later, everyone had been fed and mellowed to a suitable evening hush. Opal and Gabby were upstairs, reading to the little ones in the nursery. Jasmine was in the girls' bedroom, locked in mortal combat with the demon long division. Amber and her friends were down in the basement rec room planning moves that, from the conspiratorial whispers and giggles, had nothing to do with cheerleading. Drew slumped in his long-term parking spot in front of the big-screen TV set in the den. In the kitchen, Caro poured another round of coffee and trained her soft green eyes on Thea.

"So? How's it going?" she said seriously.

"Fine."

"Your mouth says fine, sugar, but that pretty face of yours is singing the blues."

"I'm just a little worried about Gabby. That's all. Any problems with her while I was in the— while I was away?" Even with Caro, Thea found it hard to talk about her stay at Brook Hollow and what had come before.

"Problems? Not at all. Gabby was a perfect angel. Why?"

"Hard to explain. She's just different somehow. Please, Caro. If there was anything that concerned you, anything at all, I want you to tell me."

"Of course I would. But there wasn't anything. She

and the girls get on beautifully, and she dotes on the babies. Nothing wrong in school either. Dearest teacher came in to substitute when Mrs. Carlisle left on maternity last month. Simply adores Gabby."

No sign that Caro was withholding anything. Thea had to consider that the problem with Gabby could be in her own mind. Or could it be *her*?

"Did she seem upset about my coming home?"

"Upset? Lord, no. Girl's been gushing like a fresh well since she heard you were leaving that place."

"Maybe we just need some time to get used to things. . . ."

"Sure, honey. Bet that's all there is to it."

A hand snaked into the kitchen and doused the lights. Gabby strode in from the dining room proudly carrying a large cake capped with sizzling sparklers. An assortment of smiling Millports, a couple of neighbor kids, the golden retrievers, and half the Staples High cheerleading squad accompanied her. The Rossners, Hobermans, and D'Andreas, three neighborhood couples, drifted in to join the celebration. There was a boisterous chorus of welcome homes and a round of hugs.

Shoving aside her worry, Thea made a proper fuss over the cake, then did the slicing. Everyone was so warm and enthusiastic, she couldn't help but catch the spark. Even Gabby seemed back to the old self Thea only dimly remembered. Maybe the initial awkwardness had passed and they were really on the road back to normalcy.

In her new, improved mood, Thea didn't even mind the unfortunate presence of Glenda Rossner and the heat-seeking missile that passed for Glenda's mouth. But this evening, the woman was determined to outdo herself.

"I'm so glad my floor man was able to get everything out," she crooned.

Dead silence. If only Glenda had been able to provoke the same reaction in herself.

"Blood's so difficult," she went on. "Stains like
crazy."

Caro was bearing down on Glenda, herding her and
her mute marionette of a husband toward the door.
" 'Night, Glenda. Mark. Don't let the door hit you on
the way out, now."

Glenda shrugged. She looked like an aging, oversized
Betty Boop and tended to affect that character's brand
of cartoon innocence. "But I was just saying——"

Relentlessly, Caro shooed them onto the front porch.
"That's the trouble with you, Glenda. You're always
saying. 'Bye, now. And mind you don't keep tripping
over that tongue of yours."

Shutting the door with a satisfying thwack, Caro
wiped the unfortunate incident off her hands.

But the party mood had plummeted. The other
neighbors made stilted excuses and swiftly departed.
Drew was muttering angrily. Amber and her friends
drifted off in a self-conscious pack. The younger girls
were shocked silent. Poor Gabby looked stricken.

Caro herded Gabby and the twins toward the stairs.
"You girls go pick up that room, now. From the sound
of things, I'd say it's at least a four-alarm mess."

Refusing to meet her mother's eyes, Gabby trailed
her friends upstairs. As soon as they'd rounded the second landing, Caro took Thea by the elbow, led her into
the kitchen, and sat her down.

"You all right, sugar? I swear, that woman's so busy
talking she's got no time left to use her brains."

Thea nodded numbly and kept her real feelings to
herself. She couldn't attribute Glenda's attacks to simple thoughtlessness. For some reason, the woman had
had it in for her.

Thea swallowed back a hard lump of despair. "I

don't know, Caro. . . . How can I ever make things right for Gabby?"

"Only way is to put it behind you, darlin'. Simon's murder was a terrible thing, but it wasn't the real you who did it. You've got to stop blaming yourself, Thea. That's the first step."

Exactly what Dr. Forman kept telling her. Good advice, but oh so difficult to follow. "I'll try."

Thea hugged her friend and called upstairs for Gabby. "We'd better get home, sweetie. School tomorrow."

"Coming, Mommy."

"Thanks for everything, Caro."

"For what?"

Linden Street was shaped like a light bulb. Craving fresh air, Thea turned left out of the Millport drive and followed the block to its spreading circular end. With a pang, she realized Gabby had grown so much she didn't have to skip and scurry to keep apace.

Thea took her daughter's hand. Little bird, warm and weightless. "I'm so sorry, sweetie."

"It's okay."

"No. It's not okay. But there's no way to fix all the mean and thoughtless people. All we can do is try not to let them hurt us."

"Don't feel bad, Mommy. It's not your fault."

Was she really blameless in her daughter's eyes? In Caro's eyes? Could her best friend and her little girl honestly solve the impossible moral conundrum that kept confounding Thea? Her actions had caused all this pain. She had wielded the weapon that killed Simon. Whose fault was it if not hers?

A bitter lump of sorrow lodged in Thea's throat, but, as usual, no tears followed. After Justin's death, she found herself unable to let the grief well up and melt away. Even Simon's murder and the ensuing horrors had failed to dislodge the jam. Her sorrow was dried rock in a riverbed. Unchanging.

They had skirted the end of the block. Heading home, their shadows shifted to the straightaway. Two seeking forms on the silent road.

"I'm so sorry, Gabs. So very sorry."

"It's all right, Mommy. It's over now."

Impulsively, Thea caught the child in a hug, drawing precious strength from this feisty little miracle she and Justin had produced. It would be all right, she resolved. Whatever it took, she would make it all right.

A car turned onto Linden Street. Thea shielded her eyes against the glare of the approaching headlights and made out the shape of a stately black Bentley. A liveried chauffeur was at the wheel. Definitely not your typical neighborhood traffic.

As Thea and Gabby neared their house, the big car eased to a stop beside them. Stepping out, the pewter-haired driver raised a hand to the peak of his cap.

"Mrs. Harper?"

"Yes."

He reached into his uniform pocket and extracted a square linen envelope. "For you, madam." Hard to miss the white gloves he wore and the killing frost in his tone. "My apologies for the intrusion, madam. Good evening."

Before she could ask any questions, the man bowed crisply and drove off.

Gabby was duly impressed. "Maybe it's a million dollars, Mommy. Maybe we won a sweepstakes or something."

Thea carried the sealed missive inside. She didn't have to look at the monogram to know the source. And she didn't have to read the contents to know it was anything but a harbinger of good fortune.

CHAPTER
SIX

Her appointment with Dr. Forman was in thirty minutes. Thea tossed on her jeans and a sweatshirt, downed her antiseizure pill with a slug of orange juice, and headed out.

On the way to the garage, she had the uneasy sense that she was being watched. Wheeling around, she spotted a figure running behind the Hobermans' house two doors away. Her view was partially obstructed and fleeting, but she had the distinct feeling she was being tailed by the rat reporter, Harlan Vermin.

Thea went hot with fury. Nothing would have given her more pleasure than to catch the bastard in the act and nail him, but she didn't want to be late.

Dr. Forman's office suite was in the Landmark Towers, a stark, modern complex of shops, movie theaters, and office buildings in downtown Stamford. Thea found a space in the crowded garage and took the elevator to the ninth floor.

Arriving fifteen minutes early, she settled on one of the plump brown chairs flanking the bay window. The space was neat and sparsely furnished: beige Berber carpet, tweed love seat, twin occasional tables capped by russet ginger-jar lamps. The magazine rack was filled with back issues of *Smithsonian* and copies of the *Harvard Alumni Magazine*. A Chopin sonata wafted through speakers embedded high in the walls.

Despite the music, which was intended as conversation camouflage, Thea could hear the shrill of the patient's voice from inside the doctor's office. The words were muffled, but the woman's anguish came through clearly. Her pained diatribe was punctuated by screams and wrenching sobs.

Curious, Thea leaned closer to the connecting wall, but she couldn't get a better fix on the words. She considered strolling over casually and pressing an ear to the door, but thoughts of nosy Glenda Rossner kept her in her seat. And before her own snooping tendencies had a chance to assert themselves further, Thea caught a shift in the sounds from the inner office. The patient's voice dimmed. The doctor's soothing lilt was interjected. There was the beat of retreating footsteps and a rear inside door smacked shut. The session was over.

Precisely ten minutes later, Dr. Forman opened the connecting door to the waiting room. As always, Maxine Forman was the portrait of brusque professionalism with her cropped auburn hair, hazel eyes framed by bookish glasses, stern mouth, and slim patrician nose. Her skin was factory pale, her figure lathe perfect. She wore a navy suit, cream silk blouse, ivory hose, and spectator pumps. No makeup except for the palest pink lipstick. No jewelry except for the modest strand of pearls at her throat and a simple watch on a leather band. The doctor's expression was inscrutable.

"Good morning, Thea. Come in."

The inner office was a generous square. A maple desk fronted the bay window. Opposite was a burgundy leather couch and a pair of matching armchairs. Two banks of gunmetal gray filing cabinets flanked the door at the center of the rear wall. That had to be the sobber's exit route, Thea thought. Dr. Forman caught her curious gaze.

"For my more reticent patients," the psychiatrist explained. "Have a seat."

Thea settled in an armchair. From the outset of Thea's treatment, the doctor had offered the couch as optional, and Thea had opted out. She liked her conver-

sations face-to-face, even when they weren't exactly conversations.

To indicate the official start of the session, Dr.
Forman pressed the "record" button on her ultramodern
cassette machine. As always, the initial silence was
Thea's to break. After nine months of biweekly
meetings with the psychiatrist, Thea was more than familiar with the drill. If she failed to fire the opening
shot, the entire meeting could expire without a word.
"It's been a little strange," she said finally.

"Strange how?"

"With Gabby mostly. She's changed."

Dr. Forman offered her standard response: a noncommittal nod.

"She's gotten so moody. And secretive. Half the time
I feel as if I've been locked out, as if I'm watching her
through a peephole."

"Gabrielle is how old now?"

"Almost ten. But if you're thinking this is normal
preadolescent stuff, that's not what I'm talking about.
It's different. Yesterday, she came home dressed like a
ragamuffin and reeking of cigarette smoke."

"And you felt?"

"Terrified, angry, guilty, sad. All the standard parent
stuff. Know what I mean?"

Dr. Forman nodded as if she did, though she probably would have offered the same empathetic gesture if
Thea had been bemoaning her wrenching decade-long
struggle with infertility. The shrink revealed nothing
remotely personal. After nearly a year of regular sessions, Thea had no idea whether the woman had a family, friends, or the vaguest semblance of a civilian life.

In truth, it wouldn't have surprised Thea to learn
that this particular doctor suspended herself in the coat
closet at the end of each work day and simply hung
there until her next precisely scheduled appointment. It

was difficult to picture the woman having anything as messy and uncertain as a relationship. Dr. Forman was the most controlled, most *in* control human imaginable. She acted as if her psyche had been drawn to exacting specifications in utero promptly set in cement.

At first, Thea had found the doctor intimidating, but she soon learned Maxine Forman had a keen, almost cutting intelligence. She was sharp and demanding and sometimes brutally direct. Thea suspected the woman could cause egg whites to form stiff peaks by sheer force of will.

As difficult as it was to like the shrink, it was impossible not to respect her. And in Thea's case, the respect was capped by a considerable debt of gratitude.

Thea had met Dr. Forman a month before Simon's death at a group gallery show including her work. After Thea's arrest, the esteemed doctor had agreed to conduct a psychiatric evaluation for the defense. While the state's panel of shrinks was prepared to label Simon Gallatin's murder the vicious and deliberate act of a woman scorned, Dr. Forman quickly picked up the subtle signs of an organic problem.

Thea's personal and family medical history provided the first clues. Twice, as a small child, she'd experienced seizures associated with high fevers. Her mother's brother, who'd died of a strep infection in his teens, had suffered from what Ellie remembered to be "fits." Thea's own brother Jimmy's problems with paying attention in school may well have been a case of absence epilepsy, the modern term for petit mal. The condition involved tiny, imperceptible interruptions in the flow of consciousness that could occur hundreds of times each day.

The specifics of Simon's murder had given Dr. Forman a further clue to Thea's medical problem. Thea had no memory of the bloody assault. Not even hypno-

sis or the administration of sodium Pentothal, a so-
called "truth" serum, could help her remember. Hers
was not the normal repression of a traumatic event. The
savage killing was buried in a secret place, blocked
from Thea's conscious mind.

Dr. Forman had insisted on a full neurological battery, including electroencephalographic studies, a CAT
scan, and an MRI. The sum of the behavioral and physical findings led to the diagnosis of complex partial seizures, formerly known as temporal lobe epilepsy. In
nearly all cases, the doctor explained to Thea, the condition was controllable and benign. Persistent myths
and biases against epileptics were baseless and unreasonable, she continued.

But a seizure of the type Thea had experienced could
trigger repetitive acts. And though Dr. Forman's medical opinion in the case sparked considerable contro-
versy, she had argued convincingly in court that the
savage beating Thea had inflicted on Simon Gallatin resulted from an extremely rare, highly acute episode of
the seizure disorder.

"Aside from your concerns about your daughter, how
are things?" Dr. Forman asked.

"All right, I guess." Thea considered mentioning the
disturbing letter she'd received last night, but decided
against it. Nothing in the medical books could help her
with that issue. She knew what she had to do in response; she didn't want or need Dr. Forman's input on
the subject.

"Have you gotten back to work yet?"

"Not exactly."

"It's important, Thea. As we agreed before your discharge, work is part of the return to normalcy. You
should be painting."

"I've tried. I haven't been able to concentrate."

In fact, Thea had spent the better part of the morning in her airy studio behind the house. She'd set a large Masonite board on her easel, prepared the necessary pigments, brushes, solvents, and wipes. And then, she'd spent hours staring at the blank space, willing her mind to stop its frantic racing and settle on some worthwhile image.

But nothing came.

The experience astonished and unnerved Thea. All her life she'd had a head full of compelling visions. As soon as she'd exorcised one by brushing or sketching it on canvas, another would appear. Often, several ideas gripped her simultaneously, whimpering like a litter of hungry pups for her attention. During the terrible weeks of her trial, there had been no time for painting. And at Brook Hollow, she'd lacked the necessary space and solitude. But now, fresh out of reasonable excuses, the only place her mind would settle was on the horrific image of Simon's battered body in the den. Simon's bashed skull. Simon's unseeing eyes.

"If you're not up to tackling a painting, why not try something simpler? Illustrations, caricatures, sketches. Whatever. The point is to get started."

Easy for her to say. Dr. Forman hadn't committed a lurid murder, spent a year clawing out of the rubble, and come home to a temperamental nine-year-old, a nasty-tongued neighbor, and an even nastier hand-delivered note. All that and the giant cauldron of simmering self-doubt were more than enough to keep Thea occupied full time.

"I'll try," Thea said.

"You sound awfully tentative."

"All this hasn't been easy, Doctor."

"Whether you take control or not is entirely up to you, Thea. Self-pity is a poor substitute for positive action."

"I know that."

"Of course you do. And I'm sure you understand how critical it is to put the circumstances of the past year behind you, to move forward."

"You make it sound ominous."

"That's your perception. All I've done is point out a basic fact of human enterprise. You move on or risk falling back into the past."

"Meaning?"

"What does it mean to you?"

That was the doctor's infuriating way. Answer a question with a question. Offer nothing but added fuel to the raging bonfire of misgivings.

"I thought you said the medication would prevent any possibility of another problem," Thea said.

"Thea, do you honestly believe medication is the solution to your problems?"

Fear iced Thea's bones. Her past was littered with dead eyes and spattered gore. The past was illness and mindless violence and the morbid curiosity of blood-sucking strangers.

"Each of us must grasp control, Thea. Otherwise, we all have the capacity to surrender to unfortunate impulses."

"I won't," Thea vowed in a grim whisper. Her hands clenched in her lap. "Never again."

"That's precisely the sort of attitude I want to see." The ice queen managed a tepid smile. "Remember, it's all up to you, Thea. You must take charge of your life and get on with it. You mustn't allow anything external to dictate your behavior."

Thea didn't have to check the clock to know that their truncated hour had expired. "Good-bye, Dr. Forman."

The doctor rose and extended a firm, cool hand. "See you next week. I'll look forward to a full report of your progress."

Thea took the Connecticut Turnpike to Greenwich and exited at the business district. The center of town boasted pricey boutiques, personalized pharmacies, and the occasional chain outlet, subtly packaged to suit the rarified milieu.

Greenwich was vintage money in vast quantities. True citizens of the community wore their affluence close to the understated vest. They drove generic suburban vehicles and selected their wardrobes with an eye to avoiding such unforgivable vulgarities as fashion or style. Eager newcomers tended to commit such predictable misdemeanors as buying Mercedes station wagons for the maid to drive to the supermarket.

Turning off Greenwich Avenue onto the Post Road, she followed Maple onto North Street. Her anxiety rose as she tracked the meandering route for several miles until it crossed the Merritt Parkway.

This was horse country. Sprawling estates, many home to thoroughbreds of both the two- and four-legged variety, were ensconced behind towering stands of evergreens and discreetly electrified fences.

Thea had visited several of the grander mansions in the heady weeks after Simon discovered her and her art at the gallery. A number of Gallatin family friends and acolytes, curious about the senator's newfound interest, had purchased her paintings and sought her personal assistance in their installation. She remembered feeling that much of the time it was she, and not her work, that was being scrutinized and critiqued; it was she who was placed on display.

Still, those uneasy episodes had been nothing compared to the one she was about to confront. Her throat was parched, her head pounding. Her entire being screamed for an immediate U-turn. But she had to clear the rubble before her life could be rebuilt. Dr. Forman's warnings echoed in her mind. She would not risk slipping into reverse. Whatever it took, she was going to put the past in its proper place. And she would leave it there.

A wrought iron gate marked the entrance to the Gallatin property. Interlocking iron *G*'s were woven into its design. With a red-eyed wink, the security camera acknowledged her arrival. A clipped voice sounded through the intercom, advising her to enter. After a moment's hesitation, the gates silently parted. Thea's pulse raced as she navigated the interminable chevroned drive.

The main house was a mammoth beaux-arts structure. There was a stately front porch buttressed by squat carved columns. Escutcheons, quoins, and sculptural figures adorned the elaborate facade. Thea parked her ancient Volvo beside the granite fountain centering the stone courtyard and drew a shaky breath for courage.

Climbing the stairs leading to the high-arched entrance, her face was flushed, her heart stammering. Trying to compose herself, she hesitated at the door.

Countless times since Simon's death, she'd agonized over finding some way to express her regret and remorse to his family. She'd visualized a thousand unwritten letters, rehearsed hundreds of unplaced phone calls. Her profound fear of the confrontation had not been the biggest hindrance. The problem was the laughable inadequacy of words. How could she begin to apologize for the monstrous thing she had done? What could she possibly say to ease these unimaginable circumstances?

She was about to find out.

The door swung open as she raised her hand to ring the bell. A young man with slicked-back hair and a funereal gray suit eyed her contemptuously; mutely he led her through the spacious entrance hall to a sunlit morning room. His stony silence forestalled any introductions, and none appeared to be necessary. Apparently, she was expected. Odd, Thea thought, given that the note requesting this visit had mentioned no specific time. People like these must be accustomed to having their wishes taken as immediate commands. Wordlessly, the man motioned her toward a faded rose-toned settee and withdrew.

Moments later, Lily Gallatin entered. She was followed by a young woman who bore a startling resemblance to Simon. This was his younger sister Marielle.

By report, the legendary matriarch of the powerful Gallatin clan was seventy-five, but the old woman looked at least a decade younger. Her coloring was striking: steely blue eyes, deep tan, hair so thick and gleaming white, it resembled a snowdrift. Her posture was stick straight, her bearing a cross between regal and unabashedly arrogant. She wore a black silk dress, midheel pumps, heirloom emerald jewelry, and a stern expression. Smoothing her skirt, she lowered herself onto a tapestried armchair. Her daughter stood with a hand on the chair back, still as a statue. Thea felt herself shriveling under the young woman's fixed, hostile gaze.

"You were wise to come, Mrs. Harper," Lily Gallatin said. Her voice was a hammer strike, cold and harsh. "It would not have pleased me to have to pursue you further."

"I'm glad you sent the note, Mrs. Gallatin. I've been wanting to talk to you since Simon's death, to tell you how terribly sorry I am."

The patrician look went sour. "Then why haven't you?"

There was a timid knock.

"Yes, Margaret. Come in," Lily Gallatin said.

A uniformed maid entered. She bore a formal tea service on an ornate silver tray. Thea accepted a delicate porcelain cup filled with freshly steeped Earl Grey, then set it carefully on a side table. She felt like the china, fragile and nearly transparent. The two women's faultless control only served to intensify Thea's mounting discomfort. Anything would be better than this strained civility, Thea thought. She would have preferred to have the scalding tea tossed at her, the porcelain shards raking her flesh, the burning rage out in the open, where she could see the size and shape of it.

Mrs. Gallatin sampled a sip from the teacup she had balanced effortlessly on her lap. Satisfied, she dismissed the maid with a backhanded wave and fixed her cold blue eyes on Thea.

"Tell me about yourself, Mrs. Harper. I understand you're a widow."

Thea felt the familiar tug of sorrow. "My husband died six years ago. He was teaching first-year medical students how to analyze a blood sample. To demonstrate, he drew his own first. When he viewed the slide, he knew he was looking at acute lymphocytic leukemia. It was past any hope of a cure. He died a month later."

"You have a child?"

What was the purpose of this inquisition? After Simon's death, the press had placed her life in all its most minute detail on public display. Undoubtedly, Lily Gallatin knew everything there was to know about her. But Thea was here to satisfy the old woman's agenda, whatever it was. "Gabby's nine. She's a beautiful little girl. Very bright. And sensitive. This has all been very difficult for her."

Lily Gallatin set the cup down on a marble-topped table. Rising, she crossed to the window and pushed the heavy brocade curtain aside. Her daughter's cold, un-blinking gaze remained on Thea, making her squirm. She wished the young woman would say something, *do* something. Marielle was like a weapon, aimed and wait-ing.

"Have you ever *lost* a child, Mrs. Harper?"

Losing Gabby was unthinkable. Unspeakable. And yet, Thea had taken this woman's son from her. Her throat closed. "No."

"It's a most excruciating experience, I can assure you. The pain is so deep and pervasive, it's quite impossible to describe."

If only there were a right thing to say. If only Thea could do something to make the nightmare disappear. "I can imagine," she whispered.

The old woman's composure abruptly snapped; she wheeled to face Thea. "No. I don't believe you can, Mrs. Harper. I don't believe you can begin to know what it was like to view my beautiful son in his coffin, to touch his cheek and feel the chill of death." Lily Gallatin raised her cupped hands, cradling a vision. The large emerald on her finger emitted a cold, green light. "That boy had everything: charm, looks, intelligence. Simon was a born statesman. A born leader."

Thea's heart was racing wildly. "I don't know what to say. I cared for Simon. Very much. I would never have hurt him purposely."

But you did worse than hurt him, Thea. You took his life.

The ice blue eyes narrowed to menacing slits. "I was at that trial, Mrs. Harper. I followed every word, heard every shred of testimony. You had a clever lawyer. Con-vincing experts. A pretty face and a dozen sympathetic fools on the jury. Our legal system allows such things to substitute for the truth."

"I'm sorry you feel that way. I'm sorrier than you can imagine. Believe me, Mrs. Gallatin, I'd give anything if things could be different."

The woman nodded her silver head. A murderous smirk curled the corners of her mouth. "And so you shall, Mrs. Harper. And so they will."

Marielle's approving nod was nearly imperceptible. The young woman's eerie stillness was worse than her mother's seething fury.

"I don't understand," Thea said.

"Don't you? Allow me to explain, then." Settling back in her chair, Simon's mother flared her fingers like spider legs and tapped the tips together as she spoke. The emerald ring glinted.

"My faith in our judicial system has been utterly destroyed, Mrs. Harper. Your trial proved to me that the courts are inadequate and utterly unreliable. Juries and judges are mere mortals. They are subject to whim and to irrelevant emotions. You murdered my son in cold blood, and you were found not guilty. But that in no way wipes Simon's blood off your hands."

She's right, Thea thought, feeling panic rise. *Sick or not, I'm responsible for her son's murder.*

The tapping stilled. "I shall succeed where the courts have failed so miserably. In retribution for my son's death, I plan to destroy every shred of pleasure and happiness you have. You shall be left with nothing. *Less* than nothing. What you did to my Simon will seem a gentle deliverance compared to what I see in store for you."

Lily Gallatin balled her hands in bloodless fists. Her aristocratic face flashed fury. Thea sat in numb silence. She'd expected this venomous hatred, even, perhaps, invited it, but its poisonous enormity chilled her to the bone.

"Think of me as you find your life disintegrating in

useless fragments, Mrs. Harper," said the relentless steely voice. "And think of Simon."

The old woman lifted an ornate silver frame from the end table. With a trembling finger, she traced her dead son's smiling face.

"My boy was destined for greatness. He was to be our finest president, the one to unite our fragmented country behind the common cause of our collective betterment. Simon had a genius for bringing people together. A *genius*."

Staring at the picture, her luminous eyes went vague. "Even as a small child, my son had the most engaging manner. An easy, natural charm. Everyone adored him. Even his jealous detractors couldn't help but admire Simon personally. . . ."

A flicker of pain pinched her expression. Straightening abruptly, she pressed the picture to her bosom. "Justice will not be denied, Mrs. Harper. You will find yourself devoutly wishing that the courts had meted a suitable punishment in your case. I can assure you, my vengeance will not be tempered by the slightest trace of mercy."

Thea shivered, still almost mute in the face of Lily Gallatin's rage and her daughter's bristling silence. "All I can offer you is my apology, Mrs. Gallatin. I am sorrier about Simon's death—about all of it—than you can possibly know."

"Your apology means nothing to me, Mrs. Harper. And though I agree that your life has pitifully little to offer, you may rest assured that I intend to destroy every bit of it."

He'd caught her unprepared again. Third time since lunch. A cloud of consternation crossed the teacher's face. Humiliated, Gabby scrunched lower in her seat.

She was one of the best students in the class, always one the teacher could depend on to fill the clumsy silences with a thoughtful response. But today, her attention kept straying out the window. All she could think about was whether any of the older boys would show up before the closing bell.

"Could you please repeat the question?" Gabby said.

"I asked if you could tell us about the Lewis and Clark expedition."

The information was buried in the muck. Gabby's mind was tuned to the Silly Channel. Lewis was that old comedian who made dumb faces and acted in movies with a guy named Martin. Clark was a candy bar. Peanutty center covered with chocolate. Zit food, Amber called it. Guaranteed to stick in your teeth.

"Were they the ones from China who discovered spaghetti?" she proposed hopefully.

The teacher's lips tensed. He called on Caity Cohane, and the uneasy spotlight shifted to the other side of the room.

Now, Opal Millport was vying for Gabby's attention. *Explorers out west*, Opal mouthed silently with something akin to exasperation. "Thomas Jefferson sent them to look around after he bought all that land. You know."

Gabby hitched her shoulders. One of those days.

Or was it? She ventured another peek outside. Still

no sign of the Greens Farms boys or Dylan Connable. At this point, she wasn't certain which she dreaded more. Eddie, Rod, and Brian might be dopey jerks who'd been torturing her for months about her mother. But there was a nameless something about Dylan that made her stomach go funny.

Not that he'd done anything bad. In fact, he'd treated her like some kind of a princess. With a shudder, she remembered how he'd clasped her hand to help her up the last few rickety stairs leading to his garage room. At the top, he'd worked the trail of locks and gently guided her inside.

The room was black as a moonless night. Dylan flipped a switch beside the door, illuminating the single bare bulb that hung like a disembodied head in the center of the ceiling. There was a mattress on the floor, a torn beanbag chair patched with tape, and a tall stool with a broken cane seat. A battered door on sawhorses held Dylan's boom box, a clock, a stack of CD's, and several stacks of shoe boxes. Ugly posters were tacked to the walls. A huge hairy spider stared at her from one of them. Another featured a weird-looking guy with visible bones, veins, and muscles. Gabby's eye automatically gravitated to the vein- and muscle-ridden penis, and her face went hot.

The single shabby room contained everything. In one corner, a rusty tub, sink, and toilet were set behind the same kind of folding screen they had at the pediatrician's office. No sign of a closet or dresser. Piles of junk littered the floor. Dipping into a couple of the heaps, Dylan extracted a plaid flannel shirt and a pair of grungy jeans.

"They're clean," he said, holding them out to Gabby.

Her stomach fisted as he turned his back. He obviously expected her to change right there with him in the same room. She stood immobile, frozen by fear and

embarrassment. Maybe she could pull out the folded
screen and hide behind it. . . .

"Go on. I won't look," he said. His voice held a trace
of annoyed amusement that made her feel small and
silly. Defiantly, she slipped off her torn blouse and ex-
changed it for his soft worn shirt. She hitched up the
jeans and tugged her soiled skirt over her head.

The shirt was all right, large but not ridiculous. But
she could have invited Opal and Jasmine to share the
pants. Gabby clutched a mass of fabric to keep them
from slipping over her slim hips.

"You ready yet?"

"They don't fit."

Turning, Dylan eyed her critically. Rummaging
through several more mounds of debris, he found a
length of ratty rope. Gabby's nose filled with the smell
of stale cologne and tobacco as he bent to fasten the
makeshift belt around her waist.

A tiny refrigerator hummed under the blacked-out
window. Nothing in it but soda, Yodels, and beer.
Dylan extracted two cans of Coke and steered her by the
shoulders to the stool.

"Sit." He popped the soda tab with his teeth and
thrust the can at her.

Queasy, careful not to spill her drink, Gabby perched
on the high seat and coiled her dangling feet around the
uprights.

With surprisingly deft fingers, Dylan quickly unfastened what remained of her braid. The brush was a
shivery tickle as he drew it in long, languid strokes
through her hair. His touch was the creepy trail of
crawling bugs. Gabby clenched her teeth to keep the
tremors from showing.

Moments later, he'd combed out all the tangles and
gathered her hair in a ponytail. He fastened the clump
high on her head with the coated rubber band. After he

put the barrettes back in place, he straightened her collar. Leaning close, Dylan plucked a speck of something off her shoulder. She caught the smell of minty gum and soda on his breath.

"There. That's better," he said.

"Thanks. I'd better go now."

"In a minute. I have something to show you. Something wonderful."

He reached into one of the shoe boxes.

"This is the most amazing of all things in the universe. Can you guess?"

"No."

"A miracle bigger than life itself. Guess anything. Go on. I know you're smart."

"Some kind of god?"

Dylan laughed. As he spread his fingers, Gabby saw that he was holding a dead mouse. The thing had shriveled skin and black bead eyes. Twig legs and a puff-bellied body. She gasped and had to keep herself from falling backward off the stool.

Dylan was cradling the revolting creature. Stroking it. His voice dimmed to a creepy hush. "Death is the other side, little one. The *better* side. Can you see?"

She stiffened. "Get it away. Get it away from me!"

Dylan looked startled. Tenderly, he replaced the mouse in the box, then raised a finger to his lips. "Ssh. It's all right, sweetness. Don't worry. I'm going to help you understand."

His words were wispy soft, a kisslike tickle on the back of her neck.

"I'm going to teach you," she heard him whisper. "I'm going to make you see."

The closing bell sounded, jolting her back to the classroom. Chairs scraped. A noisy, jostling mass of kids pushed toward the door. Opal was among them, toting her violin in a case covered with stars and rainbow stickers. The Millport twins had orchestra practice three days a week after school.

Gabby wished she had Opal to walk with to the bus. No one else from the class took the number seven except Neil Lufkin, who snorted milk out of his nose and turned his eyelids inside out so you could see the slimy parts. Walking with Neil would be every bit as nasty as mean teasing or dead mice.

She stole a final glance out the window. Still no sign of Dylan or the Green Farms geeks. So maybe she'd gotten lucky for a change. She swiftly packed her book bag and pushed her chair in.

"Gabby Harper. Please wait a minute. I'd like to speak with you."

She slumped back in her seat. The teacher didn't sound angry, but no one was asked to stay after school for anything good. It seemed forever until the last departing kid was out the door and the teacher strode over to close it.

Returning, he perched on top of the desk beside her. Gabby stared fiercely at the traces of chipped red polish on her nails.

"Having a bad day?" the teacher asked.

"I've been thinking. That's all."

"I've noticed. Anything you'd like to talk about?"

"No. It's nothing."

"I heard your mom's home from the hospital. That must be nice for you."

Waiting for the falling ax, Gabby could only shrug.

"I'd like to meet her."

"Please, please, Mr. Perry. Don't tell her I've been bad. I'll always listen from now on. Every word. I promise."

His face softened in a smile. "What I want to tell your mom is what a pleasure it is having you in class, Gabby. And what a talented writer you are."

"You mean it?"

"Of course, I do. Soon as she has the time, I'd like her to hear how well you've been doing. Of course, I understand she must be busy."

"Not really."

He scratched a note on his memo pad and handed it to Gabby. "If you'd give her this, she can let me know when it'll be convenient."

Gabby was happy enough to float. Mr. Perry was the nicest, best teacher she'd ever had in her whole life. Handsome, too, with his wavy dark hair and kind brown eyes and the cool way he dressed in jeans and wore a T-shirt under his sports jacket instead of a dress shirt and tie. Gabby remembered how nervous she'd been when she heard he'd be subbing while Mrs. Carlisle was out with her new baby. Mr. Perry was Gabby's first man teacher. And she hadn't known what to expect. Before his arrival, she and Opal had spent long hours discussing what it might be like having Mr. Perry in front of the room.

"I'm sure she'd like to meet you very soon. Maybe even tomorrow," she told him.

"Great. Whatever's good for her. You let me know."

"Oh, I will, Mr. Perry. First thing."

Gabby charged out to the bus. Grinning, she settled in a rear seat, savoring Mr. Perry's words. Mom would be bursting proud when the teacher repeated all that praise.

Your daughter is such a pleasure, Mrs. Harper. And so talented.

She couldn't wait to tell the twins. Everyone was crazy about Mr. Perry, especially the girls. Opal had a page of hearts inside her notebook inscribed with his initials. For weeks, Jasmine had been desperately trying to figure a way to transfer out of Miss Levine's class and into Mr. Perry's. Last week, after hearing the twins and

Gabby carrying on about the man, Amber told them about this program she'd seen on TV about a boy who'd fallen madly in love with his teacher and wound up shooting her husband. Hearing that, the younger girls all agreed how lucky it was that Mr. Perry was single.

Which set her thinking. After what happened with Senator Gallatin, Gabby had prayed and prayed that her mom would never meet another boyfriend. But now, they knew about Mommy's sickness. The medicine would keep her well. The bad thing could never, ever happen again.

Then Gabby's smile crumbled. She remembered coming home that night. Mommy had been painting when she left, and Gabby had noticed the glow from the studio lights behind the house when Amber walked her home. At first, she figured it was weird for her mother to be working so late. But sometimes, Mom got started on a picture and lost track of the clock. Her father always used to tease her about it.

The front door was unlocked, so that night Gabby said good night to Amber and let herself in. It felt spooky walking into the dark, empty house alone, but she wasn't about to act like a scared baby in front of Amber. She refused to start yelling for her mother or to run around flipping on the lamps as if she was afraid of the dark. Amber would never do dopey things like that. All Gabby had to do was follow the soft beam of light from the studio and get her mom to come inside.

Halfway across the murky foyer, a weird feeling stalled her. She'd wanted to turn on the lights, but something held her back. Something was wrong in the house, something she didn't want to see any clearer. Gabby could feel it like the spooky change before a bad storm. A dangerous shift in the air that settled deep in your bones and made your head ache.

Part of her wanted to run out back and get Mommy.

But again she considered what Amber would do. Once, the older girl had been sitting for all the younger kids when her parents went out to a wedding. Near midnight, Jasmine heard a noise. It sounded like a burglar tripping over something in the living room. Frightened, Jazzy had awakened Amber from a deep sleep, and still the older girl had the courage and presence to grab her field hockey stick and go downstairs to have a look around. It turned out that one of the cats had knocked over a lamp. And Opal and Gabby had slept through the whole incident.

So Gabby knew better than to make a big deal about some silly feeling.

She drew a deep breath, stiffened her shoulders, and entered the room. The silence was bristling thick. And there was the rank, musky smell of an animal in the woods. Maybe a stray cat had gotten in through the open door. Wouldn't that be funny?

But something told her it wasn't nearly that simple or innocent.

Forcing herself to keep moving, Gabby trained her eyes on the familiar shapes: the chunky back of the sofa, the fat arm of the blue easy chair, the dark, gaping mouth of the fireplace.

She was almost at the couch when she spotted him.

At first, she thought it had to be some kind of a joke. His face was all strange, his limbs stiff and twisted like fallen tree branches. But then, she saw the dark spreading puddle around his head. The mess was spattered over everything. The rug, the blanket, the wall. Gabby didn't feel the scream rising. She didn't feel anything until much, much later.

The bus was moving now. Gabby squeezed her fists until the nails nipped her palms. The pain turned her mind away from the bad thing. It was a trick she'd figured out months ago, while her mom was on trial. Bet-

ter not to remember. Much better to think about Mr.
Perry wanting to meet her mother. Maybe they'd really
like each other.

With a smirk, Gabby thought how the twins would
perish if she got to have Mr. Perry as a stepfather. Forget
the twins. *She* would perish.

Fingering the slip of memo paper the teacher had
given her, she closed her eyes and tried to envision that
amazing possibility. Imagine Mr. Perry living in her
house, Mr. Perry eating breakfast and dinner with her
every single day. Imagine calling the teacher Daddy and
getting to kiss him good night in her pajamas! The
thoughts were so dazzling, they made her dizzy.

Struck by a terrific idea, Gabby crumpled the note
and buried it deep in her bag. When Mom and the
teacher got together, it had to be exactly right.

CHAPTER
NINE

The chief of Westport's detective squad was wearing a warpath in his office carpet. As he paced, Inspector Buck Delavan had the comical look of a lapsed marine with his medicine ball belly, jangly jowls, and sparsely populated flattop.

"I don't appreciate getting my news thirdhand. Don't like it one damned bit, you read me? You hear?"

Sergeant Daniel Biederman recoiled from the roar of his boss's displeasure. Of course, he'd heard. Neighboring nations had probably heard. Delavan was not what anyone would describe as soft-spoken.

And the tirade had yet to reach its crescendo. "I get home last night after a long, hard day. All I'm after is a tall frosty one and a hot meal. So, I sit at the table, and I ask my wife what's new. Just making conversation, you understand. And she tells me how she was playing in her regular canasta game this afternoon, and she hears from her friend Nora that the Harper bitch is out of the loony bin and back on the street. Seems Nora's eldest boy is a dispatcher for the taxi company. He heard it from one of his drivers who drove the murdering liar from the nut hatch this very morning. Now, I'd like to know why in the hell *I* wasn't informed."

Biederman didn't respond. At six-six, Daniel Biederman towered over his boss and everyone else on the Westport force. From his unique perspective, he could observe the angry scarlet blotches mottling his boss's scalp. Sure sign of an impending eruption. From hard experience, Biederman knew there was no percentage in trying to rea-

son with an active volcano. But his partner, Vince
Passerelli, managed to miss the signs.

"The Harper woman walked, Inspector. She's not our
problem," Passerelli rashly volunteered.

Delavan snorted. "No, Passerelli, *you're* our problem.
You're freaking unbelievable sometimes, you know
that? Regular Polly Freaking Anna. Seeing what a small
town we are, you probably figure we're real lucky to
have our very own homicidal lunatic."

Passerelli scratched behind his ear. "Come on, Inspector. I know you were a big fan of Senator Gallatin's.
We all were. But you don't have to take it out on me."

"Who, then? I goddamned have to take it out on
somebody." Delavan smacked a fat copy of Connecticut's
penal code on his desktop. "Six months in a five-star
cracker factory, and that woman is home free. What's
this goddamned world coming to anyway?"

"Jury found her not guilty. What can we do?"
Passerelli shrugged.

"What can we do? What can we *DO!*"

Biederman cringed. His partner had this real unfortunate talent for turning up the heat on Delavan's in-
cendiary temper. Not that it took much.

"Right. What can we?" poor Passerelli persisted.

The inspector's complexion was flaming rare. He
lowered his tone to a poison rasp and braced his meaty
palms on the desk. His pale eyes bulged. "I'll tell you
what we can do, Vincent. *Nothing,* that's what. Not a
goddamned——sonofabitch——stinking——single
thing!"

Passerelli caught his partner's eye and passed a silent
plea for help. Biederman was sympathetic, but the guy's
only possible salvation was his missing mute button.
Passerelli was like an overgrown kid. Wide-eyed, eager.
Hopelessly honest, open, and relentlessly optimistic. Man
had missed his calling. Strong Italian background and

spaghetti-western looks aside, Passerelli would have made one hell of an elf for Santa.

"We could keep an eye on her," suggested Passerelli meekly.

Strike three. "No, Vincent. We can *not* put Mrs. Harper under surveillance."

"Why not?"

"Three reasons. Money, money, and money. Budget's tighter than a clam's ass. If we had two homicides in town tomorrow, we'd have to defer one until the next goddamned fiscal year. You hear me, Passerelli? Do you goddamned *understand*!"

"You called us in, Inspector," Biederman interjected quickly. He and Vince were partners, after all. He figured it was his job to protect and defend Passerelli, even from himself.

Momentarily distracted, Delavan exhaled noisily. "Yes, I did. You two were on the Gallatin case from the first call. You got to know the principals as well as anyone on this force."

"Probably," Biederman said, cautiously.

"Especially the Harper woman. She took right to you, Danny boy. Ain't that so?"

Biederman shrugged. "She was in rough shape. I knew to go easy on her, so she opened up to me a little. That's all there was to it."

He didn't bother to mention that Thea Harper had struck him as real and decent. Not to mention possessed of a luminous beauty verging on the irresistible. Nor did he volunteer that he'd stopped by to visit the woman from time to time during the months she'd spent at Brook Hollow. He'd justified the trips to himself as casual courtesies.

In a way, Thea Harper reminded Biederman of his kid sister, Marna. The Harper woman aroused the same

protective instincts he'd felt decades ago when a neighborhood bully knocked Marna off her first two-wheeler.

Well, maybe not *exactly* the same instincts.

The night the case broke, Biederman and Passerelli
had been on their way back to the station after investi-
gating a possible break-and-enter on Kenwood. Turned
out to be a false alarm, some high school girl trying to
sneak into her house after a forbidden date. But the incident had put them right in the neighborhood. When
the homicide was radioed in, they'd caught the squeal
two blocks from Linden Street.

They arrived to find the door to the Harper house
wide open. Lights blazed. No response when they
knocked. Not knowing what to expect, they'd entered
with guns drawn, in crouch-ready position. After stumbling on the horror house in the den, they'd found the
Harper woman and her little girl huddled together on
the living room floor.

As long as he lived, Biederman would never forget
the scene. Thea Harper's face was bone white; her eyes
were wide and rimmed with dusky circles. Her hands
and clothing were crimson with blood. Hunched on the
floor with her daughter, she clutched the small child on
her lap as if some evil wind threatened to blow apart
their universe.

And so it had.

Biederman had been struck immediately by the
mother-daughter likeness: same rich manes of dark
curls, same oversized eyes, fine features, and slender
frames. Both were in deep shock. Passerelli, great with
kids, had moved forward to claim and soothe the little
girl. Biederman offered what minor comfort and reas-
surance he could to the mother. For an instant, he'd
thought she was coming around, starting to respond to
his help. But before he could fully reach her, the med-
ics, the evidence techs, and a team from the M.E.'s of-

fice stampeded in like a herd of crazed bull elephants. They'd trampled any stray chance for calm or reason.

"That's good, Danny boy," Delavan sneered. "Can't hurt for you to have the bitch's confidence."

"For what?" Biederman worked to keep the irritation out of his tone.

"I *want* that woman, Sergeant. I'm going to nail Harper's sweet ass to a jail cell if it's the last thing I ever do."

"For what?" Passerelli took up the refrain.

"Shoplifting. Spitting on the sidewalk. Puffery. Intent to gawk. I don't give a damn what we get her for, as long as we get her. If a dead fly lands on a windowsill within the town limits, Thea Harper's our prime suspect. Catch my drift?"

Biederman caught it and didn't care at all for the smell. Even Passerelli was rendered speechless for a welcome change. Delavan was a card-carrying hard nose. Always known to play strictly by the book. Hard to imagine the chief throwing the rules away, no matter how big a hard-on he had for Thea Harper.

"I want you two to buddy up to her," Delavan ranted on. "Strictly informal. Off-duty stuff. Drop by. Play the sympathetic ear. Concerned neighbors. Whatever the hell it takes. If anything's not kosher. I know you'll pick right up on it, Danny boy."

Biederman bristled at the ethnic jab and the general idea. Undercover was one thing. There was nothing in his contract that said he had to go underhanded.

"What if she's clean?" he asked.

"Clean, my butt. That bitch got luckier in court than anyone has a right to be. She drew Let-'em-off Offley for a judge and a bunch of bleeding hearts on the jury. But my bet is her luck's about to run out."

"And if your bet's wrong?"

"It won't be. We're going to get that murdering

bitch. Period. You read me, Danny boy? Or do I have to spell it freaking *out*!"

Biederman was startled by the violence in Delavan's tirade. Made no sense.

Or did it?

A nasty notion crept under Biederman's skin. The inspector had two ex-wives and a dizzying assortment of step- and regular kids. He complained nonstop that his money was tight to the point of strangulation.

Then suddenly, a couple of months back, he bought his pricey new young wife a new car. He started talking about building an addition to their house; he planned a Christmas trip to the Caribbean. His trademark rags were suddenly replaced by a spiffy new wardrobe that didn't even hint at polyester.

Now, Biederman tried to dismiss the ugly implications. But it was hard to set aside the obvious results of simple addition. And if the chief had been bought by the Gallatin family or any of the dead senator's pals, he and Passerelli were being played for jokers in a very high-stakes game indeed.

But he couldn't imagine a reasonable way to pass or fold. Bent or not, Delavan was clearly determined to nail Thea Harper. If Biederman found a way to turn his back on this, someone else would just step in and see the dirty deed done. No way that woman was going to be hung out to dry as long as Biederman kept one hand firmly on the clothesline. He didn't know why he was so solidly on her side, but suddenly, he did know one thing: He intended to remain there until he had it figured out.

Passerelli cast a longing look at the door. Excellent suggestion.

"If that's all, Chief, we'd better get rolling," Biederman said.

"I'm counting on you, boys. Don't let me down."

"We'll keep our eyes open."

"I know you will." Delavan nodded grimly, waggling his jowls. His face was still ruddy with anger. "Do it right, Passerelli. Eyes and ears open. Mouth shut."

Five minutes later, the partners left the station and headed out to investigate a domestic violence complaint. A raw wind was blowing. Looked like it was going to rain.

SECOND

THE
SECOND

CHAPTER
TEN

His pocket was chirping. With the fluid moves of a dueling gunfighter, he hit the mute button on the big screen remote, flipped the VCR to pause, and plucked his midget cellular phone out of his shirt pocket.

Big star, he was. Walking toy store.

"Yes?"

"Great news, kid. I got them to go to thirty. Thirty with a promise to review in ninety days."

His ten-percenter. Get big in the business and they slice you up like a birthday cake. Everyone took a piece: agent, manager, lawyer, accountant, voice coach, personal trainer, publicist, secretary, assistant, bimbo-du-jour.

"I told you forty-five, Lowell. Forty minimum. They say I'm an A player, let them pay me like an A player."

"Come on, baby. You know how it is. Times are tough."

"Who're you working for, Lowell? Them or me?"

"Look, I'll try, kid. I'll do my best. You got to trust me. Do you trust me, or what?"

"Tell them forty-five an episode, or I walk."

Low whistle. "You nail them to the wall like that, they're liable to kiss you off, kiddo. There's lots of other fishies in the sea would be glad to hop on this hook for fifteen or less."

"I'll take my chances."

"I'm serious. Those boys don't do well with ultimatums."

"I know what I'm doing, Lowell. Just tell them."

"You got big brass balls, baby. That much I'll say for you."

Folding the phone, he thought about the whole thing crumbling. Going back to square one. It could happen. He knew he was offering disaster an engraved invitation.

Two years ago, he'd been busing tables at the posh Snubnose Club in exclusive Bigot City outside of Chicago. There, he'd played fawning servant for minimum wage plus tips.

Some gig that was. He sneered at the memory. Fat-assed ladies would waggle their manicured mitts at him to fetch more rolls or iced tea or sugar substitute to put in the coffee they slurped with their cheesecake. Bald guys with leather skin and matching accessories would slip him a brand-new buck or two while they sipped their martinis, sucked their cigars, and discussed their pay-per-view mistresses.

They'd called him kid, too, but only because they were too polite to say, *Hey, Nobody.*

Two years ago, he was living with his parents. Playing sponge. Getting those world-weary looks from his mother when he'd come home from an open call with nothing to show for his efforts but another bruise on his ego. Weekly, his old man would sit him down and remind him, in case it had slipped his puny mind, that he was a useless, unrealistic, no-talent bum.

But his old man had been dead wrong. The guy had even been humble enough to admit it the first time he came around with his hand out and a grin so big you could count his second row of teeth.

He'd pulled out the roll of hundreds he always carried now. Peeled off a few while his old man stood there dripping saliva like an overheated dog. That had been the best payoff of all. Better than forty-five an episode.

Still, maybe it wouldn't be so bad going back.

The work had its moments, but it was definitely work. You were always out there in the wide open. Sitting like a clown in a pie-throw booth, waiting to take one in the eye. The bigger you got, the more of them there were aching to play you for a target: critics, rivals, producers, fans.

Fans were the worst. Fans figured they owned you. Treated you like one of those all-you-can-eat specials at a truck stop. Nibbling. Biting chunks. Grabbing and tearing until you were stripped to the naked carcass, and still they weren't satisfied. They made it so you had to stay in hiding. Give up the basic human pleasures: privacy, dignity, walks in the park. When was the last time he'd had a quiet dinner out with friends? An anonymous night at the ball game? The pleasure of pursuing some unknown woman at a bar?

Big star.

Screw that.

His insides were jangling. Whole damned business was getting to him. His mother had warned him to watch what he wished for or he might just get it. And he'd gotten it but good. Hit series. *People* cover nod as sexiest man of the year. Ferrari in the garage, Malibu beach house, sprawling ranch in Montana, East Coast getaway.

He was burning hot. Avalanche of offers. Pile of scripts. Women lined up for a shot at him, took numbers.

Sounded pretty good, actually.

So why was he about ready to toss it all in the trash?

Gripping the remote, he turned on the sound again. His own chiseled face stared back at him from the gargantuan screen. His own honeyed voice, boosted by months of coaching and Dolby stereo, dripped from the speakers. He peered at his now famous eyes: hooded,

bold, hard-wired to the baby blues in the surgery-
perfect face of his costar. Critically, he watched himself
kiss her, recalling the director's barked criticism. *"I said
make it a tease, hot shot. Looks like you're trying to give the
girl a tonsillectomy."*

Maybe that was the problem. He was good at it. Too
good. A couple of crazies had mistaken the act for reality. One in particular had been after him for months.
Calling. Writing letters. Even showing up at the goddamned door.

At first, he'd taken it as some kind of a joke. But her
attentions had turned sick and sour. In the instant before he could shut the door on her or slam down the receiver, a shot of her bitter hatred would seep through.
The danger was electric. You could touch it. Nothing
he could even pretend to laugh off.

Tense as a drawn bowstring, he slumped in the plush
chair and rolled his neck to ease the kinks. He sensed
his sweetheart coming up behind him. Anticipating, he
drew a long, languid breath.

She played across his back and draped herself across
his shoulders.

"That's my girl," he crooned, feeling his muscles
ease. "What would I do without you, baby?"

She was the perfect companion. Sweet, affectionate,
quiet, undemanding. He felt the press of her muscular
body against his neck. So relaxing.

Sensual.

Reaching back, he stroked her silky flesh. She responded by nuzzling his ear, planting her own special
brand of cool kiss on the back of his neck.

"You're all I need, sweetheart. You and me. Perfect
together."

She was massaging him, miraculously pressing
away the tension. A few minutes, and he was rag-doll
limp. Nearly asleep. She kept at it, applying rhythmic

pressure to his shoulders, down his arms. Around his neck.

The pressure was building. Edging past pleasure now.

"Easy, sweetheart. That's too tight."

Why wasn't she listening?

"Stop. Cut it—"

The vise grip squashed his protests. Crushed his windpipe. Not like her, he thought with his last gasp of conscious thought. *Why?*

Sinking into the bubbling blackness, he strained to see her, to pass a final plea.

But the eyes he faced were the stranger's, filled with madness and a fury beyond reckoning. At least, it wasn't my sweetheart, he thought.

There was a moment of startling clarity. The world was revealed to him in its infinite, kaleidoscopic complexity. Amazing, he thought, struggling to hold the moment. But in a blink, his strength failed him, and the scene went fade to black.

PERSONAL JOURNAL

25 September

My surface is thick ice over a winter pond. Smooth, cool, reflective.

The danger swirls beneath. Wicked creatures slithering in the blackened depths. Graceful. Hypnotic. Deadly.

I am aware of these undulating denizens. But they remain unseen by others. I am forced to keep them submerged. Invisible. To survive, I must deny any knowledge of them.

Only in dreams do they slip from my reach and gobble greedily at the thin blue air. In dreams, awake and sleeping, they rise and flourish, growing to an all-consuming screaming mass.

The unspeakable things are only dreams. Nothing real is ever touched by them.

Anything touched by them simply ceases to exist.

*C*HAPTER
ELEVEN

Cassie Rodbury smoothed her platinum chignon and straightened the skirt of her beige Chanel suit. Armed with a studied smile, she crossed the length of her posh, paneled law office to greet her unexpected visitors at the door.

At nearly six feet tall, Cassie cast an imposing shadow. Three weekly sessions with a personal trainer kept her body in peak condition. Regular visits from a hairdresser, facialist, and personal shopper guaranteed perfect maintenance of the rest of the facade. Weeks shy of her forty-fifth birthday, Cassie could have passed for thirty.

For all of which Cassie was particularly grateful at the moment. She prized what she viewed as her personal armor: scrupulous good looks, expensive trappings, an unmistakable aura of success. Representing Mrs. Lily Gallatin was akin to fronting for a tornado. No matter what you did to tame or track the situation, there were bound to be nasty surprises. As Cassie saw it, looking and living well was the best, and most satisfying, defense.

Ordinarily, when she had business or other matters to discuss, Mrs. Gallatin summoned Cassie to the family's estate. Having her turn up unannounced at the office was both unusual and highly disconcerting.

Cassie opened her office door. Trailed by her slim, bespectacled secretary, Mrs. Gallatin and her daughter were striding haughtily toward the office. Noting the high color in the old woman's cheeks and the tight set to her jaw, Cassie braced herself for the worst. Dismiss-

ing her cowed secretary with nod, she ushered the two
women inside and shut the door behind her.

"Hello, Mrs. Gallatin, Marielle. To what do I owe
this delightful surprise?"

"Cut the crap, Cassandra. That twit girl of yours all
but swallowed her pencil when we showed up."

"Valerie is accustomed to functioning by the book,
Mrs. Gallatin. If she was rude—"

"She was not rude. Stunned is closer to the point.
And so are you, if truth be told. If your eyes were gaping any wider, they'd slip their sockets. Now, why don't
you collect yourself and offer us a cup of tea?"

"Of course, of course, Mrs. Gallatin." Holding fast to
her eroding composure, Cassie motioned the women to
a pair of leather armchairs and buzzed for tea. "Now
tell me. What brings you both here?"

The wizened face went coy. "I thought you'd like to
hear about my morning. You'll never guess who accepted my invitation and stopped by for a chat."

Cassie paled. "You didn't. I advised you—"

"I don't recall seeking your counsel in this matter,"
Lily Gallatin snapped.

"I understand, but—"

"But nothing." Frowning, she caught Cassie in her
steely gaze. "Your dear father, rest his soul, had a far
better grasp of the parameters of our professional relationship, Cassandra. An impeccable grasp. In case you
are unaware, that's one of the main reasons my husband
and I retained him to handle our affairs."

Cassie bit her lip. The threat was hardly veiled.
Rodbury, Carswell & Barr would be nothing without
the Gallatins. Virtually all of their important clients
had come through Gallatin connections or by Gallatin
referral. At Lily Gallatin's request, those same clients
had remained loyal to Cassie after her father's retirement a dozen years ago. With a snap of her gnarled fin-

gers, the old woman could turn Cassie's flourishing
career and the opulent lifestyle she so prized into ashes.

"Of course, Mrs. Gallatin. I hope the *chat* was satisfying."

"Satisfying? Hardly. Though I must say Marielle
seemed to derive some enjoyment from it. My poor girl
finds so little pleasure in life, don't you, dear?"

As usual, there was no response from Marielle. She
sat like a wax figure except for the flashing anger in her
eyes.

Cassie kept a tight rein on her expression, too. Lily
Gallatin's daughter was nobody's notion of a poor little
girl. Since early childhood, the Gallatin's youngest child
had demonstrated a cruel, verging on sadistic, streak.
More than once, Cassie had been called upon to mollify
the parents of classmates and playmates whom young
Marielle had allegedly attacked. And though the young
woman rarely spoke, faced with other people's pain or
suffering, she showed visible delight.

"The visit this morning was merely a beginning,"
Lily Gallatin went on. "I wanted to place Mrs. Harper
on notice, to advise her of my intentions. And that I
clearly did."

Cassie stifled her objections. Threatening Thea
Harper was foolish and dangerous. If anything happened to the Harper woman, Lily Gallatin would fall
under immediate suspicion. The woman had made no
secret of her feelings about her son's murderer.

Knowing about her client's lust for vengeance placed
the lawyer in a highly precarious position as well. Professional ethics required her to report any knowledge of
criminal intent. But a voracious personal appetite for
continued success kept Cassie mute. She could only
hope that Lily Gallatin's rash acts would be limited to
words and the hiring of snoops and informants. Thinking about the unsavory pair of pigeons the old woman

had already enlisted in the effort to bring Thea Harper down, Cassie frowned.

"Why the sour face, Cassandra?" Lily Gallatin demanded.

"It's nothing, Mrs. Gallatin. A little indigestion. That's all."

Her icy eyes narrowed. "If things aren't settling well with you, perhaps you should change your diet. Maybe you need to shift to something a bit *lighter.*"

Cassie Rodbury forced a smile. "Not at all. I'm fine now. Just fine."

"I'm glad to hear that. Now that all the elements are in place, I want you to monitor the situation closely, make certain that things progress with speed and efficiency."

The smile stiffened. "Of course. I'm at your service as always."

"The young man in particular bears watching. He seems a bit tentative."

"Certainly. I'll keep tabs on him." Determined to uncover incriminating evidence against Thea Harper, Lily Gallatin had recruited two sympathetic locals with ready access to the Harper woman and her little girl. The old woman was utterly unconcerned about the litany of laws she was breaking: harrassment, bribery, conspiracy, attempted assault, to name a few.

"I suspect you'll have to keep him *motivated* as well, Cassandra."

"Yes, Mrs. Gallatin." *Whatever you say, Mrs. Gallatin. Your wish is my demise, Mrs. Gallatin.*

Abruptly, Lily Gallatin and her daughter rose to leave. Cassie hastened to escort them out. On the way, they encountered Cassie's flustered secretary. Valerie bore a silver tea service and a hastily ordered platter of finger sandwiches and pastries. All were at a dangerous tilt.

"Thanks. We won't be needing that, Valerie," Cassie said.

The secretary sighed.

"We won't be needing *that* either, young woman," Lily Gallatin snapped. "It would seem your subordinates could do with instruction in fundamental courtesies, Cassandra."

"S-sorry, Mrs. Gallatin. I didn't mean—" the secretary blithered.

"Never do anything you don't mean, young lady. That's the best way to avoid being dangerously misunderstood."

"Wait in my office, Valerie," Cassie ordered.

"Yes, ma'am." The girl's voice was suspiciously sarcastic.

Tossing the secretary a withering look, Cassie followed her two most valuable clients down the carpeted hallway and escorted them out to their waiting limo.

CHAPTER
TWELVE

Where had the time gone?

Gabby was home already. From the house, Thea could hear the child's shrill summons. Checking the clock in the studio, she struggled to shake off the fog.

"Be there in a minute, sweetie." She winced at a tinny tremor in her voice.

How could it be after three already?

Thea had returned home from the Gallatin estate shaken and distracted. She distinctly recalled the announcer starting the midday news as she flipped off the car radio in the garage. More than three hours had passed, and all she had to show for them were pages of garish paint blots and a headache several sizes larger than her head.

Had she forgotten to take her pill? Worried, she checked the dated plastic medication packet. No. The space for today's dose was empty.

The light on the answering machine was blinking madly. Pressing the playback button, she rubbed her throbbing temples and listened to the quartet of messages. As usual, Pru Whittaker had called to nag. Caro had left one of her frequent dinner invitations. The third call was from the loathsome reporter, Harlan Vernon. The rat man was escalating his offensive. *"If you won't talk to me, Miz Harper, I'll have no choice but to get my story from other sources. . . ."*

Thea didn't see that as much of a threat. Vermin's stories had never been limited by anything as trivial and confining as the truth. The last message on her machine was a breather. She listened to half a minute of wheezing before erasing the tape in disgust.

Looking down, she noticed that her hands were spattered with repulsive rust-colored pigment. Her eyes smarted as she scrubbed off the splotches with a rag soaked in turpentine. Rinsing her hands in the scrub sink, a horrible thought assailed her. The last time she'd experienced a gaping hole in her life like this was the night Simon died. The night she *killed* him.

The tremor was spreading. Folding her arms, Thea struggled to contain the internal groundswell. But reminders of that dreadful episode were everywhere. She was surrounded by too many eerie echoes.

That night, too, she'd been in the studio. Pru Whitaker had encouraged Thea to tackle a series of works reflecting the motion theme from the painting she'd done of the girl on horseback. If she could produce a suitable body of paintings, a major midtown gallery had promised extensive publicity and a star-caliber opening reception. It was the sort of event likely to attract broad media coverage and major reviews, Pru promised. This was definitely the long-awaited big break, the one that could catapult her to the top level of professional respect and recognition. And Thea knew that Pru was anxious to cash in on the rumors linking Thea's name with Senator Simon Gallatin's.

For a week, things had been going beautifully. Her muse was working overtime. Thea had three pieces in progress at once. One, featuring three young dancers at the barre, was near completion. Another she called "Child Running Through the Wildflowers" was assuming the lovely, luminous quality of a perfect summer day. When the Millport twins invited Gabby to dinner that night, Thea seized the opportunity to put in a couple of extra hours at the easel before the light failed.

But the time, nearly three hours, had been swallowed

whole. One minute she was dabbing bits of ivory on the flared skirt of a young dancer. Next thing she knew, the studio was steeped in shadow. There was nothing but the inexplicable darkness and an expectant hush. As Thea tried to reason through the disturbing lapse, she heard the piercing blade of Gabby's scream.

Heart pounding, she raced in and found Gabby in the den. Simon's battered body. The blood. Her little girl's face blanched to a terrifying pallor. In a nightmarish trance, Thea looked down to find her hands, her clothing, caked and splattered scarlet. Simon's blood was everywhere.

Panic chilled her. This couldn't be happening. She couldn't survive the horror again.

Forcing a deep breath, she struggled to think rationally.

Take it easy, Thea. This is nothing like that other time. You were just absorbed in your work, that's all.

The studio was a mess. Holding her breath against the acrid fumes, she scrubbed the soiled sink and spattered easel with a wad of paper toweling dipped in turpentine. Hastily, she crumpled the abused sheets from her sketchbook and tossed them outside in the trash barrel. She couldn't find the soiled paintbrush. But for someone capable of misplacing half a day, losing a dirty brush was no major accomplishment.

Case closed.

She found Gabby in the kitchen, spooning the remains of the ice cream directly from carton to mouth. Appetite intact. Better.

"Hi, sweetie. How was school?"

"Good." Gabby looked up and her brow furrowed. "Are you okay, Mommy?"

"Fine, why?"

"You look kind of—"

Catching her reflection in the oven door, Thea didn't

need to have the blank filled. Her hair was frenzied, her face smudged with more of that repugnant rusty paint. Startled by the image, she forced a dry chuckle.

"Guess that's what they mean when they talk about really getting into your work."

Gabby's frown deepened. She held out the ice cream carton like a life preserver. "Here, Mommy. You have the rest."

"No, thanks, sweetie. What I need to do is go clean up and put on some fresh clothes."

"You sure you're not sick or something?"

"Positive." She leaned down and hugged the child tightly.

The shower was heavenly. Turning the water up full, Thea luxuriated in the warm spray pelting her back. Her shoulders ached, and a sticking pain had lodged at the base of her neck. Tension central.

Clearing the steam off the mirror with her palm, she towel-dried her hair and combed out the tangles. Big improvement. A few strategic swipes of blush and a trace of her standard lip gloss, and she looked better still. Fresh jeans and a red turtleneck, and there was a decent chance she could pass, in dim light, for human.

Downstairs, Gabby sat hunched over her composition book at the kitchen table. With a puff of pride, Thea noted the concentration etched on the child's face and the graceful flow of her handwriting.

"Big assignment?"

"I'm working on a book," the child said absently.

"Sounds *very* big."

"It's not homework. I'm doing it on my own. I've decided to be a writer. Biographies or mysteries, I think. I'm not sure yet."

Thea suppressed a smile. Big dreams, oversized ambitions. If only those delightful childhood excesses were shrink-proof.

Gabby gnawed at the end of her pencil and bowed to draft another line.

"What's your book about?"

"It's about this girl who finds out she was adopted, so she runs away from home and tries to find her real mother."

"And does she?"

"I'm not sure yet. She's still on the bus to Indiana."

"Sounds interesting."

The child frowned. "If I was adopted, you'd tell me, right?"

"Of course. But you're not."

Gabby added another line to the story. "Amber says they sometimes mix babies up in the hospital, and the parents don't even know until the kid has to have a blood test because she's got this fatal disease or something."

Thea claimed the ice cream carton and scraped out the last runny spoonful. "You're my own real flesh-and-blood daughter, Gabrielle Harper. I promise."

"How do you know? Did I have a blood test?"

"I just know."

"I hope you're right, Mommy. Because it turned out that the kid with the fatal disease really came from this family where the mother was dead and the father was busy with a new wife and baby. So now, I guess nobody wants her."

Thea snaked her arms around the child and squeezed. "You're going to make a *terrific* writer, my child. No question."

Giggling, the little girl squirmed loose. She poised her pencil over the next line. "Let me finish, okay? I'm almost done with the chapter."

Shamed by the child's industriousness, Thea resolved to make productive use of what little remained of the day. But for some reason, she felt reluctant to return to the studio. Armed with a sketch pad and charcoals, she headed for the dining room table to get started on some viable project.

Staring at the blank page, she weighed the possibilities. During her years of training, she'd explored every imaginable artistic medium. Contrary to Dr. Forman's snooty assessment, there were not more and less challenging art forms. In Thea's view, a brilliant illustrator or cartoonist simply had talent for that particular vehicle. The commercial outlets were not art's equivalent of stupid pet tricks. They were equally valid and challenging expressions of a personal vision.

But the shrink *had* been on the right track when she suggested that Thea might not be up to tackling a painting yet. She desperately wanted to be whole and wholly capable again, to return to the work she dearly loved. But her studio was still too firmly interwoven with the persistent horrors of the past year. Until she was over that nightmare, Thea would have to find something else she could call work. In truth, she wondered if she'd ever be over it.

As she thought, a demonic image slithered into her mind. Timber rattler. Thea could see the menacing coil; she could hear the creature's bone-chilling chatter.

Often, as a little girl, she and her brother camped out in a grassy field near the edge of the ranch. On one such outing, in the middle of the night, Thea had been startled awake by a sound like dried beans shaking in a gourd. Intrigued by the unfamiliar noise, she poked Jimmy awake. Hearing the rattle, his eyes went slick with fear. Jimmy was never afraid, at least not visibly so, and his reaction had multiplied Thea's nameless terror.

"Don't move," he rasped. Slowly, *slowly,* he reached for the shotgun he had propped against a pole. When Thea tracked his aim to the tent's open flap, she saw the enormous gray diamondback viper writhing toward her. Almost at her bare foot. Inching forward. Seeking with its darting tongue.

When the blast came, the slimy thing was so close, the gory remains splashed Thea.

She was repulsed by the ugly memory, but the vision of that five-foot-long timber rattler refused to disappear.

With her fingertip, she traced a long flowing prototype on the page. Substituting a charcoal nib, she sketched a few broad preliminary strokes. Satisfied, she started adding features. Smiling at the whimsical character taking shape, she enjoyed a fresh surge of energy.

Switching to a soft pencil, she added shading and cross-hatching to give the image depth and dimension. Stopping briefly to retrieve her pastels from the studio, she worked in strategic color accents. As she was roughing out the background, she thought of the perfect use for this particular creation.

Finished with her chapter, Gabby was chatting on the phone. From the sound of things, the conversation was top secret. The child's voice muted when Thea entered the kitchen. When Thea sat at the table, signaling her intention to stay, Gabby abruptly ended the conversation.

"I have to go now, Opal. See you tomorrow."

"Wait," Thea exlaimed. "Let me speak to Caro."

When her friend came on the line, Thea gratefully declined the immediate invitation to dinner. She'd already trampled far too hard on the Millports' generosity.

"You sure, Thea? We'd really love for you and Gabby to come."

The baby wailed; something crashed clamorously. Caro sighed. "Drake, sugar. Didn't Momma tell you no climbing on the china cabinet? And don't squeeze your

brother so hard, darlin'. You wouldn't want to dent the
boy, would you, now? Sorry, Thea. I'd better go."

"Sounds that way."

After she hung up, Thea asked Gabby to sit for a serious discussion.

"Is anything wrong, Mommy?"

"Not at all. I have a business proposition for you.
How would you like to be my collaborator?"

"Sure. What's that?"

"Partners, sort of. It means we work together. You
do part, and I do part."

"Of what?"

"A children's book. I drew this character."

Thea presented the sketch. The new, improved snake
had large eyes lit with a glint of mischief, high arched
brows, and a full-lipped mouth. The diamondback pattern had been translated into a tailored blouse with a
diamond print. The reptile wore diamond-shaped
glasses. A string of mock diamond beads graced the
scaly neck, and an oversized marquise-shaped solitaire
was settled on her ring finger. Arms, hands, and a cur-
vaceous feminine shape had been added courtesy of
broad poetic license. The rattle was now a whimsical or-
nament on a pillbox hat.

"I call her Sophie, but you can change it to something else if you'd prefer."

Gabby's reaction was precisely what Thea had hoped.
The child was captivated. "She's *excellent*. Sophie the
snake. I love it."

"Think you can make up a story about her?"

"Sure." The child's face tensed with concentration.
"I'd make it so she runs this ice cream store like the
one on the Post Road. And all these kids are always
coming in to hang out. They're mostly teenagers like
Amber, so Sophie keeps an eye on them, makes sure

they behave and stuff. Still, she's really cool and nice, so the kids really like her."

"Sounds great." Thea flipped a page in the sketchbook. Quickly, she drew Sophie in an apron standing behind a counter filled with tubs of ice cream. Price list on the wall. Flavor chart including all their favorite indulgences. In front of the counter, she swiftly roughed in a line of waiting customers and several tables filled with teenagers.

Gabby nodded her approval. "And there's this one kid who's sort of creepy and weird, so no one likes him. He comes in for a sundae sometimes, but he hardly talks to anybody."

Like magic, the creepy kid grew under Thea's pencil. Short, nerdy, chinless character with big ears. "Like that?"

Gabby tipped her head, thinking. "Scarier, sort of."

Flipping to a fresh page, Thea rapidly replaced the nerd with a long-haired, greasy-looking character with dark glasses and a tattoo.

"Right. And he's always smoking, so you should give him a cigarette."

Thea dangled a smoldering butt between the creep's skinny lips.

"Perfect." Gabby beamed. "This is fun."

It *was* fun. The most fun Thea had had in longer than she cared to consider. It was pure pleasure to observe her daughter's nimble mind and inventive imagination.

They continued that way for hours as the tale took shape, stopping only long enough to down a makeshift dinner of tuna sandwiches and leftover salad. At the climactic moment near the story's end, a customer tossed a lit cigarette in the trash bin, setting the ice cream parlor on fire. In a panic provoked by the roaring blaze, one of the fleeing customers accidentally knocked poor

Sophie to the floor. The unconscious snake lay trapped in the inferno. Someone had summoned the fire department, but it seemed they'd be too late to save Sophie.

The situation appeared hopeless. But at the last possible second, the weird kid, grateful for Sophie's past kindness, braved the flames to rescue the serpent. To Thea's delight, Gabby had the creepy boy put out the fire threatening Sophie by smothering it with buckets of melted ice cream.

"The end," Thea proclaimed. "Lord, look at the time. You'd better hustle up to bed, Miss Coauthor. I'd say we have a pretty fantastic first draft."

The child's eyes flashed with excitement. Her face was glowing. "How do we make the covers?"

"Maybe we can get a publisher to do that for us."

"How?"

"I'll explain tomorrow, partner. Now get going. It's way past your bedtime."

But Gabby lingered. "Can I have a friend over for dinner tomorrow?"

Thea's reluctance yielded quickly to the child's pleading look. "Okay. But it's a school night. So make it early."

"Can you cook lasagna?"

"Well, maybe. If you make it worth my while."

Gabby threw her arms around Thea and plastered her with fawning kisses.

"Okay, lady, okay. I give up. You met my price. Lasagna it is."

"Great!"

Long after lights out, Thea could hear the restless squeal of Gabby's bedsprings. Too keyed up to sleep herself, she dimmed the lights in her room and turned on the television. Most shows had the power to put her right out.

She awoke hours later to the clipped tones of a late-night newscaster.

". . . Repeating our major story. The mutilated body of TV heartthrob Brandon Lee Payton was discovered in his Bedford, New York, home this afternoon by his manager." A file photo of the young star flashed on the screen. Video footage of his bagged body being wheeled from the house followed as the announcer continued.

"Payton, star of the hit series *Last Ditch*, was a collector of exotic pets. One of Payton's snakes, a five-foot-long western timber rattler, was savagely hacked to death in the brutal attack by an unknown assailant. Police have launched a full-scale investigation."

There was another file photo of the smiling actor holding a thick reptile up for the camera's eye. Then the announcer switched to a story about a train derailment in Philadelphia.

Thea went numb. Her mind bristled with disbelief. It was the snake from her vision. Same gray scales and heavy diamond markings. How would she have known unless—?

Stop, Thea! That's crazy. Impossible!

Or was it?

Bedford was twenty miles away, no more than a half hour's drive each way. The gap in her day was more than three hours long.

Her thoughts raced. She remembered the repulsive pigment she'd washed off her hands. That ugly red-brown color. The color of dried blood.

Terrified, she ran downstairs. Barefoot, she retrieved the studio key from its hook near the kitchen door and stole out of the house. The damp chill raised a rash of gooseflesh under her thin nightgown. But she was beyond caring. Wracked by shivers, she opened the lock, entered the studio, and turned on the light. No sign of any remaining rusty spatters on the easel or the surrounding floor. She'd wiped the scrub sink clean. Remembering that she'd discarded the soiled pages from her sketchbook, she went outside and lifted the lid on the nearest trash barrel.

Empty. The garbage had been picked up.

Back in her room, Thea huddled under the covers, shivering, and tuned to the all-news cable channel. There was a story about a meningitis outbreak in a Chicago high school. Next came a piece about the trial of five college football stars on charges of raping a retarded girl. News of the Payton murder followed. The announcer repeated the same information she'd heard earlier. But he went on to report that police were seeking information about a woman who'd been stalking the murdered actor for months. The stalker's link to the killing was uncertain, but the overzealous fan was believed to be dangerously disturbed. She had made serious threats several days ago when a security guard ordered her off the set where Payton's series was shooting.

The graphic accompanying the story was an amateurish composite sketch. Generic female. Dark glasses, wiglike hair. Nothing distinguished the features except their foolish likeness to the parts kids poked into the plastic skull of a Mr. Potato Head.

Nothing to do with me. Nothing at all.

Thea had been safely tucked away at Brook Hollow while that deranged admirer was tailing the object of her obsession. She had never even watched Brandon Lee Payton's show. The famous victim's face was familiar to her, but she could reasonably attribute that to his widespread publicity. She'd probably seen his picture in the paper or while flipping through a magazine. There was no rational link between her and this murder.

None.

So how had she known about the snake?

Forcing herself to stay calm, she pieced together a logical explanation for that, too. She'd probably had the radio on in the studio this afternoon. She often listened for the companionable drone while she was working. The news of the young actor's death must have been reported. Somehow, the details had penetrated her fog and the description of the mutilated snake had stuck in her mind. Understandable, given that terrifying childhood incident on the camping trip with her brother.

That had to be it.

Exhausted, Thea fell back on her pillow. Fumbling for the remote control on her nightstand, she plunged the screen into darkness.

CHAPTER
THIRTEEN

The murdered actor haunted Thea's dreams. In one vivid nightmare Brandon Lee Payton and his timber rattler were chasing her across a soundstage. Thea tried to run, but her father caught her by the arms and held her immobile. While she flailed in a hopeless struggle to break free, the snake coiled around her ankle, then started slithering up her leg—

She awoke with a start, her pulse pounding. Banishing the ugly dream from her thoughts, she showered quickly and downed her pill with a cup of instant coffee. Time to get to work.

Thea spent the morning converting one of the preliminary Sophie sketches into a polished product. As usual, Dr. Forman was right. Being absorbed in the project did make Thea feel centered and serene. For a welcome change, she was focused on the future. While she sketched and painted, she mused about ways to connect with a publisher. Did the children's book market require that they get an agent? Was her art agent, Pru Whittaker, likely to know a suitable counterpart in the literary field? What were their real chances of turning this pleasant pastime into Gabby's dream of a real book with a genuine cover and their paired names slithering along the spine?

All right. It wasn't only Gabby's fantasy. It was hard to resist the tempting notion of visiting a bookstore with her charming little coauthor and seeing Sophie the Snake right up there on the shelf among the hotshots: the Grinch, Winnie the Pooh, Babar. Big time. While Thea had no delusions about the likelihood of Sophie rising to cult or classic status, it would be an enormous kick to see their creation in actual print with their very own Library of Congress number and a bona fide copyright.

But even if that didn't come to be, producing the prototype was very enjoyable. And diverting. Halfway through refining the second illustration, she was so engrossed, she barely heard the phone.

Monitoring the message tape, Thea was delighted to hear her mother's voice after the beep. "Hey, Checker. Hope I'm not bothering you, honey."

Thea picked up quickly. "You're not bothering me at all, Mom. What's up?"

Long hesitation. "You doing all right?"

Tension pinched her mother's tone. "Yes. What is it, Mom? What's wrong?"

Thea imagined Ellie fiddling nervously with the phone cord. "It's probably nothing . . ."

"What is?"

Hard breath. "Ada Martin called last night. Seems her Walter's on the run again. This time, he robbed a liquor store and shot the clerk. Poor man's in critical condition."

Walter Martin.

The name alone was enough to fill Thea with dread.

"Don't worry, Mom. He's not about to come three thousand miles out of his way to bother me." Thea sounded far more certain than she felt. In truth, there was little she'd put past Walter Martin, especially when it came to his long-standing fixation on her.

Things had started innocently enough. Walter's mother and Thea's mother had been friends since high school. Walter was the same age as Thea's brother, Jimmy, and the two women had encouraged a friendship between their sons. But it soon became evident that the little boys were poorly suited for each other.

Jimmy Sparks was a gentle soul, quiet and unassuming, enamored of animals and the outdoors. Walter's consuming hobby was trouble, finding or creating it and jumping in with both feet. As a small child, Walt was forever headed for the woodshed, the emergency room, or the principal's office. Later, he graduated to drug and alcohol abuse and increasingly serious brushes with the law.

At some indefinable point, Walter had trained his devil's eye on Thea. When she repelled his advances, he became sullen and threatening. For years after that, he'd trailed her like an ominous shadow. She'd only found real respite when she moved east for college.

Even then, the menacing calls and letters had continued periodically. Walter's timing was uncanny. He'd called hours after she and Justin got home from the hospital with newborn Gabby. He was on the phone again moments after she returned to the house from Justin's funeral.

"If he does turn up, you get the police right off, Checker. I don't want you taking any chances."

"Sure, Mom. But I know he won't come here."

"Just so you keep an eye out, honey."

"I will, Mom. You take care."

Hanging up, Thea turned back to the illustration on the easel. Sophie was in the ice cream parlor, scooping from the bin of chocolate cookie crunch ice cream. The unsavory character Gabby had dubbed Willy Dillon was on the other side of the counter. Where had the child come up with such a perfect name for the scary kid who turns hero at the end?

Thea eyed the picture critically. Sophie's skin tones needed softening. More blue in the gray and a dab of peach should do it. She tried to concentrate on mixing the right shade. Difficult when Walter Martin's pugnacious face kept glaring up at her from the palette.

"Please, no, Walter," she said aloud. "I can't handle you and your craziness. Not now . . ."

Trying to piece things back together would be hard enough in a vacuum. But her world was far from that. She had Gabby's erratic behavior to worry about and the relentless reporters and the menacing spectre of Mrs. Gallatin's threats. In addition, since hearing the news report of Brandon Payton's brutal slaying, Thea had been beleaguered by self-doubt. What if the medicine had stopped working? What if the violent monster in her had somehow managed to break loose?

Stop, Thea. Don't think about that.

Still, she had at least done a good morning's work. Thea cleaned her hands and brushes. Wincing from the turpentine stench, she rubbed her stinging eyes.

In the kitchen, Thea called the Millports to see if Caro and the little ones were up for lunch at the local deli. But Drake had just settled in for his nap, and Raleigh was expecting a play date. The trouble with Caro's three-ring existence was that it left her with precious little time for play dates of her own.

Staring at the phone, Thea tried to think of someone else to call. She didn't want to be alone right now. Her unoccupied mind kept drifting back to the murdered actor.

But there were precious few friends in her life. Incredible how your life gets pared to the naked core by a few strokes of tragedy's ax. When Justin died, several of her so-called friends had paddled off to smoother waters. It was as if she bore some invisible taint, as if the dry rot of grief and early death might prove contagious. After Simon's murder, most of the remaining few had followed suit. Thea had become an alien being. Inexplicable. Dangerous. Only the unreasonably brave or foolhardy or recklessly curious would dare to venture close.

At least, Thea's mother and the Millports had remained squarely in her corner. Steel shoulders. Thea supposed she was fortunate to have that many.

Playing a long shot, she dialed Brook Hollow and had Billie paged. Thea missed the jocular nurse. During Thea's time as an inpatient, Billie's steady support and encouragement had been far more effective than the hospital's more orthodox therapies. Her voice alone was a boost. "Hey, girlfriend. What's going on?"

"Nothing much, Billie. I was wondering if I could lure you away from the kitchen from Hell for a real lunch. My treat."

"Wish I could. But Doc Forman's coming by tomorrow with some big mucky-mucks from state mental health. Woman left a pile of orders like you wouldn't believe. Wants me to finish two weeks' work by closing today. Or else."

Thea was all too familiar with Dr. Forman's unreasonable demands and edicts. "Sorry, Billie. Doesn't sound like fun."

The nurse sighed. "My feet aren't laughing. Tell you that much. And then there's the Vita mess."

"What Vita mess?"

"You don't know? I figured folks could hear Doc Forman yelling about it all the way to Canada. Vita Negrone got it in that nutty mind of hers to up and walk out on us. Doc Forman called in the cops and everything, but there hasn't been a sign of her. Seems the woman's up and vanished."

Remembering Vita's lunatic ramblings, Thea shuddered. *"Chop you up, I will. Flush your pieces down the toilet."*

As if reading her mind, Billie chuckled. "Lucky thing Vita's bark is worse than her bite."

"I hope so, Billie. Another time, then."

"How about I stop by Saturday morning before I go

visit my folks. They're in Bridgeport, you know. Have to pass right by you on the way."

"That'd be great."

Hanging up, Thea's thoughts turned to a more immediate issue. Six months of low-fat, low-salt, no-taste meals had left her with a serious craving for a hot dog with the works and a double side of sour pickles. Her mouth watered at the thought. She decided that a plate of pure decadence would be sufficient company for today.

Thea shrugged into her denim jacket and retrieved her purse from the kitchen counter. She was halfway out the door when the phone rang again. Instinct urged her to pay no attention, but she ignored the caution.

The message stopped her cold. After Thea picked up, he asked if he could drop by to see her in a few minutes. Nothing critical, he said. He was in the area and simply wanted to say hello. But a hard catch in his voice told her that was not the sum of it.

Dully, Thea said she wasn't busy. Her appetite had yielded to a sick sense of impending doom. Setting down her purse, she sat at the table to wait for him.

CHAPTER FOURTEEN

Biederman pulled into the Compo Acres strip mall and deposited Passerelli in front of the bakery.

"A chocolate bagel, you said?"

"Right, Vince."

"You sure, Danny? I never heard of chocolate."

Biederman worked his face in a frown. "You trying to tell me you know more about bagels than I do?"

"No, but—"

"But nothing. I'll defer to you when it comes to Italian food, and you don't play bagel expert. Deal?"

Passerelli shrugged. "Okay."

"And if they're out of chocolate here, take a walk down to Gold's. They don't have any, come back to the bakery and order me half a dozen for tomorrow. I'm going to run over to the post office for some stamps."

"Sure you don't want to wait? It'll only take a second."

"I'm sure. Shut the door, Vince. See you in a couple."

Biederman swung out of the shopping area before his partner had time to voice any further reservations. He was about to climb way out on a creaky limb. Last thing he needed was company.

Weaving through the tangled traffic on the Post Road, he considered the best approach. He'd gotten hold of the proverbial tiger's tail. Only way to deal with such a thing was very, very carefully.

Five minutes later, he was knocking on the door. Dressed in jeans and an oversized blouse, Thea Harper looked even better than he'd allowed himself to remember. Wide copper-flecked eyes. Jungle of hair you could get lost in. Model's face. Dancer's body.

"Hello, Detective."

"Ms. Harper. Hope it's not a bad time."

Her brow furrowed as she led him into her living room. "So do I."

He took a seat on the peach-colored couch. She perched opposite on a patterned armchair. The room was warm and attractive. Lots of light. Plenty of perfect little touches. Family pictures, paintings by the resident artist, muted Oriental rugs, lacy plants in ceramic vessels. Settling against the plump cushion, Biederman made a hopeless stab at getting comfortable.

"Must be nice to be home," he ventured.

"Mostly."

"Brook Hollow didn't seem too bad."

"It wasn't."

"Chilly out. Real fall day."

She blew a breath. "Look, Detective. I get the feeling you came here for more than a casual chat. If you have something to tell me, please tell me."

Biederman leaned forward and wove his fingers together. "Only that I'm on your side."

"My side of what?"

He cleared his throat. Woman wasn't making this any easier. "If anything should come up. If you need anything, you can call on me. I *want* you to call on me." He scrawled his home number on the back of his card and handed it to her. "Anytime."

She glanced at it, then looked up to meet his gaze. "Sounds like you're expecting me to run into trouble."

"I didn't say that, Ms. Harper. But if there is any, I'm available. That's all."

She eyed him warily. "Are you telling me I can count on my friendly neighborhood policeman?"

"This one, yes."

She trained her gaze on him, trying to read the fine print. "I got that part way back in kindergarten, Detective. What's the rest of the message?"

"That's all of it."

"How come I don't believe you?"

"Please, Ms. Harper, don't push it. There's nothing more to tell."

"I'm a grown-up, Detective. You don't have to soften the facts."

"I'm not. I'm just telling you you've got an ally if you should happen to need one."

"But you don't have any particular reason to think I will. Is that what you're expecting me to swallow?"

"I come from a long line of chronic worriers. Chalk it up to that."

She looked eager to probe further, but after a few seconds of uneasy silence, to his relief she let it go. "Have you eaten? I could make you a sandwich or something—"

"Thanks. Unfortunately, I've got to run. Can I take a rain check?"

"Sure." She walked him to the door and proffered a graceful hand. Biederman took it briefly. Hated to give it back.

"Look. I don't mean to spook you, Ms. Harper. It'll probably all come to nothing. Like I said, I'm a worrier."

His card was in her other hand. She glanced at it briefly.

"Daniel's a nice name."

"Thanks."

"Wasn't it Daniel who was tossed to the lions and came through without a scratch?"

"That's the one. Lucky guy had someone watching over him."

Her smile was rueful. "Would have been luckier if he hadn't needed the protection in the first place."

Biederman couldn't argue with that. But in his line of work, you learned to make do with reality. His biblical namesake had survived the lion's den. That other Daniel had also gotten away with pointing out that his boss had feet of clay. If Biederman managed nearly that much and survived intact, he'd consider himself way ahead of the game.

"Nice seeing you again, Ms. Harper," he said.

"You, too, Detective. I appreciate the interest. Really."

Leaving the block, Biederman spotted a woman peering out at him through what looked to be a living room window. The eyes were wide and unblinking. The rest of the face was sliced by the window mullions and shielded by the closely held receiver of a cordless phone. Biederman knew the type. Big-time Buttinsky. Investigator's dream, nightmare neighbor. The name on the mailbox was Rossner.

As he drove on Imperial toward the Post Road, a souped-up Chevy hybrid honed in close enough behind him to kiss his neck. Biederman recognized the wise ass at the wheel. Kid was on everyone's list. Had a world-class collection of black marks: truancy, petty theft, DUI, assault. Biederman had paid him a visit a couple of years ago after a complaint from the lady who lived next door. Woman had no hard evidence, but she swore this kid was behind the recent rash of pipe-bombed mailboxes in the area.

Biederman hadn't been able to prove it either, though he'd spent a couple of hours grilling the boy, trying to crack his adolescent titanium facade. Biederman had looked around the kid's living quarters and checked his record too. All he'd come away with was the pitiful family portrait and a dangerous case of sympathy for the suspect.

Poor kid had been saddled with an abusive alcoholic father and an abused mouse of a mother who was forced to run a day-care center and work nights and weekends as a waitress to pay the bills. Another child in the family, a daughter, had died at age seven under suspicious but inconclusive circumstances. By default, the death had been ruled accidental. From what Biederman could determine, this one's survival had been something of a chance event as well. No one had actually raised the boy. It was more accurate to say he'd been planted and left alone to grow up, like a weed.

About two years back, the kid had added suicide attempts to his self-destructive repertoire. Only attempts so far: slashed wrists and a mild overdose of barbiturates. But plenty on the force were hoping he'd improve with practice.

Biederman couldn't help but continue to feel sorry for the kid. Nothing behind him, nothing promising ahead. Little jerk had dropped out of school. No permanent employment, no caring relatives, no visible sign of friends. Not that the boy did anything much to make himself lovable.

As Biederman approached, the light at the Post Road intersection turned red. He eased on the brakes, trying to give the jerk sufficient back-off time, but no luck. Steeling himself, he felt the rear-end jolt and heard the harsh crunch of dueling bumpers.

Stepping out, he surveyed the damage. The kid's car had suffered nothing but a small ding in the front fender. The slow drip under the Chevy's chassis was probably not new. But Biederman's Toyota had sustained a major blow to the rear bumper. The tailpipe was mangled, a back-up light shattered in a rain of ragged glass.

Kicking the rubble to the side of the street, Biederman thought about all the reports he was going to have to fill out in triplicate. He considered the time he'd have to waste with the damned insurance adjustor. He pondered the extra helping of crap he was going to have to take from Buck Delavan, who was always looking for excuses to dish it out. Adding up all the annoyances, Biederman tried to muster some decent anger at the kid. But it wouldn't come. Life was too short, the world too big and bumpy.

Something told him he was losing his edge.

The teenager swaggered out of his dragon-painted smutmobile. Sullenly, he faced Biederman.

"You stopped short, man."

"License and registration, please."

"You're a cop?" The coal eyes narrowed. "Yeah, right. I remember you. Shit."

"And I remember you, Mr. Connable. Now, let's see the license and registration."

With infuriating deliberation, the kid eyed the wreckage, then he ticked his tongue before strutting back to his junk heap to rummage around for the papers.

Biederman looked them over. The license was miraculously intact. The registration had expired six months ago.

He handed it back. "Renew this. Cut out the tailgating, and have someone check that leak. Looks like transmission fluid."

Biederman was at the door to his car before the kid found his bearings.

"You're not giving me a ticket?"

"No."

"How come?"

"I don't think it'd help, do you?"

The kid looked confused, off balance. Like a kid. Biederman was encouraged enough to keep talking.

"You're probably not going to hear this, Connable,

but I'll say it anyway. If I thought there was a way to kick your butt back in line, it'd be my pleasure. But in your case, I'm convinced nothing's going to work until you're good and ready. You ever get there or even close, let me know."

"Like you really give a shit."

The boy sniffed and strutted back to his car like a posturing peacock.

Biederman flashed his empty palms and followed suit. "Nice bumping into you," he muttered under his breath as he angled his car onto the Post Road.

He found Passerelli where he'd left him. Guy was holding a bakery bag and a triumphant expression. Getting into the car, he set down his bundle and started ticking off the facts on his fingers. "They make bagels in sesame, poppy, oat bran, onion, garlic, salt, whole wheat, raisin, pumpernickel, and plain. No chocolate. Never had chocolate. Never will."

"You try the other place, too?"

"Never heard of chocolate bagels. Said they sound disgusting."

Biederman shook his head mournfully. "And they claim this town is sophisticated. Thanks for trying, Vinnie boy. Come on, I'll buy you lunch."

After the detective left, Thea tried getting back to her Sophie sketches. But she couldn't concentrate. Nothing like unidentified flying warnings to make a person jumpy. She didn't doubt Sergeant Biederman's excellent intentions. He'd always struck her as one of the good guys. Decent and caring. Solicitous. But the cop's visit had left her feeling like a prize buck in hunting season.

She could imagine exactly what her mother would advise under the circumstances: *Anytime you see the buzzards circling, Checker honey, you make sure you keep on moving.*

She did have a pile of errands to run, and now seemed as good a time as any to get started. But her vintage Volvo was acting cranky; the ignition refused to catch. Yesterday morning, it had taken her a full ten minutes to resuscitate the old heap.

During her stint at Brook Hollow, Drew and Caro had turned the engine over periodically. And once every couple of weeks, Amber had cautiously ferried the ancient auto around the block. But the wagon, purchased used more than a decade ago with the proceeds from Thea's first significant commission, was accustomed to far more lavish attention.

When the car was new to them, she and Justin had dubbed it "Bessie" in memory of the pony Thea had ridden around the ranch as a little girl. Naming inanimate objects was a proud Harper family custom. So was caring for them. She and Justin had always been scrupulous about the car's upkeep and appearance. They figured Bessie had earned the TLC for all those years of faithful service.

After Justin's death, Thea had done her best to maintain the tradition. But now, poor Bessie was long overdue for a tune-up and an oil change. Her proud midnight blue finish was dulled by a six-month accumulation of mud, dust, and water spots. Thea didn't claim to have a mechanic's ear, but the hacking hesitation under the hood sounded like a nasty case of bronchitis.

"Come on, girl," she urged. "You can do it."

Again, she stomped and prodded the gas pedal, offering crooning words of encouragement. When all else failed, she clicked the side of her tongue, a verbal prod that had always worked with the pony. Another hard pump on the pedal, and the reluctant motor finally caught.

Relieved, Thea patted the dusty dashboard. "Good girl."

As she backed out of the drive, Thea spotted a shifting shadow across the street near the Millports'. Harlan Vernon again. She was sure of it. Fueled by fury, she resolved to catch the slime trespassing and have him arrested. Flooring the accelerator, she aimed Bessie down the block.

Nearing the Millports', she spotted the skulking shadow beyond Caro's hedge. Veering into the driveway, she kept her eye peeled for Vermin. But as Bessie rolled up the gravel path, what Thea saw instead was little Raleigh riding his tricycle directly in her path.

Slamming the brakes, she came to a screaming stop a foot from the startled toddler. A beat later, his face screwed up and he started howling like an ambulance. Shaking hard, Thea got out and hugged the screeching child to her chest.

Caro came bustling out. "What's all this?"

"I'm so sorry," Thea blurted. "I thought I saw that

reporter watching me again. I almost hit Raleigh, Caro.
My God! What's wrong with me?"

Caro gently took the little boy from Thea's quaking
arms. "There, there. It's all right, sugar. You're fine."
She trained her steady eye on Thea. "No harm done.
Take a breath now, darlin'."

"I'm so sorry, Caro."

"Nothing to be sorry for. Cup of tea?"

"I can't. I have some things to do."

"See you later then. Wave bye-bye, Raleigh honey.
Stop that howling and blow Mrs. Harper a nice, big
kiss now."

"You sure he's all right?"

"He's just fine. Aren't you, darlin'?"

"Ha-puh go bye-bye now," the child angrily demanded between tics of anguish.

"Come now, darlin'. That's not nice."

"It's okay," Thea told Caro. "He's got every right to
be angry at me. I'm sorry I scared you, sweetie."

"Ha-puh *go*," Raleigh commanded, pointing a pudgy
finger toward the car.

Heart thwacking, Thea drove out of the neighborhood. She reviewed the list of errands she had to run.
First, she headed for the car wash, where Bessie
emerged damp and shiny. From there, she drove to the
discount art supply place on Route Seven in Norwalk
where she picked up a spray fixative for the Sophie
sketches and a presentation binder to hold the finished
book.

Next, she doubled back to downtown Westport. She
stopped at the Italian deli for a fresh bread, homemade
mozzarella and sauce, ricotta, and broad curly noodles
for tonight's dinner. Gabby hadn't mentioned who was
coming, but Thea knew it was either Opal or Jasmine
or both. The three girls had always been best friends.

Gabby's stay at the Millports' during Thea's absence had rendered them virtual triplets.

Her thoughts keep returning to the sight of little Raleigh on his trike. The car bearing down on him. *But the child is all right, Thea. Put it behind you.*

In honor of the book project, Thea stopped at the Baskin-Robbins near the house for an ice cream cake for tonight's dessert. She watched as the pimply youth behind the counter piped on the requested message: "Happy Birthday, Sophie!"

From the ice cream parlor, she crossed the Post Road to her favorite store. Artifax housed a delightful hodge-podge of child and adult toys, gimmicks, geegaws, and beautifully designed accessories. The small shop was one of those too-tempting places you entered at your own considerable financial risk. Coming here with Gabby had always guaranteed an excruciating bout of acquisitive wheedling followed by an extended sulk. But now, Thea could think of nothing she'd rather do than indulge her daughter in something totally frivolous. After all the child had been through, some serious spoiling seemed entirely in order.

A bell sounded as she entered. The salesperson, a slim young man Thea didn't recognize, stood in the rear of the narrow shop with a pair of fiftyish female customers in warm-up suits. The clerk shot her a bored look, then returned to the sale at hand.

Grateful for the browsing time, Thea scrutinized the closely packed displays. Clocks, kitchen gadgets, crystal objects, building blocks. Soon, she was locked in a heated debate with herself over whether to buy Gabby the mock-leopard wallet and matching change purse, the Tweety and Sylvester watch with the polka-dotted band, the prism that was firing a round of perfect rainbows, the antique yo-yo, or all of the above.

She was weighing her options and impulsively add-

ing others when she caught the overwrought whispers
from the trio in the rear.

"Can't believe she's out already."

"Thought they'd put her away for good."

"Lunatic like that ought to be locked up."

"Wouldn't trust my kid around her. That's for sure."

Thea's face caught fire. She dropped the items in a
bin and hurried out of the store. Gulping a greedy
breath, she raced across the busy street to her car. A
speeding van narrowly missed hitting her. She was ac-
costed by angry honks and screamed obscenities. Desperate to shut out the taunting humiliation, she
wrenched the car door open, got in, and locked the
world outside.

Her head felt ready to explode. She clutched the
wheel, trying to ward off the tidal flood of remembered
horrors. The infestation of reporters and the heinous
banner headlines had been bad enough. Worse was the
small-town gossip. Ugly speculation had pursued her
everywhere she went like a swarm of pecking birds.

Even before the trial, she'd been sentenced to the
roughest brand of hard time. Her hometown had become a hostile place, a minefield of killer looks and
cruel comments intended to be accidentally overheard.
Thea had been steeled to deal with it all, but some of
the nasty barbs hurled her way had ricocheted to hit
and harm her blameless little girl. With an aching
heart, she remembered her daughter's pain and tearful
bewilderment after one shrieking mother wrenched her
child away from Gabby as if she had the plague.

Why is that lady mad at me, Mommy? What did I do?

Soon, they couldn't go anywhere. Couldn't risk the
briefest outing. Vicious strangers had made Thea a pris-
oner in her own home. They'd stolen Gabby's peace and
what precious little remained of the child's hopeful innocence.

When was it going to end? Hadn't she and Gabby suffered enough? Why couldn't the whole rotten lot of them simply back off and leave her and her daughter alone?

Overwhelmed with fury, Thea wanted to annihilate every one of the hateful ones. She ached to rip out every vicious voice box and chop off every pointed, accusatory finger.

But then she'd be exactly what they thought she was. *Stop, Thea. You can't surrender to their mindless meanness.*

Gradually, her breathing settled. She'd hoped things would be different after her stay at Brook Hollow, but a six-month absence was clearly no cure for the malignancy of intolerance. She'd been foolish to expect such a miracle. Apparently, the tiniest minds had the longest memories.

At the hospital, she'd been protected, kept at long arm's distance from cruel reality. But hiding was not the answer.

Nor was running. Many times, Thea had considered moving away, trying to regain her lost anonymity. But Simon's murder had made national, even international, headlines. There was no place she could go to hide from the vicious spotlight. Anyway, this was her home, the place she'd shared with Justin. She and Gabby had important roots here, blighted or not.

And there were plenty of positives, Thea sternly told herself. She had her daughter, a few precious friends, her freedom. She and Gabby would simply have to find a way to ignore the meanness and focus on the important things.

Pushing the bitter incident out of her mind, she vowed to tackle the pile of necessary chores she'd been neglecting. After six months, there was more than plenty of catching up to do.

The car had to be serviced and winterized. Gabby

was past due for a number of regular checkups: pediatrician, dentist, eye doctor. Thea had to hire someone to
clean the gutters and paint the peeling trim on the
house. The alarm system in the studio was overdue for
its annual servicing. Given the flammable solvents Thea
used in her work, the insurance company had insisted
on a fire alarm and automatic sprinklers before they'd
agree to cover her paintings.

And there were the standard autumn chores. Leaves
to be raked. Flower beds to be bedded down before the
first serious cold snap. The storm windows had to be
hauled out, cleaned, and put in place. She had to load
the log holder in the basement and call the chimney
sweep.

Dr. Forman had warned her to keep busy and productive. There was too much sludge lying around, waiting to fill the gaps.

Thea knew she had to muscle her way through the
bad moments. She'd made Justin a deathbed promise to
take care of herself, to make a good life for herself and
their daughter without him. After he'd died, that
promise had kept Thea going, helped her muddle
through the swamp of grief to the other side.

She'd managed to continue then, when it had seemed
worse than impossible. And she would do it again. She
would set things firmly in order and keep them there.

Now was as good a time as any to get started.

Gabby was at bat. Last inning, and the Word Wallopers were leading the Super Scrabbles five to three. Opal was on second, Jeff Chartier on third. If Gabby scored a homer, she could turn the game around.

"I'll go for it," she told Mr. Perry and watched with mounting trepidation as he flipped through the vocabulary list to the four-base words.

A crackling tension filled the room. The Wallopers were one win away from the coveted championship pizza party. A victory today would put the Scrabbles back in serious contention. With two of the opponents' top players out sick with the chicken pox, this was her team's best chance to stage a comeback.

Gabby watched the exaggerated movements of Mr. Perry's lips as he pitched her word. "Stupor," he said.

"Stupor, S-T-U-P-O-R," she blurted. But then came the hard part. She had to give the definition. Stupor. Stupor?

The kids were starting to fidget.

"She doesn't know, Mr. Perry. Call her out."

"Stee-rike *one*," Mark Opler taunted from the Wallopers' bench.

"Shut up, Mark," Opal said. "Come on, Gabs. You can do it."

"Gah-bee, Gah-*bee*!" Her teammates were cheering her on. Turning up the pressure.

Gabby had some idea what the word meant, but her heart was pounding with terror. A few alternative ideas jousted in her brain for recognition. Gabby settled on her Mom's basic rule: Always go with your first guess.

She fixed her gaze on Mr. Perry and drew a breath. "Stupor means in a daze. Sort of out of it."

"Home run!" Mr. Perry called. "Nice going, Gabby. Congratulations, Scrabbles. Everybody scores."

Gabby trotted around behind Jeff and Opal, touching her toe to each of the bookmark bases. Back at home plate, she enjoyed the eager approbation of her teammates.

"Attaway, Gabby."

"Good going, Gabs."

"All *right*, dude!"

Gabby felt helium-filled. Best of all was Mr. Perry's smile as he flashed her a thumbs-up sign. This day was going even better than she'd dared to hope.

Next up: math test. Mr. Perry wrote the problems on the blackboard. Most of it was review. Three-column multiplication, short division with remainders. Only two were long division, and she had taken pretty well to that. Gabby felt another hundred coming on.

She was halfway through the first column of problems when the intercom crackled awake and Miss Nardino barked through the speaker.

"Mr. Perry? Would you please send Gabrielle Harper to the office immediately."

The teacher nodded at Gabby. "Go on. You can finish the test another time."

Gabby froze inside. Something terrible must have happened. Last year Julie Morris had been called down to the principal's office during gym class. Turned out her father had dropped dead of a heart attack.

What if Mom had been in an accident? Gabby could picture the tangle of wrecked cars. Mangled metal, shattered glass. Sirens screaming. Her bleeding mother being lifted inside the ambulance.

Worse, what if Mom had gotten sick again? Yesterday, she'd come in from the studio looking so messed up and out of it. In a *stupor*, Gabby thought, recalling the frightening look of distance that had webbed her mother's gaze.

Gabby's mind swarmed with ugly possibilities. But she kept settling back on the most terrifying one of all: Mommy's sickness. The notion of the bad thing happening again was an ape-sized terror. Gabby thought of Senator Gallatin sprawled on the floor in the shadows. She pictured his wide, empty eyes and the dark puddle of blood seeping out from under his head. She conjured that awful scared animal smell of him, and her stomach lurched. Pressing her nails hard into her palm, she tried to make the picture disappear.

"Gabby?"

Mr. Perry's look was expectant. Everyone had turned to stare at her.

"I'm going," she said. Her voice was hollow. Conscious of all the kids watching, Gabby squared her shoulders, took the pink pass Mr. Perry was holding out for her, and left the room.

The corridor was empty. Her footsteps slapped the checkerboard tiles, and her ears roared with the tidal rush of her breathing.

Don't let it be anything bad. Please, don't!

When she entered the main office, Miss Nardino was working at her computer. The old witch leaned toward the monitor, squinting through her thick, black-framed glasses at the screen.

"You called for me?" Gabby said.

In response, the secretary pursed her lips and raised a cautionary finger. Gabby noticed the slack mottled skin on the back of the woman's hand. Looked like a dirty hammock.

The waiting was unbearable. "We're having a math test," Gabby ventured. "So, if you don't need me—"

"All right, all right." Miss Nardino's face went all pinched and bothered. "Name and homeroom?"

"Gabrielle Harper. Room one-thirty-seven."

Mean old witch. She already knew Gabby's name and homeroom. Miss Nardino knew everyone in the whole building. She saw every single thing that happened and heard every sound down to the last burp and hiccough. But her favorite thing was to torture kids by making them wait and worry. Amber said that was probably why she'd decided to work in a school.

"You called for me a minute ago," Gabby said. Her fear and impatience were vying for top bunk. "On the intercom."

The woman rifled through the large pile of paper scraps on her desk. Moments later, she held one out to read at full arm's length. "You have a dentist appointment, Gabrielle. You're to wait outside to be picked up."

Gabby felt a molten wash of relief. Not that she was all that crazy about the dentist.

"Now?"

"No. Next Tuesday," the woman snapped. "Of course, now. Go on. Get where you're supposed to be and let me finish this report."

She shooed Gabby away. Giddy with relief, the child practically flew out of the main office, down the front hall, and out the door.

The day was cool and crisp. A sharp sun crouched low in the sky. Shading her eyes, Gabby scanned the street for her mother's car. But Bessie wasn't there yet. A fancy black car drifted by, slowing as it passed the school. It looked exactly like the chauffeured limo that had stopped at her house to deliver that letter to Mommy. Gabby squinted, trying to see the driver. But she couldn't make him out through the dark tint masking the shiny windows.

Kicking through the leafy hillocks dotting the path, she dawdled her way to the street. Mom would be here any minute. Why hadn't she arrived already?

The question was answered a beat later with the stertorous roar of an approaching car engine. Gabby squinted through the glare, expecting to see old Bessie rounding the corner.

But the car was not her mother's.

He rolled down the window and fixed her with a peculiar smile. His hair looked as if he'd doused it with salad oil. A blue earring winked from his left lobe.

"Get in," he said.

"I can't. I'm waiting for my mother."

He chuckled. "No, you're not, little one. You're waiting for me."

"But—"

Her protests were squelched as he raised an imaginary receiver to his ear and tuned his voice to an eery feminine lilt. "Hello? This is Mrs. Harper calling. I need to pick up my daughter Gabrielle for a dentist appointment. Would you please ask her to wait for me outside?"

Gabby stepped away. "You shouldn't have done that, Dylan. I'm going back to class."

"You can't. I only called because I saw those little jackasses who were bugging you the other day. They're on their way over."

"So why can't you just take care of them like you did the last time?"

"The Adelman kid made a noise, that's why. I get involved again, his old lady says she'll sic the cops on me."

Dylan Connable lit a cigarette and blew a feathery plume through the open window. "Come on. I'll get you out of here before they show up."

"I can't. I'll get in trouble."

He blew a smoke ring. "It's called self-defense, little one. No one would expect you to hang around and wait for those creeps to come pick you apart."

Gabby stood rooted by indecision. She didn't want to go with Dylan again, but she certainly didn't relish the notion of another run-in with the Greens Farms boys.

"Hurry it up. They'll be here any minute."

Gabby allowed his insistence to draw her into the car. They were several blocks down East Avenue before he spoke again.

"It's good we've got some time to kill. I have something to show you."

She cringed, remembering the dead mouse. "Is it from one of your shoe boxes?"

"No."

"What, then?"

"Be patient and you'll see."

They crossed the road that led off toward the Merritt Parkway. East Avenue melted into Main Street. Dylan's car sped along the curving pavement. Tossed from side to side, Gabby braced her feet hard and clutched the door handle.

Mercifully, he slowed as they passed the cemetery. A broad concrete square was being erected at the far end of the burial ground. Dylan stopped the car beside it and pointed out the hivelike cubicles inside.

"It's a mausoleum. Ever seen one before?"

Gabby tried to melt into her seat. When she was a little kid, she'd thought the grave markers in a cemetery were actual dead people turned to stone. She used to shiver at the notion that her very own father was like that now, a squat stone lump with his name and birthday carved across his chest. Now, of course, she knew better, but the very idea of a graveyard still gave her a major case of the creeps.

"A maw-so-what?" She tried to sound brave.

"Mausoleum. It's for above-ground burial. Some people don't like the idea of having their carcasses planted six feet under. Or popped in the incinerator. Truth is, the body is nothing but water, air, and a bunch of other crap. Whole thing would be worth about eighty-five bucks if you could separate out the component parts and sell them to some chemical company or whatever. But since you can't, the average corpse is worth zilch."

"Okay. You've shown me."

"Not this. Something way better."

Dylan pulled away from the curb.

"Fancy mausoleum like that, figure they'll add a granite finish, decorative fencing and landscaping, goes for about a hundred thousand bucks. Plus maintenance, of course. Annual basic upkeep is probably in the five thousand range, minimum. Goes up every time another family member bites the dust. Pretty dumb, don't you think?"

"I guess." In fact, Gabby didn't know what to think. Generally, she chose to close her mental shutters against such grisly musings.

But Dylan seemed wholly absorbed. "Problem is, most people can't separate the significant stuff, the self and human consciousness, from the hunk of junk we call the body. All the flesh and bone and connective tissue and other organ systems are just the package. You get what I'm saying?"

Gabby refused to admit her ignorance, but the whole body thing remained a major mystery to her. She remembered learning about the pituitary gland in science last year. "Traffic control center," the text had called it. For days before the chapter test, she'd tried to figure out how the whole business worked and why some of the zillions of hormones and signals and reactions didn't simply crash and burn in the mayhem.

"Just a package," she repeated dutifully, though

what Dylan was saying made the pituitary gland look as simple as Dick and Jane.

"Right. And after death, the package is nothing but useless trash. Think how totally stupid some people are. Imagine spending a hundred thousand bucks to build some fancy place to put your potato peels and stale bread."

"Sounds pretty stupid," she agreed, but her mind flashed to the dead Senator Gallatin on the den floor. Just a package, she repeated silently, hoping to quash her rising terror.

Dylan switched the cigarette to his other side and reached over to pat her hand. "You're catching on, little one. I knew you would."

He veered off Main at the intersection of the Post Road. Gabby hoped he'd changed his mind and decided to take her directly home.

But as they approached the turnoff to Imperial, he eyed her slyly. "Almost there. Close your eyes."

"Why?"

"I want to surprise you, that's why. Trust me."

She didn't entirely. But going along with him seemed the quickest way to be done with this. Gabby squeezed her eyes shut. The old car bumped over a ridge, drifted for a few seconds, and lurched to a stop.

"Keep those eyes closed. I'll guide you," Dylan said. He blew out slowly. She could smell the smoke.

He steered her by the shoulders. Gabby stepped carefully, awkward without the visual cues. Her foot came down on a fallen branch, and without thinking, she opened her eyes.

"No looking!"

Quickly, she scrunched her eyes shut again. The anger in his tone chilled her. Careful not to peek, she tuned to the shifting sensations. Rush of wind. Rustle of leaves falling. Whiff of wood smoke. Three steps up.

Squeal of a rusty hinge, and they were inside a building.

The feel underfoot went soft and squishy. Some kind of thick carpet. Dylan's fingers bit into her shoulders as they turned left and quickly turned again.

"In here," he rasped. "Keep quiet."

Another door opened; Dylan prodded her inside. Taut with expectation, Gabby forced her wavering eyelids to stay shut. Dizzy sparkles danced against the darkness. There was a musty smell, and the muffled sound of voices filtered through a neighboring wall. They were grown-up voices, deep and grumbly. But Gabby couldn't tell what they were saying.

"A couple more steps," Dylan whispered. "Okay. Here we are."

Gabby opened her eyes. It took a second for her murky focus to clear.

Dylan made a courtly gesture. "Gabrielle Harper, I'd like you to meet the former container of the late Elwin Brock."

Blinking hard, she took in the sight of the old man lying on the raised metal table in the center of the room. He had a thick white beard and hair the yellow-white of a dirty dog. His face was the pink of a nasty sunburn, and he was all dressed up in a dark striped suit and white shirt.

"Go on. Get closer. Touch it if you want," Dylan said.

"No. We should get out of here." Gabby's voice was pinched to a squeak.

Dylan chuckled. "Don't worry. You're not going to wake him or anything. The man's *dead*."

Prickles of fear crawled up Gabby's spine. She stiffened and backed away. "I'm getting out of here."

"Easy. It's nothing. He's nothing. Just an empty box. Garbage. Don't you see?"

She bolted for the door. Before Dylan could stop her, she was charging down a dim corridor. Her heart was pounding like a sledgehammer, her breaths sharp and painful. In a mad rush, she tugged open the door. Outside, she'd be able to breathe again.

Instead, she found herself in a hushed room lined with plush crimson carpeting and fat, dark drapes. Another pink-faced man was lying in a shiny wooden box in the corner. A younger guy and a weeping woman were standing alongside. A tall man with puffy gray hair watched from across the room.

As Gabby burst in panting, the gray puff-headed man pivoted toward her. His face went sour.

"What do you think you're doing in here, young lady? What's your name?"

With giant strides, he came at Gabby. Terrified, she bolted. At a dead run, she followed the shadowy corridor to its opposite end. Outside, Dylan was waiting.

Scowling, he grabbed her painfully by the wrist. "Come on, dippy. I'll get you out of here."

Gabby ran with him to the car. She kept looking back toward the building, expecting the gray-haired man to come charging after them any minute. Or maybe the police. The door she'd come out of was the back way into the funeral parlor. Going in there when you weren't dead or invited by a dead person had to be some kind of a crime. Her heart pounded with terror.

Dylan bumped his car out of the parking lot and barreled up the street. When the funeral home was safely out of sight, he reached for a cigarette.

"You blew it," he said angrily. "Big time."

"You shouldn't have taken me there. I don't want to look at dead people."

"Not *people*, child. Empty boxes. Junk piles. Slabs of rotting meat. That's the whole point."

Gabby felt the sting of tears. "I don't care. Just leave me alone."

"I can't. It's the only way you can understand about your father and the senator. I've been there, sweetness. Believe me, I know."

The tears were flowing freely now, Gabby's grief rising in hard pulses. She didn't understand any of it. Why did people have to die? Why couldn't she have a father like the other kids? Why hadn't Mr. Gallatin stopped Mommy from hurting him when she got so crazy mad? He was so much bigger and stronger than Mommy was.

It was all so unfair. She always tried her very best to be a good girl. But these awful things kept happening to her. Wasn't God watching? Didn't He care?

The car screeched to a stop at a street corner. Unexpectedly, Dylan reached over and caught her in a gentle, tobacco-scented hug.

"It's hard, I know. But I'm here to make it easier. That's why I came around in the first place, little one. You need someone like me who really knows." His hand touched her hair.

"You have to believe me, little one. You have to go along with what I tell you. It's the only way."

He kept rubbing slow circles on her back. His hand was warm and soothing. Slowly the biting anguish started to recede. Gabby was getting so sleepy. Felt like hot syrup pouring into her limbs. Pulling back, Dylan raised the bottom of his black T-shirt and dabbed away her tears.

"Will you think about what I've said?"

She nodded. More than anything, Gabby wanted to understand. It was all so difficult. So painful and confusing.

"Next time, I know you'll be ready, sweetness. Go home, now. I'll come for you soon."

PERSONAL JOURNAL

26 September

For so long, the foul memories lurked beneath my
awareness like a dormant disease. Flashes began resur-
facing a year ago, after I learned the full extent of his
treachery.

I'd be going about my normal routine, and I'd feel
the echo of his gruff fingers against my bare baby skin.
Or, in the middle of a busy day's work, when the forward flow of my creative efforts was at its most potent
and exhilarating, I'd be stopped by the remembered
sensation of my tiny child's body on his lap.

He called it our special game. We had to wait to
play until we were completely alone and in no danger
of discovery. Then, he'd take me to what he called the
Secret Place. Days, he worked there, surrounded by foul
animal scents, immersed in filthy physical chores.
Nights, his space was transformed. Vacated. His tools
cast eerie shadows. The air went thick and still. A ticking clock was the only noise. It sounded like the beating of a broken heart.

The special game was cloaked in serious rules. Each
time, before we began, we had to turn off all the lights
and swear an oath of perfect silence. At first, to thwart
my infantile fear of the dark, I would crave the thick
feel of his hairy arms encircling me. I would settle will-
ingly on his broad lap where the demons wouldn't dare
reach out and grab me away.

For a few moments, there was comfort in that. Each
time, I managed to convince myself that this night
would be different. Safe. This time, I would tell myself,
he would only sing to me or tell a gentle story.

But soon, I could feel the hard thing twitching and
prodding beneath me. The gentle fingers would turn

into rough, seeking pistons jolting me up and down. His breathing would go so raw and ragged he could barely speak.

When I tried to squirm away, he would hold on to me. *It's just a dancing doll in my pocket*, he'd wheeze. *Sit still!*

The poking would get faster and faster. The pain was large and terrible. If I cried out, he would squeeze the blood out of my arm and press his palm so hard over my mouth, my teeth ached for days afterward.

I learned not to cry out.

I learned to leave my insensate self on his lap in the secret place and go off somewhere soft and sunny where the music was playing and the cat was curled contentedly on the windowsill and my mother was stirring a fragrant pot of pea soup at the stove.

I learned to stay removed until he pressed his hard mouth against the back of my neck, his signal that the game was at an end.

I learned to peel off the ugly times like a dirty bandage and drop them in my mental refuse bin, where they no longer had the power to harm or touch me.

What I could not do was get rid of them for good and all. There is only one way to achieve that total cleansing. And finally, now that I have discovered the means and the method, I am halfway to the end of him.

CHAPTER SEVENTEEN

Obsessively, Thea kept reading and rereading the articles in the paper about the investigation into Brandon Lee Payton's murder. So far, no solid suspects had been found. The stalking fan who'd openly threatened the young actor had presented an ironclad alibi for the day of the murder. A special task force had been created; a posted reward had prompted a flood of leads. But the brutal slaying remained unsolved.

Hearing Gabby come in, Thea quickly refolded the paper and put it aside.

"Hey, sweetie," she said brightly.

"Hi."

Gabby's moods kept shifting with startling speed. They were like capricious weather systems on the plains. The child had left for school this morning on an updraft and returned this afternoon in a trough. Her look was tight, and her voice was thick with worry.

Thea tried to draw her out, but the child immediately retreated to her room. She claimed she had a load of homework to do, but the book bag remained where she'd dropped it in the hall.

So she needed to be alone, Thea thought. Nothing wrong with that.

Or was there?

Should she go upstairs and insist that the little girl open up and air her acrid feelings? Or was it better to respect the child's obvious desire to brood in solitude?

And why did the choices seem so overwhelming?

Thea wondered when she'd begun to doubt her maternal instincts. Lord knew she was more than capable of making her fair share of motherly mistakes without all this agonizing. By default, she reluctantly decided to leave her little girl alone.

When Gabby resurfaced two hours later, Thea was at the stove fixing the pasta sauce. She was using one of the many prized culinary secrets Caro Millport had passed along years ago: dump store-bought sauce in a pot, stir, and ditch the container. Caro's cooking methods suited Thea perfectly. On the ranch, her mother had made everything from scratch, which took an astonishing amount of time. According to Ellie's way, if you wanted roast chicken, you started with the egg.

"Hi, Mommy."

"Hey, sweetie. You look lovely."

Gabby's face had a dewy, fresh-washed look, and her damp hair fell in graceful tendrils. She'd traded her school outfit for a favorite pair of printed leggings and the oversized pink sweater she'd gotten for her last birthday from the Millports. Thea caught a suspicious trace of blue on the eyelids and a heavy whiff of her own favorite cologne.

"Special occasion?" she asked.

"No. I was just sweaty from gym, so I took another shower." The child peered into the stockpot. "Are we having salad?"

"Salad, bread, lasagna, ice cream cake for dessert. Sound okay?"

Gabby frowned. "Shouldn't we have something first? An apple-tizer?"

Thea suppressed a smile. "What kind of appetizer did you have in mind?"

"A shrimp cocktail, maybe?"

"Maybe not. Don't worry, sweetie. I promise no one will go away hungry. Besides, the twins are not exactly what you'd call big eaters."

"It's not Opal and Jazzy."

"Who, then?"

"Somebody new." Gabby eyed the place settings Thea had already arranged on the kitchen table. "Can't we eat in the dining room?"

"All right. If you fix the table, we'll move the party in there."

"Great. I'll move the stuff while you go change. Why don't you wear your blue dress and those real high black heels?"

Thea's patience was fraying. "Look. I understand your wanting to impress your new friend, but this is getting ridiculous. I am not dressing up or calling in a caterer or hiring a string quartet. End issue."

"But—"

The doorbell chimed, cutting off the child's protest. Gabby charged out of the kitchen to welcome her hallowed guest. Thea gave the sauce another stir, then tossed some of her annoyance out on the salad. She wasn't ready for a fledgling adolescent. Sooner or later, she knew Gabby was bound to find her mother inadequate and painfully embarrassing, but later would be more than soon enough.

She checked herself out in the stove door. Nothing odd or unusual she could see. Regular face and hair. Standard hang-around outfit. No more than the typical ration of paint smears and charcoal blotches on the blouse. Their little visiting dignitary would simply have to accept her as is. And so, for that matter, would her daughter.

"Mom?"

Gabby was back with her guest in tow. Before she turned, Thea caught a glimpse of the pair in the glass oven door. Definitely a new breed of fourth grader.

"Mom, I'd like you to meet my teacher. Mr. Perry, this is my mom."

"It's Max." He flashed a dazzling grin. "It was nice of you to ask me to dinner, Mrs. Harper."

She tossed Gabby a chiding look, but the innocent eyes were stubbornly trained elsewhere.

"It's Thea." She knew exactly what her mother would say at a time like this: *When you're trapped, stay still, Checker honey. Wriggling around will only get you in deeper.*

Gabby ushered everyone into the living room and positioned Thea and the teacher on adjoining chairs.

"You guys talk. I'll be right back," the child said. She skipped out of the room, a broad smile plastered on her face.

Max Perry broke the clumsy silence. "Gabby's a terrific kid. Very bright."

"Thanks."

"And talented. She's a wonderful writer. Imaginative. Expressive. I've tried to encourage her."

So that explained the sudden literary ambition. The teacher's appearance explained much of the rest of Gabby's overzealous behavior. Max Perry had soulful eyes, deep dimples, great mouth. Fine chassis, too, from what Thea had casually observed. Definite crush material.

He smiled at her. "I really believe that talent like Gabby's should be nurtured. If it's all right with you, I'd like to work with her. Act as a sort of mentor."

"Sounds like you're doing that already."

"When I can, yes. But it's not easy to offer her the special attention she deserves when there are two dozen other kids in the class."

"So you're talking private tutoring?"

The notion revived poignant memories. Thea's mother had invented the "magic" casserole to fund the art lessons her family could ill afford. Somehow, the dish had magically stretched their meager food budget to cover tuition and supplies for the nearest art school.

"Not really." Max Perry shook his head. "I'm not looking for a formal arrangement, and I certainly don't want to be paid. I'd just like your permission to come by once or twice a week, when it's convenient for you. And maybe take Gabby to an occasional book signing or a reading at the library."

Sounded too good to be true. "Why would you want to go out of your way like that?"

If she sounded suspicious, Max Perry politely ignored it. "Because I think Gabby has real promise, and I'd like to see it developed," he answered earnestly. "Selfishly, she's the kind of child I enjoy working with, the reason I got into teaching in the first place. There aren't many kids who respond to learning experiences the way Gabby does. Of course, if it's not comfortable for you—"

It wasn't entirely, though Thea was reluctant to admit the true reason, even to herself. Max Perry didn't arouse any real anxieties. The teacher seemed honest and honestly interested. But with the gap already widening between her and her little girl, Thea resisted having this too charming, unfairly attractive man adding to the pull on the other end of the rope.

Gabby strode in, ceremoniously toting a plateful of raw vegetables. Pepper slices, cucumber rounds, carrot sticks. The child had even thought to peel the carrots and wash the bulk of the grime off the celery. In the center of the plate was a small dish full of something white and fluffy. First time Thea had ever seen crudités served with whipped cream.

"Would you like one, Mr. Perry?" Gabby's courtesy was elaborate.

"Thanks. They look delicious." He selected a leafy stalk of celery from the corner of the plate and munched with exaggerated appreciation.

"Mommy could make you a cocktail," she suggested.

"We have wine and Scotch and that green stuff Mommy likes. What's that called again, Mom?"

"Thanks. I'm fine," he said.

Gabby passed the tray again. Child was beaming. Nothing like blind adoration to improve the manners and raise a healthy glow in the cheeks.

Nudging aside her infantile jealousy, Thea forced herself to keep an open mind about this dedicated teacher who had tapped her child for special opportunity. As dinner progressed, the remnants of her guard evaporated. It was difficult not to like the guy. He was warm and funny and easy on the eyes. Easy to be around, also. Refusing to play guest, he entered automatically into the normal flow of serving and clearing and washing the dishes. By the time the last pot hit the drying rack, Thea's petty jealousies had been overthrown.

Max Perry eyed his watch. "Guess I'd better hit the road. Thanks for the dinner, ladies. Best meal I've had in weeks."

"Anytime," Thea said, and found herself meaning it.

"See you tomorrow, Mr. Perry," Gabby said. "Two more wins and the Scrabbles get that pizza party, right?"

"Right." At the door he stopped and turned to Thea. "And you'll let me know when you decide about that other matter we discussed?"

"I've decided already. It's fine."

"What's fine?" Gabby demanded. "What matter?"

"Mr. Perry would like to come over and help you with your writing once in a while. Would you like that?"

Gabby's eyes rolled in a near swoon. "*Would* I? You mean it, Mr. Perry?"

"Definitely. In fact, there's an author I think you'd like coming to speak at the library on Saturday afternoon. I'd love it if you'd come with me. In fact, I'd like both of you to come."

"Can we, Mommy?" Child looked carbonated. About ready to fizz over. "Please!"

"I suppose it's all right. Good night, Max. It was nice meeting you."

His smile was magnetic. "You, too, Thea. I look forward to Saturday."

Closing the door behind him, Thea caught the sheer contentment on her daughter's pretty face. If only the child's existence could always be like this, full of wonder and anticipation. But as Thea's mother often said: Life was what happened when you were busy making other plans.

After the past year, Thea didn't trust things to go nearly the way she hoped they would. She wondered if she could ever really trust anything or anyone again.

Herself included.

CHAPTER
EIGHTEEN

Twice a week, minimum, Passerelli invited Biederman home to dinner. Biederman hated to hurt the guy's feelings, but his wife's cooking was punishment on a plate, his kids acted like incoming mortar rounds, and frankly, Vinnie's company five or six days a week was more than plenty.

"Gina would really love it if you'd come, Danny. We're having sausage and peppers."

Heartburn with a side of gas. "Thanks anyway, Vince. I'm busy tonight."

Actually, he did have a full evening planned. He'd barely have time to finish dinner with Tom Brokaw before the Sox and the Yankees were slated to join him in the living room.

Passerelli was all smiles. "You got a date, Danny? No kidding?"

"Would I kid about such a thing?"

"Good for you. I got to admit Gina and I've been a little worried. It's been, what? Two years since the divorce?"

"Three a week from Tuesday at ten past four Eastern Daylight time. Give or take."

"Right, three. And you've had, what? A handful of dates?"

Actually, there had been more than a dozen, all well-intentioned fix-ups or brief cases of mistaken intensity. But no handfuls so far. At least, none that hadn't evaporated as soon as the alarm went off.

"I'm doing fine, Vinnie. Tell Gina she can put away the rosaries and quit lighting the candles."

In truth, Biederman's marriage had left him with a slightly bitter taste toward women. He suspected it might have something to do with the strychnine his ex-wife had sprinkled over his Cheerios every morning.

Actually, Biederman thought, Elaine's disaffection was understandable. He had stubbornly refused to become the international shipping magnate or corporate tycoon or grand larcenist of her dreams. Biederman's bride had meant it sincerely when she'd vowed the "for richer" part. But when it had started to look like a permanent cop career and "for poorer," Elaine had done the only sensible thing and taken up with the prosperous tax lawyer who lived down the block.

"How about next Tuesday, then?" Passerelli persisted. "Tuesday's eggplant parmigiana."

Sautéed filet of dishrag in a light gasoline sauce. Gina's specialty. "I'd really hate to pass that up, Vince. But first, let me see how things go tonight. Okay?"

Passerelli shrugged and maneuvered his minivan out of the lot. Biederman was preparing to follow when Buck Delavan came barreling across the blacktop.

"Hey, Danny! Wait up!"

The inspector was seriously out of shape. A fifty-yard sprint left him florid and gasping. Surprising that one of the more enterprising boys in the squad room hadn't taken notice and started a myocardial infarction pool. Sports betting was big around the station house. The work tended to attract risk-taking types.

"What's up, Buck?"

Pant. Gasp. "Just been a while since we got together on the outside, Danny boy. You have time for a brew?"

A while was actually never. Delavan was not one to socialize with the riffraff. Which made Biederman curious enough to suffer a sudden thirst. "Sure, Buck. Hop in."

They drove to Mario's, an Italian restaurant and

longtime Westport fixture opposite the railroad station.
As soon as they entered the busy bar, Delavan peeled off
to glad-hand the milling crowd of local businessmen
and politicians. Biederman hung back and entertained
himself with two of the dubious benefits of his height:
observing the dust on the tops of things and noting the
creative ways balding men sculpted their remaining
tresses to mask the sparse spots.

Westport's mayor had worked one five-inch, dyed-
brown ribbon into a tight coil on the crown of his head.
Built-in yarmulke.

Carl Medici, who ran two local gas stations and a
high-stakes poker game, had grown the entire right
side of his spotty mane so that it vaulted the top of his
lumpy scalp and landed over his pendulous left ear in a
rakish fringe. On a windy day, hair like Medici's tended
to billow like a mainsail. Under water, he could probably pass for the Little Mermaid in drag. Fascinating.
By the time Biederman shifted his attention to the su-
perintendent of schools, whose hair had dropped from
the top of his head to chin level, Delavan was back.

The inspector passed Biederman a frosted mug of domestic draft.

"Here's mud in your eye," he said.

Exactly what Biederman was hoping to avoid.
"*L'chaim.*"

Delavan took a deep pull on the beer. He surfaced
with a foam mustache and a grateful sigh. "You know,
Danny? I've always been partial to you."

Man could certainly keep a secret. "Is that so?"

"Way back when you were a rookie, I could see you
had that special something."

The inspector had that special something, too. And
Biederman resolved not to step in it and soil his shoes.

"What is it you want from me, Buck?"

Delavan's teeth were clamped so hard, he had to force out the chuckle.

"I want to know why you haven't come through for me yet, Danny. Passerelli's not worth the paper he's printed on. But I expected a damn sight better from the likes of you. I told you I want that Harper woman. And I meant fast."

"I can't find what's not there, Inspector. Can't and won't."

Delavan clamped a hand on the back of Biederman's neck. Felt like he was out to crush a mosquito.

"Smart boys like you. Ivy League education and all. Bet your old man was a doctor or lawyer. Am I right?"

"Actually, Dad ran a frame shop. He begged me to go into the family business."

"Smart mouth, too. Smart all around. That's why I know you're not going to let me down here. Maybe I didn't make myself clear enough, Danny boy. I won't rest easy until that bitch is locked up where she belongs."

"Why are you so hot on this, Buck?" Biederman asked the poison question with all the innocent goodwill he could muster. Which wasn't much.

"You've got no need for reasons, Sergeant. Let's not forget who works for who here. I give the orders; you take them."

"Fine. If Thea Harper steps out of line, I won't hesitate to take her down."

Delavan snorted. "*Thea*, is it now? Since when are you and that murdering bitch on a first-name basis? Not very professional, if you ask me."

That was not what Biederman had asked at all. "I do my job, Inspector. That's what I'll keep doing."

"I'd say that depends on your performance, Sergeant. Like I told you, times are tight. With the ship about to sink, last thing we can afford is to hang on to any drift-wood."

Biederman had been threatened by rabid dogs with more subtlety. But there was far more on the line here than his modest livelihood.

Biederman's bewildered parents had battled his career choice with a vengeance. They would have preferred to see him in any white-collar profession, stock fraud and embezzlement included. His wife had considered his job preference a crime punishable by the ultimate penalty: death by tax attorney. He himself was hard-pressed to explain the lure of law enforcement. The field had simply gripped and held him. Or, as his mother preferred to put it, "Don't ask."

Even as a little kid, he'd always chosen the cop side and let his bad-assed buddies play the robbers. He'd always suffered an overblown sense of fairness and justice and a tendency to care too much about other people's problems. It still drove him nuts to see the scum prevail or watch a nice guy finish last (especially when the nice guy was himself).

His parents loved to regale him with the litany of lost opportunities. He'd graduated from Brown with honors. Double major in psych and biochemistry. Phi Beta Kappa junior year. Fellowship offers. "You could have been something, Daniel," they liked to say, as if working in law enforcement was tantamount to impersonating a barber pole.

Delavan sucked down the rest of his beer and swiped the foam off his lip with the back of a beefy hand. "No need for me to be telling you how it is, Danny boy. You know the score."

Biederman also knew how to avoid hanging himself with his own tongue. Instead, he took a more subtle tack. "Nice suit, Buck. Must've cost a bundle."

Delavan's grin was a crooked line. "What can I say,

Danny? Little lady likes me to dress spiffy. Woman has champagne taste and married a suds man. Lucky thing her old man came before her."

So an affluent father-in-law accounted for Delavan's sudden solvency. Or was the neat explanation a convenient dodge?

Delavan tossed a ten on the counter and steered Biederman out the door. On the street, the chief stalled. He tuned his look to total sincerity.

"I know you think I'm being unreasonable, Danny boy, but I've been in this game a long time. Way longer than you. You think I've got some sort of personal vendetta against Harper. But the thing is, I know she's trouble. I can smell it. We don't put her away, she'll do in another poor sap. Mark my words."

"What do we charge her with, Inspector? Giving you the heebie-jeebies?"

"If something happens, it'll be on your hands, Danny. You don't help bring her down, it's like you're writing the death sentence for some innocent soul."

"Why me, Buck? You've got a whole building full of boys who'd love nothing better than to be sent out on a nice witch-hunt and stake-burning."

"It's like my sainted mother always told me, Danny boy. Because I said so. Because I know what I'm doing and how I want it done. Because it's my job to protect the public safety, and that woman is dangerous, and you're the one I've chosen to take her out of the play. Period."

"But I happen not to agree with you, Inspector. And neither did the court. Thea Harper was tried by a jury of her peers and found not guilty. She deserves to be left in peace."

Delavan's response was a very brief round of applause. Three loud claps. Slow and nasty. "Fine argument, Counselor. Real articulate. Unfortunately, bullshit in a tuxedo is still bullshit!" The chief's eyes narrowed. "It's a personal thing, isn't it, Danny? You've got the hots for the bitch. Why didn't I see it before?"

"I've got plans tonight, Buck. So, if you'll excuse me."

Delavan puffed his contempt. "Man starts thinking with his dick in this business, it's worse than stupid, Danny. It's downright dangerous. I—"

Biederman interrupted. "If you need a ride, I'll drop you off at headquarters."

"I'll find my own way, Sergeant. You'd best worry about finding yours."

Biederman watched his boss amble back toward the restaurant. Delavan's parting shot stuck like a burr. Was he letting his infatuation with Thea Harper cloud his judgment? Or had the chief's disturbing observation been a fortunate guess?

Either way, Biederman was already in this thing far deeper than he cared to be. And still, he had the sorry sense that he hadn't hit the bottom of it.

CHAPTER NINETEEN

In the still gray dawn, Westport's Compo Beach was deserted. As planned, they met behind the elaborate playground and trudged together along the littered sand. Wordlessly, the two women settled on a weathered bench facing the fog-shrouded face of Long Island Sound. Screeching gulls orbited overhead. A strident wind blew. Chill mist spattered from the roiling surf. Shivering, he sat beside them and huddled into his flimsy denim jacket.

"I trust things are progressing well," the old woman said. There was never a word from the daughter. She just followed her old lady around like some shadowy spook.

"Absolutely, Mrs. Gallatin. Moving right along."

"How soon do you anticipate having the necessary information for me?"

Clad in a black, hooded coat, she resembled a roosting vulture. She did not look at him. She never had.

"Hard to say exactly. I'm working on it. Giving it my best."

"I warned you. I am not, by nature, a patient person."

"I understand. Should be soon, now. Anytime." He shot a furtive glance at her. The hood obscured most of her face, but what showed was sharp and forbidding. Still, it was the daughter who gave him the larger case of creeps. Why the hell didn't she ever *say* anything? She was like a time bomb, saving it all for the big explosion.

"Tell me what you've discovered so far. Leave nothing out," the old woman commanded.

He offered the full report, plumping the details to give the package added weight. From the outset, the old lady had made it clear that she expected a hefty return for her unsolicited favors.

Lucky thing he knew how to pad a story. He could fine-tune assumptions into credible truth. Toss in the necessary twists and transitions to keep things interesting. To listen to him, you'd think he was actually getting somewhere. It was impossible to tell he had nothing significant to show for all his spying and deceit but a serious and growing case of the guilts.

He had no grudge against Thea Harper, no reason to want her destroyed. Quite the opposite.

Truth was, he was heartily sick of the whole damned business. Lily Gallatin was a nasty old bird. Thought she owned the world, including the meager parts that weren't actually in her family's name. She treated people like disposable diapers, to be dumped on and discarded. The old crone wouldn't even deign to call him by name. She made him feel small and worthless. The whole enterprise diminished him, which was clearly *not* what he'd pictured at the start.

When the old bird first took him under her gilt-edged wing, he'd been overwhelmed by his good fortune. All he had to do was deliver a little incriminating evidence, dig up a few shovelsful of harmless dirt, and rich old Mrs. Gallatin would see him safely out of a nasty legal quagmire.

Unbeknownst to the old lady, he'd planned to squeeze the contact for every cent of its considerable worth. Having access to the Gallatins, even the restricted, humiliating access allowed him, was priceless. His ticket.

And about time.

For the past few years, he'd had more than his fair share of rotten breaks. Time and again, he'd been passed over. Misunderstood. Through no fault of his own, a series of his hottest leads fizzled. A couple of sweetheart deals soured. And finally, he'd been primed for a lethal fall by experts. They'd left him with his neck in a noose and the floor wobbling dangerously under his feet.

At the time, he couldn't imagine who in the world might help him. His family had written him off as a useless loser. Shut him out.

But at his nadir, when his person and future were locked in a squalid holding cell, old lady Gallatin's lawyer had materialized like a genie to spring him. After the shock wore off, he'd been overjoyed. He could all but feel the fates shifting. Never occurred to him that the tilt could be in the wrong direction.

"I've been keeping a close watch on her," he concluded. "And I can tell you she's not in a good way. Very jumpy."

"What I want is to see my son's murder avenged. I can assure you I am not in the least interested in Mrs. Harper's emotional well-being."

"I understand, Mrs. Gallatin. I'm close. Honestly." He winced at the whine of desperation in his tone.

"I certainly hope so. I do *not* take well to disappointment."

At this point, all he honestly wanted was out, but that option wasn't anywhere on the menu. These rich, famous types got whatever and whoever they wanted. If he didn't come through, the Gallatins could annihilate him with a phone call.

"You won't be disappointed," he said, wishing it to be true.

"I will if this isn't resolved quickly and to my satisfaction. I expect to hear from you by the beginning of the week."

"Listen, Mrs. Gallatin. You have to understand, I'm moving as fast as I can—"

She and her weird daughter stood and strode away without a word. He eyed the swerving worm tracks the pair left in the sand. Turning back to face the churning water, he gave them ample time to disappear in their chauffeured Bentley.

After the car's sounds faded in the distance, he stood. Heading back to the parking lot, his head was bowed by the weight of his predicament. Thea seemed a kind, decent person who didn't deserve the assault. Neither did her little girl. Poor kid had already suffered more than plenty with her daddy's death and all. No matter what a self-serving bastard he could be, he had no desire to do that child any harm.

But the Gallatins were a tidal force, battering the meager remains of his sandcastle dreams into a sodden, defenseless mess.

And when it came down to basics, he had to look out for number one.

CHAPTER
TWENTY

Billie kneaded her swollen feet and propped them on one of Thea's bentwood kitchen chairs. The abused extremities looked like twin loaves of risen dough.

"Doc Forman can go out as herself come Halloween. Tell you that much," the nurse groused.

"Sorry she's giving you such a hard time," Thea said.

"Not just me, girl. Hard time's all that woman *knows* how to give. Got half a mind to quit on her. Whole damned staff should up and quit, you want my opinion. Don't imagine the doc could even stand to put up with her own damned self, if it came right down to it."

Thea bridled at the injustice. Billie was the glue that held the hospital together. The good-natured nurse was always available in a crunch or crisis. She knew how to defuse a frenzied patient, soothe a troubled relative, or placate a simmering bureaucrat. Billie was always the one to track down a crucial missing form or bridge the perilous ellipsis in a failed communication. A born diplomat, she knew how to mediate the inevitable staff conflicts, so that everyone wound up pulling in the same direction. Without Billie, it was impossible to imagine the place running at all, much less smoothly. But since Dr. Forman's appointment as Brook Hollow's medical director two years ago, the nurse's extraordinary contribution had been largely ignored.

Dr. Forman had no concept of gratitude or positive reinforcement. Her management style was courtesy of the Juiceman. She squeezed all she could from every employee and discarded the desiccated pulp. At best, she'd reward an outstanding job with indifference.

"Do what's right for you, Billie. If she's making your life miserable—"

"I won't let her, that's all. Woman's got a problem, it's her problem." The nurse took a long pull at her coffee. The four spoonsful of sugar had an instant calming effect. Billie's shoulders drooped as the tension drained from her.

"That's good. Brook Hollow would fall down without you, pal. Brick by brick."

"Wish Doc Forman saw it that way. You listen to her, you'd think I was behind every bad thing ever happened at the hospital. Woman even blames me for Vita Negrone walking out."

"They haven't found her yet?" Having Vita at large made the world seem even shakier.

"They will, girlfriend. Got a few more rocks to look under. Old Vita'll turn up."

The smile crept back into the nurse's eyes. With a hearty slurp, she vacuumed another mouthful from the mug. "How 'bout you, girlfriend? You keeping your bricks together okay?"

Thea had planned to maintain a firm, stoical facade, but Billie had a way of honing in on the raw spots. "Ups and downs."

"The ups you can handle yourself. Maybe there's a down or two I can help with."

"I doubt it, Billie. How about we talk about something more pleasant?"

"I want pleasant, I'll go see a Disney movie. Now spill, girl. Get it off your chest."

Thea did. Maybe it had been a mistake to try to reclaim her life in this town. She recounted Glenda Rossner's acid-tongued comment at her homecoming celebration and the nasty remarks she'd caught from those women at the store. She described the constant harassment from the reporters. Harlan Vermin won the chief scum award. He kept leaving message after mes-

sage on her answering machine; he shadowed her relentlessly. Thea shivered at the memory of how she'd almost
run over little Raleigh Millport in her desperation to be
rid of that heinous man.

And he wouldn't quit. Just this morning, she was
certain she'd seen him lurking outside her studio,
though he managed to disappear before she could nab
him in the act. But he was far from the only pest on the
list. Word of her release had spread to the other tabloid
rats like garbage-borne disease. Now, every time she
checked, the answering machine was flashing like a fes-
tering boil. And most of the messages were from filth-
hungry reporters.

*I'm the one to tell your side of the story, Thea. And I can
make it worth your while.*

*Give me a call, Ms. Harper. I can guarantee you a front-
page spread.*

Maybe she and Gabby would be better off fleeing like
turncoat mobsters, having their faces redone, slipping on
fresh identities, and changing their name to Smith.

Thea poured out her concerns about Gabby. What if
all the past year's craziness had inflicted permanent
damage on the child? Why else would a little girl be so
sullen and moody all the time? And why would she
swaddle herself in so many secrets? What was she really
hiding or hiding from? How could Thea hope to help
her daughter at all when her own emotional state was
about as steady as a three-legged piano?

Thea had asked Dr. Forman about therapy for Gabby,
but, after interviewing the little girl on a number of occasions, the psychiatrist concluded that formal treatment wasn't necessary. The child was functioning well
despite adverse circumstances, Dr. Forman reported.
The changes Thea was seeing were the first gathering
clouds that presaged the storm of adolescence.

Thea sighed. "I don't know, Billie. Maybe it *is* all in

my imagination. Dr. Forman thinks I'm overreacting to normal kid stuff."

"Well, the woman does know her business. That much I'll give her. She says the child's rolling straight, I'd leave it at that."

"I suppose. But it's so hard to watch my little girl pulling away, turning into some kind of stranger. Why can't things be the way they were, Billie? Why is everything so damned hard?"

It felt wonderful to unburden herself, to run through her own mental grove screaming like nutty Mrs. Argersinger. The only significant difference was that Thea's sky was falling for real.

Lucky thing Gabby had taken off over an hour ago to visit the twins, Thea thought as she drew a snuffled breath. She must sound like a crazed hyena.

But Billie was the perfect listener. The nurse readily accepted Thea's rambled angst. She responded with unerring expressions of support and understanding. Billie allowed Thea ample ranting room. There was no one else Thea could let loose with like this, not even Caro. Having a nice no-holds-barred breakdown around Caro Millport was too much like trying to stage a hurricane in a tropical lagoon.

"If only I could get a decent night's sleep," Thea said. "When I'm not having a nightmare, I'm up worrying." She could not bring herself to tell the nurse about her stubborn preoccupation with the Brandon Lee Payton murder. Thea picked over every scrap of news about the killing like a starving scavenger. She dwelt mercilessly on the terrifying open questions. How had she known about the snake? Where had those missing hours gone?

"There, now," Billie soothed. "Gonna take time for all the pieces to fall in just so, girlfriend. Seems to me you're being overly hard on yourself."

"Maybe. I'm just so desperate to get everything right

for Gabby, to start making things up to her. She's been through too much, Billie. It's not fair."

"All you can do is love the child, girl. And Lord knows you do that."

Thea sighed. "Feels like it's not enough."

"Sure it is, honey. It's everything. You'll see. I've watched that little one of yours. Child's got way more bounce in her than you think. Got to agree with Doc Forman there. Gabby'll come through just fine. You'll see."

"I hope so."

"You listen to old Billie. Tonight before bed, you have yourself a nice cup of hot milk with a spoon of sugar and a big shot of brandy."

Thea couldn't help but smile. "What's that? Punishment for my hysterical outburst?"

"Nothing of the kind." Billie shook her head with vehemence. "Old family remedy. Guaranteed to put your lights out and keep them out. You get a good night's sleep, things'll brighten up considerable come morning."

"Okay. I'll give it a try."

"You do that. Meantime, I'd best be running. I show up two minutes late, my folks'll be calling the hospitals and sending out the dogs."

Ten minutes after Billie left, Gabby came home looking like an escapee from Elizabeth Arden. Her nails were polished pink, her hair arranged in a vampy do with a deep dip over one eye and the opposite side drawn back in an ornate comb. She was dressed in a short mock-leather skirt and turquoise turtleneck sweater, courtesy of Opal or Jasmine or both. Black tights, black flats, and a double strand of black beads completed the ensemble.

Thea sucked in a whistle. "You look like you should be sitting on top of a cake."

"I do? Should I change?"

"That's a compliment, sweetie. I mean you look beautiful."

The child's cheeks pinked to match her nail polish. "So, what are you going to wear?"

"For the big outing to the library with Mr. Perry, you mean?"

"Yes. You're not going like *that,* Mommy. Are you?"

From the child's horrified expression, Thea brilliantly deduced that her vintage gray sweats with the cropped sleeves and rakishly ripped knees were unacceptable. She didn't argue, though in her view the outfit made a definite fashion statement: something about Alcatraz.

"Would my black slacks and a sweater ease the humiliation?"

"Which shoes?"

"Which will you allow, General?"

"Those low boots with the skinny heels would be great, Mommy. And your silver buckle belt. And wear those dangly earrings: the silver with the black-and-blue shiny stuff."

"It's called lacquer."

"Right. Those. And a silver bracelet."

Thea sighed. "I don't have a silver bracelet."

"Amber does. I'll call and ask to borrow it."

Thea signaled for a time-out. "That's not necessary. *Really.* I promise to look presentable in my own things."

Gabby eyed her dubiously. "Okay, but you'd better go get ready. Mr. Perry will be here soon."

Soon was almost two hours, but Thea yielded to her daughter's mania and headed upstairs. Fifteen minutes later, she reappeared in the kitchen for official troop review and inspection.

Gabby gave her a serious once-over. "You look nice," she pronounced solemnly.

"You mean, I pass? Praise the Lord."

The child frowned. "Only you forgot your lipstick and eye stuff."

"I don't wear eye stuff, my sweet. A touch of lip gloss and some blush in the event of illness is the best you're ever going to get from me."

The child issued a gusty sigh. "Okay, Mommy. But you really could use one of those makeovers they do at the department store. . . ."

The remaining time until Max Perry's arrival passed like the countdown to a nuclear strike. Gabby was frantic with anticipation. The child wouldn't touch her lunch for fear of soiling her clothing. She held herself stiff as a mannequin to keep from wrinkling anything. Thea proposed several activities designed to distract her, but Gabby's sole interest appeared to be staring at the clock.

"You won't make it any sooner that way, sweetie. A watched pot never boils."

"That's only an *expression*, Mommy. You're not supposed to believe it's really true."

When the doorbell finally rang, Thea was relieved and more than ready to let Max Perry grab the reins on Gabby's galloping enthusiasm. And the teacher pulled it off masterfully. All he had to do was step into the front hall, and the child was instantly transformed from heavy metal to easy listening.

The man was a veritable magician.

The rest of the day passed without a hitch. In her teacher's presence, Gabby was a model child: bright, polite, and beaming. She was thrilled when Perry introduced her to the visiting author after the library lecture. Her name was Madge Salner, and she'd written more than a dozen titles aimed at the preteen set.

The woman had kindly brown eyes, sandy hair drawn back in a headband, and the sort of boneless face and plump body that made her age unreadable. Max had the author autograph a copy of her latest work "To

Gabby, fellow writer." Apparently, the speaker was a longtime acquaintance, though Max seemed reluctant to explain the connection.

Afterward, they stopped at a fair at the local Y. By then, Gabby was sufficiently free of her wooden vanity to participate in the apple-bobbing contest and have her face painted. She even succumbed to the lure of a barbecued burger and a caramel apple. To cap the occasion, Max won a wall-eyed panda in the ring toss game. With a gallant bow, he presented it to Gabby.

"Thank you *so* much! He's *excellent*! I'm going to call him Perry, after you." Gabby hugged the bear so hard Thea feared the poor thing would pop its stuffing.

With startling speed, day drifted into evening. Max insisted on taking them to dinner at Sole e Luna, a popular Italian restaurant near the Westport Playhouse. Though the library visit and the fair had gone smoothly, Thea remained hesitant about public outings. But she finally yielded to Max's persuasive charm and Gabby's unabashed begging.

It turned out to be a fortunate choice. The food was delicious, the atmosphere pleasantly boisterous, the company made to order. Max Perry had an infectious smile and a terrific sense of humor. Gabby was deeply entranced. Thea had to admit she was having a wonderful time, too. If there were gawking onlookers or nasty gossips in the packed house, Thea didn't notice them. Didn't notice, and found she honestly didn't care.

Maybe happiness was like bike riding, a skill somehow retained despite prolonged disuse. Thea dared to imagine feeling like this more often, enjoying herself, watching the delicious gleam of excitement in her little girl's eyes.

For a lovely moment, Thea saw a slim ray of hope ahead of her. Could she dare to believe it might mark the end of the long, dark tunnel?

T H E
THIRD

CHAPTER TWENTY-ONE

"You're a blasted cheat, Alden Gaithwaite. A cheat and a braggart."

Gaithwaite bit back the grin and waxed innocent. "What's this, Blossom? Could my dearie be turning into a poor loser?"

"Loser, my ass. I saw you slip that queen from the bottom of the deck. I may be old, but I'm not dotty. And I'm not putting up with the likes of you for another minute."

Blossom Price set her ax-head jaw, grabbed her public television canvas tote bag, and tossed on a trench coat over her flowered robe. She paused at the condo door for yet another last word. "Far as I'm concerned, you can play by yourself from now on, Alden Gaithwaite. You get lonely, you can always cuddle up with your dag-nabbed awards."

"You don't mean that, dearie. Come on now. Let's kiss and make up." Gaithwaite spread his arms and cocked his head like a hopeful puppy.

"You can kiss my butt, that's what. Can't believe I've frittered my best years on a stuck-up old card cheat. Good riddance to you. I'll send for my things."

The door slammed hard, and there was the brutish smack of Blossom's fleece-lined boots against the hall floor.

Gaithwaite finally allowed the simmering smile to surface. He and Blossom had been living in what some folks called sin for nearly thirty years now. She'd walked out on him in a huff or a whatever at least twice a week for the entire three decades, more during a full moon or back when there was still a wrong time of the month.

Not that there was ever a right time.

Never a dull moment with that girl. Gaithwaite chuckled and praised his good fortune.

Fondly, he recalled the half dozen times he and Blossom had considered getting hitched. Once or twice, they'd made it almost all the way to the altar. But Blossom's temper always stepped forward at the last minute to raise some deal-breaking objections. So Alden and his lady love weren't family—at least, not in the legal, churchly sense. But Blossom was certainly the nearest, dearest of relatives in Alden's heart.

He couldn't envision a life without her—tantrums, testy temper, and all. Blossom was his best friend and firmest supporter. It was Blossom who'd kept him going years back when the bottling plant closed and Alden was shut out of the company he'd served faithfully since his discharge from the navy after World War II.

Ten years ago, when Alden suffered the coronary, Blossom had dutifully nursed and nagged him back to health. Afterward, she'd convinced him to give up the night security job at the mall, which was killing him even faster than his elevated pressure and clogged arteries.

Gaithwaite had never planned on retirement. But as Blossom predicted, he found peace and unparalleled enjoyment right here in the condo complex, where he'd become a surrogate grandfather to legions of neighborhood latchkey kids.

"Pappy Alden," they called him when they dropped by for help with their bruises, homework, broken toys, and garden-variety childhood woes. Gaithwaite discovered he had a natural affinity for kids of all ages, and they responded with more affection and regard than a

body could hope to absorb. The public acclaim that followed had been a most unexpected, though not at all
unwelcome, bonus.

A few years back, Alden had been tapped as one of
ex-President Bush's "Thousand Points of Light." Apparently, old George didn't mind that Gaithwaite was a
lifelong Democrat and a dirty Liberal to boot, or maybe
someone in the Points of Light Department had simply
fouled up and failed to notice.

However it came to happen, Gaithwaite greatly enjoyed the flurry of public attention. His ugly mug had
been plastered on the front page of the *Connecticut Post*.
He'd been a featured guest on *The Fairfield Exchange*, a
local cable show that aired once live and then five times
taped in a single day. The award had even received
midpaper mentions in dailies outside the region.
Alden's sister from Cleveland had sent him a clip from
the national section of the *Plain Dealer*.

But the most exciting experience by far had been the
follow-up article in one of last July's issues of *People*.
Must have been a light news week, Alden figured. But
he'd reaped the benefit of inclusion in a "Where are
they now?" piece on several of the ex-prexy's honored
volunteers.

Blossom wasn't the type to let on, but Alden spotted
the glint of pride in her steely old eyes when she found
his picture and the paragraph about Bridgeport's beloved "Pappy Alden" on page seventy-two. His dearie
had snuck off and had the article mounted and framed
as if it were some fancy Harvard diploma or the stuffed
head of a prized buck.

Gaithwaite leaned back in his chair, threaded his
veiny hands behind his neck, and stared at his most
prized possessions (next to Blossom, of course). There
was the Point of Light certificate, personally auto-
graphed by the ex-president. The framed *People* piece

and the headline picture from the *Connecticut Post* hung alongside. But his favorite souvenir by far was the picture where he was surrounded by all the neighborhood kids at the surprise party they'd thrown for him after the Point of Light award was announced.

I'm a lucky old codger, Alden thought with a contented sigh. *Got all my adopted grandkids and my lady. And I'm feeling sassier than I have in years.*

Blossom surely hadn't been cranky or complaining last night when Alden moseyed over to her side of the boudoir for a little hanky-panky. Wasn't even Saturday night, Gaithwaite mused with a puff of macho pride. Must be those new megavitamins.

The *Tonight Show* theme was playing. With a start, Gaithwaite noted that it was past eleven-thirty. Blossom should have been back by now. Before now.

Standing stiffly, he lumbered to the window and peered out at the street. A van barreled by, brights beaming. A striped tabby dashed across the road. No Blossom. Where in the jeezum crow was that girl? What in the Lord's name could she be up to at this hour?

Trying to torment him, that's what. After thirty years, Alden should darn well know better than to let Blossom tweak him into fretting about her. Girl was a master tweaker, no question about it.

Well, this time, he'd go her one better. When she wearied of sulking around and came home, he would *not* be waiting up for her like some lovesick sap the way he usually did. Wouldn't Blossom just birth a cow when she found the apartment all dark and zipped up and him curled in the sack, snoring as if he hadn't a care?

Gleeful at the naughty notion, Gaithwaite brushed his teeth and snugged his weary bones under the covers. He'd intended to feign sleep, eager to catch Blossom's shocked reaction when she finally showed up, but he dropped right off as if he'd been perched at the edge of a crumbly cliff.

Some time later, he awakened to the sound of the condo door creaking open. Still groggy, he heard Blossom stumbling around the dark living room.

She spat a curse. Must've barked her shin, poor dearie. But Gaithwaite resisted the urge to hop to and go make the fuss she was expecting.

He kept his face to the wall, eyes closed, breaths slow and steady. Let the woman wonder for a welcome change. Let her be the one to make the overtures. You don't try to even things up here, old Blossom'll be glad to give you thirty more years of worse than the last ones, Alden Gaithwaite.

Not that he wouldn't be more than glad to settle for that.

Still, it was fun to be on the winning side of the practical joke for once. Blossom was forever playing tricks on him. She kept him hopping like grease on a hot griddle. *Stick with it, you old Point of Light, you. Don't let her win this round.*

Gaithwaite imagined how fired up his dearie must be. He heard her rummaging around the kitchen. Probably sucking down a pile of sweets to calm her ruffled plumes, he thought. Well, this time, he wasn't dashing in to remind her about the troubles she had digesting rich food. If she wanted a bellyache, that was her privilege.

Good. She was on her way to the bedroom. Huddled in a fetal ball, Gaithwaite made slow, deliberate snoring noises. Come on, Blossom. Come blow that pretty old stack of yours.

And he wasn't disappointed. Gaithwaite heard the steps accelerate as she approached the bed in a fury. He figured he was in for some serious torture. Blossom knew every one of his ticklish spots, and wasn't

ashamed to use them. Steeling himself, he kept up the
sleep act.

He kept it up until he felt the stinging stick of the
knife blade. The pain built to a stark, white pressure at
the center of his spine. Electric jolts seared through his
limbs. In a final, startled reflex, he struggled to outdis-
tance the agony. But the effort was beyond him. He felt
the press of her lips against his neck. Weird.

Then, his dearie had never been the least bit easy or
predictable. Part of her charm. He wanted to tell her,
but his mouth wouldn't respond to the signals his brain
was frantically sending. Too hard, dearie, he thought
with a long burbling sigh of surrender. You win.

And then, Alden Gaithwaite went to sleep for good.

CHAPTER TWENTY-TWO

Leaning on her desk, Gabby stared across the street at the Millport house, waiting for the lights to go on in the twins' room. Five after seven already. Drake and Raleigh were always up by six the latest. Those babies made more noise than the average car alarm. How could Opal and Jasmine still be asleep?

Gabby had triple-swear promised to visit the very first thing this morning with a play-by-play account of her incredible day with Mr. Perry. Opal had practically fainted when Gabby phoned late yesterday afternoon to report that the teacher was taking her and Mommy out to dinner. Jasmine had begged Gabby to snatch a souvenir from the restaurant, something Mr. Perry had touched, or better yet, eaten with.

Gabby had spotted the chance to pocket a hunk of his bread crust while he and Mom were busy talking about some museum exhibit in New York City. But she hadn't been able to muster the nerve. On the way out, when Mom was in the ladies' room and Mr. Perry was getting the coats, she could have slipped his soiled napkin into her purse, but the risk of discovery and humiliation had kept her honest. Then, from the front desk where they kept the phone, Gabby had tried to take a pack of matches with the restaurant's name. But her mother had seen and pocketed the matchbook herself. Thankfully, Mom had let the incident pass with nothing but an angry look. For a heart-stopping instant, Gabby feared she was going to get yelled at in front of the teacher.

Too bad. Opal and Jasmine would have been super

impressed by the matches. This morning, Gabby had even considered trying to slip them out of Mommy's jacket pocket just long enough to show the twins. But if she got caught, she'd be history.

Still, she had Perry the Panda to show off, and she could proudly display the spot on her left cheek where Mr. Perry had given her an actual good-night kiss. His lips were nice and dry, she would report with authority. And he made exactly the perfect amount of kissing noise. Not a thunderous smackeroo like Mr. Millport or a silent rubber stamp like baby Drake.

Mr. Perry hadn't kissed Mommy good night, but he had taken her hand at the door and stared hard into her eyes the way movie couples always did when they were about to fall deeply in love.

So things were moving right along.

Yesterday morning, when the twins were helping Gabby get ready for the library outing, the three girls had held a preliminary discussion about the wedding. Opal favored a formal Saturday night affair with several ushers and a long row of bridesmaids dressed in bright pink. Jasmine preferred an afternoon reception in the Millports' backyard, similar to the one she'd seen last spring on *The Young and The Restless*, while she was recuperating from the flu.

Gabby remained open to suggestions, but she personally envisioned a small gathering at home, probably in the living room. Nothing too fancy. If she had her way, the guest list would be limited to the Millports, Mr. Perry's closest friends and family, and Mom's parents. Mrs. Millport could handle the decorations, and, for the celebratory dinner, they could bring in Chinese food from the Panda Pavilion. Anything to do with pandas had assumed greatly increased significance since Mr. Perry's gift of his stuffed namesake.

Finally, a blush of pink light stained the Millport girls'

bedroom window. Gabby had been dressed and ready to go for hours. Heading out anxiously now, she peered into her mother's room. Still sleeping. Highly unusual for Mom, who was always up at milking time, even though the cows were now several thousand miles away.

Maybe she was worn out from the excitement of being with Mr. Perry. Gabby had been up nearly the whole night, her insides fizzing like a shaken can of Coke. But Mommy was entitled to react her own way.

Downstairs, Gabby downed a glass of juice and tacked a note to the refrigerator door. No way she could hang around until her mother awakened. She'd already done far more than her fair share of restless waiting for one day.

Quietly, she slipped out the front door and headed down the walk. Autumn had intensified overnight, framing Linden Street with lacy patches of deep yellow, russet, ginger, and grape red. Some of the border hedges had turned the crimson of a Jell-O mold. Others sported deep orange berries and a tangle of fallen leaves.

Gabby's breath rose in misty plumes, and she hugged herself to ward off the chill. She was clad in the same dark skirt and fuzzy aqua sweater she'd worn last night to dinner. Sniffing the sweater carefully this morning, she'd detected a remaining trace of Mr. Perry's citrusy cologne. She'd deliberately left her jacket off this morning, fearful that the teacher's scent might be suffocated before the twins had a chance to take a whiff.

Smoke trailed from the Rossmans' wood stove chimney. Gabby spotted Mrs. Big Mouth herself, already peering out the window. A leaf blower chattered in the distance, and there was the growl of a chain saw. Gabby quickened her pace, anxious for the comfy warmth of the Millport kitchen.

She couldn't wait to tell the twins everything. Gabby held all of yesterday like a videotape in her brain: the author's talk at the library, the fair, the spaghetti dinner.

And then there was the incredible time back at the house when Mr. Perry had actually asked if he could stop by Tuesday after school to work with Gabby on her writing.

The day had been so amazing, she could barely believe it had actually happened. Gabby was so absorbed in the wonder of Mr. Perry's attentions, she didn't notice the rustling hedge at the border of the Millports' property. She didn't spot a thing until he'd leaped out from behind the shrubbery and caught her by the wrist.

"Let go of me!" she shrieked.

Her heart started stammering wildly. Struggling loose, Gabby wheeled around and found herself face to sneering face with Dylan Connable.

"Okay, okay. Now, shush, will you? You want to wake the whole neighborhood?"

"What are you doing here?"

"Waiting for you, little one. I knew you'd be coming this way."

"How could you?" she challenged.

"I'm your guardian angel, sweetness. Here to protect you. That's my purpose. My calling."

"Why?"

"Because I *know* you, that's why. In a way, we're entirely the same, you and me."

Gabby shivered. Dylan seemed to be everywhere, a spooky shadow she couldn't shake. "I can't talk to you now. I have to go see my friends."

He lit a smoke, his palm sheltering the match. Then he threw the match on the sidewalk. "You can't put it off forever, sweetness. You know you want me to give you the answers. You *need* the answers."

"I'm cold, Dylan."

He planted himself in front of her, blocking her way. "I know what it feels like, sweetness. I've got dead people in my life, too."

"What are you talking about?"

"My old man. And my little sister. She was just about your age."

"What happened to her?"

"Death."

"I mean, was she sick or something?" Dead people were supposed to be old like the bearded man in the funeral place, or, at the very least, grown-up like her daddy and Senator Gallatin.

"I can't talk about it here. Come for a ride with me, and I'll tell you the whole story. I'll even show you my best, deepest secret."

Dylan had that same weird look in his eyes he'd gotten when he took her to see the yucky dead man. "I told you, I can't," Gabby protested.

"Sure you can. Come on. My car's right around the corner."

"My friends are expecting me." She started to skirt him, but he set himself directly in her path. Gabby was positive he wanted to show her some other creepy thing. Maybe even his dead sister. Her heart shriveled with apprehension.

"Stop it, Dylan. Get out of my way."

"Sooner or later, you've got to face it, little one. Death is part of the continuum. Neat and natural. It's something to embrace like an old friend. Certainly, nothing to fear. Come with me. I'll make it clear and simple for you this time. I promise."

"Stop!" Gabby was jangling with frustration. She wanted to be done with Dylan and all his creepy death talk. She never wanted to see him again.

"Let me go! LET ME GO!"

The Millports' door flung open, and Mr. Millport came charging outside like a rodeo bull. "What's going on here?"

Dylan raised his hands and started treading in reverse. "No problem. I was just leaving—"

"You bet you were, you little punk." Mr. Millport turned to Gabby, his face taut with concern. He was still wearing his pajamas and his feet were bare. "You okay, honey? What'd he do?"

Gabby caught the plea in Dylan's eyes. Most of the time, Mr. Millport was a cuddly bear, but he could be ferocious, especially where any of the kids were concerned.

"Nothing, Mr. Millport. He was just talking to me."

"You sure?"

"I'm sure." Dylan might have been pestering her, but he didn't deserve to be ripped apart like a messy homework paper.

"Get going, then," Mr. Millport said sharply. "And don't let me catch you hanging around again."

"Okay, fine. I'm out of here." Dylan flashed Gabby a look she couldn't interpret.

Mr. Millport frowned. "Come on in, honey. You shouldn't be out in the cold like this without your coat on."

"I thought it was warmer out," she said lamely.

At the door, Gabby cast a furtive look back at the street. Dylan had vanished.

But then she saw his head bob up from behind the hedgerow. He mouthed something and ducked down again before Mr. Millport had time to turn around.

Soon, Gabby was surrounded by warm, chattering Millports and the sloppy affections of the Millport menagerie. After a quick round of hellos, the twins took Gabby up to their room. As she started her tantalizing recap of yesterday's events with Mr. Perry, she worked to push that sneaky creep Dylan Connable out of her mind.

Unfortunately, she'd been able to read his lips when he'd popped up from behind the bushes. She couldn't fully enjoy this long-awaited moment. Not when she knew what was to follow.

CHAPTER TWENTY-THREE

Startling awake, Thea couldn't believe it was nearly ten o'clock. Shivering, she burrowed under the covers. Why was she so cold? Billie's insomnia remedy had worked entirely too well. Last night, right after Gabby turned in at nine, Thea had downed a cup of warm milk, sweetened and spiked per the nurse's prescription. Ten minutes later, she was out cold. And even with that preposterously early collapse, she'd managed to sleep hours later than she ever had in her life.

Growing up on the ranch, she'd become accustomed to greeting dawn upright. By her parents' reckoning, sleeping past five was for malingerers and invalids. Past six was for the deceased or soon to be. If Thea had ever dreamed of lying abed this late at home, her mother would have called emergency or hauled out the jumper cables.

Thirteen hours of unconsciousness, and she was still inexplicably exhausted. Slogging out of bed, her limbs hung limp and heavy as sacks of wet cement. A monstrous pain lodged behind her eyes. Strange. Thea rarely suffered from headaches, and this was the second one in the past few days.

Trembling with a bone-deep chill, she wrapped herself in a woolly robe. Rummaging in the closet, she couldn't find her slippers. She'd probably left them under the kitchen table as usual.

Downstairs, she found a note in Gabby's childish script flapping from the refrigerator magnet. The child had gone to the Millports'. Caro probably had some party setups scheduled for this morning. The twins and

Gabby loved to assist, especially with the considerable inducement of a quarter-an-hour salary.

Dressing quickly, Thea resolved to make up for the lost time. She wolfed down a hunk of cold lasagna, washed down her daily dose of antiseizure medication with a glass of juice, and headed toward the dining room. Glancing behind her, she noticed the trail of sooty footprints she'd tracked across the kitchen floor. The soles of her feet were filthy.

How many times have I told you not to walk around barefooted, Checker? If you get yourself a case of lockjaw, don't come screaming to me.

Thinking of her mother, Thea made a pit stop at the phone.

"Hi, Mom? How's it going?"

"Same old same old, honey. Everything okay with you?"

"Fine." Thea saw no reason to mention the growing attacks of self-doubt and her terrifying forays into the twilight zone. She'd had nothing to do with that actor's death. *Nothing.*

"No word from you-know-who?"

"Walter Martin, you mean? No, Mom. And I don't expect any."

" 'Course you don't. Always were one to look on the sunny side, Checker. That's why everyone's drawn to you like flies to honey. Your ears should be burning from the way they were all talking about you at bingo Thursday night. 'How's that pretty girl of yours, Ellie? You tell Thea we're thinking about her, wishing her well.' "

"That's nice, Mom."

"Remember how they voted you 'Most Popular' senior year, Checker? Right from when you were a little snip you had this way about you."

Thea warmed to her mother's words. Through all the mess with Simon, Ellie had remained an unwavering ally. Never once had her mother's expression registered that terrible flicker of distrust.

"If I had a way with people, I came by it naturally, Mom. You could charm the skin off a crocodile."

Ellie chuckled. "Go on, now, Checker. No need to be blowing smoke at an old lady."

"Old my foot. How's Dad?"

"Ups and downs. You know how he is."

Thea knew in ways her mother would never imagine. "You doing okay with him?"

"Sure, honey. He gets to growling, I toss him something hard to chew on. Best thing to do with sharp teeth is keep them busy, I always say."

"Sounds sensible. Speak to you soon, Mom."

"Real soon, Checker. Kiss Gabby for me."

At the dining room table, Thea prepared to tackle the next illustration in the Sophie series. It was the panel in which Weird Willy Dillon and the serpent have a heart-to-heart talk about the boy's dysfunctional family. This was the pivotal scene that would set up the teenager's eventual rescue of Sophie from the blazing inferno.

Thea quickly roughed out the sketch. But when it came time to flesh things out, she found herself stymied. How close together should Sophie and Willy be positioned? Sitting or standing? Should other patrons be within hearing distance? What time of day does their meeting take place? Is Willy larger than Sophie, and if so, by how much?

As she pondered these cosmic issues, Thea abruptly recognized the problem. Another artistic notion was vying for her attention. Setting Sophie aside, she flipped to a fresh sheet in her sketchbook and allowed the competing image to play across the page.

Thea fashioned a crude pyramid of people. At first, she expected to fill in the faces from Amber's cheerlead-

ing squad. But as she sketched, she realized that the
subject of her vision had nothing to do with athletics.

At the pyramid's core was a wizened old man with
impish gray eyes. That central figure was surrounded by
dozens of children. They all leaned toward him like
light-seeking plants. Adoring eyes were trained in his
direction. Small fingers sought his venerable touch.

In response, the man radiated warmth and caring. His
furrowed brow and mottled skin were oddly luminous.
Humor and kindness registered in his expression. Thea
felt the pull of this highly appealing character. The elderly
man was the perfect father figure. Strong, benevolent
Daddy minus the human flaws and complications.

The pyramid was an ancient and fascinating composition, subject to varying interpretations. The old man
could be seen as the tree from which the little apples
derived, the fountain spewing nurturance and wisdom,
the Godhead surrounded by his flourishing creations.
His gnarled hands, draped across the arms of the two
children at his sides, were the power and mortar that
held the entire composition, and its disparate develop-
ing elements, together.

At the base, the little ones furthest from the old
man's grasp were linked to him by a loose chain of seeking hands. Under Thea's pencil, the old man naturally
evolved as more textured and dimensional than his platoon of young admirers. As connected and central as he
was to the children, the greater depth and detail of his
figure defined him as a complete, independent entity.

Working feverishly, Thea took the key from the hook
beside the kitchen door and moved her act to the studio. She squeezed a rainbow of pigments onto her long-
neglected palette. Using the pencil sketch as a model,
she quickly reproduced the human pyramid in a light
umber wash. The portrait took shape as she applied
slim strokes of color to define and enliven the old man's

face. From there, she worked outward, filling in the children's faces and shapes. Each subject appeared to her as an established whole. No need to pause and ponder the arc of a jaw or the slope of a shoulder. Never had she included so many people in a single painting. And still, she had no difficulty envisioning each character down to the most minute component.

The phone rang. Pru Whittaker, art agent to the core, must have detected the brush strokes. Thea heard the woman's voice after the beep on her answering machine. She decided not to pick up. Pru certainly wouldn't want to interrupt a work in progress, especially one progressing this well and this fast.

Thea couldn't remember the last time she'd been so absorbed. She'd thought she'd lost the knack for finding immersion in her work.

Thea's mother had a saying to cover this one, too: *See, Checker honey? You never know until you know.*

The agent was still chatting with the message tape. Pru was one of those people who were just as comfortable with machines as with people. Maybe more so.

"So, Thea. That's the bottom line here. The gallery is still *very* hot on the idea of doing that one-woman show. All you need to do is to put together a half dozen or so *fabulous* new pieces. We can fill in with collection loans or whatever, but we simply *must* have a decent number of fresh oils."

Thea thought that ended the sermon, but the agent was merely pausing for breath.

"Look, I know you're ducking me, darling, but I simply *won't* be avoided where your brilliant future is concerned. This is *it*, darling. That sound you hear is opportunity knocking. Go answer it. *Now!* Speak to you, soon. Kiss, kiss. 'Bye."

"Kiss kiss yourself," Thea told the final click as the

answering device duly swallowed the agent's interminable message. "Won't you be pleasantly surprised."

Eyeing the painting, Thea knew Pru Whittaker would be closer to ecstatic. The piece was good. "Important," Pru would term it in that clipped preppie twang of hers. Few would guess that the agent had been born on the Lower East Side and graduated, Magna cum Loudmouth, from the streets of Bensonhurst.

Quite a character.

Thea smiled. Pru was right. The gallery show was worth battling for, especially now that the first essential new painting was well under way. Another couple of days at this rate, and the piece would be completed.

Stepping back to scrutinize the work, Thea noticed that the studio light had shifted. The crisp morning glow had yielded to the subtler bronze and pewter tones of impending dusk.

Impossible.

Squinting at the clock, Thea discovered to her amazement that she'd been working nonstop for almost eight hours. At least, she knew precisely how this mass of time had evaporated. Proudly, she eyed the old man's kindly visage and the eager young faces surrounding him.

Not bad, Checker honey. Seems you haven't gone and lost it all, after all.

Thea cleaned her brushes and set them to soak. Steeping a wad of paper towel in turpentine, she wiped the worst of the paint stains off her hands. As always, the strong solvent started her eyes watering. Tossing the pungent toweling in the trash, she decided that the remaining spatters and the pigment under her nails could stay. After all this time away from the easel, she rather enjoyed the visible signs of her return.

Reconnected with reality, Thea acknowledged the yawning pit in her stomach. A slab of cold lasagna and a pill did not a full day's nourishment make. Back in the house, she rummaged through the refrigerator and stilled her growling hunger with a buttered chunk of Italian bread and a generous slice of ice cream cake. Clearly, she was still rebelling against Brook Hollow's storm trooper dietician. But after such a productive day, Thea reasoned she'd earned her fill of empty calories.

No gold stars for mothering, though. Gabby was still at the Millports'. After six months as an honorary family member, the child had to relearn the reasonable limits for an ordinary visit. Caro would never object to an extra kid or two hanging around, but the woman had already extended a larger-than-lifetime supply of hospitality to Gabby. Thea decided to invite all available Millports to be her dinner guests for a change. She picked up the phone.

Amber answered. The Millports had two lines and Thea had the distinct sense that she'd interrupted the teenager in the midst of a critical call.

"I won't keep you, Amber. Would you please tell Gabby to come home?"

"Gabby?"

"Yes, sweetie. You know. Thin child, big hair. *That* Gabby."

"But Gabby's not here, Mrs. Harper."

As usual, Thea winced at the formality. She would have preferred to be on a first-name basis with the Millport kids, who were virtual relatives, but Caro and Drew clung to old southern tradition on the matter.

"Is she on the way, then?"

"No, ma'am. Gabby left hours ago. Before lunch."

"Did she go someplace with your mom?"

"No. Mother and Daddy went shopping at the mall a while ago. Far as I know, Gabby was headed straight home when she left here."

Thea's throat closed. *Don't panic. Think!* "Gabby's

not here, Amber. Would you please ask the twins? Maybe they know where she went."

There had to be a simple explanation. Gabby must have gone to play with one of the other neighborhood kids. It wouldn't be the first time she'd neglected to call home.

Amber came back on the line. "I asked them, Mrs. Harper. They have no idea where Gabby might be. Want me to take a ride and look for her?"

"No. I will. Ask the girls to please call around. If you hear anything, or if they have any ideas, leave a message on my machine. Okay?"

"Sure thing, Mrs. Harper. You think maybe we ought to call the police?"

"No. Not yet."

Fingers of fear squeezed Thea's throat. What if Gabby had been hurt? Kidnapped? What if one of the lurking reporters had cornered her? Thea imagined her terrified daughter locked in a room with some predatory stranger intent on squeezing the child for damaging information.

Or worse.

Oh, God. Please, don't let anything happen to my baby!

"I'm going to find her," Thea said.

"Okay, Mrs. Harper. Let us know."

Thea groped in her purse for the car keys. Racing to the garage, she stomped the accelerator. The old engine coughed and went still.

"Come on, Bessie. You can't let me down now. We have to bring Gabby home."

Pumping the gas, Thea coaxed the motor to life. But when she threw the car into reverse, the engine bucked, then stalled.

Thea bashed the steering wheel in frustration. *Easy, Thea. This isn't going to find Gabby.* Counting slowly to ten, she started the car again. This time the engine caught. Thea forced herself to wait another minute until Bessie had a chance to warm up.

She switched into reverse and navigated the narrow stone driveway. She was angling onto Linden Street when she spotted her little girl trudging up the block. Without pausing to turn off the motor, Thea slammed on the brakes and raced out to meet her.

"Gabby, thank God. Are you okay? Where have you been?"

"At the Millports'. I left a note."

"I called the Millports. Amber said you left there hours ago."

The eyes dipped. "I went for a walk."

Thea gripped her by the shoulders. "Stop it, Gabby. Stop lying to me."

"You never believe me. Why don't you just leave me alone?" The little girl's voice wavered and broke. Shaking free, she bolted toward the house.

Thea sprinted after her and caught up as Gabby was wrestling open the front door. She took the child in her arms and held her hard.

"This has to stop, Gabby. You have to tell me what's wrong."

The little girl strained against Thea's grasp.

"I won't let you go, Gabby. I love you too much to let you shut me out anymore."

The child started to cry. Thea clutched her little girl and tried to soothe her. "What, sweetie? How can I help you? Please, *please* tell me."

Consumed by sobs, the child could barely speak. Her words came in broken pieces. "Don't——die, Mom-my. Please——don't——die."

"Ssh. Of course not. I have no intention of dying for a long, long time."

"But Daddy died. And Senator Gallatin. Everybody dies. You can't help it."

"That's true, sweetie. But most people live until they're very, very old." The child was trembling. Thea hugged her tighter, breathing in the scent of her hair, aching to ease her terror.

"I'm so scared, Mommy."

"I know. It's scary to worry that you might be left alone. But you're not going to be, Gabby. I'll be here for you."

"What if you get sick again and have to go back to the hospital?"

"That's not going to happen."

"You promise?"

"Cross my heart." Releasing her grip on the little girl, Thea rendered an invisible X on her chest and held up the two fingers necessary to make the pledge official. "Now, will you *please* tell me where you've been all day?"

"Just hanging around. Thinking about stuff."

"Honestly?"

"Honest."

Hanging and thinking didn't begin to account for a six-hour absence, but Thea decided not to press the issue further. Maybe this was fitting retribution for all the random disappearances she'd inflicted on her own parents as a child.

Where do you suppose that girl's gotten to this time, Hugh? Would you please ride out and check her?

Gabby was safe. That was the main thing.

"I need you to promise that you won't wander off like that again, sweetie. I need to know where you are, okay?"

Gabby repeated the sign of the oath, scrawling the X on her chest and raising her fingers. "Triple-swear," she vowed solemnly.

From the road came a rattling wheeze as the idling Volvo protested Thea's abandonment. Satisfied that the crisis had passed, Thea returned old Bessie to the garage. Then she followed her daughter inside.

CHAPTER TWENTY-FOUR

Passerelli was always in a garrulous mood on Monday mornings. A weekend of his wife's nonstop jabbering and the kids' ear-splitting noise left Vince with a serious craving for genteel conversation.

"Hey. You watch the game yesterday, Danny?"

"No."

"Saturday, then? You catch the Rangers?"

"No, Vince. I was busy."

Passerelli ticked his tongue. "There was this play in the second period? Not to be believed. LaMouche goes deep, passes the puck to Deroguerre, Maitland clips Chartier with an elbow, and all hell breaks loose. I counted two busted shnozzes, a dislocated shoulder, five serious cuts, and at least one broken arm. It was terrific, Danny. Best ever."

"Sounds outstanding."

"And then, I'm flipping the channels, and, you ready for the most amazing coincidence?"

"I suppose so."

"HBO is running *Animal House,* my all-time favorite movie. You seen it?"

"Yes."

"Try seventeen times," Passerelli said proudly.

Biederman took a long, slow breath. "Actually, I'd rather not."

"What's with you today, Danny? You in a bad mood, or what?"

"I'm fine, Vince. Just peachy."

Actually, Biederman was far from peachy. He'd spent most of the weekend arguing with himself and losing.

The smart thing was to play along. All he had to do was give the appearance of trying to scuttle Thea Harper, and he could probably ride out the current storm unscathed.

But that would leave too many open questions. Somehow, he had to separate his tangled feelings about Westport's most notorious woman from the facts. To Biederman, truth had always been a sort of security blanket. Having it made him feel better, even if it provided no genuine protection.

Unfortunately, baring the facts in this case was not going to be easy. The FBI had jurisdiction over assaults, kidnappings, and homicides committed on federal officials. As soon as the corpse in Thea Harper's den was identified as Senator Simon Gallatin, Fibbie agents had rolled in swiftly and seized control of the investigation.

Normally, the feds sought or, at least, accepted the cooperation of local authorities, but Buck Delavan had no use for diplomacy and no tolerance for intrusions on his turf. In record time, the inspector had seriously alienated the team of special agents deployed out of the Bridgeport FBI office.

"Too bad the Bureau has such a terrible reputation," Buck had said in greeting the agents. "FBI. Some say the initials stand for Foolish Bunch of Imbeciles. I bet that galls you boys out there giving it your best and all, isn't that so?"

The agent in charge was named Robert Szathmary. Buck had cemented the lousy relations by saddling the guy with a nickname that was guaranteed to irk.

"So, Agent Mary," Buck said. "You figure these girl scouts of yours can outcop my men? Is that where you're coming from?"

For the duration, the general public had been privy to more information about the Gallatin murder than members of the Westport force.

Still, after a decade on the job, Biederman knew how any case was constructed. The prosecution provided one version of events along with the necessary backup experts and evidence. The defense countered with an alternative scenario and supporting detail. Anything that didn't suit one side or the other was denied, discarded, or conveniently overlooked. To divine the unexpurgated truth, Biederman would have to uncover the contents of that black hole.

And he'd have to do it flying solo. Neither side would be eager to part with evidence they had knowingly ignored or suppressed. Most interested parties were much happier keeping the lid on a closed case. Justice was never as swift or sure as it ought to be. Every time a verdict was read and recorded, the court system breathed a collective sigh of relief, then plodded on to the next one in the relentless parade.

To make matters worse, Biederman would have to do his digging while maintaining a very low profile. If Delavan found out he was poking into the Gallatin case, Biederman would be skewered and spit-roasted before the inspector sent a pink slip to his remains.

"So, *are* you?" Passerelli demanded.

"Am I what?"

"Up for a doughnut. Jeez, Danny. I asked you three times already. What's with you this morning?"

"Nothing, Vince. You want a doughnut, we'll go for a doughnut."

Passerelli swerved into the Compo Acres strip mall. Biederman went through the motions, accompanying his partner, as was his mandate, into the perilous wilds of Gold's Delicatessen. Serious danger lurked in the bakery bins. The meat section was a minefield of potential missteps. The cheese area alone was enough to lead the weak of will and strong of appetite astray.

Despite his preoccupation with graver matters,

Biederman could not in good conscience leave Vince to his own devices. This time last year, Passerelli had weighed in at a hefty two fifty-five. If not for his wife's inedible cuisine, the number might well have been higher.

At his doctor's urging, Vince had gone on a liquid protein diet. Breakfast and lunch were glasses of strawberry-flavored chalk. Dinner was a flat-chested chicken breast and a few anemic vegetables.

It had taken six months of anguish, but the extra bulk had finally melted away. Now, thank the Lord, Passerelli was back to regular food. The guy no longer spent all day, every day whining, "Gee whiz, Danny. You got any idea what I'd give for a burger (bowl of pasta, piece of cheesecake, hunk of salami, slab of cheese)?" If Vince put the weight back on, Biederman would be the one to really suffer through another diet.

Passerelli ogled the doughnuts as if they were a line of topless dancers. "The cream-filled look great, don't you think, Danny? And look at those lemon—"

"One, Vince. Make a choice."

"How about a couple of those crullers, then? They're small."

"Yes, but you're not. Now pick one, okay?"

Passerelli's face tensed, and he balled his fists in concentration. Normally, Biederman was a patient man, but at the moment he was operating on no sleep and frustration overload.

"Eenie, meenie—"

"Come on, Vince. Choose," Biederman snapped.

"Okay, Danny, okay. Take it easy. I'll have a raspberry jelly."

The blonde behind the counter reached for one of the sugary orbs.

"Not that," Vince said. "The one two to the left looks bigger."

On the verge of a felony, Biederman drifted to the front of the store and ordered a large coffee, black. Passerelli caught up a couple of minutes later. He sported a sticky red mustache and a grin.

"Nothing to eat for you, Danny?"

"No, Vince. I'm fine."

Passerelli reached up to knuckle Biederman's shoulder. "Cheer up, kiddo. Whoever she is, I bet she's not worth the aggravation."

Clenching his teeth, Biederman didn't respond. By device or by accident, his partner had hit a nerve. Biederman cared way too much about Thea Harper. He should know better than to be traveling in the wrong direction, especially when the sentiment was a one-way street full of potholes.

He should know better than a lot of things, Biederman thought grimly. But he had never been one to hesitate when fate handed him the opportunity to make a really dumb and potentially serious mistake. With two eyes open, he'd married the unfair Elaine. Without a heartbeat's hesitation, he'd opted for the down and dirty existence of a uniformed trash collector.

Life might be too short for the majority of things, Biederman figured. But it was far too long for perfection.

CHAPTER TWENTY-FIVE

For once, the car started without a hitch, and the normally sluggish Connecticut Turnpike traffic was flowing smoothly. Thea arrived at the Landmark Towers twenty minutes in advance of her scheduled appointment with Dr. Forman.

Thea considered a quick trip to the adjacent Stamford Town Center Mall to pick up some things for Gabby. The child was rapidly outgrowing her wardrobe. But any holdup in the store could make her late for therapy. The notion of Dr. Forman's stern reproach at such an unthinkable infraction was enough to prod Thea directly toward the elevator.

Entering the waiting room, she caught the tirade blasting from the inner office. It was the same screamer who'd had the appointment before Thea's last week.

Guiltily, Thea claimed a chair that backed on the connecting wall. Focusing hard, she was able to make out scraps of the woman's diatribe. The voice was a hammer strike; the accent was an odd blend of Eastern European immigrant and American upper crust.

"That *bastard*! The *things* he did. Unspeakable!"

Thea imagined a tall theatrical sort in flowing skirts and a turban. Vividly, she conjured an ornate cigarette holder poised between the woman's graceful fingers and etched silver earrings drooping from her pendulous lobes.

"I could *kill* him with my bare hands! I could tear him in bloody parts and not be a *bit* sorry." The words sounded closer to "keel" and "beet," but none of the fury was lost in the translation.

The screamer would have a name like Madame

Veruschka, Thea decided, and a family descended from a deposed Russian tsar. She pictured Madame Veruschka walking a large, aristocratic dog. Probably an afghan hound with a jeweled collar and a haughty gait.

"Killing him is all I think about. My dreams are awash with his blood."

Thea could not decipher Dr. Forman's low, controlled responses. But the shrink provided a firm counterpoint to the patient's mounting hysteria.

"He deserves to *die*. To die and rot in *Hell* for what he did to me!"

There was another muted comment from the psychiatrist. But the reasoned reply did nothing to mollify the crazed woman.

"He stole my childhood, my innocence. I can still feel his revolting hands on my body, his thick fingers crawling over me like *worms*!"

The patient's virulent pronouncements were punctuated by anguished wails. The cries reverberated in Thea's head like the jarring clashes of an Oriental gong.

As the ranting continued, Thea stole across the waiting room and claimed a seat beside the door that led to the outside hall. She did not want to give the appearance of eavesdropping. Doing it was bad enough.

Finally, the madwoman was winding down. Dr. Forman's calculated tones reentered the discussion. Eager to gain further distance from the fray, Thea scanned the pristine waiting area for something to read.

The magazine rack held nothing but outmoded issues of publications from the National Society of the Terminally Dull. Dr. Forman had provided similar scintillating diversions in her waiting room at Brook Hollow. Billie had suggested it was a form of subtle torture, but Thea didn't entirely agree. To her, the practice didn't seem all that subtle.

Scanning the room hopefully, Thea noticed a glossy

photo poking out from under the adjacent chair. Retrieving it, she was delighted to discover that the picture was a shot of Princess Di on the cover of the current issue of *People*. No doubt the magazine had been left behind by a benevolent fellow patient. Dr. Forman would never deign to be associated with such escapist fluff.

Her loss, Thea thought as she settled the magazine on her lap. Nothing like some gratuitous star gossip to take one's mind off the rigors of real life. It was no coincidence that *People* and *Us* had been eagerly circulated at Brook Hollow. For mental patients, juicy dirt was definitely a drug of choice.

Thea started leafing through the pages. She skimmed the letters to the editor and the literary, film, music, and TV reviews. Next came the standard diet of dirt from Buckingham Palace, dish on Hollywood's celluloid flavors of the week, and speculation about various marriages, mergers, and purloined secret memos.

Following were the typical human interest stories: a five-year-old Ohio girl had received a six-organ transplant, a Boston centenarian was employed full-time as an aerobics instructor, a young Oklahoma boy had raised a ten-pound tomato that bore an uncanny resemblance to an apoplectic pig.

Flipping the page, Thea found a story about a Canadian psychobiologist who had formulated a drug therapy for violent criminals. The medication had been tested extensively on Ottowan and Manitoban inmate populations and appeared to have reduced recidivism rates and diminished antisocial behavior.

Fascinating.

Could there be a magic pill for Walter Martin? Something to stabilize that lunatic's behavior would provide the long-awaited answer to one of Thea's prayers. Even with thousands of miles separating them, Walter loomed like a poison cloud over Thea's existence. There was always the vague threat of him.

Maybe a medication could defuse Walter. The experiences of the past year had greatly enhanced Thea's respect for the value of pharmaceuticals. Before her ruinous run-in with her own inner beast, she'd been an ardent advocate of medicine-avoidance. Now, she wouldn't forgo her daily dose of the antiseizure drug carbamazepine on a million-dollar bet.

The connecting door opened.

"Good morning, Thea. Come in." Dr. Forman looked prim and proper as ever, completely unruffled by Madame Veruschka's harangue. A black blouse with a stern notched collar set off her porcelain pale complexion. The pleats in her knee-length skirt were aligned like tin soldiers. Not a misplaced hair nor a lint speck marred the perfect picture.

Setting the magazine facedown on a chair, Thea smoothed the worn knees of her favorite jeans and followed the shrink inside. Again, Madame Veruschka had slipped out the rear, which was just as well. Reality was certain to be several giant steps down from Thea's melodramatic image of the woman.

Perching a pair of gold-rimmed glasses on her nose, Dr. Forman opened Thea's folder and skimmed her notes. The psychiatrist surprised Thea by starting the session herself.

"We discussed your getting back to work at our last meeting. How have things progressed in the interim?"

"Very well, actually. Gabby and I are writing a children's book together. And I've started an oil that's coming along nicely."

A brow peaked. "No problems, then?"

"A few here and there. Nothing I can't handle."

"Such as?"

Thea enjoyed having several positives to report for a

change. She wasn't about to mention her stubborn fixation on Brandon Payton's murder or her continuing concerns about Gabby and set herself up for a round of Dr. Doom's dire cautions and pronouncements.

Stifling a smirk, she said, "The car hasn't been running well, and there's a hole in the downspout near the kitchen. That sort of thing."

One eyebrow was perched so high on the shrink's faux marble forehead, it appeared poised to take a dive.

"And nothing else?"

"That's it," Thea said.

"You've resolved your concerns about Gabrielle, then?"

"Gabby's conducting a normal preadolescent campaign for independence. Wasn't that the way you put it last week?"

"Was it?"

Thea repressed the urge to sock the woman. It would not, she supposed, be the most effective way to showcase her exemplary emotional adjustment. Instead she replied, "Sometimes I think you say things just to provoke me, Dr. Forman."

"Do you?"

"Yes. That's why I said so."

"Why do you suppose you're feeling so hostile today, Thea?" Dr. Forman cocked her head.

"I'm not hostile. At least, I wasn't until you started in on me."

"In what way do you feel I persecute you, Thea? This is most interesting."

Thea drew several measured breaths. The shrink was a master goader. Give her an inch, she'll have you half-crazed. "I don't feel persecuted. And I'm honestly not in the mood for high angst or deep drama today. I feel fine, Doctor. I'm working again. Things are going well. Sorry if that disappoints you."

The laugh was three oddly musical notes. "Of course it doesn't disappoint me, Thea. Analysis is a process of discovery. It's perfectly appropriate for you to proceed at whatever pace suits you."

"If you're suggesting that personal growth only comes through pain and suffering, I don't begin to buy it. Contentment suits me fine. If my feeling better gets in the way of your so-called therapy, I'll pass."

You have to know your own mind, Checker honey. Some folks'll pee on you and try to convince you it's raining.

"Your anger is perfectly normal, Thea. Negative transference is an expected stage in the therapeutic process. You need to reject me in order to begin separating from the doctor-dependent state."

A silent ten-count did nothing to ease Thea's exasperation. "I shouldn't have come today."

"And why is that?"

"I just shouldn't have. Look, Dr. Forman. I'm not in the mood to be taken apart and glued back together right now. Actually, I don't see the need for that altogether. How about we shake hands and part company?"

The shrink pursed her lips. "I don't think that's advisable, Thea."

"That's your opinion. Mine is that I need to concentrate on my daughter and my work for a while. I've had about all the shrinking I need."

"I can't force you to remain in treatment, Thea. But I *strongly* recommend it. You're not nearly ready to terminate yet."

Thea stood. "I honestly appreciate everything you've done for me, Doctor. Thanks."

Dr. Forman blinked slowly. "You're making a mistake."

"I don't think so."

"I see no point in further debate. Meantime, I cannot

maintain you on your drug therapy unless you agree to continued blood level checks and neurological exams."

Thea had never intended to compromise that treatment. Despite Dr. Forman's unspoken diagnosis, she was *not* crazy. "Of course. I have an appointment for the usual battery of tests at Brook Hollow on Thursday morning. I'll see you then."

"Fine. And when you change your mind about therapy, call to schedule a session."

It didn't escape Thea's notice that the shrink had said *when*, not *if*.

"Good-bye, Dr. Forman."

Striding purposefully out of the office, Thea closed the connecting door behind her. She felt giddy with relief. Most of her sessions with Dr. Forman had been like doses of nasty-tasting medicine that had to be downed for punishment's sake or to satisfy some baseless superstition. Only when they'd discussed her residual guilt about Simon's death had Thea derived any real benefit. The rest, the endless probing about family relationships, past traumas, early anxieties, sexual preferences, and personal quirks, had felt like unnecessary surgery. Thea's issues were her own business. She did not care to share them, or anything else, with that stiff-assed, smug, self-important woman.

Halfway through the waiting room, Thea spotted the copy of *People* she'd left on the chair. Certain it had been abandoned by an earlier patient, she decided to help herself. That promising drug for criminals might be of some use to Walter Martin, her futile distraction. As soon as she got home, Thea would find a way to contact the researcher and get more information. If there was anything to the new medication, she'd contact Walter's mother and let her know.

In the Landmark Tower garage, Bessie had been sandwiched between a minivan and a pickup. As Thea edged out of the nooselike space, the engine sputtered and stalled six times. Thea heated a bit, but, still relishing her declaration of independence from Dr. Forman, she did not boil over.

Her equanimity was tested again on the turnpike, however. Traffic came to a dead halt as soon as she breezed past the first available exit ramp. Peering as far ahead as possible, Thea was unable to spot the source of the trouble. No blinking lights or construction signs. All she could see was a solid wall of inert vehicles from here to infinity.

Tuning out the strident honks of her fellow pavement prisoners, Thea rested the magazine she'd taken from the shrink's waiting room on the steering wheel. Idly, she started leafing through the articles she hadn't read yet.

An Oregon man, paralyzed in a riding accident, was walking again with the help of an implanted microcomputer. Five-year-old Paul Jovarty was now the proud owner of a rare and extremely valuable Mickey Mantle trading card, which the canny young entrepreneur had purchased at a neighborhood tag sale for twenty-five cents.

The honking around her grew louder and more persistent. Eyeing the gas tank, she noticed that the gauge was dipping toward the half-full mark. She'd filled up Friday and hadn't used Bessie since. A trip to Stamford and back, even with the interminable traffic, shouldn't have taken the tank that low. Either Bessie was burning more juice than she ought to be, or the pump jockey had ripped her off.

No big deal, Thea. Nothing worth fretting about.

She flipped on the radio, hoping for news about the cause of the tie-up. "That's traffic on the ones," the announcer said with irritating glee, promising another road, bridge, and tunnel update in ten minutes.

Turning back to the magazine, Thea skimmed the story of an adopted young woman named Nancy

Browne, who'd been reunited with her birth parents when she literally ran into them on an interstate highway with her new Dodge Omni. Prior to that uncanny collision, ten years of active searching had failed to unearth a trace of the woman's blood relatives.

Nice story, Thea thought. Happy ending and all.

Traffic was beginning to ease. Every so often, Thea was able to take her foot off the brake and let Bessie roll a couple of inches. Still, she was in no danger of making any significant forward progress anytime soon. Flipping to the "Passages" page at the end of the issue, Thea skimmed through the marriage, divorce, birth, death, and arrest summary.

Rocker marries model. Actor marries actress twice divorced from actor's ex-wife's ex-husband. Aging crooner has test-tube twins with young dancer. Transvestite Madonna impersonator is arrested for DUI.

Nothing out of the ordinary.

But a picture at the bottom right-hand column stopped Thea cold. Squeezed by terror, she could not believe her eyes. This simply could not be happening. Her mind must be playing a nasty trick.

The driver behind her was leaning hard on his horn. The logjam had been broken. Both adjoining lanes were moving at a normal clip. Thea was the only remaining obstruction on the road.

Dropping the magazine, she eased onto the gas. Forcing her attention to the road, she clung fast to her disintegrating grip on the world. She had to get home; she needed to think, to figure out what the hell was happening.

Something was threatening to destroy her. And she had to find a way to put an end to it.

CHAPTER TWENTY-SIX

The old bitch was squeezing him hard. Twice last night and again first thing this morning she'd had her bitch lawyer call with the same damned warnings. Deliver and soon. Deliver *or else*.

Trying to reason with her would be a foolish waste of breath. Lily Gallatin was terminally overprivileged. The crone believed she could change the Earth's orbit with a snap of her gnarled fingers. Everything had to be her way, and now.

Her escalating demands were making him nervous. This whole nasty business burrowed under his skin like an unscratchable itch.

Enough already. Time to bail out.

He'd waited all morning for his break. Determined to put the misery behind him, he strode purposefully to the nearest pay phone and dialed the lawyer's number. The firm's line made a low belching sound.

"Rodbury, Carswell and Barr," the receptionist chirped.

"Ms. Rodbury, please."

"Who shall I say is calling?"

"Mr. Holmes, tell her. Sherlock F.U. Holmes."

The pause stretched the limits of well-trained politeness. Finally, the woman cleared the astonishment from her throat and said, "Yes, Mr. Holmes. Please hold a minute."

Almost a full sixty seconds later, Cassie Rodbury's imperious voice claimed the line. He pictured the attorney in one of her uniform Chanel suits. Arrogant mouth pinched in distaste. Snooty nose perched skyward.

"I trust you are calling with good news?"

"Right, Ms. Rodbury. The good news is: I quit. I've had it."

"Hardly."

Now, he was the one at a total loss. Hardly? What the hell kind of an answer was that? "Look. I've given this everything I could, but there's just no pleasing your client. You want more or faster, call Superman. Meanwhile, I'm out."

"I think not," Cassie Rodbury said. "Mrs. Gallatin engaged you. For obvious reasons, you're in the best position to get what we're after. Like it or not, you *will* continue with this until and unless we say otherwise."

Something had to be wrong with the phone. Bad connection. *Nightmare* connection. "Listen, lady, I'm not your goddamned slave. Not yours or the old lady's or anyone's. You read me?"

The lawyer didn't ruffle. "We'll expect a full report by close of business tomorrow. I've assured my client that you are on the cusp of securing the information we seek. I suggest you press hard to fulfill that promise."

"Or else what?"

The lawyer chuckled. "Very amusing."

"Then how come I'm not laughing?"

Rodbury's good humor evaporated. "You have until tomorrow at five. I'll expect the full report on my desk by then. Good day, sir."

Slamming the phone down, he was caught between fear and fury. They were playing with him, enjoying his discomfort. Like a dumb animal caught in the trap. See how he runs in useless circles.

Across the hall, a plump redhead was waiting impatiently for the phone. Tapping her foot, she shot him a silent rebuke. Her gum cracked like a warning shot. To spite her, he lifted the receiver to his ear again and slid another quarter into the slot.

He warmed to the sound of Thea's voice, but cooled quickly when he realized he was listening to her recorded words on an answering machine.

"Leave a message after the beep, and we'll get back to you as soon as possible."

He dumped the handpiece in the cradle and turned away. Noting the snotty look on the fat woman's face, he stalled long enough to give her a proper reward for her attitude.

"Phone's out of order," he said.

She puffed her annoyance, cracked her gum again, and took off. Good. At least he could still win a hand or two when the odds were closer to even.

Unfortunately, Lily Gallatin held all the aces. But that impulsive phone call to Cassie Rodbury had given him an idea. If he told Thea what was going on, she might be able to salvage his sorry hide. She could give him enough to satisfy the old lady, maybe even enough to get the bitch off both of their backs.

Brilliant solution.

Sure, Thea would be pissed at first, but she'd cool off once she understood he'd had no choice but to go along with the Gallatins. Actually, he'd done her a favor. If he'd somehow managed to walk away, Lily Gallatin would have found someone else to do her nasty business, someone who didn't give a damn what happened to Thea or her kid.

Through him, Thea would have the chance to plant something neat and harmless. Simple. He could go in wearing a wire and prearrange for Thea to admit that she now remembered the murder. She could say that the seizure amnesia, or whatever bullshit ailment her lawyer had concocted for the jury, had cleared up. For effect, he'd have her toss in a few juicy details about the senator's death that had supposedly been withheld from the press. Reeling through the inside information he'd

managed to squeeze from the lawyer, he thought of the
lipstick smudge on the back of the corpse's broken
neck.

Perfect.

It would appear to be proof that Thea had been a
conscious murderer after all. Lily Gallatin, starving old
barracuda that she was, would swallow the tidbit whole.
He'd be long gone before the old bitch discovered that
the admission was legally worthless. Laws against double jeopardy would protect Thea from a retrial for the
senator's murder. A perjury charge wouldn't stick either,
because she'd been telling the truth as she knew it during her trial. The worst she'd suffer would be some
nasty publicity.

Hardly the worst thing.

Meanwhile, he'd get himself set up in a new town
under a fresh alias. If the past few years had taught him
anything, it was how to turn invisible. Once he was
safely out of the old bag's reach, he intended to take full
advantage of the opportunity Lily Gallatin had un-
knowingly dumped in his lap. The old lady would wet
her custom silk panties if she knew how he was planning to pay her back for making him hop through her
goddamned hoops.

His break was over. Whistling, he returned to the
job Mrs. Gallatin and her lawyer had arranged for him.
Soon he'd be out of here and finished with this whole
rotten operation.

Finally, things were looking up. After work, he'd go
see Thea Harper and turn this mess around.

CHAPTER
TWENTY-SEVEN

Thea ditched the car in the driveway and made her shaky way into the house. Shedding her coat, she hurried directly to the studio. She set the copy of *People* on the easel beside her painting of the old man and the children.

Numb with incredulity, she compared the nearly completed canvas to the photograph she'd spotted on the road. The composition was identical. The *People* shot depicted the same human pyramid centered by a wizened old man. The caption indicated that the photo had hung in the old man's apartment. Thea had reproduced the faces from the picture, feature for feature. It was all there: the children's outstretched hands, the old man's encircling arms, the rapt expressions of trust and adulation.

How could this be? How could I have painted this picture unless I was in that poor man's apartment and saw it?

Consumed by dread, she read the obituary accompanying the photo:

> *Alden "Pappy" Gaithwaite, honored last year as one of President Bush's "Thousand Points of Light" for his extraordinary commitment to neighborhood youth, was found dead early Sunday morning in his Bridgeport, Connecticut, apartment. Gaithwaite was the victim of multiple stab wounds inflicted by an unknown assailant. Blossom Price, Gaithwaite's longtime companion, was also found murdered in the corridor outside the apartment the couple had shared for thirty years.*

The picture was captioned:

Here, Gaithwaite, in happier times, is surrounded by many of the countless children he counseled and nurtured over the past decade. The picture was presented to Pappy by his "kids" after a neighborhood celebration of Gaithwaite's "Point of Light" award.

Thea was dizzy with alarm. The old man must have been murdered sometime Saturday night. She'd been with Gabby and Max Perry until nine, fallen asleep shortly thereafter, and stayed in bed until almost 10:00 A.M. Sunday.

Or had she?

Saturday night was a dreamless blank. All she could remember was drinking Billie's knockout cocktail and awakening obscenely late on Sunday morning with a hungover feeling and a massive headache. She'd felt sapped, as if she'd been out prowling the streets half the night.

And what if she had?

Prickles of terror scaled Thea's spine as she thought of several other baffling oddities. Bessie's half-empty gas gauge. Thea had filled the tank Friday afternoon. She hadn't used the car since. Something could be wrong with the indicator, or she might have been shorted at the pump. But she also lit on the horrifying possibility that she may have burned the missing fuel while driving around in a fugue state in the middle of the night.

Why can't I remember? What's happening to me?

The missing gasoline was not the only mystery. When she finally came to on Sunday morning, she'd felt inexplicably cold. It had taken hours to evict the bone-rattling frost from her bones. She'd downed several cups of hot tea and added layer after layer of clothing before she was finally able to still the shivers. The only times she remembered being chilled like that were when she'd defied the devilish elements on the ranch as a rebellious teenager and ventured out in the worst of an Idaho winter without a coat. And in the hours after Simon Gallatin's murder.

The house was warm enough, the doors and windows double-thick and weatherstripped to bar stray breezes. After a night cocooned under her plump down comforter, why would she wake up trembling like that?

Could she have left home during the night in her flimsy cotton gown? And barefoot? She thought of the soiled soles of her feet, the tracks she'd made on the kitchen floor Sunday morning.

God, no!

Her heart was hammering. An air raid wouldn't wake Gabby. Thea could easily have slipped out and re-entered the house hours later without disturbing the child's sleep.

Alden Gaithwaite lived in Bridgeport, only twenty minutes away. Thea would have had ample time to make it to his apartment and back while the entire neighborhood was asleep and heedless. Even Glenda Rossner closed her oversized eyes and ears after midnight.

No! It couldn't have happened that way.

Thea didn't know this man Gaithwaite or his girlfriend. It was insane to believe she'd somehow wandered into his building in an unconscious state and murdered two innocent strangers.

Totally insane.

And what about the blood? If she'd stabbed two people, surely she would have been covered with the grisly evidence. Wincing, Thea remembered how bloodied her hands and clothing had been after Simon's death. Her palms had been slicked with blood, her clothing smeared. There had even been blood in her hair. The police hadn't let her wash or change until they'd taken dozens of pictures and scraped samples of the victim's dried blood into a series of plastic bags.

Afterward, she'd spent an eternity in a near-scalding shower, trying to rid herself of the sight and smell of Simon's battered body, trying to feel clean again, as if the mark of such a hideous experience could ever be washed away.

It could not be happening again. Desperate to confirm her innocence, Thea hurried upstairs. Retrieving the nightgown she'd worn Saturday night from her bathroom hamper, she frantically searched the soft blue fabric. But she found no signs of soil or violence. Relieved beyond measure, she realized she could not have showered to wash any blood traces off her body. If she had, her feet wouldn't have been so dirty. They'd probably gotten soiled while she was walking around after Max Perry left, cleaning up. It wouldn't be unusual for her to step outside barefoot to take out the trash. That surely explained away that piece of the puzzle.

But where could she have seen the picture of Gaithwaite and the children?

Groping hard for a plausible explanation, she considered the timing of the obituary. The magazine piece stated that the murder of Alden Gaithwaite and his girlfriend hadn't been discovered until Sunday. The news of his death appeared in the *People* issue that went on sale Monday. In order to run the column so quickly, Gaithwaite's photograph must have been on file from an earlier article.

Thea called the magazine. The switchboard operator transferred her to an assistant editor on the "Passages" page. Thea claimed she was a neighbor of the deceased. She said she was working on a eulogy for Alden Gaithwaite and needed to know if anything else about

"Pappy" had ever appeared in *People*. A cheery-sounding young man asked her to hold. Moments later, he came back on the line.

"Found it. July thirteenth issue. Page twenty-five, last column, three graphs about Gaithwaite in a 'Where are they now?' piece about Bush's honored volunteers."

"Was there a picture?"

"Yes. Same one we ran next to the obit in this week's issue. Sweet story. Too bad about the old guy. He didn't deserve to go that way."

"No. He didn't."

"If you'd give me your name and address, I'll be glad to send you a tearsheet. . . ."

"Thanks. That won't be necessary."

Hanging up, Thea sought solace in the news. Undoubtedly she had seen the earlier article about Pappy Gaithwaite and the neighborhood children at Brook Hollow, where each new *People* issue was promptly circulated and devoured by the world-hungry patients.

But that neat explanation didn't begin to silence the remaining crowd of strident questions.

What had inspired her to paint that particular image on the day after the old man's death? Why had that particular picture, out of all of the zillions of magazines she'd skimmed to pass the time at the hospital, stuck so hard in her mind? And how could she have reproduced the photo in such intricate detail after more than two months? Thea had never been blessed with anything akin to a photographic memory. Her brain functioned much more like a sieve.

She could not deny the sickening pattern. First, Brandon Lee Payton is murdered, and she envisions a serpent exactly like the one killed in the attack. Now, Alden Gaithwaite and Blossom Price are viciously stabbed to death, and the next day, she paints a replica of a photograph hanging on the wall of the victims' apartment.

The damning evidence swam in Thea's mind, making her woozy and nauseous. Again, she thought about the disappearing gasoline. Her dirty feet. The penetrating chill and inexplicable exhaustion she'd felt after a night of supposedly uninterrupted sleep. The absence of blood on her skin and nightgown didn't clear her. She knew nothing about stabbings. A gory mess might not be inevitable.

What if the medicine wasn't working? In the cloistered confines of Brook Hollow, she'd been fine. But Dr. Forman had never adjusted the dose to account for the stresses and pressures of normal existence.

The worst thing was not knowing, lacking faith in her own behavior. The deadly seizures played beyond the arena of her conscious control. Her inner monster could be responsible for a murderous rampage, the vicious annihilation of innocent people. And she could be totally unaware.

That's how it had happened with Simon. If Thea hadn't been discovered at the scene, covered with his blood, she still would not believe she'd murdered him. A determined piece of her refused to believe it even now. So maybe the demon within her, the monster hidden from her consciousness, had killed these others, too.

Stop, Thea!

She didn't need to play her own judge, jury, and executioner. Lord knew the rest of the world would rush to condemn her immediately if even a fragment of hard evidence emerged.

Thea went cold at the thought. This time, they would cage her like a rabid animal. After the last trial, her own lawyer had confided that he viewed her acquittal as a sizeable stroke of good fortune. Few juries would buy the claim of unconscious violence, especially

when so many experts on seizure disorders had ardently
denied the possibility. The state had presented three
compelling witnesses to contradict the defense's contention that Thea had murdered the senator while suffering
a complex partial seizure. If she were tried again, the
prosecution would undoubtedly parade dozens of experts to undermine Thea's assertion of innocence. And
this time, they would succeed.

Living through another trial was unthinkable. Thea
could not bear to be a prime press target again. The
current campaign of phone calls and prying eyes was
nothing compared to what Harlan Vermin and his fellow rats had carried on before her acquittal. Thea could
not endure the stares, the relentless whispers. Yes, she
still suffered an occasional rude remark or skewed
glance, but most people had shifted their focus to
fresher outrages.

Above all, Gabby must be spared. The child was terrified of another abandonment. Thea had promised not
to leave her daughter again. Nothing short of a deadly
disease or fatal accident could force her to break that
crucial pledge. Nothing mattered more than Gabby's
trust and well-being.

*You are not a murderer, Thea Harper. What happened
with Simon was a one-time freak event.*

The only links between her and the Payton or
Gaithwaite killings were a few disturbing question
marks. She vowed to do everything in her meager
power to keep it that way.

The phone rang. Monitoring the machine, Thea was
bolstered by the sound of her mother's drowsy drawl.
"Hey, Checker. How you doing, honey?"

She ordered her tone to sound light and breezy.
"Same old same old."

"You sure? You sound frazzled."

"I was working, Mom. You know how I get."

Her mother paused a beat. "—I was thinking it'd be nice to see you and Gabby, Checker. How 'bout if I come east for a couple of days? Jimmy says he'd be glad to help out with Daddy and the ranch."

Thea's brother had a ranch of his own near Bozeman, Montana. He also had a mammoth mortgage, a frail rabbit of a wife, and four bottomless, boisterous kids to support. Taking a few days away from the overwhelming demands of his own life to attend to their father and the ranch was nowhere near as simple as Thea's mother made it sound.

"Absolutely not, Mom. You know I'd love to see you, but you and Jimmy both have your own responsibilities at home. I've been thinking that maybe Gabby and I will come out for Thanksgiving. How's that?"

"You sure, Checker? Maybe you could use the help. A few days' rest might do you a world of good."

"I'm sure."

"All right, honey. But if you change your mind—"

"I won't, Mom."

Two-thirty. Gabby would be home in an hour. By then, Thea had to piece herself and her shattered universe back together.

A hairbrush, lip gloss, and a studied smile sufficed to smooth her troubled appearance. Realizing what else she needed to do broke her heart. But it could not be avoided.

Returning to the studio, Thea squeezed a hill of black paint onto her palette. With an inch-thick brush, she layered over the pyramid of warm, hopeful faces. One by one, the charming children were buried under wretched stripes of stifling darkness. Her "important" painting was reduced to a cagelike crosshatch of ugliness and despair. Soon, no images remained but the old man in the center. Thea passed the blackened bristles over his kindly face.

A lump of sorrow filled her throat, but no healing tears followed. Her grief was a stone, cold and unyielding.

No more, she whispered. *Please, no more.*

The canvas was a muddy mess. Thea propped the ruined painting backward against the studio wall to dry. Once it did, she'd leave it out for the trash collectors.

Filling an empty coffee can with turpentine, she set the brushes to soak.

How had it come to this? A single involuntary act had turned her entire world on its ear. Her future had been eclipsed, her present shadowed by doubts and terrifying lapses.

Thoughts of her mother's relentless optimism penetrated the gloom. *Once you hit rock bottom, Checker honey, there's no way to go but up.*

Feeling sorry for herself was certainly no solution. Somehow, Thea had to find the necessary answers. Fortunately, she was scheduled for that checkup at Brook Hollow on Thursday morning. The exam would include an assessment of her medication levels, an EEG, and other neurological tests to determine whether there was any evidence of seizure activity. If everything proved normal, Thea could stop worrying about a recurrence.

Too bad the exam wasn't sooner. But if she asked for an earlier time, she'd be pressed for an explanation. Her only choice was to wait.

Meantime, she'd try to ascertain the current status of the Gaithwaite and Brandon Payton murder investigations. By now, the police might have firm suspects in one or both cases. That would be the surest way to ease her doubts.

Reflecting on his offer of help, Thea considered calling Detective Daniel Biederman. She found his card where she'd left it on the kitchen counter. She dialed

the station house but hung up hastily after the first
ring. How could she justify her interest in those homicides? Asking questions would surely only serve to
draw suspicion her way.

She'd have to find some other route to the information. She could check the local papers or call the
Bridgeport and Bedford police posing as a reporter or
whatever. She would think of something.

A sharp sun was shining. The autumn day had the
crisp clarity of a polished mirror. Staring out the
kitchen window, she drank in the magnificent display
of fall foliage.

Frantic squirrels darted across the lawn. Falling
leaves rode the insistent breeze. A pack of neighborhood
school kids drifted off the bus from the middle school.
Thea spotted Alec Goldblum, Robert Klaasens, and
lanky Mike Rossner. Lauren Rose and Arlene Pavony
drifted behind. The children were young, vigorous,
flame-cheeked with the chill. Filling her lungs again,
Thea reveled in the feast of savory sights.

Things would be all right, she promised herself. She
would claim control; she would find some way to set
her life in order. She'd always been able to handle the
curveballs, especially when she hunkered down and gave
the effort her all. And that's what she needed to do now.

*There's nothing so big you can't find a way to get around
it, Checker honey.*

But then, a noise from the front of the house caught
her attention. And she spotted the fresh nightmare
making his way up the walk.

CHAPTER
TWENTY-EIGHT

Walter Martin had aged a decade since she'd seen him last three years ago during a visit home to Idaho. His face was rough and craggy, his eyes were the dead black of burnt coal. Reluctantly, she opened the door to him. He exuded a strong scent of old sweat and stale tobacco.

"What are you doing here, Walter?" she asked.

"What kind of a greeting is that for your first love, doll face?"

"A better one than you deserve. Now please leave."

He raked nervous fingers through hair that begged for a decent cut and a washing. "I've come a long way, darlin'. Aren't you gonna ask me in, at least? Offer me a friendly taste?"

Thea caught the needy addict's shiver and felt a swell of revulsion. From the bony look of him, Walter's nourishment had been largely limited to injectibles and hard drink. "You can come in long enough to call home and let your mother know you're okay, but that's it. I am not harboring a fugitive."

Edging past her, he strode through the house, boldly scrutinizing the furnishings. "Looks like you've done real good for yourself, darlin'. That fancy doctor you married must've left a bundle when he passed on."

"Make the call, Walter."

He strolled into the den and fingered the Navaho blanket. "How's that little girl of yours doing? She must be, what? Nine or ten now? Bet I'll hardly recognize her. She still at school?"

In the living room, Walter picked up the photo album and started leafing through the pages. Thea wrenched the book from his grasp. She didn't want him tainting her precious memories.

Walter hiked his hands in mock surrender. "Whoa! Easy now, girl. Better mind that temper of yours. Last time you let her rip, that poor senator friend of yours wound up in real Big Sky country."

Thea reined in her fury. All she wanted was to be done with this and him. "What do you want, Walter?"

"Don't want nothing, darlin'. Came by to see you, that's all. Been a while."

"I'm not in the mood for your games, Walter. Tell me why you're here and then get the hell out."

He gnawed a ragged cuticle. "All right. But first give me a little taste, will you, baby? Nice shot of Jack Daniels would go down real smooth about now. Man gets mighty parched out riding the roads like I do."

"No drinks. You're trouble enough when you're sober."

Sighing, he perched on the sofa arm and hunched forward. "Fact is, I could use just the *teeniest* favor."

"Forget it, Walter. I'm not giving you any money. But if you're ready to fly home and surrender to the sheriff, I'll be glad to buy the ticket."

"Now, why would I want to go and do a thing like that?"

"Because you can't keep running forever, that's why. Because it's time to straighten up and try living a decent life for a change."

His laugh was dry and ugly. "You been reading some of them romance novels or what?"

"Nothing says you can't turn things around, Walter."

"That's a heap of prime horseshit, and you know it. I was born rotten and that's how I'll go out when the time comes. Plain and simple."

"It doesn't have to be that way."

A wicked smirk warped his face. "You know, Checker, it gave me quite a hoot when I heard about you offing that big-shot boyfriend of yours. United States senator, no less. Always knew you and me were two of a kind."

"Get out of here, Walter. I have nothing more to say to you." His words were poison darts, his aim too close to perfect.

"Sure you do, darlin'. You can say how you'd be glad to help your old friend out. 'Specially now that you know how easy it is to find yourself ass-deep in trouble." He blew a low whistle. "Murder. Even I've never stooped that low, baby. Not close."

A hot flush scaled her neck. "I want you to leave, Walter."

He stood and started toward her. Rage brightened his eyes. Thea took an involuntary step backward. "Must be I heard you wrong," he said roughly. "You saying you won't do me a simple little favor? I'm not asking for much, darlin'. At least, hear me out."

"Go or I'll call the police, Walter."

"You wouldn't dare."

"Watch me." Bolting out of the living room, she raced to the wall phone in the kitchen and dialed nine-one-one. But Walter caught up and wrestled the handset from her grip before the connection was made.

With the full force of his wrath, he pitched the receiver at the wall, dimpling the plaster and cracking the plastic casing on the phone. On the backswing, he caught Thea hard on the cheek and sent her sprawling across the room.

Her face stung; her mouth slackened with shock. At his craziest and most desperate, Walter had never laid a hand on her.

"Get out of my house," she said, her voice tight with anger.

"Hey, darlin'. I didn't mean that, honest. I'm real, real sorry, okay? How 'bout we kiss and make up."

Before he could take a step in her direction, Thea tugged open the drawer behind her and pulled out the carving knife. "I mean it, Walter. Get the hell out of here."

The smirk returned. "You want to cut me, baby? That make you happy?"

Thea forced herself to point the knife at him. "Go *now*!"

"This how it was with your senator friend? You just got madder and madder 'til you lost it altogether?"

She held her ground, wielding the blade. Walter was dangerous. She had to get rid of him before Gabby came home.

He egged her on, the dare written on his face. "That's it, baby. Show your true self. Nothing but a murdering, lying bitch, aren't you?"

The knife wavered in her grasp. Thea longed to drop the thing, to be done with this ugly scene. But she feared his response to an unconditional surrender.

With a wicked grin, Walter took another step toward her. "Go on, stab me. Anything to make my darlin' happy. Stick it in my heart, why don't you? Quick and easy."

He was getting too close. The blade danced dangerously near his abdomen. Thea backed away until she was pinioned against the cabinets. She tried to drop the knife, but his flat gut was pressed against the point. Pushing closer.

"Stop it, Walter. Enough!"

Squeezing into the blade's sharpened tip, he began to giggle. The laugh was demented. A maniacal expression stained his face.

The knife point pierced his shirt front. Horrified,

Thea saw a comma of blood seep through the tattered cloth.

The lunatic was trying to impale himself. Thea was powerless to stop him. The knife handle dug into her abdomen, making it hard to breathe. "This is crazy, Walter. Don't!"

She felt him pressing harder, saw the bloody circle spreading on his shirt.

"Mommy, no!"

Gabby stood in the doorway, her face frozen in stark terror.

Startled by the little girl's scream, Walter jerked back. Twisting free, Thea turned and dropped the knife in the sink.

"It's okay, Gabby," she gasped. "It's over now."

The child whimpered. Thea crossed to hold her, but Gabby recoiled. "You don't understand, sweetie. Walter was just acting crazy."

He was moving forward again, his fingers pressed against the crimson stain on his shirt. "She understands fine. Don't you, darlin'? Your momma was fixing to run me through like a roasting pig. Not real friendly, if you ask me."

"No, Gabby. Don't listen to him. You know Walter's not right in the head."

"But I saw you, Mommy," the child cried. Hysteria squeezed her voice. "You promised not to get sick again. You promised!" Gabby tore upstairs. Thea heard the door slam.

Pushing past Walter, Thea picked up the cracked receiver and dialed. Anger boiled in her. "Police? I need you to send a car immediately. A man named Walter Martin is here, and there's a warrant out for his arrest. The address is—"

Walter leaned close to her; his finger pressed the disconnect switch. His breath brushed her ear. "All right, baby. You win. I'm out of here."

She set down the dead receiver. "Not until you tell Gabby the truth."

This time, his grin was boyish. With a pang, Thea remembered a much younger Walter, one who hadn't yet crossed over the great divide beyond redemption. "Sure. Why not?"

Standing at the bottom of the stairs, he called up. "Gabby? You listen to your old buddy Walter, darlin'. Your momma and me was just playing is all. She wasn't really meaning to hurt me."

Silence.

"You hear me, baby?"

A tiny voice drifted down. "But I saw the knife. And you were bleeding."

"That's just play blood. Like they use in the movies. I brought it along for a joke."

Gabby's door opened a crack. "You mean it?"

"From the deep foggy bottom of my heart, baby." He held out his arms and spun in a jaunty circle. "Old Walter's right as rain, you see? I just like to play tricks every now and again."

Gabby hesitated. "Are you staying over?"

" 'Fraid I can't. Got business to see to down in New York City. I was just passing through and figured I'd stop in and say a quick how-do to two of my favorite gals."

". . . Okay."

" 'Bye, then. You be a good girl and mind to your momma, you hear?"

"I will. 'Bye, Walter."

He turned to Thea. "Walk me out, will you, darlin'?"

Thea felt Gabby's quizzical gaze. Everything had to appear normal. "All right."

On the path Walter turned to her. His eyes were glazed with fury. "I'm gonna pay you back, baby. You're gonna be real sorry you treated me so shabby."

"I'm not interested in your threats, Walter."

"But you *will* be. I'll see to it you are. Could be, I've already made it so your sweet life's about to turn sour."

The murderous glint in his eye made Thea shiver. Walter Martin specialized in the manufacture of other people's misery.

"Good-bye, Walter."

He waggled his fingers. "Remember me when it all comes tumbling down, Checker."

Thea reentered the house, closed the door, and hugged herself to still the trembling. Walter's foul hatred stuck in her throat. She'd never imagined being the target of so much venom: Walter, Mrs. Gallatin, all the angry judgmental strangers. If wishes were horses, she'd have been trampled to death by now.

As it was, she was merely scarred for life by the hoofprints.

CHAPTER TWENTY-NINE

Overnight, a dozen leather sofa beds had disappeared from a furniture store on the Post Road. Biederman and Passerelli had caught the case. They'd spent the morning in adjoining model rooms, questioning employees.

Last on Biederman's list was a cocky twerp from shipping named Paul Garraty. The guy had a pimply face and the jittery moves of a bad boxer. His nose was a pink mushroom, his forehead a cantilevered porch. Not a pretty package.

For the first fifteen minutes, Biederman and the clerk danced in aimless circles. Garraty tried to pull off an unconvincing imitation of the doe-eyed innocent, and Biederman pretended to buy it, though the jerk was dripping with guilt. Genuine gold Rolex on the wrist, silver concho belt girdling his waist, fat roll of bills bulging in his back pocket. Biederman wondered why the bozo didn't simply get himself a T-shirt saying "Heists R Us."

When he ran out of patience, Biederman extracted a crumpled Visa receipt from his pocket.

"Before we waste any more valuable time on this, Garraty, I'll be straight with you. What I've got here is a copy of an invoice for a truck rental in your name. Nice big truck. Perfect for hauling all those sofa beds and the piles of dirty cash you pocketed selling them under the table."

Garraty started to sweat. "Okay, okay. How 'bout I cut you in?"

"How about I add bribery to the list?"

"Don't get excited. Gotta be some way we can work this out—"

"Sure, Mr. Garraty. The way we work it out is I put this charge slip of mine back in my wallet, and then I haul your ugly mug to the pokey."

Garraty's face blanched. His pimples stood out in classical bas relief. "Hey, that's not fair, man," he whined.

"Feel free to register a sportsmanship complaint," Biederman said affably as he slapped on the cuffs.

When Biederman and Passerelli dumped the thief at headquarters, the sergeant at the desk informed them that the afternoon duty roster had been amended. Instead of their continuing with an ongoing embezzlement case as planned, Inspector Delavan had assigned them to work a bus safety program at the Coleytown Elementary School.

Good old Buck. Guy was a true prince: The kind descended from a bullfrog.

To Passerelli, the gig was anything but punishment. Vince was crazy about kids, and the sentiment was mutual. Passerelli had an uncanny knack for fitting in with the knee pants set. All he had to do was be himself.

"That's great, Danny. Isn't that great?"

"It's swell, Vince."

Passerelli was pumped. "Wait 'til you see, Danny. We get to use this make-believe bus. It's got blinking lights and an automatic door and a horn and everything. It's really cool."

"I know, Vinnie. I can barely contain myself."

Vince frowned. "What, Danny? You're not up for bus safety?"

"Actually, it's what I've prayed for. Only today, I was hoping to take care of some other things. I'm a little backed up."

The frown deepened. "That's what happens when you don't eat enough fiber."

Biederman shook his head. "Not that kind of backed up, Vince. I mean, I've got some work to do."

"Go for it, then. I can handle the bus program myself."

"You'd do that for me?"

"No problem."

"There would be if the inspector found out, Vince. We'd have to keep it our little secret."

"I read you loud and clear, partner. Delavan won't hear a word from me."

Biederman chucked Passerelli's dimpled chin. "You're a real pal, Vinnie. I owe you one."

Passerelli beamed. "My pleasure, Danny. Honest."

Biederman dropped Passerelli at the school with a promise to return in two hours. Vince trotted toward the building's entrance like an eager puppy. Biederman watched until his partner was safely inside before heading toward the turnpike. He often felt a tug of parental responsibility toward Passerelli. To really keep the guy out of trouble, he should have been teamed up with a nanny.

Two hours. With any luck, Biederman would have ample time to make the critical contacts and return before Buck Delavan got wind of his extracurricular activities.

Downtown New Haven was a maddening maze of one-way streets. For an irksome few minutes, Biederman bounced around like a pinball as he attempted to zero in on the Court Street Federal Building that housed the local FBI field office.

The bulky building had been constructed during the Carter administration. It reflected that era's obsession with energy conservation. There were no breaks, no windows. Nothing adorned the dull as dirt facade except the plaque dedicating the homely structure to some deceased congressman who'd delivered several prime slabs of D.C. pork to his local constituents.

The Fibbie offices occupied the fifth and sixth floors. After explaining what he was after, Biederman was passed rapidly from desk to desk like snapshots of an ugly baby. No one seemed to know how to handle a request for records from a moribund case. Special Agent Vartuli referred him to Agent Wolkowitz who handed him off to Marcantonio who went deep and passed to Makowski who finally punted Biederman to the administrative officer in charge of the closed file section.

Sylvia London was squat, square, and neckless. At fifty-something, she had the grim, pugnacious bearing of a bureaucrat who'd long been married to the unbending rule book and the uninspiring job. Her desk was devoid of pictures or personality. Seated behind it, she clutched a feedbag-shaped handbag.

From time to time, she rifled through the contents. Otherwise, she kept one hand submerged in the purse as if it were a hand puppet. As Biederman succinctly related the purpose of his mission, she kept jangling her keys in a rhythm that put him on the lookout for flying reindeer.

"What's your interest in the Gallatin case, Detective?" Her voice had the tinny timbre of a kazoo.

"Curiosity. I know some of the principles."

Ms. London smirked. "Let me take a wild guess. You've got an agent shopping a book deal? Maybe angling for a movie-of-the-week?"

"Nothing like that. I told you. I'm just curious."

"Yeah, right. And I'm the Easter Bunny."

From the jingling, Biederman would have guessed Santa's helper, but he had not come to argue.

"All I need is a couple of hours. Tell me when it's convenient, and I'll come back."

"This is a federal agency, Detective. Not a museum. We do *not* welcome browsers."

"Come on, Ms. London. All I'm asking for is a little professional courtesy."

"I heard you ask, and you heard me answer. To be perfectly frank, you Westport cops have done nothing to endear yourselves to this office."

Biederman tried to think of an effective bribe. London wasn't the type to have her head turned by a dozen roses or a silk scarf. A nice box of dog biscuits came to mind, but with Biederman's luck, the woman was probably on a diet.

His next stop was the U.S. Attorney's office. The number-two man there, an ex-navy officer named Joe Kelley, had headed the prosecution team in the case against Thea Harper. Buck Delavan hadn't had the opportunity to alienate the lawyers, so Biederman hoped his reception there would not be quite so chilly.

At the front desk, however, he learned that Kelley was recuperating from bypass surgery. The deputy's assistant, a brunette in her thirties named Penny Proctor, was easy on the eyes but tough as nails when it came to protocol.

"Sorry, Detective. Anything to do with the Harper case would have to be cleared through Mr. Kelley."

"But you said he'll be out for several weeks."

"A month or more," she said. "Honestly, I'd be glad to help you out, but my boss is a stickler. Very territorial."

"What if I ask Scarlotti?" Biederman hadn't had any direct dealings with Connecticut's U. S. Attorney, but the man was so busy spreading sound bites and grabbing photo opportunities, he seemed like a close personal friend.

"You're welcome to ask, but I'd bet he'll tell you exactly the same thing. No one's going to step on Mr.

Kelley's turf unless it's absolutely necessary. And frankly, I can't see the emergency, given that the Harper case is dead and buried."

"All I need is a quick look at the file, Ms. Proctor. Mr. Kelley wouldn't even have to know," Biederman suggested hopefully.

"Believe me, he'd know. Last week, I agreed to take a deposition in one of Kelley's active cases because the witness was due to leave the country. An hour after we wrapped it up, Mr. Kelley called from Cardiac Intensive Care to bawl me out. My lunatic boss actually got someone to smuggle in a cellular phone. The thing screwed up the monitors so badly, they thought the woman in the next bed had expired. Imagine waking up from an innocent nap to the code blue team and a crash cart."

Biederman checked Penny Proctor's eyes for signs of slack and found none. The eyes reminded him of Thea. Then, most everything did lately.

Ms. Proctor did appear sympathetic. "What exactly is it you're looking for, Detective?"

"I don't know specifically. But I believe something in that record might help me clear up another open case."

The eyes narrowed. "I take it this is an *informal* investigation?"

"That's true."

"Something you have a *special, personal* interest in, Detective?"

"I'd like to see justice done where I think it hasn't been. If that's what you call special, personal interest, I'll have to plead guilty."

A coy smile tugged the edges of her lips. It had been a while, but clearly, the woman was flirting with him.

"Are you busy tonight?" she asked.

"Actually, I am."

"Tomorrow, then?"

"Sorry. It's a bad week."

Biederman resisted the considerable temptation to leap at the offer. Best and only one he'd had in many moons. The woman was pretty, sharp, and attractively self-confident. But his dance card was already way overbooked with complications.

"Too bad." She shook her head. "My fiancé's with the FBI. The records are too hard to access in this office. But if I asked, I'm sure Warren would let you come in and have a look at the files after hours. . . ."

Biederman's cheeks flamed. "That'd be terrific, Ms. Proctor. If your *fiancé* can do that for me, I'll be glad to change my plans."

She stifled a grin. "I'll call and check Warren's schedule."

Feeling the total fool, Biederman waited impatiently while she efficiently made the arrangements. Turned out her betrothed was tied up for the evening, but he agreed to meet Biederman at the field office at eight tomorrow night. The man, whose surname was Bell, was possibly the only agent in the office who hadn't yet had the chance to slam a door in Biederman's face.

"All set," she said as she hung up.

"Thanks a million, Ms. Proctor. I really appreciate this."

Penny Proctor allowed the smile to surface. "I can't remember the last time someone mistakenly thought I was coming on to him, Detective. In your line of work, I'd think you'd avoid jumping to misplaced conclusions."

"You're absolutely right," Biederman conceded with an embarrassed grin. "And someday, I'm sure I will."

Gabby buried her face in the pillow, pressed her nails
into her palms, and tried to erase the gruesome picture
from her mind.

She kept imagining Mommy holding the turkey
knife and the bloody-looking front of Walter Martin's
shirt. On visits to Granny and Grampy Sparks's ranch
in Idaho, Gabby had overhead conversations about
Ada's son Walter and how he was always getting into
hot water. When she was a little kid, Gabby thought
that meant the guy took a lot of baths. Now, she understood that Walter was a criminal like the mean-faced
people they flashed on *America's Most Wanted.*

Still, having known Walter all her life, it was tough
to think of him as really rotten. Usually, he seemed
more or less like a regular grown-up. But if fake blood
and phony cuts were his idea of a joke, Gabby was certainly not laughing.

The movie blood and the knife reminded Gabby of
Dylan Connable's death room. No matter how she tried
to forget that awful place, her thoughts kept dragging
her back there. It was a closet really, but with all the
normal stuff removed. Dylan had taken her to see it last
Sunday after she left the Millports'.

Gabby had hoped he'd get tired of waiting around
for her and leave. But when she came to the end of the
Millports' front walk, he was still huddled out of sight
behind the shrubbery. Like a statue, Dylan didn't seem
in the least chilled or ruffled by the insistent wind.
Gabby suspected he would have crouched there indefi-

nitely had she decided to stay at the twins' house for dinner or a sleep-over.

Seeing Dylan opened a yawning pit in Gabby's stomach. He tossed her off balance like the vomit wheel at the playground. She never knew what sick, strange thing Dylan might be planning to show or tell her next. And, once he wrapped his mind around something, Gabby could not find a way to refuse him. If she tried, Dylan would follow her around like one of the Millports' dogs until she agreed to go along with his plans.

He'd parked his car around the corner on Imperial. As soon as Gabby shut the door, Dylan gunned the motor and turned a screeching circle in the middle of the road. Soon, they were shooting at warp speed down Dylan's street, bumping up his driveway.

"What is it this time?" Gabby asked.

"I told you, it's the ultimate. My biggest secret."

"What's that?"

"I can't explain, sweetness. You'll have to see for yourself."

Dylan peered through the garage door's slitted windows. "Good. She's gone. Follow me."

"Your mom's not home?" For some reason, Gabby felt safer knowing Mrs. Connable was nearby, even if Dylan didn't actually live inside the house.

"Nope. She went to visit my Aunt Jess and Uncle Eli out on Long Island. She won't be back until late."

"Maybe I should go, then."

"She has to be gone for me to show you this, little one. Don't worry. I never bite."

Dylan left Gabby at the front door and entered the house through an unlocked window in the den. An instant later, she heard the clack of the latch chain, and the front door opened. Looking smug, Dylan motioned her inside.

"Don't you have a key?" Gabby asked.

"I did, but I lost it."

"You can get another one made at the hardware store."

Dylan snickered. "I didn't lose it that way. My old lady took it away."

Gabby gaped in astonishment. She'd never heard of a parent locking a kid out of the house. It had to be against the law.

"Why'd she do that?"

"Long story," he said. "Wipe your feet. She'll have a French-fried fit if she finds out I came in here."

Timidly, Gabby trailed him down the narrow hallway. There was a living room on one side, a dining room backed by a tiny kitchen on the other. The whole place had a medicine smell like a doctor's office. Everything was so neat, it was hard to believe anyone actually lived here, especially someone related to a major slob like Dylan. Remembering the revolting mess in his car and the piles of junk all over his room, Gabby thought she understood why his mother had kicked him out.

Dylan's old room was at the rear of the house behind the kitchen. Like the rest of the place, it was pin neat and smelled of cleansers. The ugly plaid bedspread matched the window curtains, and an oval rug softened the center of the polished plank floor. Rock posters were tacked to the wall, and normal kids' books, aligned in size order, filled the bookshelves.

Looking around, Gabby spotted several volumes of the Hardy Boys, a set of Alfred Hitchcock mysteries, and *The Lord of the Rings.* If she didn't know better, Gabby would have figured that an ordinary kid used to live here.

At the rear of the room was a padlocked closet. Dylan worked the combination for a moment, then opened the door. Gabby's heart fluttered at the thought of what might be hidden inside. But in her wildest imaginings, she could never have guessed the contents.

The inside was papered with notes, newspaper clippings, drawings, and photographs. In amazement, Gabby scanned the bizarre display. There was a story from the *Westport News* about an unnamed youth rescued after a suicide attempt. A note in ragged handwriting said, *"Finally, it's over. And about time. Good-bye, World. See you in Hell."* A picture showed wrists wrapped in thick white bandages. Another displayed the wrists with the bandages removed. Stitches like a parade of spiders cinched the nasty gash circling his flesh. Gabby looked from the photo to Dylan's scarred wrists and shuddered.

"My death room," he bragged. "Everything in here is a tribute to my imminent demise."

"What does that mean?"

He patted her on the head. "It means I'm going to die soon, little one. I'm not long for this cold, gray world."

"Why? Are you sick?"

"Not in the classic sense. It's more accurate to say I'm world-weary. I've had my fill of this wretched existence. It never has suited me all that well."

"You mean you're going to *kill* yourself?" Of course, Gabby had heard of suicide, but she couldn't believe anyone would actually do such a thing.

Last year, she and the twins had agreed to become blood sisters, but when it was Gabby's turn to prick her finger with the safety pin, she thought she would throw up. She hadn't been able to wreak even that tiny degree of damage on herself. The twins had agreed to settle for mingled swipes of red Magic Marker. Fortunately, Opal and Jazzy had understood their friend's powerful aversion toward self-inflicted pain.

"We are all killing ourselves by degrees, little one.

Every breath we take is one closer to the last; every
movement erodes our basic structure. Even as you stand
there, horrified at the notion of my voluntary demise,
you are shedding millions of cells. The Earth is covered
with the residue from our relentless decay. Even my fas-
tidious mother can't keep ahead of the dead cells." He
swiped a finger over the windowsill and came away
with the tiniest trace of dust. "Human waste," he said.

Gabby wrinkled her nose. "That's gross."

"Perhaps, but it's also truth, sweetness. We begin
dying at the moment of our birth. Think about it.
Death is the common defining feature of every living
thing. I've simply decided to select my own time, place,
and method."

Gabby couldn't tear her eyes away from the death
room walls. There were poems and stories about dying,
and tracings from tombstones. One read, *"Sarah Lynn
Connable, 1977–1983. Bright angel, beckoned home. Rest in
peace."*

"Was Sarah Lynn your little sister?" Sadness shrank
Gabby's voice to a whisper.

"*Is,* not *was,* sweetness. Death simply releases a person's trapped spirit from this lowly plane. Sarah didn't
cease to exist. My little sweetness was simply spared
further suffering."

"You mean, she had a disease?"

"Not at all. Sarah Lynn was perfect. Bright and
lively and lovely to the end."

"Then, how'd she die?"

Dylan stood silent. His dark gaze was fixed on the
rubbing from his sister's gravestone.

"How, Dylan?" Gabby insisted.

"Sarah had this pair of lacy tights she wore for special occasions, church and the like. One day, she was
running into the house after a little friend's birthday

party. She tripped on the walk and tore her best tights
at the knee."

"And she died from that?" Gabby was forever rip-
ping her tights. She'd never suffered anything worse
than a skinned knee.

"When my old man saw, he beat Sarah with a stick
until she stopped breathing. Son of a bitch fractured her
skull in three places, broke seven ribs."

His voice was soft, but the terrible words felt like
blows to Gabby's stomach.

"When I got home that day, my mother was holding
Sarah in her lap, trying to convince her to come back to
us. But she was too smart for that. My sweetness had finally gotten to a better place. She wasn't about to come
back for more beatings."

The story about Dylan's dead sister kept looping
through Gabby's mind. Maybe he was just making the
whole thing up. His father hadn't gone to jail or anything, Dylan said. Mr. Connable had forced Dylan and
his mother to lie to the doctors and the police. He made
them say Sarah had fallen down the stairs. If they told
the truth, the old man had vowed to kill them also. At
the time, Dylan told Gabby, he was still dumb enough
to let that worry him.

But now, death didn't frighten him in the least. He
looked forward to dying the way Gabby couldn't wait
for her next birthday.

They had stayed at the death room long enough for
Gabby to read every note and article and take in every
horrible picture on the walls. The whole time, she'd
tried to convince Dylan that killing yourself was wrong.
Life was very important and you only got to have one.
Giving it up on purpose, even for a possible trip to
heaven, had to be a big mistake.

But Dylan argued that he had no reasons to stay
alive. When Gabby suggested that people would miss

him, he told her sourly that he had no real family or friends. The few people he hung around with from time to time wouldn't even notice he was gone.

Gabby had tried her hardest to change his mind. Wasn't he looking forward to being a grown-up? Having a wife and kids of his own? A job?

Gabby couldn't wait to be a grown-up famous writer with fans like Mr. Perry's author friend. She'd travel all over the country giving autographs and talking about her work. Someday, she'd even have a whole room full of books she'd written. Sophie the Snake was just the beginning. She could feel it in her bones.

But the future didn't mean anything to Dylan Connable. He was worthless, he told Gabby. All he'd ever become was bigger trouble, he'd grimly predicted. Much better to cash his chips now.

By the time Gabby finished examining the death room, it was nearly dinnertime. Mommy would be looking for her. To her relief, Dylan agreed to let her go.

On the way home, Gabby kept working to change the teenager's mind. "You do have a friend, Dylan. You have me."

His smile was wistful. "That's sweet of you, little one. Means a lot."

"Then you won't kill yourself?"

"Oh, I will, but I'll depart with one less regret."

The pillowcase was soggy with her tears. Gabby had to find a way to keep Dylan from cutting his wrists again or doing some other awful thing to himself. Too many people had died on her already.

Mommy was coming up the stairs. Gabby stifled the sobs and buried her wet face in the pillow. Her door opened, and she felt the warmth of her mother's watchful gaze. Holding her breath, she waited for the sword of light from the hallway to disappear.

Finally, the door softly closed. Turning her pillow to

the dry side, Gabby squeezed her eyes shut. She prayed with all her soul for Dylan to be okay. For good measure, she put in a special word for Mommy and all the Millports and Uncle Jimmy and Grandma and Grandpa Sparks. She was about to close out her requests when she thought of something else.

"It might be asking too much, Lord," she whispered. "But if you happen to be thinking about sending me a stepfather, Mr. Perry is definitely my first choice."

Somewhat comforted by the notion that a higher power had been notified of Dylan's troubles, Gabby pulled the covers to her chin. Her mind drifted from Dylan to Sophie and from Sophie to the imaginary shelves full of her own world-famous books. From there, her thoughts turned to more immediate issues.

Mr. Perry was coming over after school. Gabby had to get Mommy to wear her red sweater and short black skirt. Mom looked great in red, and the skirt showed off her legs, which were really terrific for someone who was nearly thirty-five. Mr. Perry was bound to take serious notice.

A smile played on Gabby's lips. Thinking about the wedding, she drifted off to sleep.

CHAPTER
THIRTY-ONE

Rising from the paper-capped table, Thea plucked the final lead from her temple and wiped off the remains of the fixing gel with a damp paper towel. Dr. Forman, clad in a lab coat and bookish glasses, stood across the stark examining room in Brook Hollow's medical wing. She was bowed over the hefty printout from Thea's EEG, scrutinizing the results.

Edging closer, Thea peered over the doctor's shoulder and eyed the pile of ragged lines. The portrait of her brain waves resembled a mass of cars skidding wildly on an ice-slicked road. But from countless past experiences, she knew that even the most normal EEG could pass for a study in chaos.

It's okay. It has to be.

For the last ten months, every one of her neurological tests had been negative. More desperately than ever, she wanted to hear that nothing had changed, that she was still in conscious control and free of the deadly seizures.

Impatience was a live wire, sizzling in her gut. *Tell me I'm all right. Say I'm okay!*

But Dr. Forman kept peering at the printout. Her mouth was drawn in a pensive pucker. The faintest whisper of a frown ruffled her ivory brow.

The endless waiting was unbearable. "So?"

The shrink shot her a chastening look, then returned to her maddeningly slow perusal of the test results. Drawing a breath, Thea struggled to stay on top of her mounting apprehension.

There was no way to hurry the doctor along. Thea could not express or even hint at the cause of her excru-

ciating anxiety. If Dr. Forman had any reason to suspect
Thea's involvement in a crime, the shrink would be
duty-bound to report the information to the authorities.

Thea imagined setting the wheels of a giant crushing
machine in motion. Pulverizing her own existence. De-
stroying any remaining chance she and Gabby had to
transcend the horror of Simon Gallatin's death and live
a normal life.

Tucking back an errant strand of hair, Dr. Forman
started at the bottom of the printout and made several
notations on the long snake of accordion-folded paper.
She paused to sharpen her pencil with the old-fashioned
crank-driven device mounted beside the examining
room door. She honed the point with enormous deliberation and emptied the belly of the sharpener into the
trash bin before she returned to her torturous flipping
and marking.

Thea struggled to sound calm. "Is there a problem,
Dr. Forman?"

The arched brow rose like a wind-borne leaf. "Why?
Have you any reason to suspect one?"

Thea's heartbeat quickened. "No. I was just wondering why you're taking so long."

In fact the pile of reasons was so high and precarious,
Thea feared they might slip like a raging avalanche and
bury her alive. Large chunks of time had vanished from
her life. Vivid images from two different murder scenes
she couldn't possibly have seen had somehow wriggled
into her consciousness. So many inexplicable things
were happening, she didn't know what to worry about
first.

What if the doctor detected an abnormality on the
EEG? Would that confirm Thea's terrifying suspicions
that she might have been involved in the murders of
Brandon Lee Payton and those poor old people from
Bridgeport?

Thea's heart thundered. Something must be wrong. If the tests were normal, why all the delay and secrecy? Earlier that day, Thea had taken a CAT scan and had her blood drawn to test the levels of the antiseizure medication in her system. Officially, lab technicians weren't allowed to report test results. But Al Yudis, who operated the scanner, and Phil Edell in hematology usually gave Thea some casual indication that things looked fine. A smile. A confirmatory nod. But today, both had been noncommittal. Had they seemed uneasy?

She recalled Al's abrupt departure after the CAT scan. He'd muttered something about a family emergency. Had that been an excuse to ease him out of the room before he inadvertently cued her to some abnormality?

Quit it, Thea. There's nothing to be gained by jumping ahead of the facts.

The phone rang. Dr. Forman answered and engaged in a lengthy discussion about a patient's medicare status.

Enough already. Get on with it!

But as soon as the shrink hung up, the phone trilled again. This time, the doctor listened for a moment and replaced the handset without a word. Her lips were pressed in a hard line.

"Sorry, Thea. There's something I need to attend to. You relax. I'll only be a moment."

How could she possibly relax? Thea could barely breathe. She stared at the clock for the full five minutes it took the psychiatrist to return. It felt closer to five years. This was pure torture. Thumbscrews and electric prods would have been preferable.

Dr. Forman spent nearly another ten minutes hunched over the printout. Finished at last, the shrink dropped the printout in a metal basket, slipped her glasses into the pocket of her lab coat, and wove her snow white fingers neatly together.

"Tell me how you've been feeling lately, Thea. Any unusual symptoms?"

"Why do you ask?"

"Because your physical state is part of the clinical picture. No need to be evasive. I'm your doctor."

Thea's nerves were jangling. "I'm not being evasive. I was just wondering why you're asking about symptoms. Is anything wrong?" She heard the edge in her voice and hoped Dr. Forman didn't.

The shrink pulled the printout from the basket, hesitating a long extra beat. "I'm afraid I can't give you a simple yes or no. As I've explained countless times, seizure management involves a delicate balance of many factors. I'll have to study all the test results before I can comment further."

"But why? What's the matter?"

"Perhaps nothing. Give me a couple of days, and I'll have more concrete information for you."

A couple of days? How in hell was she supposed to wait that long?

"Look, Doctor. I understand you need time to be absolutely sure. But if you suspect a problem, I'd like to know about it. Now."

Frowning, Dr. Forman tapped the paper stack with her pencil eraser. "Have you noticed any dizziness? Nausea? Headaches?"

Careful, Thea. This was a test she could not afford to fail. She thought about the monstrous spikes of pain that had followed her blackouts. Having taken an extensive history, Dr. Forman knew that Thea had never been prone to headaches. She must not add any ammunition to the doctor's arsenal.

"I've been fine."

The frown deepened. "No drowsiness or confusion or changes in your sleep pattern?"

"No."

"Well, then. As I said, I'll take everything under consideration and get back to you as soon as I have a definite answer."

Thea could not be dismissed this way, left to float in a sea of doubt and terror.

"What if you find something wrong?" *Oh God, how shrill I sound.*

"Then we'll explore our options."

"Other medications, you mean? What options are there?"

Irritation cracked the doctor's icy facade. "When and if it's necessary, we'll discuss it fully, Thea. Now, if you'll excuse me, I have other patients to see."

With a dismissive nod, the psychiatrist collected her purse and briefcase and strode out of the examining room. Her heels rapped sharply on the polished tile corridor floor. Thea stood immobile as the sound dimmed and disappeared.

Shaken, she crossed to the mesh receptacle and scrutinized the printout of her EEG. If only she could read the damned thing herself. But interpreting the blips and nuances required an expert's eye. The wave patterns were affected by the slightest variations in thought, external stimuli, and positioning. That crazy spike in the center of the top sheet might indicate a seizure. Or it might have been a simple response to an unexpected noise from the hall.

Thea had a sudden, desperate urge to scoop up the pile of paper and find some other shrink or a neurologist who could interpret the results for her. But how could she possibly explain the theft?

Never go off the deep end until you've tested the water, Checker honey.

Her only choice was to wait for Dr. Forman's diagnosis. Thea tried to comfort herself with the best-case outcome. The psychiatrist would probably call in a day or two and declare everything in perfect order. All this was probably just an overreaction to an innocent blip in the test pattern. By the doctor's own description, these things were very subtle and extremely subjective.

Leaving the medical wing, however, another nasty possibility crept under Thea's skin. Maybe there was nothing at all unusual on the readout. Might all the posturing and delay be the witch doctor's wicked way of punishing Thea for terminating therapy?

That prickly possibility made Thea furious. It wasn't a big stretch to imagine Maxine Forman acting out of spite. True, she was a fine physician, but none of the framed credentials on the wall certified that she was anything close to a board-certified human.

Approaching the reception area, Thea enjoyed the molten surge of outrage. It was a decided improvement over her earlier sense of helplessness and impending doom. Pausing at the hospital's exit, she impulsively decided to stop by and see Billie. After a dose of Dr. Forman, an antidote was definitely in order.

Thea's apprehension increased as she approached the patient wing. Quickly, she passed the familiar rooms, avoiding contact with the residents. The oppressive scents of mustiness and despair made her wince. When she was halfway down the hall, Mrs. Argersinger burst out of the TV room with her ubiquitous umbrella at the ready.

"Duck, girlie. Get your sweet ass down! Hurry!"

Past the rooms, Thea knocked at the door to the staff lounge and peered inside. Her nurse friend was lolling in an easy chair, chin on ample chest, snoring loudly.

Poor Billie looked exhausted. Hating to disturb her, Thea edged out and slowly tugged the door behind her.

When it was nearly shut, the hinge squealed like a stuck pig.

"Who's there? What's happening?"

Thea winced and poked her head back inside. "Sorry, Billie. I didn't mean to wake you."

The nurse flapped a hand. "No such thing, girlfriend. Just resting my eyes a minute. Come on in. What brings you 'round here?"

Thea entered and claimed the chair opposite her friend's. Billie's feet, propped on a mock leather hassock, looked somewhat better. But the puffy soreness appeared to have drifted to the woman's face.

"I came in for some tests."

"What kind?"

"Routine. What's up? You look beat."

Billie rubbed her bloodshot eyes with a knuckle. "Vita Negrone's still missing, and now her family's threatening to sue. Cops haven't been able to track her, so Doc Forman got it in her mind to send the staff out looking. Past two nights I got four hours sleep all told."

"That's ridiculous, Billie. You'll get sick."

"Already am, if you want the truth. Sick and tired of Doc Forman, anyhow."

"I can certainly relate to that." Thea frowned. "It's strange that Vita hasn't surfaced." Strange and disturbing.

"Oh, she'll turn up. Meantime, what's going on with you? Looks like you got something real heavy setting on that pretty head of yours."

The ready shoulder was tempting, but Thea held back. She couldn't trust anyone with her blackest misgivings, not even Billie.

"Same old same old," she said, trying to invoke her mother's breezy tone.

Billie looked skeptical, but she didn't push. "You need me, I'm here."

"I know that, and I'm grateful. Believe me."

Frowning at her watch, the nurse labored to her feet. Yawning, she rubbed the small of her back. "Time I got going again. But you're welcome to come along and keep me company. Truth is, I miss having you around."

"I miss you, too, Billie. But I *don't* miss this place. I belong home with Gabby. Not here!"

The declaration was far more emphatic than Thea had intended. Billie's dark eyes widened.

" 'Course you do, girlfriend. No one's suggesting any different, are they?"

"No. Sorry. I guess I'm just wound a little tight today."

"You *sure* you don't want to tell old Billie what's wrong? Everything feels better once you get it off your chest."

"I laid it all on you Saturday, Billie. Seeing Dr. Forman makes me edgy, that's all."

Billie nodded emphatically. "Join the club. That doc's like a nasty bug you can't slap away."

Thea declined the offer to accompany the nurse on her rounds. The hospital walls were closing in on her, cutting off her air.

At home, she could do her work, take care of her little girl, get on with her life. Here, she was reduced to patient five-three-nine-six-seven: a strange clinical case of electrical brainstorms and mindless mayhem.

The test results *had* to be negative. She had to be free of this place forever.

Slipping into her denim jacket, she quickly retraced her steps to the front hall. Outside, she drew a greedy breath and hurried across the parking lot toward the Volvo. The sky had darkened. She thought she felt a drop.

PERSONAL JOURNAL

2 October

The final time, I was eleven years old, and my body was undergoing a startling metamorphosis. Over the summer, I had grown half a foot and taken on the lean, leggy appearance of a newborn foal.

One day, while toweling off after a bath, I discovered that small bumps had risen on my chest, tender as bee stings. When I brought them to my mother's attention, seeking her assurance that I had not contracted a serious malady, she somberly reported that I would soon *become a woman*. By her grave description, the process would involve pain and bleeding and the need for embarrassing devices of the sort she kept hidden behind the spare toilet tissue under the bathroom sink.

In my juvenile explorations, I had come upon these secret contraptions: thick scented hammocks and slim cardboard torpedoes stuck on strings. As she spoke, I tried to imagine placing such things near the intimate parts of my body, and I flushed with molten shame.

Boys would behave differently toward me, she cautioned. And I would need to be perpetually on my guard. Males had base and powerful instincts. They would take advantage of any girl who was soft or compliant or foolishly unaware.

I didn't tell her that I already knew. I feared she might demand to hear who'd taught me.

For days afterward, I lived in dread fear of my father. The change in me was bound to inflame him further. But when he finally came to my room one night and took me to the secret place, a startling thing occurred.

For a long time, he stared at me as if I were an alien being. Running his hand roughly over my chest, he felt the bee stings. Revulsion twisted his face. Pushing me off his lap, he ordered me out of his sight.

He never touched me again. I suspect he turned his heinous attentions toward my brother, who was two years older but still a child in form. My brother never dared speak of it. But the light in his eyes went out like a spent bulb, and he grew grim and silent.

My wounds were left to heal. I reveled in guilty relief. Gradually, layers of soothing distance swaddled the hideous memories. The pain dimmed to an occasional flicker. Eventually, I was able to wrap the ugliness in thick layers of denial and stash it in the deepest recesses of my mind.

That might have been the end of it. But my father continued to sow the seeds of his evil. His issue flourished like weeds, choking off my final chance for peace or love or happiness. Evil untamed multiplies with startling rapidity. I learned that well, though it was a lesson that came far too late for salvation.

The source, in all its forms, must be eradicated. The last, and most difficult, is yet to come.

Biederman was being annihilated by degrees. Yesterday it was bus safety; today, the message desk. Nowhere to go from here but potty patrol at the town park, or rabid dog registration.

Passerelli, who'd been temporarily reassigned to team with a rookie detective named Herb Sinkinson, empathized completely. "Message desk. Geez. Better you than me, Danny."

"Thanks, Vince. I feel much better knowing how deeply you care."

"Sorry. I didn't mean that the way it sounded. I just meant I'd *really* hate to be sitting at that desk all day answering phones. It'd probably bore me right to death."

"I understand, Vince. Each to his own. Personally, I've always fantasized about front desk duty."

"You're kidding."

"Would I kid about such a thing?"

"Then it works out great." Chuckling, Passerelli left Biederman at reception and went off in search of his interim partner.

The chair fronting the switchboard was a rickety number with an arthritic swivel base. The brown mock-leather upholstery had the look and consistency of beef jerky. Biederman donned earphones redolent of hair pomade and surveyed his command post.

Heavy duty.

For this entire ninety-two-hour day, he would serve as the department's primary link to the outside world. He would bear the sole responsibility for directing incoming complaints and fielding pleas for assistance. When the good citizens of Westport wanted to bitch about traffic tie-ups or protest the volume of their neighbors' stereos or domestic disputes, he would be the man to handle the call. Ditto when Kitty scaled a phone pole or Fido fled the yard. Biederman tried to absorb the full magnitude of his new responsibility. He found himself completely underwhelmed.

The switchboard was peppered with indicator lights and extension numbers. A cross-referenced personnel roster, sheathed in yellow plastic, dangled from the board by a frayed shoelace. Buck Delavan's direct line topped the list. Extension fifty-three. Biederman tried the two-digit combination. F-sharp followed by a resounding B-natural on the touch pad. Music to his ears.

A light flashed on the board. It was a woman calling to inquire about the status of a bridge construction project. Biederman rang it through to Delavan's line. Next, a little girl wanted to know if she could come by with samples of the wrapping paper her fifth grade class was selling to raise money for a trip to Mystic Seaport. Delavan again.

Three calls in a row reported a downed electrical wire on Long Lots Road. Biederman passed them all on to the inspector. He did the same with an inquiry about the state sales tax on interior design services and another about the possibility of hiring off-duty cops to monitor traffic flow at a yard sale. Delavan was the department's top detective, after all. Who was better qualified to unearth the answers to all these perplexing queries?

Biederman's shift commenced at nine. By nine-thirty, he'd gotten through to his boss but good. Delavan stormed into the lobby. He pounded his fat fist on the desk, sending a hill of message slips fluttering through the air.

"I am *not* amused, Biederman. Stop ringing my god-damned phone!"

"Sorry, Inspector. I guess I'm not very good at this."

"Then, get better! This is legitimate duty. You handle it properly or forfeit the day's pay."

Biederman kept his tone even. "With all due respect, Inspector, you're an asshole."

The inspector turned the color of a rare steak. "I'm not taking any more of your crap, Biederman. Consider yourself on probation as of right now. Another step out of line, you can turn in your badge."

For the rest of the morning, Biederman obeyed Delavan's edict. He directed the steady stream of incoming calls to P.R. and Dispatch and Human Relations and Internal Affairs. Westport was hardly a hotbed of criminal enterprise. The most serious reported offense was a complaint about the possible theft of an evening purse and two boxes of spaghetti from a house on Old Road. The babysitter was suspected, though it might have been the window washer or the painter or the laundress or the cook.

"The purse wasn't new, but there's a sentimental attachment," the caller insisted.

Personally, Biederman would have waxed more sentimental about the noodles, but he duly noted the pertinent information and promised to send out the first available car.

At noon, he was spelled for a half-hour break by a young dispatcher named A.J. Tesler. Biederman used the time to pace the relative tranquility of the parking lot. Under the best of circumstances, he was not a phone enthusiast. After three hours of incessant calls, bells were jingling in his head, his ear felt chafed, and his jaw was stiffening with charley horse.

Perils of police work.

Armed with a can of Coke and a Snickers bar,

Biederman resumed his post at twelve-thirty. The afternoon passed with excruciating slowness. During the lulls, Biederman amused himself by picking the lint out of his pockets and rearranging his credit cards in order of size of debt.

By four, he'd contracted a serious case of prison fever. The earphones were a ball and chain, the desk a rank stone dungeon. Biederman couldn't bear to sit still any longer, but any shift in position sent the chair into perilous spasm. Worse, a particularly vicious crack in the seat upholstery had opened and taken to nipping at his rear end and family jewels. Every so often, in the midst of a conversation with one of Westport's concerned citizens, Biederman's voice jumped an involuntary octave.

"Yes, ma'am. We'll send someone RIGHT out."

Still another hour to go. The inspector's punishment was beginning to have the desired effect. Between calls, Biederman pondered his sins against power and authority. He'd directly defied his boss's irrational orders. He'd refused to fabricate a case against Thea Harper. He'd had the audacity to concern himself with something as trivial as the woman's civil rights.

Still, he held the unwavering conviction that Thea deserved his support and, if necessary, his protection. If he had to provide it from exile, so be it. Delavan might own his professional future and his job security, but Biederman wasn't trading those for his self-respect.

As the clock edged toward four-thirty, he focused on his upcoming appointment at the FBI field office. Finally, he would have a chance to inspect the records in the Gallatin case. Somewhere in the mountain of reports and other documents, there had to be overlooked proof of Thea Harper's innocence. If he knew anything about human nature, that woman was *not* a murderer.

Thinking of Thea, his tension eased. He pictured her gold-flecked eyes and the way the light played on her hair. He thought of her lovely body and the way she moved with fluid grace and dignity.

Another call came in. Tugged from his reverie, Biederman answered. An outraged man had damaged the mag wheel on his Porsche in a North Street pothole. The city was responsible, he railed. He would sue. He would get his influential friends to write nasty letters and articles in prestige publications. He would see to it that everyone responsible got fired.

Nothing like a little hysterical overreaction to cut the monotony. Cheerfully, Biederman noted the necessary details and referred the apoplectic caller to the city engineer. Only fifteen minutes to go.

Passerelli and Sinkinson came strolling in at ten to five. Sinkinson headed to the locker room. Vince paused at the desk.

"How's it going, Danny? You have a good day?"

"Fine, Vince. You?"

"Great. Herb and I finally dug up the banking records on that embezzlement suspect in the Hawkins case. He made a deposit for every one of the company's withdrawals. The dates and times match perfectly. Can you imagine a neater collar?"

Biederman forced a smile. That was *his* case. He'd been working it for three weeks, and now Vince and Sinkinson would share the credit. "That's nice for you, Vince."

"Thanks. Listen, Danny. I got to run. Herb's coming over for dinner. Gina's making chicken cacciatore. You're welcome to join us."

Gina's chicken was truly foul. Delicate chunks of library paste in a zesty salmonella sauce.

"Thanks anyway, Vince. I'm busy tonight. See you tomorrow."

Another incoming call. Biederman plugged the flashing line.

"Westport police. How may I help you?"

"This is Detective Ray Edwards calling from Bedford, New York. I need to speak to someone in Homicide."

The tone read serious. "This is Detective Dan Biederman. Go ahead."

There was a pause. Biederman supposed Edwards was wondering what a homicide dick was doing on the switchboard. Good question.

"All right, Detective. I've been working the Brandon Lee Payton case."

"The actor?"

"Right. The press has really been crawling up our butts on this one. We've put half the county on it, and so far, nothing solid. But a few minutes ago, a peculiar call came in from a woman posing as a reporter. She wanted to know the status of the case. Did we have any suspects? That sort of thing. We have reason to believe the perp is female, and this call set off alarm bells, so we put a trace on it. Turns out it came from a Westport exchange."

By the book, Biederman knew the matter should be patched through to Delavan. But that would contradict the inspector's strict orders that he not be disturbed by any more calls. Anyway, Biederman was way too curious to let this one go.

"What's the number? I'm about through here. I'll be glad to check it out for you."

"Thanks. Sooner the better. We can't waste any time playing jurisdiction games. If she's the one, we don't want to give her any running time."

Biederman promised to get back to the Bedford squad as soon as possible. He copied the anonymous caller's phone number on a message slip and hung up uneasy. The number was familiar. Too familiar. Checking the reverse directory, Biederman's apprehension turned to alarm.

A fresh light winked on the switchboard. Setting the earphones back in place, Biederman plugged in the matching lead and answered the call.

CHAPTER THIRTY-THREE

Why was her mother being so impossible? When Gabby came in from the bus, Mommy was in the living room, hugging the old picture album and staring at the wall. Her face was sweaty pale, her eyes distant.

When Gabby asked, Mommy swore she wasn't sick or anything. But she didn't do any of the normal stuff. She didn't offer Gabby a snack or ask about how her day had gone at school. Mom had acted a million miles away, as if someone had stolen her insides and shipped them off to Tahiti.

Worse, she'd refused to change out of her ratty blouse and jeans or fix her hair for Mr. Perry's visit, even though it was all gooey on the sides and tangled.

After the teacher showed up at four, Mommy had barely said hello before making some lame excuse about needing to work and heading outside to her studio. Ever since, Gabby had been keeping an eye on the door, expecting Mom to reappear at any second. But it was after five already and still no sign of her.

Mr. Perry eyed his watch. "Good work, Gabby. I think you've done enough for today."

"No, really. The story's nearly done. Please can't you stay until I finish it?"

She simply couldn't let him go before Mommy came back inside. Sooner or later, she'd have to leave her dumb studio and do something about dinner.

Gabby feared that the teacher was about to refuse, but instead, he asked a question about the story.

"Okay. What does Eleanor do after she finds out her

friend Connie is planning to jump into the Long Island Sound and drown herself?"

Gabby frowned. This was the part where she kept getting stuck. How did you stop a person from hurting herself?

"What if she tells the police, and they go to the beach and stop Connie from jumping?"

"That's one possibility. But how would the police be able to watch every part of the beach all the time?"

"Well. What if Eleanor finds out when and where Connie expects to drown, so she can tell the police?"

Mr. Perry nodded. "That's fine if Connie's willing to confide all that to Eleanor."

"Well, they *are* best friends." Gabby never kept secrets from Opal or Jazzy, except for the time Caity Cohane said the twins were stuck-up. Gabby didn't want to hurt their feelings by repeating it to them.

Gabby leaned over the lined tablet. She clutched the pencil hard.

Connie said she was going to drown herself at Compo Beach at five o'clock on Saturday. Eleanor called the police station and asked them to stop her.

"Nice job, author. Sounds like we're getting to the conclusion," Mr. Perry said.

Not before her mother showed up. "No, wait. I have to *revise* that."

Mr. Perry had taught her the word today. Serious writers *revise* all the time, he said. That way, the work keeps getting better and better.

"What you have sounds fine to me."

"No. It's not right. I don't think Eleanor would call the police and rat on her best friend. She wouldn't want Connie to get in trouble or anything."

"What would she do instead?"

Gabby sensed that the teacher was running out of

patience. His voice was pinched, and there was a hard
set to his mouth. But Mommy couldn't be much longer.

"What do *you* think she'd do, Mr. Perry?"

"This is your story, Gabby. You have to figure out
the ending by yourself."

"Oh, I will. But I don't know that much about people killing themselves." She wondered if all of them had
death rooms and wormy scars around their wrists and
said weird things like Dylan Connable.

He smiled. "If a writer doesn't know, she has to do
research." Catching Gabby's puzzlement, he added,
"That means you have to look it up in the library or
talk to an expert and find out the answers. There's a suicide prevention hot line right here in town. I'll bet if
you called, they could give you some suggestions and
maybe send you a brochure."

"Research and revise," she said, savoring the words.
Mr. Perry's assignments were very grown-up, almost
like the ones Amber got to do in high school. "Okay.
I'll try them now."

"You do that, and I'll see you tomorrow." Mr. Perry
was rising from his chair, taking out his car keys.

"No, wait. Maybe they can tell me the answer on the
phone, and then we can finish the story—"

"We'll finish next time, Gabby. I'll call and see
what's a good day for your mom."

He was putting on his sports jacket now. Gabby
wanted to tug his arm out of the sleeve.

"No, really, Mr. Perry. I just *have* to finish this story
today. You know what? I bet Mommy would love it if
you'd stay for dinner. I'll go ask."

Ignoring his protests, she raced out of the kitchen
and rushed into the studio without knocking. There
were strict rules against bothering Mommy while she
worked. Unless Gabby was sick or hurt or the house
was on fire, she was not allowed to barge in on Mommy

in the studio. Painting took serious concentration. An unexpected interruption could cause Mommy's brush to slip and ruin the whole canvas. But as far as Gabby was concerned, this was an emergency.

Her mother was on the phone. A Sophie picture was propped on the easel. It showed the part of the book when the other kids warn Sophie that weird Willy Dylan is a troublemaker and advise her to ban him from the ice cream store. To Gabby, the painting looked finished and dry. So why was Mommy still hanging around out here instead of coming in to visit with the teacher?

Muffling the receiver with her hand, her mother scowled. "What is it, Gabby?"

"Can Mr. Perry stay for dinner?"

"Tonight's not good. Another time."

"Please, *please!*"

"I said no, Gabby. Now please go. You know better than to come in here while I'm working."

"But you're not. You're just talking on the dumb phone."

"I asked you to leave."

The voice was low but packed with anger. Gabby knew she was stepping into serious trouble, but she couldn't stop herself. "Why are you being so mean to Mr. Perry? He took us out to eat and got me the book and the panda and everything."

"I'm busy now. We'll talk about this later."

"No, Mommy, *now*! Mr. Perry is leaving. You have to come in and ask him to stay for dinner."

"You know the rules, Gabby. We can discuss this after I'm finished here."

Her mother pressed the phone to her ear and started talking again. It was as if Gabby were invisible.

"Yes. I'm working on an article, and I wanted to know the status of the Gaithwaite case. There's no one

I can talk to now? All right. I'll call back after nine tomorrow. How do you spell his name?"

Gabby was a trapped head of steam. As soon as the receiver hit the cradle, she grabbed her mother by the hand and all but dragged her into the house.

"I told you, another time, Gabby. I'm not up for dinner company tonight."

"Just *ask* him. We can order in Chinese or something."

But the kitchen was deserted. Mr. Perry had left a note on the counter.

Dear Gabby, Had to run. See you tomorrow in class. M.P.

Tears pooled in Gabby's eyes. "Now, it'll never work. He probably thinks you hate him."

"Now *what* will never work? What are you talking about?"

"You and Mr. Perry. He really liked you, Mommy. I could tell."

Her mother's angry face melted into a smile. "Sorry to disappoint you, sweetie. But there's nothing between me and Mr. Perry. He's interested in helping you with your writing. That's all."

"That's not true. He looked at you like Miss Piggy did when she fell in love with Kermit in *The Muppet Movie.* I saw, Mommy. Honest. Call and ask him to come back. Please!"

Instead, her mother opened the refrigerator door and peered inside. "What do you feel like for dinner, Gabs? Chicken or pasta?"

"Mommy, I *mean* it!"

The smile evaporated. "Sit, sweetie. Let me try to explain."

It was the same story Gabby had heard dozens of times, the one about how Mom was still in love with Daddy, even though he wasn't alive anymore. Mom

claimed she wasn't interested in having a new boyfriend. She was happy with things the way they were.

"You and me are all I need for right now, Gabby. Anyhow, you can't push those things. When it's right, they
just happen."

"Then, how do you know it won't just happen with
you and Mr. Perry?"

"I don't think so, sweetie."

"But you're not absolutely, completely, totally,
without-a-doubt positive. Right?"

"Not to that degree. No."

"Good. Can he come to dinner tomorrow night?"

She sighed. "I told you, I'm really not up for company."

"Please, Mommy. He was so nice to us."

Her mother was bending. Gabby knew the signs.

"I'll set the table and do the dishes and everything.
I'll even cook the salad."

This time, the sigh was filled with sweet surrender.
"All right. You can ask if he's free. But no pushing."

Gabby held up three fingers. "Triple-swear."

Reveling in her victory, Gabby sprinted upstairs to
wash for dinner. Afterward, she would call Amber and
seek her advice. Boys went nuts over Amber. Zillions of
high school guys and even some college ones were forever calling and coming over and asking for dates. Mr.
Millport treated most of them like mosquitoes, but
they simply took their swats and kept coming back for
more.

Amber had the knack, no question. She'd know exactly how to make things "just happen" between Mom
and Mr. Perry. Maybe there was a magic potion or some
kind of love medicine Gabby could sprinkle on their
food.

Delighted with that possibility, Gabby made a mental list of all the things she had to do. First, she'd con-

sult with Amber. Then, she'd call the suicide prevention hot line and ask them how to keep a friend from killing himself. She'd pretend she only needed to know for the story she was writing, but she was sure she'd learn something she could use to help Dylan.

So much to do. Before bed, she had to pick out an outfit for tomorrow and make a dinner invitation for Mr. Perry. She decided she'd draw a picture of Perry the panda on the cover. Also, she had to have a serious talk with her mother about the menu and what she ought to wear. After the way Mom had looked and acted this afternoon, tomorrow night's dinner had to be *extra* special.

Rinsing her hands, Gabby scowled at her own uncertain expression in the mirror.

"I don't care what anyone says," she told her reflection. "Mom and Mr. Perry can still fall in love."

Her stomach rumbled. Lunch was so long ago, Gabby could barely remember what she'd eaten. Whatever they were having for dinner, she hoped it would be ready soon.

Gabby raced down the stairs, planning to grab something to snack on in the meantime. But she was stalled by a knock at the door. Mr. Perry must have changed his mind or forgotten something and come back. Excellent!

The door opened with a rush of wind and a startling spatter of raindrops. On the front stoop stood a man so tall Gabby barely reached his waistline. She couldn't remember ever seeing someone so big, not counting the old King Kong movie she and the twins had watched on cable.

But when he said his name and asked to see her mother, Gabby realized that she'd seen this particular giant before. And like the last time, she knew he spelled serious trouble.

CHAPTER THIRTY-FOUR

Driving over from the station house, Biederman had rehearsed a dozen alternative approaches. He didn't want to come on like a sledgehammer, but there seemed no delicate way to phrase this. What the hell was he supposed to say?

So, I hear you called the Bedford police about Brandon Lee Payton's murder. What's the deal, Ms. Harper? You a Payton fan? Plain old morbid curiosity? Or could your interest be more personal?

Before he could agonize further, however, the little girl returned to the foyer with her mother in tow. Even scowling and disheveled, Thea Harper made his heart dance the merengue.

"Sorry to bother you," he began awkwardly. He was acutely conscious of the child's bright eyes on him. "But there's something we have to discuss."

She seemed to grasp his predicament immediately. She turned to the child. "Take something to eat and wait in your room for a few minutes, will you, sweetie?"

The little girl paled. "What's wrong, Mommy? Why's the policeman here? Are they taking you away again?" The fear in her eyes was enough to break Biederman's heart. "Please don't take my mommy away!"

"There's nothing to worry about, Gabby," Thea assured her calmly. "Detective Biederman just stopped by to discuss a painting."

"Honest?"

Biederman could only nod. The lie caught in his throat along with the rest of the situation.

Forgoing the snack, Gabby climbed the stairs. Every few steps, the little girl paused to peer down at them warily. Thea waited until the child's bedroom door smacked shut. Then she led Biederman inside and motioned him toward the couch. Her face was pale.

"What's the problem, Sergeant?"

"You called the Bedford police to inquire about the Brandon Lee Payton homicide. They traced the call. They've asked me to check you out."

The barest flicker of surprise crossed her face.

"They didn't think you were a reporter, Ms. Harper. They're looking for a female suspect."

"What exactly do you want to know, Sergeant?"

"Why you called, for starters. What's your interest in Payton's murder?"

Her gaze was level. "I know it must look strange, but after all that's happened, I find I pay much more attention to such things."

"That's understandable. May I ask where you were the day Payton was killed?"

"That was last Thursday, right?"

"Yes."

She hesitated no more than the expected beat. "Right here. I did some painting. Spent time with Gabby. The usual."

"Wasn't your daughter in school?"

"During the day, yes. But she gets home a little after three."

Biederman figured the child must have caught the elementary school bus at 8:00 A.M., give or take. That left Thea on her own for seven hours.

"You didn't go out at all?"

"I did have an early appointment with my psychiatrist."

He wrote down the doctor's name. The visit accounted for one floating hour.

"Afterward you came directly home?"

"I might have run an errand or two. I don't remember exactly."

"The bank? Cleaner? Supermarket?" he prompted.

"I probably stopped at the Italian grocery on Main Street. And maybe at Baskin-Robbins."

That accounted for another hour, tops, even if she'd taken her sweet time to stop and smell the rigatoni. "Anywhere else?"

"I may have browsed awhile at a shop or two on the Post Road. I wanted to get something for Gabby."

"And did you?"

She shrugged. "I considered a few things. Couldn't make up my mind."

Biederman noted the store names. Another hour down, four to go. Unfortunately, those were the crucial ones. The M.E. had fixed the time of the attack that killed Brandon Lee Payton somewhere between 12:30 and 3:00 P.M.

"Is there anyone who can verify the time you spent at home? A neighbor? A workman, maybe?"

"Not that I know of. I was alone in my studio."

"And you were still here when Gabby got home?"

"Yes. I make it a point to be. I don't like her coming into an empty house."

Biederman reviewed the particulars. All the bases had been covered, though in no way well enough to prevent a possible slide. But if he didn't present the Bedford cops with a quick conclusion, Thea would be subjected to a lot of hard, messy scrutiny.

Biederman sensed her nervousness. But who wouldn't be under the circumstances? The woman makes one unfortunate phone call, and the next thing she knows, Big Brother comes barging in firing a round of questions. He took a hard look at her eyes. There was intelligence in them, softness, a hint of sorrow, and maybe a trace of fear. But murder was nowhere in the picture.

Thea Harper had not whacked Brandon Lee Payton. Biederman would stake his life on it. In fact, that's exactly what he was about to do.

He got to his feet. "I guess that covers it, then. I'll tell the Bedford police this one was a false alarm. Sorry to bother you."

"That's all right. You're just doing your job."

That was either the understatement or the overstatement of the year. Either way, the future of his so-called job had never been in more serious jeopardy.

Biederman hesitated at the door, hating to leave.

"Has everything been going all right for you, Ms. Harper?"

"Fine." Her voice was firm. She was clearly anxious to have this unsettling visit concluded.

"The offer still stands. If you need anything, anything at all, just holler."

"Thanks. I will." Her tone did not soften.

"Take care, then."

"You, too, Sergeant."

The rain had picked up. Head ducked against the damp slap of the wind, Biederman ran to his car. He headed directly to a gas station pay phone on the Post Road and put in a call to Detective Ray Edwards at police headquarters in Bedford.

"I just spoke with your phony reporter, Edwards. Turns out to be a curious amateur, that's all."

"You sure?"

"Positive. Her alibi for the time of the murder checks out. She's not your suspect."

"Damn. I was hoping we were finally on to something."

"Sorry," Biederman said. "Let me know if there's anything else I can do for you."

"Sure, Detective. Thanks for the assist."

He still had plenty of time to kill before his appointment at the FBI field office in New Haven. Biederman stopped in front of a nearby deli.

Scanning the sandwich list, he discovered that his appetite had deserted him along with his senses. But he tended to think more clearly on a full stomach. So he ordered a pastrami on rye with a side of slaw, a potato knish, and a celery tonic. His mother's notion of brain food.

He ate in the car to the sweeping rhythm of the wipers. While he chewed, he thought about trying to forge a fresh career if this thing went sour or caught the inspector's eye. After Buck Delavan finished with him, he figured he wouldn't be in shape to do much. Maybe he'd see if any of the neighboring communities had an opening for a speed bump.

After he'd choked down as much of the food as possible, he headed toward the turnpike. Traffic was light but skittish. The rain was falling in driving sheets, reducing the visibility to near zero. Low-lying sections of the road were flooded and swagged with fog.

Biederman slapped on his portable cap light and worked his siren, clearing an instant path. Twenty minutes later, with his brakes soaked to a perfect *al dente*, he was off the pike at New Haven and through the weave of streets to the federal building.

As promised, Special Agent Warren Bell was waiting for him on the otherwise deserted fifth floor. Penny Proctor's description of her betrothed didn't begin to do the guy justice. Ms. Proctor had termed him fit and attractive. A bomb shelter with ears said it better. Bell's neck was a hitching post, his arms a tower of bowling balls. You could have launched an Olympic ski jump off the guy's abdomen. Even his teeth looked strong.

"You Biederman?" His voice wasn't exactly a bark, but close enough.

"Yes. You must be Warren Bell."

"Guilty. Penny said you wanted a look at the Gallatin file. I've got it in my office."

Biederman followed the agent to a small windowless room in the rear. The Gallatin case records, six broad cartons' worth, were stacked beside the gunmetal desk. Bell glanced at the clock.

"I can only give you two hours. There's a security check at around eleven. We'll have to be gone by then."

"That's great, Agent Bell. I really appreciate this."

"Anything for Penny." The mushy smile gave the big guy the look of a lovesick ape.

Bell posted himself beside the door. Biederman would have preferred to work in private, but he wasn't about to ask the guy to relocate. This was his office, after all. If he wanted to park his tank here, that was his privilege.

Shaking off the self-conscious feeling, Biederman started leafing through the records. There were the usual technical reports: crime scene analysis, autopsy findings, latent prints and trace evidence summaries. Two of the boxes contained transcripts of witness interviews. Everyone with any conceivable knowledge of the crime had been thoroughly questioned: Thea Harper's friends, family, and neighbors; Senator Gallatin's relatives, staff, and social acquaintances. Another carton was filled with evidence analysis by hired experts for the prosecution and defense.

Time was flying. Returning to the first box, Biederman skimmed the coroner's report. Much of the medical minutiae made his eyes glaze over. There were pages and pages of mind-numbing data, including toxicology findings, microscopic and spectrographic analyses of tissues and fluids, internal organ status, rigor and livor of the mortis, and so forth.

To Biederman, the M.E.'s description of the senator's injuries was both more interesting and much harder to swallow. How could a slender, delicate-framed woman like Thea Harper be responsible for the fractured skull, the three shattered cervical vertebrae, the broken femur, the horrifying array of lacerations and contusions, the multiple facial fractures that had caused the left half of Simon Gallatin's face to crumple like a used paper bag?

Biederman could not put the woman and the crime in the same frame. The picture refused to gel, even though he had personally arrived at the murder scene moments after the squeal hit the police band. Biederman had witnessed the damning tableau with his own eyes. Thea Harper had been caught, quite literally, red-handed.

And the evidence techs had found plenty to bolster the prosecution's case. A clear set of Thea Harper's prints, and only hers, had been lifted from the trophy used to bludgeon Gallatin. Microscopic and DNA analyses had concluded that a hair found embedded in one of the corpse's wounds was hers. There were no unidentified latents or other signs of anyone else having been on the premises that evening, except the suspect's eight-year-old daughter.

It was a classic open-and-shut case, the kind that played well in one-hour TV format, but almost never happened in life.

The quantity of material was staggering. With almost an hour down, Biederman was still plodding through the first carton. He cast a longing eye at the copier in the hall, a move not lost on Special Agent Bell.

"Sorry, Detective. It'd be my ass if I let you take those records out."

"Sure. I understand."

Speeding his pace, Biederman skimmed the witness reports. One of Thea Harper's neighbors had seen the senator's car arrive close to seven. Another claimed that the studio lights had been off when she glanced that way at about six. Several attested to Thea's conscientious parenting, pleasant nature, and good character. It was a pity, several mentioned, that her husband had died so young.

The crime scene photo riveted Biederman. The techs had taken countless close-ups of the corpse and Thea's bloodied hands and gore-streaked clothing. Staring hard, Biederman sensed something out of place. But the clock was running out. No time to dwell on it now.

Glancing up, he noticed that Special Agent Bell had vanished. No trace of him down the hall. Across from the office, the copier had been fired up and left running. The ready light was winking coquettishly.

Twenty minutes to eleven. Biederman grabbed the M.E.'s report, the crime scene summary and photos, several of the expert interviews, Thea's interrogation report, and prime segments of the trial transcript. Quickly, he fed the salient data into the yawning mouth of the copy machine. By the time Agent Bell noisily reappeared at a couple of minutes to eleven, Biederman had made a fat stack of copies and tucked them discreetly under his Windbreaker.

Bell eyed the pregnant bulge. He nodded approvingly. "Time to go, Detective."

"Thanks, Agent Bell. I'm grateful to you."

"For what?"

"Nothing."

"Exactly."

Biederman followed the incredible hulk off the floor and out into the rainswept night. With a silent nod in the parking lot, they went their separate ways.

T H E
FOURTH

CHAPTER THIRTY-FIVE

"Mommy! Daddy!"

Her throat was screamed raw. Lindy Zesch howled her frustration and pummeled the mattress with her fists.

She wanted her daddy to come back and read another story. She wanted Mommy sitting on the rocker beside her bed. She hated being alone like this. After Mommy and Daddy left the room, the night-light got so scary. The mean plastic clown kept making that bad face at her, flashing that wicked grin as if it couldn't wait for her to fall asleep. As soon as she did, Lindy knew that awful clown was planning to jump out of the wall and burn her all over.

Burning worried her all the time now. Lindy shrank in terror if someone lit a match or smoked a cigarette. She couldn't stand to be anywhere near the stove. Even when the burners were off, the stumpy flames that blazed deep in the oven's belly like a row of fiery teeth terrified her. Even the teeniest baby fire could keep growing and growing until it was big and strong enough to eat an entire house.

She had seen it happen.

Mommy and Daddy never talked about their old house anymore, but Lindy remembered everything about it. Her room there had a strip of rainbow wallpaper and a fat ruffly quilt with puffy rainbows sewn across the top. Sunshine paint colored the walls, and the ceiling was the blue of a clear summer sky.

Squeezing her eyes shut, Lindy pictured her old room and smiled. Best room ever.

Every day, while Lindy was at kindergarten at the
Montessori Center, all her favorite dollies used to sit on
the bed and wait for her to come home. As soon as she
finished her lunch, Lindy would race upstairs, close the
door, and tell Mollie and Druselda and Winnie and Ve-
ronica everything that had happened to her during the
day. The dollies would laugh when she'd learned a new
joke and get angry when Lindy reported that one of the
other kids had pushed her or called her a bad word or
refused to share with her in the dress-up corner.

The new dolls Mommy had bought for her after the
fire were no good at all. They looked exactly like the
old ones, but they refused to pay attention when Lindy
talked. They didn't laugh or ask questions or anything.
The dumb dolls just sat there staring at the wall.

Fueled by fresh anger, Lindy grabbed Baby Sweet
Stuff by the ankle and flung her to the floor. The doll's
patent leather strap shoe came off and her lacy bonnet
went flying, but Lindy didn't care.

"Please, Daddy! Mommy! I'm hungry! Can't I have
a cookie? Just *one*?"

Lindy quieted to listen for a response. She couldn't
hear any approaching footsteps. But her parents had to
come. They had to *save* her.

"My tummy hurts," she wailed. "I have to go to the
bathroom!"

How could she make them listen? Lindy kept telling
them about the clown light, warning that it was going
to jump out of the wall and set the house on fire. But
they refused to believe her.

Mommy and Daddy kept insisting that the house
they used to live in was very, very old, older than
Grammy Ellen even, and had faulty wiring. They said
this new house was built in a special way, so it could
never, ever burn down.

But Lindy knew better. Right after they moved in,

Daddy had set fire to some construction junk in the fireplace and the stuff had gone up like crazy. The fierce blaze had so terrified Lindy, they'd had to take her over to stay at Grammy Gwen's house until the fire was finished burning.

"Please!"

"Please!"

All the crying had made her hot and sweaty. Stopping to catch her breath, she remembered what Grammy Gwen had told her that time.

When she was a little girl, just Lindy's age (which was really, really hard to imagine), Grammy Gwen had been terrified of ghosts. Grammy's mother, Greatgrammy Ada, who was dead now, had shown Gwen a special magic dance she could do to scare the ghosts away.

Grammy Gwen taught Lindy the special steps, which were very complicated. You had to put one foot exactly in front of the other, kick twice, and then do the same thing with the other foot. Next, you had to turn around and repeat the whole dance again facing backwards. Grammy swore that it worked for ghosts, and she promised it would have the same effect on burny things.

Lindy liked the idea of scaring away the mean spirit inside the clown light. She wanted to get even with all the bad burn devils who had lit up her old house and gobbled up her dolls and gotten her stuck in her chokey smoke-filled room until the fireman came and carried her down his ladder.

She stole soundlessly out of bed so Mommy and Daddy wouldn't catch her and get mad. Concentrating hard, she worked the dance steps. The carpet tickled her soles as she very, very carefully positioned her feet, did the kicks, and turned to perform the steps again facing the wall. Lindy aimed her eyes toward the ceiling,

where she couldn't see the clown light. Just thinking of
that nasty thing made her shiver.

Had she done the second kick in the second se-
quence? Grammy Gwen's dance had to be followed exactly perfect if she wanted to destroy the clown's power.

Pivoting back toward the window wall, Lindy started
the dance all over again. That was when she saw the
lady.

"Who—?"

Her question was cut off as the stranger grabbed her
hard by the arms and clamped a hand over her mouth.
Lindy couldn't speak. She could hardly breathe.

The woman's arms were strong as the monkey bars at
the playground. A furious growl rumbled deep in her
chest. With one arm, she held Lindy tight against her
body while she used the other to search for something
in her giant purse.

Horrified, Lindy watched as the lady took out a slim
yellow can, flipped off the tiny cap, then squeezed a
stream of liquid onto her mattress. No! She didn't want
Mommy and Daddy to think she'd wet her bed like a
little baby. Flailing in the stranger's grasp, Lindy struggled to protest.

The can was empty now. When the woman pressed
it again, nothing emerged but a burpy sound. A strong
stink rising from the mattress made Lindy's eyes water.
She could barely see what the woman was holding after
she dipped into her purse again. Blinking away the
tears, Lindy tried hard to figure out what it was. Some
fancy silver thing with a little black wheel on top.

An instant later, the stranger ran a thumb over the
wheel. With a sharp scratching sound, the tube spat a
lick of yellow flame. In terror, Lindy thrashed and
kicked. A strangled scream stabbed at her throat.

The lady giggled viciously, multiplying Lindy's

panic. She tried to get away, to shout for help, but she was trapped in the stranger's powerful grasp.

Reaching out, the woman held the burning tube toward Lindy's bed. The sheets caught in a rush. Fat fire devils jumped and danced across the mattress. The blankets went up with a pop. The dolls on the bed started melting in the heat.

Frozen with fear, Lindy shut her eyes. The fiery heat rose around her; the fire's fierce light penetrated her clenched lids. Inside, she was a mass of screeching horror.

No! Stop! Let me go! I can't stand it!

But the stranger's hand trapped the screams inside. Only the tiniest whimpers escaped. Lindy gasped for air. Her breaths came in rapid pulses. The fire, the terror was making her dizzy. Opening her eyes, she found the room spinning in crazy circles.

Then, she felt the lady's lips on the back of her neck. It was a tickly kiss, the kind her Daddy sometimes gave her after he tucked her in. Maybe she'd put the fire out next. With all her might, Lindy prayed for the bed to stop burning and the stranger to let her go.

But the flames kept growing, and the lady started pressing her toward them. Lindy felt the searing bite of the leaping flames. The burny monsters were close enough to lick her hair, her forehead.

Drawing a breath, Lindy made a final attempt to scream and warn her parents. But before she could make another sound, she was dragged beneath the fear.

CHAPTER
THIRTY-SIX

Biederman awoke with a start. He'd fallen asleep with his head lolling on a grisly close-up of Simon Gallatin's mutilated remains.

Appropriately, he'd been dreaming about a singles dance for the recently deceased (ages twenty-five to forty). Biederman had attended at his mother's insistence, only to discover that the bandleader was Lawrence Welk. The refreshments were liverwurst sandwiches and a punch bowl full of bile-colored Kool-Aid. And worse, all the female stiffs were literal dead ringers for his ex-wife, Elaine.

He glanced at his watch. Three A.M. Since his visit to the Fibbie field office, his mind had been circling non-stop over the details of the Gallatin homicide. To divine the holes and glitches in the case, he needed to develop a clear mental picture of the events surrounding the senator's murder.

Rubbing his bleary eyes, Biederman turned to the summary of Thea Harper's initial jailhouse interrogation. Unable to recall or justify her actions, the woman had been of precious little use in her own defense.

She remembered working on a painting in her studio late that afternoon. After an unaccountable hole of over three hours, she'd been tugged back to reality by her daughter's wrenching screams. Tracing the sounds to the den, Thea had discovered the child standing next to Simon Gallatin's bloodied corpse. After dialing nine-one-one, she'd herded her hysterical little girl into the next room. Huddled together like shipwreck survivors on a life raft, the two had waited in stunned silence for help to arrive.

By her own self-incriminating admission, Thea had not touched anything in the den after racing in from the studio. Simon Gallatin was obviously dead, so she'd made no attempts to stanch his bleeding or resuscitate him. She had noticed the battered, gore-spattered trophy beside the body, but she stubbornly insisted she had not handled the murder weapon. Instinct had pressed her to call Emergency and remove her daughter from the horrifying scene at once.

Which left their leading suspect with no explanation for the presence of the dead senator's blood on her skin and clothing. She'd offered no mitigating excuse for the violence, such as self-defense in response to a physical or sexual threat. In fact, from everything Biederman had read about the investigation and trial, the defendant had remained mystified about the whole grisly event, including the very fact of Simon Gallatin's presence in her house.

From the beginning, Thea had insisted that she and the senator had no plans to get together that evening. According to her unwavering testimony, Simon Gallatin never dropped by unexpectedly. His schedule was tight and rigorously maintained. There was no room for social spontaneity.

Examinations of Thea's personal diary and the calendar she kept on her desk confirmed that no appointment had been formally scheduled between her and Gallatin for the night of his murder. The senator's secretary found no record of such a proposed meeting either.

But a search of the phone company computer revealed that a forty-second call had been made from the Harper house to Gallatin's office at 5:36 that evening. The U.S. Attorney trying the case had neatly concluded that the defendant had phoned to lure the victim to her place. By the lawyer's reckoning, that brief call was sufficient evidence of premeditation.

Exhaustion fogged Biederman's brain. In dire need of a jump-start, he made himself a strawberry-slathered English muffin and some triple-strength instant coffee. The sugary jam and the first swig of mud got his motor running. By the third cup, his synapses were on world-record pace.

Fully wired, he turned to the trial transcript.

According to the prosecution's reconstruction of the homicide, Thea Harper had made the call and then headed upstairs to prepare for the senator's arrival. The bathtub was still damp and soap-streaked when the evidence techs inspected the house. A hair dryer and an array of makeup tubes littered the bathroom sink. A lacy black negligee had been laid out beside the pillow.

Gallatin's local staffers confirmed that the senator had left his Greenwich office at six-thirty. Given the light traffic and clear road conditions that night, he was presumed to have arrived at the Harper home at approximately 7:00 P.M. The M.E. set the probable time of death at somewhere between seven-fifteen and seven-forty-five, when the little Harper girl happened in from a neighbor's house and discovered the body.

What took place during the critical intervening thirty minutes was deemed self-evident by the assistant U. S. Attorney assigned to try the case. The defendant had obviously invited the victim in. She had then offered him the glass of wine that turned up in the dead man's stomach contents on autopsy.

According to an oenologist hired to testify for the government, the wine was the same moderately priced California merlot that was confiscated from the sideboard in the defendant's den. Given the amount missing from the bottle and the victim's low blood-alcohol level, the prosecution argued that Thea Harper had imbibed enough to send a highly susceptible woman of her height and weight into a drunken rage.

The Assistant U.S. Attorney had thoroughly milked that possibility during his summation. *The defendant consumed nearly three quarters of a bottle of wine, ladies and gentlemen. And then, full of liquid courage and blind fury, she brutally murdered this fine, talented young man who devoted his life to serving his country.*

No one had tested Thea Harper's blood-alcohol level at the time of the arrest. And Biederman cynically suspected that the omission had been deliberate. In court, unfounded theory was far more useful than contradicting fact.

At some point, Thea had left Simon Gallatin seated on the sofa in the den. According to the prosecution's version, she had then proceeded to the living room where a golf trophy won by her deceased husband occupied a prominent place on the mantelpiece.

Returning with the heavy statuette, she struck the senator on the skull. It was a blow sufficient to cause his death. But the defendant had relentlessly continued the vicious attack. She'd struck Simon Gallatin six more times before her savage wrath was sated.

Afterward, she'd returned to her studio, where she'd likely intended to change her soiled clothing and wash the senator's blood off her hands before attending to the disposal of the corpse.

But that plan was thwarted when her daughter returned from the neighbor's house earlier than expected. By the prosecution's reckoning, Gabby's arrival had forced Thea to concoct the preposterous tale of temporary amnesia.

The government's case was neat, tidy, and, as far as Biederman was concerned, completely incredible.

To be honest, he wasn't all that impressed either by the defense contention that Thea had committed the murder in a state of seizure-induced unconsciousness. Aside from one highly convincing lady shrink who'd deftly sold that version to the jury, Thea's attorney had offered nothing substantial to support the claim.

Several respected experts on epilepsy had testified for the prosecution that seizures did *not* cause violent behavior. One impassioned neurologist argued that attributing the Gallatin murder to a seizure could set back the cause of tolerance toward epileptics hundreds of years.

People with seizure disorders still suffered from damaging misconceptions and cruel discrimination, the neurologist explained. Epilepsy does not predispose a person to crime or antisocial behavior. Suggesting otherwise was an affront and injurious to people with the disease.

Staring at the photographs again, Biederman focused on Thea Harper's gentle features. Sensitive mouth. Guileless eyes. That woman could not have caused those massive injuries. No way. There had to be another explanation for Simon Gallatin's death, one that did not require a complete revision of the book on human nature.

With every fiber of his being, Biederman believed in Thea Harper's innocence. And he knew he would pay with every fiber of his being if his instincts turned out to be mistaken.

CHAPTER THIRTY-SEVEN

Frowning, Thea swiped a trace of pink over Sophie's cheekbones and darkened the serpent's extravagant eyebrows. She'd been working on this panel for hours, and Sophie still looked in desperate need of a vacation. Poor snake had no zest.

The same held for Thea. She felt logy and bleary-eyed. Last night, after turning in early and falling instantly unconscious, she'd awakened at one o'clock in the morning with a racing heart and a piercing headache. Unable to fall asleep again, she'd spent the rest of the night staring at the ceiling. When she wasn't worrying about the test results, she kept busy reviewing her growing litany of regrets.

She was sorry she'd ever caught the fancy of Simon Gallatin and his fancy friends. If they'd never met, her life, Gabby's, and most important, Simon's, might still be steeped in blessed normalcy.

She regretted leaving her parents' ranch and the precious obscurity one could only enjoy on several hundred acres of stubborn, unforgiving land. Growing up, she'd been chronically restless and eager to move on to keener, greener pastures. Now, she fervently longed for a way to recapture that silence and solitude.

If only she could shed twenty years and return to the comfort of her mother's protection. Add growing up to the list. Kids wouldn't be nearly so anxious to collect extra years if they fully grasped the potential consequences.

Who would have imagined that little Thea Sparks, bright, sensitive, artistic soul that she'd been, would someday find herself up to her ears in blind violence and vengeful wrath?

And dumb. "How could I have been stupid enough to call the police about that actor's murder?" she asked the snake.

Sophie maintained her noncommittal posture and a look of utter apathy.

"No more," Thea vowed with all the conviction her muddled mind could muster. "That's the last time you'll catch me getting in my own stupid way."

If the declaration impressed Sophie, the serpent kept it to herself.

"You'll see. From now on, I'm going to focus on Gabby and my painting and keeping my head on straight. No more runaway imagination, no more opening my big mouth."

You don't need to go out looking for trouble, Checker honey. Lord knows plenty will find you on its own.

With a sigh, Thea set down to work in earnest. This panel for the book, which depicted the outbreak of the fire in Sophie's store, began to take shape. Finally, proper alarm registered on the serpent's face. Thea filled the foreground with panicky, fleeing customers. A gaping crowd gathered on the street.

Still, something was missing. Stepping back to scrutinize the work, Thea decided to enhance the drama of the event by having the fire occur on the eve of the store's anniversary celebration. Certain that Gabby would approve, she festooned the shop with balloons and twisted streamers and added a costumed clown with a bright, bulbous nose to the mob crowding the exit.

As she painted, her attention kept straying to the phone. Why didn't Dr. Forman call? She'd had plenty of time to study the damned test results. Increasingly, Thea believed that at least part of the delay could be deliberate retribution for her decision to terminate therapy against doctor's orders. Or maybe the ice queen figured that driving people crazy was a clever way to drum up business.

Put it out of your mind, Thea. Don't let her get to you.

Once the Sophie panel was improved to her satisfaction, she decided to make the calls she'd been putting off for days. She had two lines, so Dr. Forman could get through if the woman was stricken by a rare humane impulse.

Thankfully, her agent was out. Thea left a message on Pru's answering machine. She said that while she appreciated the gallery's continued interest, she doubted she'd have the necessary new oils completed before late spring or early summer, minimum. Meantime, she'd nearly finished the illustrations for a children's book that Gabby had written. Thea believed the project had commercial merit, and she'd appreciate Pru's help in circulating the work to publishers.

The agent would probably erupt when she heard how Thea had been spending her time. But once the initial tantrum subsided, Pru's implacable hunting instincts would likely move her to pitch in on the Sophie effort.

The next call was to the ranch. Thea dialed the distant exchange and smiled, anticipating her mother's cheery greeting. But it was her father's shivery voice that came on the line.

"Hello, Dad."

"Who's this?"

"It's your daughter, Thea. Checker. Remember?" Her father's memory faded in and out like the reception on a cheap radio. In a way, the disability didn't seem so tragic to Thea. There were certain ugly events she'd be more than happy to forget. In fact, speaking to her father brought some of the worst of them flooding back.

"Checker? Sure, I remember. You making my lunch, Checker? Tuna sandwich be nice."

There was a clatter at the other end. A beat later, Thea's brother took over the conversation.

"Hey, Checker. What's up?"

"Nothing, Jimmy. What are you doing there?"

He hesitated. "—Just stopped by to see the folks. There's a cattle auction down at Miracle Reservoir this weekend. Good stock, from the look of things. Thought I'd pick up a couple of head."

"Can I speak to Mom?"

"She went to the market. I'll tell her you called. Okay?"

"Fine."

" 'Bye then."

Odd, Thea thought as she hung up. Idaho was a long way for Jimmy to travel for a cattle auction. Maybe he was looking for an excuse to stop in and check on the folks. Jimmy had always been a good son. Thoughtful.

Turning her thoughts back to Dr. Forman, Thea scowled at the silent phone. *Call already, damn it.*

She had a right to know what, if anything, the psychiatrist had found. Any kind of news would be better than this intolerable waiting.

She plucked the receiver from its cradle, hesitated a beat, then firmly set it down again. Calling was a bad idea. If she appeared too anxious, the shrink was bound to question why.

Forget it, Thea. A few more hours won't kill you.

Given the rate at which her anxiety was escalating, a few more hours might do precisely that. News about the unsolved Payton murder still dominated the daily headlines. Thea needed to hear that she was still in conscious control. She needed to know that she couldn't have had anything to do with that killing or the brutal slayings of that old couple in Bridgeport.

Dialing Dr. Forman's office number in Stamford, Thea vowed to sound calm and offhanded. It was perfectly reasonable for a patient to request test results. She would simply act as if Dr. Forman hadn't made it clear who was to initiate the contact.

After the third ring, Thea had the sinking sense that reaching the psychiatrist might not be as simple as she'd hoped. Another ring, and the tenor of the signal changed. The answering service picked up a beat later.

"Doctor's wire. How may I help you?"

"This is Thea Harper calling. I have to speak with Dr. Forman."

"Is this an emergency?"

Thea considered that the hand holding the phone had gone slippery with perspiration and replied, "You could say that."

"In that case, Dr. Boster is covering. He can be reached at nine-six-eight-three-three-four-seven."

"No. It has to be Dr. Forman."

The voice on the line assumed the patronizing lilt of a misguided kindergarten teacher. "Sorry. Dr. Forman is speaking at a symposium this morning, and she's tied up all afternoon."

"There must be some way you can get through to her. I only need a minute of her time to ask a question."

"I'm sure Dr. Boster will be able to assist you."

"No. It has to be Dr. Forman."

The lilt vanished. "Look, miss. You can*not* expect me to interrupt the doctor every time some patient calls with a problem. Dr. Forman happens to be a very busy, very important woman."

It took everything in Thea's power to keep her temper from grabbing the receiver. Frustration was a steamroller, stretching her words flat and hard. "When do you expect her to call in?"

"Sometime this afternoon at the earliest."

"Fine. When she does, kindly tell her that Thea Harper would greatly appreciate two minutes of her very precious, very important time."

Thea ached to pitch the phone through the window, but that wasn't likely to alleviate the situation. At least, not for long.

She had to lower the volume on her screaming anxieties. This was all a foolish overreaction. If there were anything really disturbing in the test results, Dr. Forman would certainly have called by now. The doctor might be a coldhearted control freak, but she was not about to jeopardize Thea's health, or her own precious professional reputation, by withholding crucial information.

It made much more sense to presume that everything was fine. Thea would simply have to cling to that comforting notion until she got some definite word. At least, she had to make the attempt.

Convinced that distraction was in order, she headed out for the Millports'. Caro's world was endlessly entertaining, and this visit proved no exception. Raleigh had entered a fresh developmental stage: search and destroy. While Thea watched in amusement, the toddler managed to develop and test a staggering array of original hypotheses. Would the umbrella from the hall stand fit in the baby's ear? Was it possible to climb from the end table to the mantelpiece and execute a swan dive onto the fireplace poker? How would the serving platter fare in a head-on collision with the crystal carafe?

Caro trailed a step behind her one-tot demolition squad, determined to anticipate and thwart the mayhem. With unwavering calm, she intercepted the platter as Raleigh was preparing it for lift-off.

"That plate's fine just the way it is, sugar. It won't work nearly so well in a million little pieces."

Baby Drake was teething, which prompted him to

alternate between furious crying fits and the frantic
gnawing of a crazed beaver. Caro hauled the child
around like a sack of grain, simultaneously attempting
to comfort him and keep the world safe from his kami-
kaze brother.

The woman was amazing. Absolutely nothing fazed
her. The baby stiffened in her grasp and started screaming, his face lobster red and contorted. "There, now,
sugar," Caro crooned. "We're going to have to teach you
some Lamaze techniques before your next molar comes
in. A nice cleansing breath and you'll feel much better."

Despite the good company and the extraordinary
floor show, Thea's eye kept straying to the clock. The
snit from the answering service had said Dr. Forman
wouldn't be calling in before noon. If the shrink
deigned to respond to Thea's urgent message anytime
thereafter, she wanted to be available.

Back home, she decided to start another Sophie illustration. Given Thea's current mind-set, the scene in
which the conflagration in the store threatens to destroy
the unconscious snake seemed a perfect one to tackle.
But her eyes kept straying to the phone. *Ring, damn it!*

Finally it did, startling her so badly, she knocked
over a coffee can full of turpentine. Eyes smarting, she
raced to grab the receiver before the machine picked up.
But instead of Dr. Forman, she was greeted by the
loathsome gravel of Harlan Vernon's voice.

"Thea Harper. Hal Vernon here. Listen, we've simply
got to talk. Get to know each other better. How about
I stop by for you at, say, seven, and take you to dinner."

To the cleaners was more like it. A single misplaced
word to that jackass, and Thea Harper, Westport's infamous Black Widow, would be squarely back in the sordid headlines.

"I have nothing to say to you, Mr. Vernon."

Thea hung up, but Vermin was not the type to take

that as an answer. The pushy troll called back seven
times in rapid succession. Clenching her teeth, Thea let
the machine deal with him. Meanwhile, she sopped up
the turpentine spill with paper towels and stuffed the
wadded mess into her trash can. Finished, she closed the
lid to contain the acrid fumes. One spark around those
gases and the studio could go up like Sophie's store.
With a guilty twinge, Thea realized she still hadn't
called to have the alarm and sprinkler system checked.
She'd take care of that first thing Monday.

Finally, the rodent wearied of his badgering and the
phone went still again.

Nearly two o'clock. Thea had spoken to the answering service four hours ago. By now, Dr. Forman could
have found a free second to return the damn call. Building a fresh head of steam, Thea tried the shrink's
number again. The same officious operator came on the
line.

"Dr. Forman's wire."

"This is Thea Harper. Has Dr. Forman picked up my
message?"

"Yes. She has."

"Do you have any idea when I might expect to hear
from her?"

"I'm sure she'll get to you shortly, Ms. Harper."

Before Thea could request the definition of shortly,
the line went dead.

She couldn't work. Her mind swarmed with disastrous possibilities. What if she were having seizures
again? What if she'd actually murdered that old couple
and the actor? A noose of terrible phrases looped around
her throat. Life without the possibility of parole. Death
by lethal injection. Thea thought of poor Gabby or-
phaned. She imagined the rest of her child's life soiled
by shameful association.

Enough!

"Dr. Forman's wire."

"This is Thea Harper again. When can I expect Dr. Forman to return my call?"

Audible sigh. "Dr. Forman is tied up with a serious emergency, Ms. Harper. I'm sure she'll get to you as soon as she can."

Thea's face caught fire. The "serious emergency" was probably a long, leisurely lunch. She pictured Maxine Forman at a trendy restaurant trading wacko war stories or commiserating about the inadequacy of their exorbitant fees with several of her equally empathetic colleagues.

Recognizing there was no way to hurry the shrink's response, Thea smacked the phone down. Crossing to the easel, she struggled to concentrate on the Sophie panel. She added a threatening lick of flame nearer the unconscious snake and roughed out the form of weird Willy Dillon approaching the burning store. Widening the mouths and eyes, she intensified the shocked expressions of the gawkers on the street.

This scene was nearly done. A few more illustrations, and the book would be finished as well. But suddenly, the whole enterprise seemed trivial, verging on the ridiculous. If Thea had reverted to the beast who'd murdered Simon Gallatin in cold blood, she had no future. Nothing lay ahead but a graveyard of decimated dreams.

Shame. Ostracism. Punishment.

What would all that do to her beautiful little girl? Gabby would feel abandoned, betrayed. The poor child would spend the rest of her years trying to shake the taint of her mother's madness. Thea's heart ached.

Three-fifteen. Any minute now, Gabby would come walking in from the bus. There was nothing to be gained by upsetting the little girl unless and until Thea's worst fears became reality.

Drawing a hard breath, Thea cleaned her brushes and went to the window to watch for her daughter. She craved some special time with the little girl, a cushion against the dark possibilities clouding their future. But Gabby was not the first to arrive.

CHAPTER THIRTY-EIGHT

Thea was stunned.

"Close your mouth, Checker honey. You don't want to be letting anything in or out that doesn't belong."

"Mom? What on earth are you doing here?"

Her mother chuckled. "How'd it sit if I was to say I happened to be in the neighborhood and decided to drop by?"

"Not real well." Thea's thoughts turned to the similarly lame excuse her brother had offered for being at their parents' ranch in Idaho. Thea should have suspected immediately that Jimmy was telling her a tall one. Mom had probably sworn him to secrecy.

Her mother's smile faded. "Truth is, you've been sounding a little funny on the phone, Checker honey. Figured I'd stop by for a couple of days and see for myself how you're doing."

"I told you I'm doing fine, Mom. But it's good to have you here anyway." Thea set her mother's shabby plaid suitcase in the front hall and wrapped Ellie in a long, hard hug. Her body still had the trim feel of a young girl's. Her strong-boned face, framed by a puff of graying hair and set off by large tortoise-rimmed glasses, looked youthful as well. The only clue that Ellie Sparks was closing in on sixty was the dull weariness in her brown eyes.

"How was the trip?" Thea asked.

"You know me and traveling, honey. Feels like I've been rode hard and put up wet."

"Why don't you go freshen up, then? Gabby will be home from school any minute."

Ellie bustled up the stairs. From past experience, Thea knew that her mother would recover from the journey in record time. Then she'd insist on getting right down to cooking and mending and ironing and cleaning. Ellie thrived on a relentless stream of chores. Idleness was as alien to her as a space flight. The woman's day always contained more obligations than hours.

Which was probably just as well. Given Thea's growing trepidation over the test results, she did not relish the idea of anyone sitting around scrutinizing her. She didn't want her mother's apprehensions added to her own.

"Hey, Mom."

Thea hadn't heard Gabby come in. "Hi, sweetie. Guess who's here?"

"Mr. Perry?"

"No."

"Santa Claus?"

"In October?"

Gabby shrugged. "Maybe he likes to watch the leaves turn."

Thea smiled. "It's Grandma. She came as a surprise."

Oddly, Gabby's enthusiasm faded. "How come?"

"She wanted to see us. That's all."

"Honest? Nothing's wrong?"

"Honest. She's upstairs washing her face."

Satisfied, the little girl tore up the stairs. "Gram? Where are you?"

Thea heard the excited patter of their voices overhead. Gabby and Ellie had always hit it off famously. Being around her grandmother brought out the child's otherwise invisible domestic side and a touch of incipient cowgirl.

Predictably, Thea's mother came downstairs minutes later and went directly to the broom closet in the kitchen for supplies. Bearing a full arsenal of cleansers, sponges, and rags, she mounted the stairs again. Ellie's standard mode of attack was to start at the top and work her way down. By the time she finished sanitizing the cellar, enough invisible dust and imaginary grime would have accumulated in the attic for her to rationalize starting the entire scrubbing process again. After a visit by her mother, Thea's house was always clean beyond recognition. Generally, it took a month or more of dedicated sloth to restore the place to a tolerable level of disorder.

Thea grinned. Hopefully, the local market wasn't experiencing a spot shortage of bleach or ammonia.

From upstairs came her mom's soothing drawl. The sound eased the pain in Thea's heart. Ellie had always been Thea's staunchest supporter. No matter how the rest of the world viewed her, no matter how appalling the headlines and accusations, her mother had never displayed a morsel of doubt about her daughter's essential goodness and innocence. In Ellie's eye, Thea remained whole and unchanged. When virtually all else failed, Thea had clung fast to that.

Maybe Ellie's arrival was a good luck sign. Despite the exasperating delay, the call from Dr. Forman might well bring positive news.

Thea imagined celebrating her unspoken relief with her two favorite people. That was all she wanted. A good word from the doctor would bring this hideous nightmare to an end.

CHAPTER THIRTY-NINE

Just when Biederman figured things on the job couldn't get any worse, Buck Delavan managed to concoct yet another, ever more diabolical form of torture.

Manning the message desk had been no picnic, not even the kind with bugs, botulism, and a rainstorm. But now, as he stood on the corner of North Street and Easton Road, wielding a stop sign on a stick, Biederman actually found himself waxing wistful about the switchboard.

Crossing guard.

Never again would Biederman take one of those valiant warriors for granted. Compared to this work, the most hazardous of standard cop duties seemed tame. Drug busts, explosive domestic disputes, even burglaries in progress were nothing compared to this.

Try heading off a first-grader intent on beating a speeding delivery truck to a runaway ball. Try herding a crowd of airhead eight-year-olds safely across a busy intersection when they were drunk with hilarity over the latest elephant joke. Try fencing with a lunatic mother who's willing to use her minivan as a battering ram if that's what she thinks it'll take to get her little princess to school ahead of the late bell.

But the kids were worse.

Talk about no respect. In Biederman's youth, adults, especially those in uniform carrying loaded semiautomatics, were at least mildly intimidating. No more. This morning, he'd been subjected to name-calling, pelted with fallen leaves, and treated to several snotty asides.

"Hey, look. It's the jolly green giant!"

"Doesn't look so jolly to me! More like a giant geek."

A day in school hadn't mellowed the little monsters in the slightest. Ever since dismissal, he'd been ducking the flying insults.

"Hey, Mr. Policeman. Climbed any nice bean poles lately?"

"What do you mean, climbed any? He *is* one."

"Bet your daddy was a phone pole. Right, Mr. Copperdoodle?"

Bet I'd wring your little neck if I didn't know how rotten the food was in maximum security.

The tolerant smile felt frozen on Biederman's face. Fortunately, this day had its compensations. The crossing guard gig only involved an hour's work in the morning, another split hour at the beginning and end of lunch, and an hour at closing time. In between, he'd managed to further his knowledge in the Gallatin case.

This morning, he'd paid a visit to Murray Masters at his home in neighboring Wilton. Masters, now retired, had taught the evidence course at the police academy in Meridan where Biederman trained for the force a decade ago.

Back then, Biederman had been astonished by the amount and quality of information the professor was able to squeeze from the sparest clue. From their phone conversation last night, it was clear that Masters hadn't lost the knack. Not only had Murray instantly recognized Biederman's voice after a ten-year hiatus, but he'd been able to gauge the temperature, shape, and weight of the situation from the voice, too.

"No need to explain further, Daniel. I'd guess this is regarding a murder investigation in which you have some personal, emotional stake. A romantic interest, perhaps?"

Biederman wanted to ask if Masters could already tell the woman's weight and eye color as well. But he'd caught the old man on his way out to a poker game, so further details had to wait for this morning.

Masters's ancient stone cottage was set on six acres of prime Wilton woods. The interior was a mirror of the man. Scant attention had been paid to appearances. The furniture was a hodgepodge of dull wood and shabby upholstered pieces. A massive collection of books and the latest in information storage and retrieval devices burdened every conceivable surface, kitchen counters included. Unlike many of his peers from the slide-rule-and-lead-pencil generation, Murray Masters wasn't at all put off by computers, modems, on-line data systems, fax machines, CD-ROMs, scanners, laser copiers. You name it. What the old man didn't know, which was precious little, he could find out in a keystroke.

Masters was clad in faded green corduroys, a blue plaid flannel shirt, and a vest the color of dried mud. Fishbowl bifocals magnified his razor-keen eyes. His features were hawklike and imposing, his handshake a vise. A halo of cottony hair rimmed his mottled scalp.

"Good to see you, Daniel. Come in and tell me who she is and what she's suspected of doing."

Bite to the bone. The professor had never been one to fritter time on small talk.

"Are you familiar with the Gallatin murder?" Biederman asked.

"The senator? Certainly." The triangle of frown lines between Masters's thick brows deepened. "Cause of death was a crushing blow that compressed the hypothalamus. As I recall, the case was handled by Luther Griscom. He pinned the defense on unconsciousness due to a complex-partial seizure. By the books, Griscom's not much of a lawyer, but his balls have always been oversized. Sometimes, they land him a term for contempt. But he generally manages to find some way, no matter how outlandish, to get his client off." Masters trained his piercing gaze on Biederman. "So it's long curly auburn hair and intelligent green eyes flecked with gold, is it?"

"There's nothing between me and Thea Harper, Professor. This is strictly business."

"You mean nothing between you as far as the lady is concerned. Don't tell me you wouldn't have it otherwise, Daniel. It's written all over you in large print."

"Okay. I'll admit to some attraction on my part, but that's not the point here."

"Fine. Sit and tell me what is."

Without reservation, Biederman spilled everything he knew or suspected. Masters had no ties to Buck Delavan or any of the nasty politics that might be skewing the inspector's judgment. The old man had always been a maverick. He was a feisty, independent soul whose primary passion was unearthing the unvarnished truth. Throughout his career, he'd been courted as a potential witness by countless defense and prosecution teams, a sideline that could have brought him a small fortune in fees. But he'd staunchly refused to shape his opinions to suit the purposes of one side or the other.

Masters spent nearly an hour poring over the case materials. Biederman kept quiet until the professor finished his review. Not until the old man peered up from the stack of documents did Biederman leap like a crazed kangaroo to Thea's defense.

"This woman is no murderer, Professor. You have to know her. I don't care what the defense or the prosecution said. I don't even believe she *killed* Simon Gallatin, seizure or no seizure."

Masters was nodding. "I agree with you, Daniel."

"You do?"

"The evidence agrees with you as well."

As Biederman listened raptly, Masters inquired about Thea's height, heft, and physical conditioning. Biederman's answers confirmed the professor's view. Given the angle of the blows, the senator's murderer was at least two inches shorter than Thea, probably more. And though the killer might have been a slender woman, she had to be heavily muscled to inflict the particular injuries described in the autopsy.

Masters pointed to the coroner's account of the break in Gallatin's thigh bone. "Given the specific mass and tensile strength of the femur and the size and weight of the murder weapon, a fracture of this nature would require a force at impact of at least fifty pounds.

"I'd wager your killer has engaged in a regular strength training program for a minimum of two years. He or she uses free weights in the forty-pound range and can bench-press upwards of one hundred fifty pounds. We're talking cut muscles, Daniel. Visible bulging arm veins. I see no evidence of such characteristics on Ms. Harper in this picture taken at the scene."

Biederman eyed the photo. "Then this had to be some kind of a setup. . . ."

"I would say so. Look at the blood distribution patterns on Ms. Harper's hands and clothing. What's wrong with this picture, Daniel?"

The cylinders started clicking into place. "Her hands are smeared with blood, but the techs found no evidence that she'd touched the corpse."

"Very good. And?"

Biederman forced himself to examine the picture again. He couldn't bear the look of shock and despair in Thea's eyes. The naked terror. "And except for the blood streaks, her clothes are clean. No splatters. None of the Jasper Johns effect you'd get if you smashed someone up like that with a heavy trophy. Her clothes should be a gory mess."

"Excellent. You were one of my finest pupils. Nice to see you've kept that sharp mind of yours in peak operating condition."

In fact, Biederman's sharp mind was hopping around like a manic frog. Pushing to reopen the Gallatin case would not be easy. Neither side was likely to take the word of an eighty-year-old man or a disobedient cop as sufficient cause to question the outcome of a four-month trial. The Gallatin prosecution had cost the federal government millions and left Uncle Sam with an egg-coated face. Biederman was going to need much more. Rock-solid evidence.

The old man remained several steps ahead of him. "I wish I could help you further, Daniel. But I'm off today to a conference in Amsterdam and then a month-long visit with my sister in Paris. That's why I needed to see you this morning. In fact, I think that's my car now."

He went to the window and peered out. "Yes. Sorry. Have to run."

Masters ducked into a bedroom and emerged with a battered suitcase, a tweed overcoat, and a baseball cap.

"Please, Professor. What I have isn't enough."

"Sorry, Daniel. I wish I could but I can't miss this plane. I'm delivering the keynote address."

Biederman trailed the old man out to the waiting Lincoln Town Car. "Is there anything else you picked up? Something that might at least point me in the right direction?"

Masters handed the driver his luggage and slid into the limo's backseat. "If I were you, I'd take a hard look at the trace evidence. The hair. And the lipstick, Daniel. The lipstick is most interesting."

The driver took the wheel and gunned the engine.

Biederman was trying to follow the twists and leaps of the old man's nimble brain. "What about the lipstick?"

A tiny smear of pink residue, found on analysis to be lipstick, had been retrieved from the back of the senator's neck. Amazing discovery, given the extent of the damage inflicted by the trophy. But beyond that, the investigators hadn't considered it all that significant.

A coy smile played on Masters's lips as the long, black car pulled away from the curb. "Think about it, Daniel. What does it remind you of when a killer gives the victim one last kiss?"

CHAPTER
FORTY

Lily Gallatin was possessed of a rare talent. Given sufficient motivation, the matriarch of the country's most august political clan was able to strangle a person without using her hands.

When the call came at home earlier this morning, Cassie Rodbury immediately felt the powerful press of the gnarled fingers against her windpipe. Now, seated ten feet from the old woman in the Gallatin mansion's sun-washed morning room, the asphyxiating grip was so strong, the lawyer could barely swallow.

Marielle Gallatin's eerie presence did nothing to ease the situation. As usual, the young woman stood behind her mother, silent, erect, and unblinking.

For all Marielle's stony reserve, Lily Gallatin's rage was palpable. Her opalescent eyes flashed fury and a wormlike pulse wriggled in her neck. She fisted and unfisted her wizened hands, causing the large emerald in her ring to spark a chill warning.

"I am *fast* losing patience, Cassandra. This entire matter should have been resolved by now. Why hasn't it been?"

"These things take time, Mrs. Gallatin."

"Time!" she spat. "In the year since Simon's murder, I've done nothing but wait for some minuscule shred of satisfaction. All I've sought is a meager bit of peace in the knowledge that my son's vicious killer has been made to pay. I want this thing resolved!"

"Certainly. We all do, but—"

The green stone flashed again. "No buts, Cassandra.

I want answers. If you can't deliver, I'll go elsewhere. To Clemmons and McGrath, perhaps. That firm is hungry and ambitious. I'm afraid an excess of comfort has dulled your edge."

The noose around Cassie's neck tightened a notch. She imagined the end of her career. Everything she cared about, shattering. "No, Mrs. Gallatin. Not at all. This matter will be concluded rapidly. You can count on it."

"I *do* count on it, Cassandra. You have until the beginning of next week. If you haven't been able to milk my people for results by then, I'll have no choice but to seek other assistance."

Cassie Rodbury squeezed the words past the painful constriction in her throat. "That won't be necessary, Mrs. Gallatin. As I said—"

Stiffly, the old woman rose. Her frown chilled the air. "Words mean nothing to me, Cassandra. Results are my sole interest."

"I understand."

"Do you? I think not. The fact is I will go to any length to properly avenge my son's murder. As you know, I've engaged the services of those best equipped to contribute to the effort. As you may choose *not* to know, I've been having Mrs. Harper and her daughter watched as well. I've done everything I can, Cassandra. Now I'm telling you to bring this to a swift and satisfactory conclusion."

Cassie struggled to hide her revulsion. Having Thea Harper's nine-year-old daughter followed? Her client must have taken leave of her senses.

"Leave everything in my hands, Mrs. Gallatin. I'll handle it."

The old woman's pale eyes bored into her. "We shall see."

Desperate to escape the hard, vicious voice, Cassie muttered an awkward farewell and took her leave. She had until the end of the week to shore up her world against impending disaster. There wasn't a minute to spare.

For once, Gabby was pleased to find Dylan's black bomb waiting when she exited the school. She didn't want to ride the bus, where there was bound to be more teasing. Those dumb babies in her class hadn't stopped since Mr. Perry caught her passing Opal the note during history. The teacher had insisted that Gabby read it aloud.

"If it's important enough to need saying in the middle of a class, I think you should share it with all of us."

Gabby had mumbled the words, hoping that no one would hear her. But Neil Lufkin, the dope, had caught the gist and blurted it aloud.

"Thea Harper and Max Perry request the honor of your presence at their wedding on June the first at six P.M. at their home at Twenty-one Linden Street. R.S.V.P."

Gabby thought she would melt from the humiliation. She *wished* she'd melt. She wanted to ooze through the cracks in the wooden floor and vanish. If not for Opal's sympathetic looks, Gabby doubted she could have survived the rest of the day. Even after the dismissal bell, when Mr. Perry called her over to say he'd read her note and would be delighted to come for dinner, Gabby couldn't shake the fog of shame. Actually, his accepting the invitation made matters worse.

What if he tells my mother? I'll be grounded forever.

Now, she strode past the line of kids at the number seven bus and slipped into Dylan's car. Setting her jaw, she countered Neil Lufkin's mocking gaze with a hard stare of defiance. Hopefully, the jerk would think that Dylan was her boyfriend. Imagine her having a boyfriend old enough to *drive*. Let Neil Lufkin spread *that* all over the stupid school. Everyone would forget about that dumb note in a big hurry. At least, all the kids would.

If Mom finds out, she'll know she brought the wrong kid home from the hospital.

"Hey, sweetness. You look glum," Dylan was saying.

"I'm not."

"Then, why do you look that way?"

"I said, I'm not," Gabby snapped. "Anyway, it's none of your business."

He raised his hands in mock surrender. "Whoa. Easy, girl. Pardon me for breathing, will you? I'll do my best to give it up as soon as possible."

The car was steeped in troubled silence as they drove the length of Easton Road. With a sidelong glance, Gabby spied the sadness in Dylan's face. What if she got him so upset that he actually went ahead and killed himself?

"Sorry, Dylan. It's not about you."

"What, then?"

"Nothing, really. Forget it."

"Is there anything I can do to cheer you up, little one? Buy you a soda? Shoot my brains out, perhaps?"

"Cut it out, Dylan. I hate it when you talk that way."

He ticked his tongue. "Where's your sense of humor? You leave it in school or something?"

"Were you really kidding?"

"Absolutely. I would never shoot myself. My old lady could never tolerate the mess."

Gabby thought about the conversation she'd had last night with the operator at the suicide hot line. After Gabby explained about her school assignment, the woman read her a list of warning signs and the things

you were supposed to do if you spotted any of them in
a relative or friend.

Number one was to always take suicide talk seriously. Second was to urge the person to seek professional
help.

"You really ought to go to a doctor or something,
Dylan. Killing yourself doesn't solve anything."

"Yes, it does. It solves *everything*."

"That's not true."

"Have you ever heard a dead person complain?"

"Of course not, but—"

"I rest my case."

Next on the list was to warn the person's parents,
spouse, or other loved ones. But Gabby doubted that
Dylan's mother would care. How much could Mrs.
Connable possibly love her son if she wouldn't even allow him inside her house? Dylan wasn't married, so
there was no spouse to consider. His little sister was
dead. And as far as Gabby knew, he had no other loved
ones. So who was there to tell?

What Gabby felt for him most of all was sorry. Sorry
and scared. She really didn't want him to take a bunch
of pills or cut his wrists again or breath in the smelly
gunk from his tailpipe until he turned blue. Even at the
movies, where she knew they were only make-believe,
Gabby had to bury her face in her hands when such
things happened.

Vividly, she pictured Dylan hanging by the neck, his
face the color of skimmed milk. She imagined him
walking into the ocean until the waves were roaring
over his head.

No, Dylan. Stop!

One day last summer, the Millports had taken her to
Jones Beach. There, a monster wave had knocked her
down and barreled overhead like a speeding train. By
the time Gabby managed to regain her footing, her

lungs were on fire and coughs sharp as steak knives were stabbing at her throat. It had to hurt something fierce to die like that. Most kinds of dying had to be worse than the worst pain imaginable, even booster shots.

Gabby shivered.

"A doctor could help you feel happier, Dylan. Then, you wouldn't want to kill yourself."

"You think it's that simple? Here you go, Mr. Connable. Take two of these happy pills every four hours and call me in a week or so."

"I mean a psychiatrist."

He lit a cigarette and shot the smoke through his nostrils. "You ever drop a glass on the floor?"

"Sure."

"Then you know some things are too damaged to fix, sweetness. Too damaged and too much trouble."

Gabby had used up all the hot line advice. All she could do was hope for Dylan to win millions in the lottery and forget about dying. Or maybe he'd fall madly in love and decide to get married and not want to leave the girl—ever.

Which made her think about that stupid note again. Mr. Perry simply mustn't mention it to her mom.

Please, Lord, if you make Mr. Perry forget about that fake wedding invitation, I promise never to ask you for anything again.

"So, you want to stop for that soda?"

"I can't, Dylan. I have to get home. My grandma's visiting and we're having company tonight."

At least, this time he didn't argue. There were no detours to death rooms or cemeteries or funeral parlors. Dylan took the direct route home. Gabby's bus angled in behind them as Dylan pulled over to let her out at the corner of Linden Street.

Quickly collecting her jacket and book bag, Gabby

glanced at Dylan again. His eyes were a dark, empty room. It was as if he'd been thrown into one of those ovens he'd told her about that was used to burn dead people, and nothing was left of him except the smoke ghosts floating around his head. Gabby tried to remember what the oven was called. Big word. Sounded like cream of tournament.

A lump of sorrow was lodged in her throat. No one should be so alone and unhappy. It wasn't fair. At least when her mom was sick in the hospital, Gabby had been able to count on Opal and Jasmine.

"Please don't do it, Dylan," she said desperately. "I'd really, really miss you."

He kept staring straight ahead. "Maybe for a day or two, while it was fresh and interesting. But after that, most of the time I'd be as far from your thoughts as Madagascar."

"I've never even heard of mad-a-gas-card."

"As I said."

"I wouldn't forget you, Dylan. You don't know me. I still remember my dad, and he died when I was just a baby."

"You remember him from pictures and stories and talk, sweetness. I will fade to nothingness. The burst of a bubble. Tick of the clock. Over. Kaput."

"That's not true. Anyway, you promised to help me understand stuff, which I still don't."

"You will when you will."

"But you said you were sent to take care of me, remember? If not for you, the Greens Farms kids would still be hanging around, driving me crazy."

"Go now, sweetness. I have things to do."

Gabby hated to leave him. There was an ache deep in her chest. She just knew something awful was going to happen. Dylan was planning to hurt himself soon. Maybe even today.

Please, Lord. Help me figure out how to stop him. Eyeing the heavens, she guiltily recalled her earlier bargain. *Lord, I know I said I'd never ask you for another thing if you helped Mr. Perry forget about the note. But this is really important.*

"Go, sweetness."

He was starting the engine, leaning across to open her door and let her out.

"Okay, but first you have to promise to come to my birthday party."

"When?"

"Sunday night." She hoped Dylan wouldn't notice the color rising in her cheeks. Lying always made her feel hot and stupid.

"I'll try."

"No. You have to promise."

"I said I'll do what I can."

"That's not good enough. You have to promise. You *have* to."

He went tense with irritation. "All right already. I promise. Now go."

The black car shot away from the curb. Relieved beyond measure, Gabby headed down Linden Street toward home. Sunday was two days away. In two days, things might look a lot brighter. If the Lord could help her think up that birthday fib so quickly, she figured there was no limit to what miracles the big guy in the sky might be able to arrange to save Dylan.

While Thea was dressing for dinner, her mother rushed into the bedroom, breathless.

"There's someone poking around out back, Checker. Sumbitch tried to duck and hide when I asked who it was. But I heard the footsteps, clear as day. Maybe you'd better call the police."

Thea thickly crossed to the bedroom window and peered down at the backyard. Through the curtain of vibrant leaves, she made out a skulking form. Whoever it was wore a long, dark coat and a broad-brimmed hat.

Tugging open the window, she called out. "Hey!"

The figure paused a beat, then continued, head bowed.

"Show yourself, you sneaky bastard!" Thea hollered in frustration.

By now, the interloper was nearing the privet hedge bordering the rear of her property. Tossing a paint-spattered shirt over her underwear and slipping into loafers, Thea tore downstairs and out the kitchen door.

As she rounded the studio, the intruder was momentarily caged in the brambly hedge. But before Thea could reach the spot, the privet yielded with a jarring crackle, and the dark-coated figure tore down Fielding Street.

She tried to follow, but the dense hedge raked her bare legs and caught the flimsy cotton of her shirt. As she struggled to break loose, her shirt tore and a snapping branch slapped her hard on the cheek. Another inch, and it would have been her eye that took the stinging scratch.

When she looked again, she spotted the fleeing trespasser turning onto Imperial. Her chances of catching up were next to none.

Her mother's fretful voice drifted down from the window. "You okay, Checker honey? Come on inside now. You'll catch your death out there in the near altogether like that."

Extricating herself from the brambly mess, Thea swore under her breath. It was probably Harlan Vernon again. She was sure the rodent reporter had been tailing her for days. Half a dozen times since her release, she'd spotted his hulking shadow in the neighborhood, but he'd always managed to disappear before she could catch him in the act. Once she did, Thea would demonstrate exactly what Westport's Black Widow was capable of doing.

If only the rotten bastard would slow down long enough.

Trudging back toward the house, Thea entertained a nasty notion. What if it wasn't Vermin? What if the toxic shadow was someone or something worse? She thought of Vita Negrone, still on the loose, whereabouts and mental condition unknown.

Vita had suffered a jealous snit when she heard of Thea's impending release from Brook Hollow. *Why her, not me? Both of us the same inside. Slice her up and show you, I will.*

Thea shivered at the memory of the lunatic's rambled threats. *Carve you in slices, I will, Thea Harper. Peel you like a grape.*

By now, Billie and everyone else at Brook Hollow were positive Vita had left the area. An exhaustive search by the neighboring police departments had turned up no trace of her. The Brook Hollow staff's own investigation had been fruitless as well. They'd interviewed countless people without a single reported sighting. And Vita wasn't exactly easy to overlook. People would tend to notice a wild-eyed wacko loudly holding forth on creative ways to dismember and flay her fellow man.

Thea finished dressing and set the table for dinner. Max Perry rang the bell as she was adjusting the final spoon.

As soon as the meal was served, the teacher trained his high-beam charms on Thea's mother.

"The sauce is delicious," he proclaimed. "So's the bread."

"My mom made everything," Thea said.

Ellie flapped away the praise. "Just something I threw together."

"Then your aim is exceptional, Mrs. Sparks." Max Perry flashed a dazzling grin. Ellie Sparks melted in the reflected heat.

"Go on, now," she said, flushing with pleasure.

"Have some more, Mr. Perry." In her zeal to pass the bread basket, Gabby upended Max's wineglass. Chianti rained over the white linen cloth and drizzled onto the carpet. Max recoiled instinctively, but not in time to prevent the rash of red freckles that bloomed across the front of his white shirt.

Thea exploded. "Damn it, Gabby. Be careful!"

"I didn't mean it, Mommy. You don't have to swear at me." The child's lip quivered. Her slender body stiffened with the struggle not to cry.

Thea caught her mother's startled look. "Sorry, sweetie. I didn't mean it. Don't worry. No harm done."

Gabby rarely blew the fuse on Thea's patience, but waiting for Dr. Forman's call had her circuits on serious overload.

Feeling guilty for her outburst, Thea mopped up the table, then tossed a clean napkin over the scarlet streaks on the cloth. Before she or her mother could get to the rest, Max fetched some club soda that magically lifted the remaining stains from the rug and erased the mess from his shirt.

"It's a trick I learned a couple of years ago when I was moonlighting as a bartender," he explained.

"Good trick."

"Real clever," Ellie agreed with enthusiasm. Beating dirt was her passion.

Thea was tempted to ask if Max had any similar remedies for removing the indelible blotches that killing left on the murderer's soul. She wondered if he knew of a magic poultice that might eradicate her terror of a relapse.

Why the hell didn't Dr. Forman get back to her? Thea's fears multiplied in the silence, spreading malignantly out of control. All evening, her thoughts kept swerving back to the nightmare of Simon's death.

Reliving the grotesque episode, she heard the screaming wail of approaching sirens. She felt Gabby's violent shivers and the whimpers bubbling up from the hellish depths of the child's horrified disbelief. Thea stiffened, recalling the frigid bite of the handcuffs. The blinding glare of flashbulbs. The loud, pressing throng of curious onlookers. The shame of the strip search. The sickening slam of the holding cell door.

That night, and for months afterward, shock had blunted the worst of the reality. But now nothing buffered Thea from the grisly clarity of the scene. She couldn't bear the garish memories. It was unthinkable that the nightmare might be recurring.

"May I please be excused? I'm tired," Gabby said.

"You all right, sweetie?" It wasn't like the child to volunteer for early retirement, especially in the presence of her beloved grandmother and the man she idolized.

"I'm fine. Just been a long day."

"Okay. You get ready, then. I'll be up in a few minutes to tuck you in."

"I can do it myself. You stay and visit with Grandma and Mr. Perry."

"How about I do the honors, honey? Be a real treat for me," Ellie asked.

"Okay, Gram. I'll be ready in a couple of minutes."

Poor Gabby seemed so blue and listless. Maybe she was coming down with something. Probably a case of substandard mothering. Thea had been so absorbed in her worries, she hadn't been paying nearly enough attention to her little girl.

She suffered yet another guilty pang. Before Simon's death, back in another incarnation, Thea had been a patient, thoughtful, caring mother. Could she ever hope to piece that old self back together? Was it possible to restore things to the way they'd been?

"If you don't mind, Mom, I'd like to tuck Gabby in," Thea said.

"Sure, Checker. If you two will excuse me, I think I'll turn in myself. Change of time's got me turned inside out and backward."

Leaving Max with apologies and a fresh cup of coffee, Thea followed her mother up the stairs and headed down the hall to Gabby's room. The child had already turned off her lights and huddled under the covers. Perched on the edge of the bed, Thea pressed her lips to Gabby's forehead. No fever.

"You sure you're all right, sweetie? Is there anything you'd like to talk about?"

"You should be with the company, Mommy."

"Mr. Perry's fine. Anyway, you're more important," Thea said firmly. "Tell me what's up."

"There's nothing to tell. I'm just sleepy. That's all."

"You're sure?"

"Positive."

"Absolutely sure?"

"Triple swear."

Thea kissed both silken cheeks and pulled the covers to Gabby's chin.

" 'Night, my sweet. Happy dreams."

"You shouldn't keep Mr. Perry waiting, Mom. It's rude."

"Yes, Miss Manners. I hear you. I'm going."

Max was no longer at the dining room table. No one in the kitchen, either. He must have gone to the bathroom.

As Thea began clearing the last of the dinner dishes, she heard a noise from the den. Must be Max. Padding through the hall in her bare feet, she was surprised to discover him peering into a drawer in the end table. Turning at the sound of her approach, he seemed startled as well.

"I was looking for a coaster," he blurted. "Didn't want to put that down on the wood."

She followed his gaze to a small crystal glass on the sideboard beside a bottle of ruby port. "Hope it was all right to help myself. I figured you might be a while."

"Of course."

"Join me?"

"Actually, Max, I'm pretty tired myself. Maybe Gabby and I are both coming down with something."

His face tensed with concern. "What can I do to help?"

"Nothing, really." She managed a smile. "A good night's sleep is probably what I need most."

"Look, it's none of my business, but I can see there's something on your mind. If you want to discuss it, I'm available."

"Thanks, Max. I appreciate the offer, but there's nothing to discuss. Getting back to real life is just turning out to be more complicated than I expected.

Strange as it may sound, mental hospitals have their re-
deeming virtues."

His smile was sympathetic. "Doesn't sound strange
at all. I can imagine how terrible it must have been for
you. After the trial, you were probably relieved to get
away from the flashbulbs and microphones."

"To say the least."

"I'll bet the Gallatin family didn't make it any
easier."

Good bet. "They lost someone they loved. I can't
blame them for hating me. It was the strangers I could
have done without. And the press."

Max's eyes brimmed with sympathy. "It's disgusting
what people will do to get a story. The more desperate
you are for time and space, the harder they pick at your
bones."

"You sound as if you've been there."

He placed a hand over hers. "No. But watching the
news, I could see how they treated you. Microphones
and cameras following you everywhere. Everything sen-
sationalized. It was a media circus. Made me furious.
This may sound strange, but I felt a connection to you,
Thea. Even then."

Their eyes met and held. Max Perry was charming,
caring, bright, sane, attractive, and available. Sounded
way too good to be true. But Thea found herself drawn
to the fantasy.

No one, Caro included, had been able to talk about
Simon's death and the ensuing emotional firestorm in
such an open, direct way. There was something different
about Max. Something Thea couldn't fully define.

And while she was making the attempt, he confused
things further by pulling her toward him. His mouth
was warm velvet, his tongue probing. The kneading
press of his hands on her back liquified her bones.

With the spare remains of her strength, Thea pulled away. "Max—I'm not ready for this."

"All right. I understand. No strings. Just let me hold you for a minute."

Tempting. But she could see the alligators lurking in that innocent-looking moat. The ache of longing she felt had been a long time brewing.

Give a wild horse her head, and she'll ride you right to oblivion, Checker honey.

Max's voice was soothing, seductive. "It's okay, Thea. The bad times are behind you now."

At that, Thea's thoughts swerved relentlessly to the impending call from Dr. Forman. Until she heard the test results, she couldn't be at all certain that the horror was history.

The result was better than an ice-cold shower. In a breath, Thea was back in full command of her limited senses. Until she had a firm grip on her life, there was no way she could consider taking on a fresh relationship. It wouldn't be fair or right for either of them. And it all too well might end in another disaster.

"You'd better go now, Max."

His eyes held her. "How about I move to a neutral corner and we just talk?"

Another temptation. The man had a remarkable knack for drawing her out, making it easy for her to express exactly what was on her mind.

Too easy.

And so dangerous.

"Some other time, Max. I'm really tired."

He didn't protest. Thea herded him to the door and double-locked it behind him.

After ten already. Dr. Forman wasn't likely to call tonight.

Damn that woman. This was torture.

Everything is mind over matter, Checker honey. If you don't mind, it doesn't matter.

She would not let the anxiety take her over. Somehow, she'd make it through the night. She considered a shot of Billie's magical sleep nostrum. But the last dose had been frighteningly effective. A small glass of the crème de menthe on the sideboard would probably suffice.

Heading for the den, she remembered Justin's buying their first bottle of her favorite liqueur and a variety of other cordials to offer their guests after the many elegant dinner parties they'd planned to give. At the time, they'd both taken an interest in wines and culinary arts. They'd enrolled in cooking classes and gone to tastings. But after Justin's death, she'd developed an aversion to all but the most essential food preparation.

Funny how things change.

Not so funny.

Max's glass and the port were still on the sideboard. Opening the base cabinet, she replaced the bottle in the only available space in the rear. The action raised a cloud of dust. Thea hadn't so much as looked at Justin's fledgling wine cellar since his funeral. Max had been quite the detective to unearth this musty stash.

She poured a measure of the minty liqueur into a cordial glass and started turning out the lights. Halfway out of the den, she spotted Max's cordovan briefcase propped against the sofa. Thea wasn't the suspicious type, but she did entertain the fleeting notion that he might have left the case on purpose.

If so, good try, Max. Morning would be soon enough to call and have him come for it. He wasn't likely to be correcting any homework or working on his plan book tonight.

Anyway, early on, every rancher's child learns that it's best to let sleeping dogs lie.

CHAPTER
FORTY-THREE

Biederman landed a vacant spot in the heart of Westport's shopping area and ventured into The Hair Lair. The salon was packed with women of all ages in varying stages of completion. Most wore the customer uniform: a raspberry toga trimmed in battleship gray. Many had odd gadgetry aimed at or appended to their heads. Biederman made some of the machines as miniature satellite dishes and circuit boards. One three-pronged monstrosity appeared to be a brain-tanning machine.

What price beauty?

At the front of the shop, a dozen waiting women on wicker chairs pored through fashion and fitness magazines. Beyond, a row of washing stations faced the line of cut-and-style seats. Mirrored walls caught and echoed the frenetic activity. Hairdressers deftly juggled combs and scissors. Clients confessed their most intimate secrets at the peak volume necessary to outshout the blow dryers. New-mown hair rained and hair spray hissed angrily.

The pungent stew of dyes, sprays, and hair repair products made Biederman's nose itch. The curious eyes trained his way inspired him to turn and flee. Squaring his mind on the mission, he strode to the reception desk and stood behind a meticulously coiffed redhead who was settling her sizeable bill with a Visa card.

A host of items for sale lined the display cases flanking the cash register. Biederman identified several as glorified barrettes, combs, and headbands. He could only imagine the purpose of others. For the fashion-

conscious angler, there were miniature fishnets capped
with velvet bows. The giant clips appeared suitable for
resealing potato chip bags or performing do-it-yourself
vasectomies. While he was scanning the selection of
jewel eye-gougers, the customer ahead of him stepped
aside.

The willowy brunette receptionist turned his way.
"Help you?" she purred.

"Name's Dan Biederman. I have an appointment
with Mr. Thomas."

Tracking with a two-inch nail, she located his name
on the appointment roster. "There you are, Mr.
Biederman. Will that be highlights or single process?"

Biederman flushed. "Neither. I'm just here to talk to
him."

"A consultation, then?"

"Right."

"Here's a robe. Changing room's around to the right.
Mr. Thomas will be right with you."

Biederman declined the toga and retreated to a vacant sliver of space in the waiting area. Ten minutes
later, a pallid woman with hair the red of cough syrup
arrived to shepherd him to a small private room in the
rear. She wore a tiny black leather skirt, a black spandex
turtleneck, and thigh-high boots replete with buckles
and studs. If this was the day job, Biederman figured
she spent her nights posing for layouts in *Hurt Me* magazine.

The assistant instructed Biederman to sit on the
plush pink recliner and offered him a choice of bever-
age. "Relax," she ordered brusquely as she slipped out
and shut the door behind her.

Another several minutes passed before Mr. Thomas
breezed in. He trailed a trio of fawning assistants and
the heavy scent of bay rum spiked with lavender. The
Hair Lair's expert in trichology—defined as the science

of the scalp and whatever should happen to grow on it—wore his own lemon tresses in an Elvis do complete with pompous pompadour and sideburns of sufficient magnitude to upholster the arm of a chair.

Mr. Thomas made a rapid circuit around the chair, gravely scrutinizing Biederman's head.

"I can see why you called this urgent. We're talking *serious* dehydration here. Those little follicles of yours are just crying out for relief. 'Help, I'm so thirsty!' they're saying. Do you hear?

"And we simply *must* do something about the color. A henna rinse, perhaps. Or, better yet, a few face-framing highlights in a warm gold tone."

His tone went brusque. "Danielle, mix me two parts of G-thirty-seven and one B-five. And see if Mr. Barry has time for a deep conditioning in half an hour. Tell him it's an emergency."

Biederman raised his hands in defense. "Time out. I'm not here about me. I'm a cop. I need your expert opinion for a case I'm working on."

The trichologist smirked. "Look. I didn't buy the one about the attorney general wanting to fly me to D.C. for a makeover, and I'm not about to fall for this. You can just tell my joker friend, Jeff Leichter, that I saw right through you."

Delavan had neglected to strip Biederman of his department-issue photo ID. When Mr. Thomas examined the credential, his smirk yielded to a gap-toothed grin.

"My goodness. It'd be an honor to help serve the cause of law and order in these dreadfully violent times. How can I help you, Detective?"

Biederman rummaged through his jacket pockets. He extracted the photocopied blowup of the long, curly hair found embedded in one of Gallatin's savage wounds. Analysis by the FBI's forensic pathologist had confirmed it as Thea Harper's. The prosecution had presented the hair as damning proof that Thea Harper had wielded the bludgeon. Given the defense plea—not guilty by reason of unconsciousness—Thea's lawyer let the evidence stand. They weren't denying that Thea had murdered Simon Gallatin, only that she'd done the deed willfully or with premeditation.

Magnified by giant multiples, the auburn hair resembled a bubble-headed, wriggling worm. The trichologist mounted the page on a light box, and his cadre of assistants clustered to peer over his shoulders.

"This image was captured on a transmission polarizing light micrograph," Thomas said. "Excellent quality. Fine quality hair as well. Given the eight-micron diameter and the absence of breaks in the color bands, I'd say we're dealing with a youngish white female who has never subjected herself to harsh perms or coloring. She washes with a mild shampoo and avoids temperature extremes. Smart. Rare to find so little damage in an adult."

Biederman couldn't imagine how any of the above might boost a claim of Thea's innocence. But with Murray Masters in mind, he persisted. "This particular hair was found on a murder victim. Supposedly, tests showed it came from the killer. Can that really be proven beyond a doubt?"

"Well, forensic pathology isn't my field, but there has been lots in the trichological literature recently. They're using DNA testing now. State of the art. I'd say a hair match is pretty reliable."

"So you'd agree with the prosecution that this hair was probably tugged out during the attack?"

"Oh, no. Absolutely not."

"But I thought you said—"

The trichologist pointed to the worm's transparent head. "See here? The bulb is round and healthy. That's

characteristic of a hair shed during the telogen or resting phase of the normal growth cycle. If that hair had
been pulled out during the anagen or growing phase,
the bulb would have been distorted by the tug-of-war
with the follicle."

Biederman weighed that one. "So you're saying the
hair fell out naturally and happened to land on the
corpse?"

"That depends." Mr. Thomas frowned. "How long
after the crime was this micrograph taken?"

Biederman checked the date on the photocopy. "The
next day."

"No way it fell out during the crime, then. You're
looking at a hair bulb that was exposed to the air for a
week. Maybe longer. The specimen is all dried out, almost as bad as that hay crop of yours, Detective."

"You're positive?"

"Absolutely. Now how about those treatments for
you? A couple of hours, and you'll look like a new man.
Guaranteed."

"Sorry. No time."

"You sure? You could *really* use some help in that
department—"

Driving home, Biederman wavered between elation
and outrage. The trichologist's analysis meant that
Thea's hair had been planted on Gallatin's corpse by the
killer. The son of a bitch hadn't been content to whack
the senator in Thea's house and smear her with the dead
man's blood. He'd taken extra pains to make the prosecution's case airtight.

Fortunately, the defense had come up with the seizure angle and the shrink to back it up, but justice had
yet to be served.

And Biederman still lacked sufficient proof to force
a reopening of the case. Given that the murder occurred
in Thea's home, finding her hair on the body could rea-

sonably be dismissed as insignificant. Biederman rubbed his eyes. Something was missing here. Probably a serviceable brain.

Back in his apartment, he pored over the Gallatin case materials piled on the rolltop desk in his bedroom. If only the pages could cry out to him the way his long-neglected tresses had wept for Mr. Thomas.

He needed Murray Masters. Or failing that, he needed to think with the professor's unique brand of clarity.

Which brought to mind the way Masters used to tame the convoluted elements of a case, dazzling his students as he sorted, segregated, and arranged the facts in rational order. The professor's insights and intuitive leaps were legendary. Even the most baffling events could be explained with persistent applications of a stubborn, nimble mind, the old man insisted.

As Masters often said, logic was the most powerful of all forensic tools. Apparently, it was also the first to fail in the presence of an acute infatuation or the bared fangs of a rabid employer.

Buck Delavan, Biederman thought. Bless the man's heart, if only he had one.

Forget it, Danny boy. Stick to business.

Trying to follow the professor's methods, Biederman started laying out the facts and unknowns.

Fact: The bloodstains on Thea's hands and clothing could not have resulted from her wielding the trophy that crushed the senator's skull.

Fact: The angle and force of the blows also eliminated Thea as a suspect. Someone else, notably someone about five feet four inches tall, who'd engaged in an intensive, extended strength-training program, had committed the Gallatin murder.

Or maybe not.

Biederman detected a potential flaw in the professor's deduction on that score.

What if the perp had inflicted the blow from other than a full upright stance? A taller person might have been in a semicrouch to counter the heft of the trophy. To reduce the risk of back injury, weight lifters were taught to assume a bent-knee stance. A seasoned body-builder would never hoist a heavy object with straight legs.

Crouching as he would to lift a barbell, Biederman marked the wall at the top of his head with a felt-tip pen. Stooping subtracted six inches. So the killer was probably closer to five-ten. Maybe taller. Made more sense, given the senator's massive injuries. Hard to imagine a really little guy or even the strongest woman dealing that much damage.

Anyway, women weren't bashers. They tended to prefer more genteel weapons, like poison or pistols or, in his ex-wife's case, asphyxiating the victim by shoving another man down his throat.

Luckily, justice had prevailed in Elaine's case. She'd gotten what was coming to her. Life with herself.

Keep your mind on the case, Biederman.

He shook his head like a wet dog, trying to clear the distractions.

Somehow, the perp had lured Simon Gallatin to Thea's house, bashed him, and then arranged the physical evidence to turn Thea into an instant, irresistible suspect. Regular prince. Biederman couldn't wait to meet the guy and break his hand.

By some means, Thea's memory for the hours preceding the murder had been erased. Drugs or hypnosis, Biederman figured. He scrawled a note to himself and made several question marks in the margin. It would be interesting, though probably impossible, to determine the method a full year after the fact. Again, he wished

that samples of Thea's blood had been taken at the time
of her arrest. That could have filled several yawning
blanks in the story.

Forget it, Daniel. Monday morning quarterbacking isn't
going to solve this thing.

Rolling his neck to ease the kinks, he started on the
list of unknowns. Topping the hit parade was the identity of the real killer. Biederman ached to nab the scum
and have a serious fist-to-face chat with him. He
wanted to pay the guy back for every bit of the agony
Thea had suffered. Homicidal maniacs deserved plenty
of things, but a stand-in wasn't among them.

How could someone have set Thea up like that? And
why Thea?

Interesting question.

He wondered if the perp had had any prior connection to her and added that to the list. A man like Simon Gallatin knew hordes of people. Any one of them
might have been tapped as the patsy. Was Thea a random selection, or had she been chosen deliberately?

Biederman weighed the possibilities on both sides of
the ledger: jealous other woman, disapproving relative,
angry constituent, disgruntled employee, a lunatic sore
loser Gallatin had trounced in some past election? A
man with the senator's long public history and
nosebleed-high profile was bound to have collected
quite a few enemies along the way. Unearthing them all
and checking the lot for loose screws was far too much
legwork for a solo practitioner, even one with a thirty-
six inseam and size fourteen shoes.

He considered enlisting the aid of an ally. Passerell
was the likeliest candidate, but good old Vince had several major strikes against him. For one thing, the guy
couldn't keep a secret. Letting Vince in on this unauthorized investigation was akin to posting a progress report on the station house wall. Plus, every millimeter of

Passerelli's spare time was crammed with family obligations. When the guy wasn't cheering one of his kids on
at a ball game or ballet recital, he was mucking out the
gutters or raking the leaves. Truth be told, Biederman
had long suspected that mud and leaf clippings were secret ingredients in several of Gina Passerelli's prized
recipes.

Nearly one o'clock already. Biederman was fast running out of steam and ideas. Aside from a sticking pain
behind his eyes, he had nothing solid to show for all the
sleep he'd lost over a case the department officially considered closed.

He needed more expert input. But where was he
supposed to find the time? Predictably, Delavan had
shifted him from off- to on-duty for the rest of the
weekend. In an hour, he was due at the local Y to direct
the crush of traffic expected at a benefit house tour. Tomorrow, he'd be making sure that no one absconded
with the two-ton crane idling at a municipal construction site. The rest of the week was similarly packed
with scintillating assignments. How was he going to
find the hours it would take to dig up and question the
necessary consultants?

As if in answer, the doorbell chimed. Biederman
wasn't expecting anyone, especially not Buck Delavan
in the apoplectic flesh.

"Inspector?"

Delavan muscled his way into the apartment. The
chief was snorting like a dyspeptic bull.

"I told you, Danny boy. I warned you, but you
wouldn't freaking listen."

"About what?"

"About going with the program. About doing what
you were freaking told."

"Sorry, Buck. I don't follow."

The chief's eyes narrowed to menacing slits. "No you

don't, Biederman. You don't follow orders. You don't follow directions. Not following is your whole freaking problem."

"Let me make a wild guess here, Buck. Sounds to me as if you're upset about something."

"You're freaking right I'm upset about something. And that something is you, you arrogant, overgrown, hymie bastard."

Holding his temper hard, Biederman nodded impassively. "You didn't have to go out of your way on a weekend to show me what a small-minded, hotheaded, anti-Semitic fool you are, Buck. I already knew that."

Delavan chuckled sourly. "You think you know it all, don't you, Danny boy?"

"Actually, no. I have no idea to what I owe the displeasure of this visit."

Still chuckling, the inspector paced the room. "There I am having my coffee this morning. The sun is shining and all is right with the world. But then, I ask my wife how was canasta last night. Just talking, you understand."

"So far."

Delavan shot a warning glare and resumed his pacing. "Turns out one of the regular players was out with the flu and sent her sister-in-law to substitute. The sister-in-law is a paralegal. Works for the U.S. Attorney's office in Bridgeport. When my wife mentions that she's married to Westport's chief of detectives, this woman says, isn't that a coincidence? Seems a tall man from my office has been asking around about the Gallatin case, sticking his big nose in where it doesn't belong. That would be you, wouldn't it, Danny boy?"

"Actually, I never thought of my nose as all that big."

"Always the wiseass, aren't you, Danny?" Delavan snarled. "Well, this time you've wiseassed yourself right out of a job. Bring me your piece and your shield. If I have to look at the likes of you much longer, I'll puke."

Biederman couldn't see a way out and found he didn't much care. After a ten-year diet of Delavan's bullshit, he was more than ready for a break. The badge was on his nightstand, his department-issue Glock nine-milly was tucked away in his top dresser drawer. He retrieved both and handed them over.

"If you thought your insubordinate crap was going to help that little bitch you've got the hots for, you're dead wrong, Danny boy. I've put some real men on that murdering slut. A couple of days and I'll have her."

With a parting sneer, Delavan slammed out. In the silent aftermath, Biederman waited for a twinge of regret. Instead, he found himself oddly pleased by the fresh twist of events.

CHAPTER FORTY-FOUR

Thea loaded her brush with a glob of mud brown paint, cocked the handle, and let fly. She repeated the assault several times until the canvas propped on the easel resembled a mudslide into a swamp. Still, she found it an improvement over the clumsy mess she'd made of the panel depicting Sophie's successful rescue from the fire. By the time Thea had finished with her, the poor reptile looked as if she'd have been better off taking her chances in the flames.

Still no word from Dr. Forman about the test results. Desperate, Thea had waited until her mother was firmly ensconced in her cleaning, then made two more attempts that morning to reach the shrink by phone. The same officious twit at the answering service had picked up both times. Her voice was tack sharp and dripping with sarcasm, as if the calls were an unforgivable intrusion.

You're an answering service, lady. Answering is your goddamned job.

"I *told* you, Ms. Harper. Dr. Forman is unavailable at the moment."

"When will she be available?"

"I really can't say."

"Will you please tell her I'm *very* anxious to hear from her?"

"I'm sure she knows that. You have called *five* times."

But who's counting?

Much of Thea's terror had been displaced by a burgeoning rage. The test results had to be in by now. If they weren't, Dr. Forman should have called to offer an explanation for the holdup.

It was an obvious power play, the shrink's means of demonstrating that she held all the cards and wouldn't hesitate to flog a recalcitrant patient with them. But Thea wasn't anyone's naughty child. And she wasn't about to hold still for Maxine Forman's version of a spanking.

Thea peered at the house through the studio window and spotted her mother in the master bedroom. Ellie was in her spray-and-wipe mode, attacking stray dust particles with a near religious zeal. The woman wouldn't move on to the next room until the place looked and felt uninhabited.

Propping a fresh Masonite board on the easel, Thea started sketching the rescue scene again. This time, she tried to muzzle her temper and concentrate.

I won't let Dr. Forman ruffle me. If I do, she wins.

Still, the rhythm of the work eluded her. Her fingers felt stiff. The brush was a dead branch, the pigments dull and defiant. Once, she could lose herself in a painting, abandon reality and unite with the graceful sweep of the bristles, the capricious play of color and tone, the mesmerizing emergence of an image out of the void.

But again, Sophie began to resemble something closer to a flabby foot-long wiener than a voluptuous serpent. Maybe Thea was being derailed by the taunting memory of the snake image that inspired the Sophie story in the first place. The diamondback viper she'd envisioned was identical to the one mutilated in the attack on Brandon Lee Payton. How could that be if she'd only heard about the assault on the radio?

Stop, Thea. It's just a coincidence.

A crowd of distractions buffeted her. The flames were the sharp, erratic lines of Thea's EEG. Weird Willy

Dillon's eyes kept slipping out of sync. Poor kid appeared more tipsy than heroic.

Hopeless.

This time, she saturated a large brush in turpentine from the coffee can and worked over the ugliness until the images dribbled off the canvas in a dark, soupy broth. Satisfied, she tossed the mess into the trash barrel.

Catching a strong whiff of the turpentine from yesterday's spill, she capped the barrel tightly. Heavy fumes like that were a conflagration waiting to happen. The next garbage pickup was on Monday. She'd have to remember to set this can outside on Sunday night. She also reminded herself to call first thing Monday to have the fire alarm and sprinkler system tested.

Determined to break her slump, Thea propped yet another board on the easel, then spent ten minutes staring at the white space.

Useless.

She wasn't likely to accomplish anything productive today. At least, not until she heard from Dr. Forman. Thea left her studio and headed for the house. Upstairs, she found her mother in the bedroom, ironing her underwear.

"That's not necessary, Mom. Really."

"Can't ever have things too straight, Checker."

"How about taking a break. I could use a walk."

Ellie frowned. "Maybe later, honey. That closet of yours could do with some tidying, and I want to get to the mess in the studio."

Thea's head was swarming with turpentine fumes and dread possibilities. She decided to take the walk alone and try to clear the rubble.

Hurricane Imogene, having vented the worst of her fury on the coast of South Carolina, was due to hit the area later tonight. In a cliché prestorm lull, the air hung still and expectant.

Thea's thoughts drifted back to similar times on her parents' ranch. She imagined the animals, driven by instinct to the meager protection of the barn. Horses, sheep, even barn dogs, detected the approach of dangerous weather hours in advance of the National Weather Service. Growing up, Thea had learned to read the fear in the critters' eyes as clear warning to board up and hunker down for the duration.

The same eyes had confronted her in the mirror this morning.

Gabby had left hours ago to help Caro and the twins set up for a bridal shower. As soon as the little girl came home, Thea decided she'd make a cozy fire and put up some soup for dinner. She'd make split pea, Gabby's favorite. She'd even do it her mother's way: Start from scratch—carrots, onions, dried peas, spices and broth—and let the pot simmer for hours.

Later, the three of them could curl up in front of the fireplace and play cards or tell stories. Gabby never tired of hearing about herself as a small child, especially the tales that included her father. Ellie would be able to add her own stock tales to the collection.

Wistfully, Thea remembered Justin at the town park kiddie pool, teaching Gabby to swim. She conjured the image of tiny Gabby perched on her father's broad shoulders as the three of them trudged around the Bronx Zoo on a sweltering June day in search of a pink unicorn. She also recalled their visit to the ranch the spring before Justin's death. It had been the first time on a horse for both Daddy and daughter. Gabby had taken to the saddle as if she'd been born to it. Justin had barely hidden his abject terror.

"Where's the parking brake?" he quipped nervously.

"That old nag's only got two speeds, son: slow and stop," Thea's father had assured him.

"Oh, no. Watch out. I think she's thinking about moving."

Ellie laughed. "Riding's easy, Justin honey. You just keep one leg on each side and your mind in the middle."

Thea was so steeped in reveries, she didn't notice Glenda Rossner's approach. The neighborhood busybody bustled up behind her, leading, as usual, with her mouth.

"Thea? That you?"

Reluctantly, Thea stopped. "Hello, Glenda."

"You okay? You look awful."

"Kind of you to say so."

Glenda ticked her tongue. "Well, it's no wonder. If it was my kid, I'd be a wreck, too."

"If what was your kid?"

Glenda was on autopilot, barely pausing for breath. "The first time I saw them together, I figured, it's probably nothing. But it's been almost every day for more than a week, now. I have to tell you, I wouldn't even let my Mikey hang around that kid, and Mikey's a *boy*."

"What on earth are you talking about, Glenda?"

"I'm talking about Dylan Connable and your Gabby."

"Gabby and who?"

"Dylan Connable. Look, I know you've been through a lot, Thea. And I'm sorry for you, really. But to let your little girl hang out with that juvenile delinquent . . . I mean, everyone knows the kid's plain rotten. He looks like hell. Smokes like a fiend. Dropped out of high school a couple of years back, and he's not much better than a bum. Even tried to kill himself a couple

of times. Wouldn't surprise me if he was on drugs or
something."

"I never heard of anyone by that name," Thea said.
But even as she struggled to deny what the witch was
saying, she felt a chill. Gabby's lies and evasions. The
sudden secretiveness. An alliance with someone she
knew her mother would find objectionable could explain all of it.

Glenda eyed her with open contempt. The woman
obviously delighted in Thea's discomfort. "It's about
time you *did* hear, then. If you don't put a stop to it,
there's no telling what might happen, Thea. I mean,
what would a boy like Dylan Connable, he's eighteen—
maybe nineteen—years old by now, want with a pretty
little thing like your Gabby?"

"I'll look into it, Glenda. Good-bye, now."

Thea turned to walk away, but the vicious snoop had
more shots to take.

"If she were mine, I'd have her checked by a doctor.
In this day and age, you never know."

"Good-bye, Glenda."

"Kids need supervision, Thea. You don't keep a close
eye on them, you're asking for trouble. *Begging* for it."

Finally, Thea managed to break away. Hurrying
home, she thought her head would burst from the
loaded accusations.

Unfortunately, it all rang true. According to Glenda,
the Connable kid was a heavy smoker. That would account for the time Gabby came home reeking of tobacco. The child had been so distant and secretive since
Thea's release from Birch Hollow. Hiding in her room.
Disappearing for hours. Turning up preoccupied and
grim without a reasonable explanation.

Gabby had even concocted a similar name for that
creepy character in the Sophie story: Weird Willy
Dillon.

Dylan Connable?

Desperately, Thea searched her memory, but she couldn't place the name. How had this teenager wormed his way into Gabby's life? And, as Glenda had so aptly put it, what *did* he want with her?

Thea thought of Gabby coming home in those strange, scruffy, oversized clothes. Facing the possible implications, she went cold.

God, no. He can't have abused her. She's just a baby.

Her throat closed. She ached to see her little girl. She longed to cup Gabby in her hands like a fresh-hatched bird and protect her.

Please, don't let it be too late!

Luckily, Ellie had gone out to straighten the studio. Thea spotted her mother through the window, lining up the brushes. This Dylan Connable thing could turn out to be nothing but a figment of Glenda Rossner's tiny mind. Thea didn't want to burden her mom with unnecessary aggravation.

Thea found the detective's card on the kitchen table. He could help her learn the truth. Dialing the station house, she drew a measured breath.

"Sergeant Daniel Biederman, please."

She was put on hold. Minutes later, the cordial voice on the other end returned. "Sorry, ma'am. Biederman's not available. May I help you?"

"It's personal. Can I leave a message?"

The voice cleared itself and dipped to a conspiratorial whisper. "You'd better try Dan at home, ma'am. The sergeant's on leave."

On leave?

"Could you give me his home number?"

"Sorry. That's against regulations."

The desk officer hung up, forestalling further questions. Thea's hopes sank. A cop's home number wasn't likely to be listed. Biederman was her only reliable ally on the force. To the rest of the cops she was Westport's infamous black widow. Dangerous. Crazy.

Replacing the receiver, she accidentally brushed the detective's card onto the floor. Stooping to retrieve it, her heart leaped. He had scrawled his number on the back. Biederman answered on the second ring.

"This is Thea Harper. Sorry to bother you at home, Detective."

"Not at all."

"I called headquarters, but they said you were on leave."

"Leave's as good a word for it as any."

"Are you all right?"

"Fine. Are you?"

She hesitated, trying to find the words. "You said I should call if I needed help, and I'm afraid I do."

"With?"

"It's complicated. I hate to put you out, but it'd be easier to explain in person."

"No problem. Ten minutes be okay?"

"Yes, only my mother's visiting. Maybe it'd be better if I meet you somewhere."

"That's not necessary. If Mom asks questions, you can pass me off as a plumber or whatever."

"You sure?"

"No problem."

Thea was too jittery to sit and wait. Pictures of Gabby and some chain-smoking delinquent kept snaking through her thoughts. She'd never really been able to relate to herself as a killer, but the notion of someone hurting Gabby filled her with a murderous rage.

Pacing like a caged beast, she spotted Max Perry's briefcase still propped against the sofa in the den. The detective had been the right person to call about Dylan Connable, but it would be nice to have the comfort of Max's sympathetic ear as well.

Oddly, she couldn't recall his ever mentioning where he lived. Directory assistance had no listing for a Max or an initial "M" Perry in Westport or any of the surrounding towns. Beyond her selfish wish for his reassuring presence, Thea was concerned that Max might not remember where he'd left his briefcase. She imagined him wracking his brain, worrying.

She lifted the case onto the sofa. There was no luggage tag on the handle. Feeling uneasy, she flipped open the latches. She hated to breach Max's privacy, but something inside would likely provide her with his address or phone number or, at least, a clue to how she might be able to track him down. She didn't feel right entrusting Gabby to deliver the case to him at school on Monday. The child had a genius for losing things.

Thea had expected the briefcase to contain mostly teacher trappings: lesson plans, test papers, memos from the principal's office. Instead, it was neatly fitted with a microcassette recorder, a steno pad, extensive notes penned on legal pads, and an array of newspaper clippings.

Horrified, she eyed the sickeningly familiar headlines on the clips:

GALLATIN BLUDGEONED TO DEATH
WESTPORT WOMAN CHARGED IN SENATOR'S MURDER
BLACK WIDOW MURDER CASE GOES TO JURY
UNCONSCIOUS PLEA STANDS.

Thea's stomach fisted. She flipped through the stack of letters tucked in a side pocket. There was a dues bill from the American Society of Journalists and Authors, an invoice from a computer search operation, and a flyer announcing an upcoming conference entitled "The New News."

With mounting horror, Thea spotted the monogram on the back of the next envelope. It was the same set of interlocking G's she'd observed on the gate fronting the Gallatin estate.

She slipped out the folded sheet of stationery inside. *The enclosed is for services rendered through September 30*, the pinched, elegant handwriting said. The check was gone. Max had obviously cashed it.

Bristling with disbelief, Thea mouthed the unthinkable. Max Perry was a shill, a reporter working in league with Lily Gallatin. Somehow, Simon's mother had arranged for Max to substitute as Gabby's teacher. No doubt they'd viewed it as a surefire way for Perry to insinuate himself into Thea's life and squeeze whatever damning information he could from the contact.

With mounting fury, Thea thought about his phony interest in furthering Gabby's writing abilities. She replayed his bogus attentions to both of them: the smiles, the flattery, the sympathies, the seeking press of his lips.

Lying son of a bitch.

Hefting the case, she flung it across the room. It slammed the stone hearth, raising a cloud of ash. The contents scattered. Thea was tempted to take a match to the papers. Better yet, she'd like to barbecue the bastard himself. She'd like to see him skewered and spit-roasted.

Suddenly a wave of dizziness overcame her. The room started spinning. Staggering to the couch, Thea sank in terror. What was happening to her? Could this be the start of another lethal seizure?

Gulping a breath, she struggled to focus. Gradually, the walls settled and the double images coalesced.

Better.

A few minutes more, and the crisis had passed. Still shaky, she crossed to the fireplace and started cleaning up the mess.

As she finished scooping up the last of the ashes, the

doorbell sounded. Peering out the window, Thea spotted the detective's Toyota at the curb. On the way to the door, she brushed her fingers through her hair and pinched color into her cheeks. She didn't want the policeman to view her as a raging wild woman.

Ensuring Gabby's safety from that predatory delinquent, Dylan Connable, was all that mattered right now. Selfish pleasures, such as the castration and dismemberment of the duplicitous Mr. Perry, would have to wait.

CHAPTER
FORTY-FIVE

Dylan Connable's black bomb was parked at the end of the driveway. Biederman's knock at the front door brought no response, and a quick circuit of the house unearthed no sign of life. But that didn't mean the little scum wasn't hiding inside.

Biederman remembered the time two years ago when he came to question Dylan about the mailbox bombings. It had taken thirty minutes for Mrs. Connable to coax the kid out of his room. And even then, the teenager had stayed silent as a tomb.

Hammering harder, Biederman barked a warning. "Open the door or I'll break it down, Connable!"

Still no sound from inside. Casting around, Biederman's eye was drawn to the narrow window over the garage. He took in the black drape centered by a crude painted skeleton. Definitely Connable's sicko style.

His old lady had probably banished him from the house. Understandable.

Before the little creep had a chance to bolt, Biederman sprinted to the garage and took the stairs three at a time. Catching his breath, he pounded on the door.

"It's Detective Biederman, Connable. Open up. I need to talk to you."

Nothing.

Biederman pummeled the door harder. "Come on, Connable. I'm in no mood for games."

Steaming, Biederman knew the kid was inside. He could even picture the smart-ass look on Connable's mug. Time to bust in and wipe that smirk away.

So he wasn't on the force anymore. So he didn't have a warrant. Since when did wild animals have civil rights?

"That's it, Connable. I'm coming in."

Trying to assess what he was up against, Biederman jiggled the knob. To his considerable surprise, the handle turned freely; the door creaked open.

Inside, the room was steeped in shadow. Clothing littered the floor. Squinting, Biederman took in the makeshift furniture. A tower of shoe boxes burdened a table fashioned from an old door on sawhorses. For seating, there was a beanbag chair and a bar stool with a broken cane seat. Two ratty mattresses stacked on the floor passed for a bed. The bathroom was a trio of fixtures half hidden by a hospital screen.

"Connable?"

Groping around, Biederman located the light switch. He flicked it on. The screaming glare momentarily blinded him.

Where in hell was the kid? Could the little scum be crouching in ambush? From ancient reflex, Biederman groped for his piece. But the cupboard was bare. Cursing Buck Delavan, Biederman tossed caution and sense aside.

"Sing out, Connable. Let's play this straight and easy."

As his eyes adjusted, he scanned the wreckage for the hidden teenager. He poked through several of the junk heaps that seemed large enough to camouflage a crouching body.

"Come on, Dylan. Give it up. I know you're here."

Biederman knew Connable's mentality. A kid like that would sooner leave one of his limbs behind than venture out without his wheels. If his car was here, so was he.

"*Now*, Connable. I'm running out of patience."

Only two piles left. Biederman stomped them in turn. No Dylan.

Crossing soundlessly toward the hospital screen, he tensed. He wouldn't put it past the Connable kid to be packing a piece of his own. Guns were all the rage with miscreant minors these days. Bigger than Nintendo, and way more bang for the buck. For the price of a few weeks' allowance, any tot with a lethal chip on his shoulder could vent his adolescent frustrations through the barrel of a thirty-eight.

Biederman was in striking range of the divider. The stained toilet and half of the filthy sink were fully visible. A ceramic claw poked out from the bottom of the screen. Connable could be crouching behind the tub, using it as a barricade. Shielding his head with an arm, Biederman lunged and knocked the partition aside.

Dylan Connable was splayed out in the tub, but the teenager wasn't bathing. There was a sickly gray cast to the kid's skin, and his eyes had the cracked look of old porcelain. Searching wildly, Biederman spotted the empty vials. Valium, Seconal, Halcyon, and Darvon. Jesus. No way to know for sure how many pills the kid had ingested. But from the look of him and the shallow rasp of his breathing, it had been more than plenty.

No phone in the room. Biederman draped the unconscious boy across his shoulders and hustled him down the stairs. Awkwardly, Biederman laid Dylan's limp body out on the backseat of his Toyota and slipped behind the wheel. Slamming a portable gumdrop on the hood, he hit the siren.

On route, he directed a steady pep rap at the unconscious kid.

"Hang in there, Dylan. Keep breathing. In with the good air. You can do it, son. Just a few minutes, and we'll be there. Breathe, Dylan. Thatta boy."

Swerving around a car in his path, Biederman veered

into the hospital drive and barreled toward the Emergency entrance. Racing the clock, he tugged open the back door and pulled Dylan out.

Kid was limp as a water balloon. His color had deepened to an ominous blue-gray. A thread of spittle trailed from the slack corner of his mouth.

"No croaking on me, Dylan Connable. You *breathe*, damn it. Take a breath!"

Within seconds, a code blue blasted over the loudspeaker, summoning the emergency team. A trio of white coats appeared pushing a gurney and swiftly hustled the kid into the treatment area.

Biederman tried to follow, but a burly security guard blocked him at the door.

"Sorry, buddy. Gotta wait out here."

Biederman saw no reason to argue. All he could do was pray for Dylan's survival, and that didn't call for a front row seat. Unexpectedly, he found himself rooting hard for Connable. All things considered, he seriously doubted there was anything sinister about the kid's attentions to the little Harper girl. The teenager was a sad case, true. Misguided, no question. But Biederman couldn't place him anywhere close to evil. He'd never seen Dylan as mean or vindictive either, except when it came to the destructive impulses the boy aimed at himself.

You'd better pull through, Connable. I want you strong enough so I can wring your stupid neck.

After one of the longest hours in the history of time, a blond resident emerged with a weary smile and an upturned thumb.

"We pumped his stomach and brought him around. Give him a couple of days' rest and observation, and he'll be ready to head home," she said. "You his dad?"

"No relation. I just happened to stop by his place and find him."

"Lucky thing. Much longer, and we would've lost him."

"I'm glad he's okay."

She removed her gold-rimmed glasses and rubbed the narrow bridge of her nose. "I wouldn't go that far. That young man needs long-term psychiatric help and a strong support system. According to our records, this was his third attempt."

"I know."

"You think the family would cooperate in a treatment program?"

"There's only the mother, and from the look of it, the relationship isn't what you'd call close."

The doctor frowned and replaced her glasses. "Sounds like he might be a candidate for the new program here. We just opened a psych unit on the adolescent wing. It's geared to young people like him who've got a lot on their minds and not much behind them. The team provides long-term counseling, job training, and the kind of supportive atmosphere these kids so desperately need. They're booked to capacity, but by fortunate coincidence, my husband happens to be head of the department."

Biederman thought about Connable's record. "This kid's no angel, Doctor."

"That's fine, because I'm not talking anything close to heaven. Fighting back from that level of depression isn't easy. He's facing a long haul and a lot of serious hard work. I'll stop up and check on him tomorrow. See if I can get him interested."

"Sounds good. Thanks."

Biederman gave the doctor his number and asked to be kept informed. From the lobby pay phone, he called Thea to bring her up to date. She sounded tighter than a drumhead. Even worse than she'd been earlier when she unloaded her concerns about her daughter's secret attachment to Dylan Connable.

He did what he could to reassure her. The Connable kid had plenty of problems, but Biederman honestly couldn't imagine him as a child molester.

Heading for his car, Biederman wondered if there was really any way to set the suicidal teenager spinning in the right direction.

Meanwhile, there was work to do. Thea deserved to have her name cleared. Time to pin the tail on the real donkey.

He spent the morning wandering the downtown streets aimlessly, trying to think past the utter futility of his situation. Returning to the room, he found his message light blinking like an eye full of cinders. He dialed the desk, and Molly, the pudgy day receptionist, connected him to the voice mail recording.

"You———have———three———messages," the robot operator intoned.

His pulse quickened. Three calls? Aside from the Gallatins' lawyer, no one had this number. Since signing on with the old lady, his world had shrunk to this: a seedy motel room overlooking the turnpike off-ramp. A job he loathed and an obligation he hated worse. The package was all-inclusive: snowy TV, sway-backed mattress, unlimited helpings of humble pie.

"First———message."

As expected, the lawyer's clipped tone chilled the line. *"This is Cassandra Rodbury calling at one-oh-five P.M. Saturday. As you know, your full report was due at my office by five P.M. yesterday. At this juncture, I have no alternative but to presume you are unable to fulfill your obligation to us. Unless I hear from you by noon Monday to the contrary, you may consider yourself terminated."*

"Fine, Ms. Rodbury. Out is what I wanted in the goddamned first place."

He raised a triumphant fist. Finally, there was a snippet of good news. If he'd known it was as easy as screwing up, he would have used that exit door long ago.

"Second———message," the robot voice droned.

"*Cassandra Rodbury again. I neglected to mention that our mutual employer is highly displeased at this unpleasant turn of events. She wishes for me to inform you that unless you meet our Monday deadline, she fully intends to turn over certain unfortunate information about you to the appropriate authorities.*"

He blew a breath. A few years back, he'd spent six months in Mexico, working on an exposé about a U.S. pharmaceutical firm that was relabeling and dumping expired and substandard medicines across the border.

Shortly after his arrival in Mexico City, he'd met a knockout young local named Yolanda. The connection was instant and intense. Advanced chemistry. When he'd collected enough to hang the drug company in print, he'd headed home believing his lady love would follow in a couple of weeks after her kid sister's high school graduation.

Yolanda had insisted on seeing him off at the airport. As they were about to separate at the security gate, she handed him a gift-wrapped package. In her halting English, she'd shyly explained that it was a gift for his mother, a special surprise.

He'd floated home on a lazy cloud of contentment. But the stroll through customs in New York brought him in for a nasty landing.

Turned out that his beautiful Yolanda worked for the drug company he'd set out to trip. The real special surprise was the contents of the so-called gift for his mother: two kilos of top-grade coke. Faster than you could say "Hands up and spread 'em," he was staring down the throat of fifteen-to-life for possession with intent to sell.

One of the arresting cops had summed things up neatly. His story was about as believable as a three-dollar bill. With his brain finally back from vacation, he quickly realized exactly how things were destined to go. Authorities attempting to check his version of events would find no Yolanda, no romance, not a shred of proof to back his strident claim of innocence. Instead, they'd turn up any number of credible witnesses willing and extremely eager to link him to one of the major drug cartels. Through the steel bars, he watched his bright future winging out the window.

But after two days in the federal lockup, a guard simply opened the cell door and let him walk. At first, he thought it a miracle, or, at least, some incredible stroke of good fortune. Turned out he'd simply been tapped by Lily Gallatin's scouts for a different brand of imprisonment.

As soon as he walked out of that cell, he became old lady Gallatin's puppet. How had he ever been dumb enough to imagine he could regain possession of his own strings? Like it or not, he had to deliver what the old bitch wanted. It was either Thea Harper's head or his. Make that Thea's or the matched set. One way or the other, old lady Gallatin was determined to avenge her son's murder. Nothing would be gained by his joining Thea under the blade.

"Third——message," the mechanical voice intoned.

"Max, it's Thea. The game's over. I know who and what you are. First thing Monday, I'm calling to let Gabby's school know, too.

"You are hands-down the most despicable person I've ever had the revolting misfortune to meet. I hope you crawl back under whatever rock you came from and stay there."

"End——of——final——message."

With a groan, Max Perry sank onto the bed and flung an arm over his eyes. Final message was right. With Harper onto him, how could he possibly redeem himself with the old lady?

What had tipped Thea? And why now?

He played over every second of their time together

last night. Lust squeezed him as he recalled the melting softness of her mouth and the lean press of her body against his. She certainly hadn't found him despicable then.

So, what changed her mind?

Suddenly, it dawned on him. A frantic search of the room and his car confirmed his idiotic mistake. He'd left his damn briefcase at her house. The thing was crammed with incriminating evidence of his true purpose and identity.

Flopping back on the bed, Max Perry stared at the stained ceiling in disgust. How had he come to this? He'd been a rising star. Unlimited future.

Fresh out of Columbia journalism school, he'd landed a plum job with *Newsweek*. One of the first pieces he'd worked on, an undercover insider's view of a militant religious cult in Oregon, had made the short list for that year's Pulitzer.

After that, the offers came fast and furious. *The New York Times, People, Vanity Fair, Chicago Trib,* NBC television. But he'd turned them all down, convinced he was destined to set the world ablaze as a maverick freelancer. Max Perry was going to do the important stories, profile the key players. He would not be muzzled by sponsor sensitivity or front office politics.

But he'd hit a series of false starts and unfortunate dead ends. Tight finances forced him to accept a number of third-rate assignments. He'd found himself beholden to the very system he'd vowed to avoid. He was no longer viewed as a first-team player. Few viewed him as a player at all.

The pharmaceutical company story was supposed to mark his comeback. He'd saved his pennies for over a year and finally scraped up enough to strike out on his own again. But in the end, corporate greed and a fork-tongued Latin beauty had capped his pen for good.

By far his strongest talent had turned out to be tossing away his best chances. It was exactly what his father had predicted during the old man's frequent drunken tirades. Old sot must've had the crystal ball hidden inside his omnipresent Wild Turkey bottle.

You're nothing, Maxwell Perry. And nothing's all you'll ever be.

He spoke to the foul-breathed memory. "You were right, Dad. Pity you drank yourself to death before you had a chance to watch all your fondest wishes for me come true."

If he didn't deliver tomorrow, Lily Gallatin would push the necessary buttons. She'd get the drug case against him reopened. She'd destroy him. His sole future writing would be for the *Danbury Federal Penitentiary News*. It was over. He was over.

A wave of fury overcame him. "No!" he bellowed.

The outcry drew a protesting bang from the adjoining room. Probably some illicit lovers in a midday tryst. Whole goddamned world was full of cheats and liars. But, considering what his reward had been for going it straight and honest, who the hell could blame them?

This was his last chance. He simply could not play dead and let it escape him.

There was only one sure way to please old lady Gallatin and get the bitch off his back for good.

Thea Harper had to be sacrificed.

CHAPTER FORTY-SEVEN

Ellie was in a full-fledged cleaning frenzy. She'd been at it nonstop since early morning, pausing only long enough to wolf down a cheese sandwich and a cup of tea for lunch before returning to the studio. Normally, Thea would have tried to get her mother to slow down and relax awhile. But today, she was glad to have Ellie preoccupied and unaware of the nasty turn of circumstances.

Caro's minivan paused at the curb. Peering out, Thea caught the high-pitched chorus of farewells. The twins urged Gabby to come by later for a sleepover. A moment later, her daughter trotted toward the house smiling broadly. Must have been a pleasant morning, Thea thought. Rotten shame she had to kill the child's afternoon.

Thinking of the hideous news she was duty-bound to report, Thea's mouth parched. But she couldn't risk having Gabby hear from someone else about her treasured teacher's duplicity or her clandestine friend's suicide attempt. Sordid tales spread faster than flu germs in this town, as Thea knew all too painfully. At any moment, the phone could ring or a little friend might stop by to recount the nasty stories.

Spying Thea's troubled look, Gabby stopped cold. "What's the matter, Mommy?"

Thea had planned to ease into the difficult revelations, but the child's antennae had picked up the distress signals at once.

"Come on in and sit down, sweetie. We have to talk."

"You're sick again, aren't you? You promised me, Mommy. You promised!"

Thea quickly caught her panicked daughter in a fierce hug, then dried the trail of tears. "Ssh. It's not that. Come inside, and I'll tell you."

She tried to temper the blows. Stretching as far as she could, she glossed over the matter of Max Perry's false face. The teacher had been working on a story for a magazine, she told Gabby. Now that he was finished collecting his material, he'd be leaving the class. Soon, Mrs. Carlisle would be returning from her maternity leave, so Mr. Perry's stint as substitute was bound to end one way or the other.

Softening the Dylan Connable story was harder. At the very mention of the teenager's name, Gabby stiffened. Her mother's gentle probing about the duration and nature of the friendship inspired a stream of lies and defenses.

"I don't know what you're talking about. Who told you junk like that?"

"Stop, Gabby. Mrs. Rossner saw you with Dylan several times. It's okay. I'm not angry with you. I just want to know how you got to know him and how you spent your time together."

"Mrs. Rossner's a stupid, dirty liar! I hate her. Everyone does."

Thea didn't press it. "All right. You'll talk to me about it when you're ready. But I have to tell you Dylan has very serious problems. Today he tried to hurt himself by taking a bunch of pills."

Gabby paled.

"He's okay," Thea added hastily. "They pumped his stomach at the hospital. Hopefully, he'll agree to enter a special program they have for troubled teenagers. With the right help, he can get well."

"But I said it was my birthday and he promised," the little girl muttered.

"What?"

"Nothing. Can I go to my room now?"

Again, the child was retreating, running away from her. Thea ached for the way things used to be, when she was the prime source of her daughter's comfort. "Please don't, sweetie. I know you're upset about Mr. Perry and your friend Dylan. It's better if we talk things out together."

But the little girl recoiled and headed for the stairs.

Thea heard the too-familiar sound of the door slamming overhead. So much for her cozy plans for a special family evening. She'd be lucky if she managed to pry the child out of her room, much less the clam shell.

Casting around for a distraction, Thea realized it had been several days since she'd written in the journal she'd brought home from the hospital. At Brook Hollow, daily entries were encouraged. The writing was viewed as a means for patients to stay in touch with their thoughts and feelings.

Skipping to a vacant page, Thea allowed her meandering thoughts to lead her hand. From the journal, there were no secrets. Here, the only judgments that mattered were her own.

PERSONAL JOURNAL

4 October

Thus far, the path has been clear and level. Three times, I have confronted and eliminated my tormentor. Only the first exposed me to the vicious glare of public view, and still I managed to escape harsh punishment. Only the fourth and final reckoning remains incomplete. That scrap of rotting, useless flesh clings stubbornly to its pitiable existence. But surely, the struggle will soon be surrendered.

Beyond that, I must remain unfettered and untarnished. My sacred mandate transcends petty human enterprise. It is beyond justice, beyond such trivial questions as guilt or innocence, right or good, past or future.

I have been chosen as the agent of cleansing.

I must rid the world of my father's evil presence in all its myriad forms.

Anything that blocks my path must be thwarted. Anyone who bars my way will be leveled to blood and ash.

CHAPTER FORTY-EIGHT

Armed with the evidence tech's report, a photo enlargement, and the spectrographic analysis of the lipstick
smudge lifted from Simon Gallatin's corpse, Biederman
visited the laboratory of Dr. Cyril Hammond.

Hammond, a biochemist, served as director of product development for Lucy Glenn Cosmetics, a small
Stamford-based concern specializing in eco-friendly face
paints.

The contact had been arranged through Biederman's
kid sister, Marna, whose oldest son, Greg, played soccer
on the squirt squad Hammond coached. Biederman had
gone to cheer his nephew's team a couple of times, and
the coach had impressed him as decent and supportive.
Hammond was the type who taught and encouraged the
kids rather than egging them on out of misplaced ma-
chismo or some warped passion for victory at any cost.

Rare breed.

From Biederman's observation, most suburban team
leaders were in it solely for the kill. So were the majority of the kids' misguided parents. At the typical game,
any number of charming moms and dads could be heard
urging their little Jason or Tiffany to murder the defense or kick the goalie in the head.

The cosmetic firm occupied the first three floors of a
squat cement-block building in Stamford's Research
Park. As promised, Hammond was waiting at the entrance when Biederman arrived. A slight, balding man,
he was clad in the orange-and-white uniform of his
team: the Sorrento's Pizzeria Pirates. He'd come directly

from the kids' stunning four-to-two upset over the formerly undefeated Springdale Dry Cleaner Devils.

Biederman reveled in Hammond's recap of the game. Marna's kid had been credited with a goal and two assists. The Devils' star center, a steamroller named Bobby, had been exposed by the referee as an overaged ringer. Turned out the kid was pushing eleven, and the coach had been trying to pass him off as just past eight. Best of all, the Pirates had survived the heady triumph with their sportsmanship intact. As Hammond proudly told it, every one of the runts had remembered to line up and shake hands with the grumbling losers before running off to pat themselves on the backs.

Right makes might.

Hammond unlocked the main door and led Biederman through the lobby. The ground-floor lab was a spit-shined square filled with futuristic machinery. Biederman took in the endless racks of trial formulations and the mountainous stacks of computer-generated data. Seemed like an enormous amount of energy and brainpower to expend in the dubious interest of stamping out facial nudity.

"A private facility like this is a rarity today," Hammond told him. "Most cosmetic companies do nothing more than package and promote. They simply buy the innards from one of the major fabricators.

"We manufacture from scratch because of our commitment to the environment. Everything that comes out of this facility is nontoxic and strictly natural. Of course, no animal testing." Proudly, he ticked off the features of the line on his fingers. "We're dye-free, additive-free, fragrance-free, and hypoallergenic."

Biederman figured the products must be big ticket. These days, the more you were guaranteed not to get, the higher the freight.

"Let's see what you've brought." Hammond took the

copies of the reports and the blown-up photo and settled down to study them at his desk.

While he did, Biederman embarked on a cautious stroll around the lab. The place held miles of delicate glass tubing and dozens of scrupulously calibrated devices. An errant sneeze might mean a serious setback for such critical causes as blemish concealment or eyelash conditioning.

"Dan? What exactly were you hoping to get from this?" Hammond called. His words ricocheted off the polished metal surfaces, raising a perilous vibration along test tube alley.

Biederman would have answered honestly, but the truth was too ridiculous to express aloud. What was his real hope? He wanted the killer's name and address. He wanted Thea's innocence proven and all traces of guilty shadow eradicated from her life. He wanted her, overwhelmed by gratitude and instant adoration, to fling herself onto the back of his majestic white steed, loop her eager arms around his suit of shining armor, and ride off with him into the sunset.

The vials were still shivering from the sound of Hammond's voice. Treading lightly, Biederman returned to the scientist's glass-walled office in the rear. "I'll take whatever you've got," he said in a cautious hush. "Anything and everything you can tell me about the person who left that smudge."

Th scientist frowned. "I'm afraid there's not much. The lipstick is your basic P-three fifty-eight with a sunscreen additive. Pale pink with a subtle blue undertone and a trace of frost. It's a staple. Any number of companies market it under a variety of names. There's Pretty in Pink, Pink Sunset, and Blushing Beauty, just to name a few."

"How about the print itself? You must be able to tell something from that."

Hammond stared at the blowup of the smudge. "There's no sign of the color bleeding into the orbicularis oris. In other words, no wrinkles in the surface around the lips. So, it's a pretty safe bet that this came from someone fairly young. Under forty anyway."

Turning to the spectrogram, he went on. "Also, whoever left this print presents a lower than normal pH balance. The skin's acidic. You can tell that from the intensified blue cast."

"Which means?" Biederman prompted.

"Any number of things could account for it. Might be a form of anemia or a side effect of a medication or it may simply be that the kisser is partial to citrus fruit or pops a lot of vitamins."

Biederman's hopes were going under for the third time. "Can you tell anything else about the person? Gender maybe?"

"Not really. Obviously, women are the typical lipstick users, but there's nothing to indicate that this print couldn't have been made by a male."

"Especially if it was a male trying to frame a woman for the crime."

"True."

"Anything else?"

Hammond mused awhile. "Well, from the sunscreen, you might conclude that you were dealing with a sensitive, fair-skinned individual. But our research shows that a decent proportion of medium and even dark-skinned consumers are buying into the sun protection craze. And, of course, there are those who just pick up cosmetics on impulse or buy by package, brand, or color and have no interest in the contents whatsoever."

"Can you tell anything about the person's size or physical condition?"

Hammond shook his head. "Nothing like that. If you found the mouth that made this print, an expert might be able to determine whether there's a reasonable probability of a match. But even then, I don't know if a court would consider it admissible evidence. Lips are too easy to alter surgically or by collagen injection."

"There must be something else," Biederman urged desperately.

Again, the scientist peered at the photo enlargement. Trading his glasses for a magnifying lens, he held the picture up to catch the fluorescent light.

"Hmmm."

"Hmmm what?"

"The print was made with the lips flaccid. No pucker. If the musculature had been engaged, you'd never be able to see the outline of the underlying tooth. See here?" With his finger, he traced a vague tulip shape in the center of the smudge.

"What is it?"

"Right lateral incisor. And an interesting one at that."

Biederman's patience level was lolling in emergency reserve. "Interesting how?" he demanded.

"There's a visible medial striation." Hammond pointed to a groove down the center of the tulip. "Very distinctive."

"So we're looking for a person with a dented tooth."

"Right. And should you find that tooth, you've got convincing evidence that the lips in front of it were the ones that left this smudge."

Biederman thanked the scientist and hit the road. The tooth angle was a step in the right direction. There was ample legal precedent for the admissibility of dental evidence. The fact that the killer had left a clear impression of a tooth with an oddity was convenient. What was highly *inconvenient* was his continuing need to track down this particular mouth.

There had to be an easier way, something he was overlooking. *Damn it, Daniel. Think!*

Which reminded him of Murray Masters's parting words. *Think about it, Daniel. What does it remind you of when a killer gives the victim one last kiss?*

One last kiss?

He rummaged through all the logical associations: a kiss good-bye, a kiss good night. In this case, it had been the kiss of death. But that neat link told him nothing meaningful.

A good-bye kiss certainly described it best, but Masters had been trying to point him toward something that would help to unmask the killer.

A kiss good night?

The phrase propelled him back through time and circumstance to his parents' split-level home in Lynbrook, Long Island. He was a gangly kid of seven or eight, about the same age as his nephew Greg. Every night at eight-thirty on the nose, his mother would enter his room, corral his lanky limbs under the covers, and plant the ritual succession of busses on his forehead, cheeks, chin, and nose.

"Sleep tight, my little genius," she'd say. "Rest well, so you'll be fresh and alert and keep making straight A's so they'll accept you at the very best medical school."

Woman would have made one hell of a soccer coach.

Evicting Mom from his thoughts, Biederman retrained his focus on Murray Masters's teasing question: *What does it remind you of when a killer gives the victim one last kiss?*

No contest. One last kiss made him think of a parent's bedtime ministrations to a child. But how was that significant in the case of Simon Gallatin? Did Masters honestly believe the senator's mother had committed the murder?

No sale.

No matter how hard he tried, Biederman couldn't make the addition work on that one. If, for some bizarre reason, old lady Gallatin had wanted her son eliminated, she would have used her considerable means to get the job done professionally. People like the Gallatins did not attend personally to menial tasks. Lily Gallatin wouldn't know which side of a dust rag to use, much less how to go about personally whacking a wayward offspring.

Plus, it was impossible to imagine a woman in her midseventies wielding the hefty trophy that had splattered the senator's brains. The scant solid evidence Biederman had uncovered made the perp as a young person in peak physical shape.

One last kiss?

A pair of sleepless nights had left him dull and foggy. He needed a nap to recharge his mental batteries. An hour or two would put his brain back in decent operating condition. Yawning broadly, Biederman eased the Toyota into his designated parking space and headed for his apartment.

$\mathcal{C}$HAPTER
FORTY-NINE

Finished with her journal confessional, Thea settled on the living room sofa with the family photo album. She turned to her favorite picture of Justin and studied his warm green eyes.

"Pity they don't have an Olympics for foul-up parents, Justin my love. I'd win the gold hands down."

As always, Thea warmed to the sight of him. The powerful connection was still there. And it was still a comfort.

"I must have said something to drive Gabby away like that. Said something or *done* something."

Thea imagined Justin's arms encircling her, his voice firm and reassuring. *It's not you, sweetheart. Gabby's just going through a stage.*

"But what if it's more than that? I don't think she trusts me, Justin. How can a little girl grow up in a world where there's no one she feels she can trust?"

She's just worried because she loves you. Give it time and she'll get over it. You know how resilient kids are.

Yes. Thea knew. But she also knew how easily small kids could be damaged. Sometimes irrevocably. Shaking her head sadly, she closed the album and set it aside.

Turning, she was surprised to find her mother standing in the doorway.

"Hey, Mom. I didn't hear you come in. You finally ready for a break?"

"What's going on with you, Theodora?"

Thea cringed at the unexpected use of her given name and the unaccustomed hard edge that had invaded her mother's tone.

"What do you mean?"

Ellie pulled several odd objects out of her apron pocket and held them out accusingly. "I found these in your red Windbreaker in the studio. Jacket smelled of fire something awful."

Thea eyed the strange display. There was a black doll's shoe, an empty can of lighter fluid, and an unfamiliar house key.

"I have no idea where those things came from," she said softly. "I've never seen them before."

Her mother's frown deepened as she set the objects down on the coffee table. "And how about all those paintings you messed up? What's gotten into you?"

Thea recoiled from her mother's suspicions. Ellie had always stuck by her without reservation, even after Simon's murder. That unconditional support had helped Thea through some of the worst times. How could Mom suddenly pull the rug out now?

"What are you saying, Mom?"

"I'm not *saying* anything, Theodora. I'm asking. Ever since I came, you've been acting mighty strange. If something's not right, I'd rather hear it directly from you than find it out in some newspaper or on the six o'clock news."

Her mother's distrust seemed more than she could bear. "It's just been difficult getting things back to normal with Gabby, that's all," Thea said dully. "My coming home has been a tough adjustment for both of us. Maybe this wasn't such a good time for you to visit."

Her mother stiffened. "Maybe you're right. Probably be best if I get back to Daddy and the ranch anyhow."

"It probably is. I'm sure Jimmy is anxious to get back to his place, too."

Ellie glanced at her watch. "I'll go pack. If you wouldn't mind calling me a cab, I can likely make the five o'clock flight."

"Fine."

Thea ached to back up and replay the scene to a better conclusion. She hated to have her mother leave like this. But she knew it was for the best. It really would be easier to sort things out with Gabby alone. And if the report from Dr. Forman was bad news, having her mother around would only make things more complicated. Despite the throbbing ache of loss in Thea's heart, she decided to keep still and let her mother go.

She eyed the odd objects on the coffee table. A doll's shoe? Lighter fluid? A key? Where *had* those things come from? What did they mean?

In under ten minutes, Ellie Sparks trudged down the stairs toting her suitcase. Five minutes later, the cab Thea had called pulled into the drive. The driver leaned on the horn.

Thea walked her mother out and wrapped her in an awkward embrace. Ellie pulled back and met her daughter's anxious gaze.

"Sorry, Checker. I didn't mean to upset you. I was just—"

"It's all right. I'd rather have you speak your mind than let things fester."

Sorrow filled the older woman's eyes. "You know I'll always love you and stand by you, honey. No matter what."

"I know."

Ellie nodded firmly. "Guess I'd best be going, then. Talk to you soon."

Thea watched until the cab drifted out of sight on Imperial. Folding her arms against the chill of loneliness, she walked into the house.

CHAPTER FIFTY

Reluctantly, Gabby had agreed to join Thea at the dinner table. But a toxic silence loomed between them. Her attempts to draw her daughter out fell flat. The conversation was the toss and parry of dead balls.

"Don't you like the soup, sweetie?"

"It's fine."

"If it's too hot I can get you an ice cube."

"I'm not hungry."

Thea had no appetite either. She felt wrung out and bone weary. Maybe she really was coming down with something.

Or maybe she'd succumbed to an acute attack of bleak reality. For once, she found her optimistic nature completely overwhelmed. At best, she could envision the glass as half full of arsenic.

The sorry facts were undeniable. Her career was in a persistent vegetative state, her personal life was in shambles. Even her foundation of close family support had developed a web of dangerous cracks.

To the general public, she remained an object of derision and disgust: Westport's black widow. Strangers, Simon's family, and her old nemesis, Walter Martin, wished her harm. Others, including Harlan Vernon and the king of all snakes, Max Perry, sought to mine some nuggets of personal gain from her mother lode of misfortune.

As if the legions of detractors weren't enough to drag her down, her own psychiatrist was playing cruel mind games, forcing Thea to wait endlessly for the results of a routine examination. Now even her daughter was shutting her out.

Not that she could blame Gabby. She had caused the child so much pain and confusion. Naturally, the little girl felt abandoned and betrayed. Distancing herself from the specter of further disappointment was a logical protective response.

Regaining Gabby's trust would not be a simple matter. Thea had to repair the shattered bridge between them. The bond had to be mended, inch by inch.

"How about dessert?"

"No, thanks. Can I go to the Millports'? The twins asked me to stay over."

Thea stifled her protests. Let the child enjoy herself. "Okay, sweetie. Have fun."

In record time, Gabby bounded upstairs, packed her overnight bag, and left. Standing in the doorway, Thea watched until the little girl was absorbed by the well-oiled family across the street.

Pinched by envy, Thea pondered Caro's crammed existence. The big sloppy lapdog of a husband. The noisy crew of flourishing kids. The burgeoning business. Everything Caro touched blossomed. All Thea had managed to raise was a bumper crop of thorns.

After the front door closed at the Millports', Thea continued to stare at the striking display of nature's temper. The predicted storm had passed in a brief, angry rush. An hour of driving rain had polished the sky and dotted the ground with puddles. The road was dark, the air fresh and settled. Now, against dusk's muted canvas, the autumn hues were garish bloody slashes, violent spikes, bolts of startling flame. Chilled by the unwelcome images, she turned and went inside.

Thea cleared the table and dumped the remains of the disastrous meal into the trash. In the living room, she flipped through the cable channels, trying in vain

to find something that might absorb her. Turning off
the set in disgust, she picked up her precious photo album. But tonight, the smiling snapshots offered no
comfort. Instead, they seemed a mocking reminder of
all the things she'd lost.

Only six-thirty. How was she supposed to fill the
rest of this godforsaken evening? She considered and re-
jected her favorite pastimes in turn. Formerly an avid
reader, she hadn't been able to lose herself in a good
book since Simon's death. Snuggling required a partner.
So did engaging in stimulating discussion. Painting
called for a normal attention span and some inspiration.
She couldn't muster either at the moment. Normally,
she loved soaking in the tub, but given her current
mood, she might be moved to dive in headfirst.

*Can it, Checker honey. Nothing's sorrier than a body feel-
ing sorry for herself.*

Rummaging through the linen closet, she found her
favorite bath salts. Perched on the rim of the tub, she
fiddled with the taps until the water temperature was
perfect. As the bubbly brew approached the top of the
tub, she tuned her bedside radio to soft classical music.

Sinking into the warmth, Thea's aching muscles un-
coiled like slipknots. Her weary mind drifted. All the
weighty problems turned to helium balloons. She imagined them catching the wind and bobbling off toward
oblivion.

So relaxing.

She was floating herself, dangling at the fuzzy edge
of consciousness. Languishing in the sensuous moment.
The perfumed water played against her like knowing
fingers. Pressing, probing.

Thea worked the currents with her hands. Eyes
closed, she conjured the warmth of Justin's body.
Justin's seeking lips and stroking fingers. A groan of
pleasure escaped her as she surrendered to the luscious

sensation. It was building, consuming her. Sounding a jarring shrill.

Ringing?

The phone!

Sloshing out of the tub, Thea sped into her room to pick up before the tape machine. Slim chance it was Dr. Forman calling on a Saturday night, but she didn't want to blow the possibility.

"Hello?" The towel she'd grabbed in her haste was hand size. She blotted what she could of the soapy swells coursing toward the rug. Her bare, wet skin caught a draft that made her shiver.

"Thea Harper?"

"Yes."

"Hold, please."

Great. Probably someone trying to sell her tickets to a benefit concert or shares in a mutual fund. Those people had an uncanny knack for sniffing out the prime time for unwelcome intrusions.

Talk about cold calls.

Thea was about to hang up when she heard the unmistakable starch of the voice she'd been awaiting.

"Thea? Dr. Forman calling. Sorry I couldn't get back to you sooner. Before we spoke, I wanted to have a colleague review the results of your tests. Unfortunately, he wasn't available until late this afternoon, but I thought it was important to wait for his input."

"Why? What did you find?"

"I'd prefer to discuss it in person."

"Whatever it is, I'd rather hear it now."

The starched voice softened. "I understand your anxiety, Thea. But there are issues here that we need to address at some length. I'm in the office for a session right now. I can meet with you in forty-five minutes."

"All right."

Thea toweled off, tossed on jeans and a sweatshirt, and headed out.

Bessie was acting her cantankerous worst, stubbornly refusing to start. Railing in frustration, Thea stomped the gas pedal. After several fruitless attempts, she was rewarded by the sorry groan of a flooded engine.

Pounding the steering wheel, she accidentally hit the horn. It stuck, raising a strident scream. Anxiously, she dug at the depressed button. A commotion like this was bound to bring the neighbors. In her current state of mind, a single round from Glenda Rossner's mouth might prove lethal.

Desperate, Thea rummaged through the glove compartment and found a screwdriver. The metal point liberated the horn; the blaring stopped.

Take a breath, Checker honey. Running like a headless chicken isn't going to get you there any sooner. Anyway, what's your fat hurry? The badder the news, the longer it's guaranteed to wait.

Still, she had to learn the truth and find some way to deal with it. Whatever it was couldn't be worse than the dark sludge dredged up by her own imagination. These past few days she'd been no good to herself and less than useless to her child. Time to face the facts.

Thea was no mechanic, but she'd mastered a few necessary tricks over the years. To clear the glut of fuel, you had to keep the gas pedal floored while charging the motor.

Two long, slow stomps cured Bessie's constipation. The old engine churned to life. Breathing a prayer, Thea backed down the drive and drove toward the turnpike.

Twenty minutes later, she turned into the Landmark Towers garage and found a vacant spot near the elevator entrance. On the way to the ninth floor, she worked to tame her growling terror. Soon enough, she'd have the answers. No need to torment herself when a seasoned professional like Dr. Forman was so willing and able to do the job.

A small pool of light leaked from under the door to the office suite. Thea let herself into the waiting area and crossed to knock at the inner sanctum. After a beat, Dr. Forman opened the door a crack and peered out.

"We're just finishing up, Thea. I'll have to ask you to wait five minutes."

The doctor had neglected to turn on the music. Distinctly, Thea heard the sound of her retreating footsteps followed by Madame Veruschka's plaintive wail.

"Miserable bastard refuses to die! Again and again I murder him, and still he returns to ruin my life. I can't bear it. No more!"

The woman was in rare form tonight. Her anguish surged like a swollen river. Thea imagined the hands gesticulating in grand dramatic fashion. The chiseled face pinched with overstated pain.

"With every breath I despise him. My veins run hot with hatred."

As always, Dr. Forman's piece of the dialogue remained smooth and muffled. Either the shrink had been impeccably trained to swallow her feelings or, as Thea strongly suspected, she'd been born without any.

"This time, I'll see him dead for good. Once more will surely be the finish of him. Tell me so, Doctor. Tell me *this can't go on*!"

Soon, Dr. Forman drew the session to a close. As always, Madame Veruschka exited through the inner door.

In the ensuing silence, Thea imagined the shrink seated primly at her desk, penning a neat note to the loony woman's chart. That done, she'd slip a fresh cassette into the tape recorder and extract Thea's folder from the rack of patient files beside her chair. Frowning ever so slightly to avoid wrinkling her pristine complexion, she would shift her focus to the next case. Madame Veruschka's torment would simply slip from her ice-slicked mind.

Nothing moved that woman. The shrink probably enjoyed observing other people's miseries. Strange job, being paid by the truncated hour to witness a string of amateur horror shows.

Too bad no popcorn.

"Come in, Thea." As always, the doctor's garb was prim and professional: pleated black skirt, sedate white blouse with a ruffled jabot, pale hose, black midheel pumps. Not a hair out of place, not a preview of things to come in her guarded expression.

As Thea claimed her customary seat, she wished she'd taken the time to fix her hair and put herself in better order. She must look like a madwoman.

How appropriate.

The doctor donned a pair of gold-rimmed glasses. She flipped silently through a stack of reports.

"Have you been taking your medication regularly, Thea?"

"Of course."

"You're sure?"

"Positive. Why?"

The shrink pursed her lips. "The tests showed a significant dip in the blood marker for your antiseizure drug, and an oddity in your EEG. If it isn't a dosage error, we have to assume the medication has lost its effectiveness."

Fear squeezed Thea. She thought of the misplaced hours, the eerie images from homes of the murdered actor and the old couple, the strange unfamiliar things her mother had found in her Windbreaker. Her throat was so constricted she could barely speak. "Are you sure?"

"Sure enough to switch you to a different anticonvulsive drug. As I mentioned on the phone, I've consulted with a colleague. He's in complete agreement. Dr. Ronald Kriedman was involved in the development of a new medication for seizure management. It's highly effective and has few reported side effects. I think we should start you on it immediately."

"All right. I'll have the prescription filled first thing tomorrow."

"I'm afraid it's not that simple. The precise dosage has to be determined through constant monitoring. You'll have to check into Brook Hollow for several weeks, possibly a month."

Thea shook her head vehemently. "I can't. I can't leave Gabby."

The shrink allowed a trace of visible sympathy. "I understand it's difficult."

"Not difficult, impossible. I promised I wouldn't leave her again. I can't break my word."

"You can't afford not to, Thea, and you know it. As soon as this came up, I thought of Gabrielle. Why don't you bring her in and let me work this through with her?"

Thea felt torn in a million useless scraps. Dr. Forman was right. She couldn't ignore the test results. She knew too well what bloody havoc the electric storms could wreak. The image of Simon's battered corpse surfaced in her mind. So did the terrifying unknowns.

Does this mean I killed Brandon Payton and the people in Bridgeport?

She had no choice but to check into the hospital and take the new medication.

Dr. Forman's offer to temper the blow for Gabby was irresistible. Thea couldn't bear to be the one to break her promise and her little girl's heart. Maybe the shrink's training had included the mastery of some magic words.

She drew a ragged breath. "Okay. When do you want to see her?"

"I think it's best to address this right away. Why don't you bring Gabrielle in tonight? I can meet with her again tomorrow if necessary. Then, I'll arrange to admit you first thing Monday and get started."

Leaving the office, Thea was tormented by the doctor's words. The time was long past for getting started. Having spent a year inside the nightmare, all she longed to see was the end of it.

CHAPTER
FIFTY-ONE

Thea was getting nowhere. Gabby staunchly refused to leave the Millports', especially not without a compelling explanation.

"That's not fair, Mommy. You said I could stay over. We're right in the middle of putting on a play."

"I'm sorry, sweetie. We have to go now. Something's come up."

"Why can't you tell me what it is?"

"I'll explain on the way."

But the little girl set her jaw and folded her slender arms defiantly. "You said I could stay, and I'm staying."

At that, Caro returned from putting the little ones to bed. "There now, sugar. Mind your momma and run along now. You'll come sleep over with the girls another time."

Caro's honeyed manner had a miraculous way of dissolving even the stubbornest child's resistance. Gabby instantly let her arms drop and issued a sigh of surrender.

Thea caught her friend's reassuring smile, but she wasn't able to return it. "Thanks, Caro. Sorry for any trouble. Come on, sweetie."

Caro's smile yielded to a look of concern. "What's wrong, Thea?"

"Nothing."

"You sure?"

"I'll be fine."

The worried frown didn't waver. "Call me first thing tomorrow, sugar. You hear?"

"All right."

That conversation was not going to be easy. Again, Thea would have to impose on her friend's generous nature and ask her to care for Gabby while she was at Brook Hollow.

Gabby slammed the car door and jammed her seat belt into the buckle. "Okay. We're on the way now, so where are we going?"

"Dr. Forman wants to talk to you. She had some free time tonight."

"What about?"

"She'll tell you herself."

The child settled in an angry silence. Grateful for the reprieve, Thea trained her shaky focus on the road.

Ever since Dr. Forman confirmed the medication failure, Thea had been wavering between paralyzing self-doubt and desperate defensiveness. She still couldn't imagine herself hurting innocent strangers. But a seizure had reduced her to the Frankensteinian monster who'd brutally beaten Simon Gallatin to death. Was there any certain way to silence the beast for good? Could she never hope to regain some semblance of a normal existence?

Useless questions. Right now, all she could do was take the doctor's advice and get stabilized on a different drug. But first, things had to be smoothed over for Gabby.

Only a scatter of cars remained on the side of the Landmark Towers lot nearest Dr. Forman's building. Thea led her brooding daughter into the elevator and down the ninth-floor corridor to the psychiatrist's suite. As they entered the waiting room, the shrink emerged from her office. Spotting Gabby, Dr. Forman offered a warm smile and an effusive greeting. The moves were so uncharacteristic, Thea was tempted to demand the woman's identification.

"Come in, Gabrielle. I'm delighted you've agreed to come talk to me."

"No problem," Gabby said, trotting after the shrink like an obedient pup.

"I hope I didn't disrupt your plans, dear," Dr. Forman said.

"That's okay."

The door shut behind them. The camouflage music was playing at peak volume now, making it impossible for Thea to catch anything but the vaguest hint of Gabby's youthful voice and the doctor's level tone. Claiming a seat against the far wall, Thea settled down wearily to wait.

Several advance sections of tomorrow's Sunday *New York Times* were tucked into the magazine rack beside the antique *Smithsonian*s. Retrieving the newspaper, Thea leafed through the magazine and the Book Review.

Turning to the Connecticut section, she started reading a story about a little girl from Bethel who'd been injured when her bed caught fire.

Wincing, Thea glanced at the picture of the child's charred bed and smoke-blackened room after firefighters extinguished the blaze. Her thoughts swerved to the odd items her mother had found in her Windbreaker. A doll's shoe? Lighter fluid? Could she have been involved in this, too?

No! That's crazy. All this is crazy.

Dr. Forman slipped through the connecting door and closed it behind her.

"How's it going?" Thea asked.

"Fine. Can I ask you to do me a favor?"

"What?"

"There's a book I'd like to read with Gabrielle. I thought I'd brought it up, but apparently, I left it in the trunk of my car. It's the black Mercedes. You mind?"

Thea took the keys she offered. "I'll be right back.

"Thanks. I'll let you know when we're ready for it.

The doctor's gleaming black car occupied a reserved spot right near the elevators. In the trunk were several cartons packed with testing materials and other professional supplies. One box, marked "pediatric," contained dolls and puppets and the volume Dr. Forman wanted. It was an annotated story entitled *Good-bye for Now*.

Back in the waiting room, Thea set the book down beside her and paged through the Travel section of the *Times*. Then she started on Arts and Leisure. She checked her watch. The shrink had been with Gabby for almost an hour, and she still hadn't gotten around to the story she'd sent Thea down to retrieve.

Maybe she'd misunderstood and Dr. Forman was expecting her to bring the book inside. It couldn't hurt to ask. Anyhow, Thea wanted to take a firsthand look at the situation. She knew her daughter well enough to assess at a glance how things were progressing.

Thea knocked at the inner door. She listened for a response, but it was impossible to hear over the music. After a beat, she opened the door.

The office was empty.

Where could they be?

Maybe they'd taken a walk down the hall. That must be it. Gabby had probably gotten restless, and the doctor had encouraged a seventh-inning stretch.

Thea headed for the rear exit favored by Madame Veruschka. But when she opened the door, she was confronted by rows of shelves packed with office supplies.

A closet?

Searching the room, she confirmed that there were no other doors except the one leading out to the waiting area. But that was crazy. She'd heard Madame

Veruschka's bitter voice and the sound of an inner door closing. How had that patient left the office?

Thea was drawn to the stack of used cassettes on the doctor's desk. On top was the neatly labeled tape of her meeting with Dr. Forman earlier that night. Madame Veruschka's session tape must be underneath. Slipping the unlabeled cassette into the recorder, Thea pressed the play button.

After a pause, Dr. Forman's voice filled the room. *"The following is a self-session, recorded at seven P.M. on the fourth of October, 1993."*

Self-session?

"Tell me how you're progressing," Dr. Forman began in dispassionate tone.

"I am filled with hatred for that bastard. Again and again I must kill him!"

Without the music or the obstructing wall, Thea caught the similarities in the two voices. Despite the affected accent and the thick layer of raw emotion, it was still the shrink talking.

This was insane.

There was no Madame Veruschka. The crazy woman spewing poison hatred was Dr. Forman herself.

Thea's mind reeled. That lunatic had Gabby! She must have spirited the child out while Thea was downstairs getting the book. Nearly an hour ago.

Where did she take my little girl?

Thea had no idea where Dr. Forman lived. Maybe Billie knew or could find out from someone at the hospital.

She lifted the phone to make the call, but the line was dead. Tracking the cord, she spotted the severed end coiled on the floor like a sleeping reptile.

A rash of terror scaled Thea's spine. This whole thing had been a setup. The delayed test results and the re-

ported drug failure were a deliberate means for th
shrink to get her hands on Gabby.

But why?

Frantically, she tugged open the desk drawers, de
perately searching for a clue to the doctor's home ac
dress. The top drawer held nothing but paper clip
pens, extra cassettes, a letter opener, and note cards. I
the center drawer were memo pads, typing paper, a
sorted envelopes, and stamps. The bottom drawer w
locked. Thea picked up the letter opener. Without he
itation, she pried the drawer open.

Inside she found a photo album. Next to it was
pebbled notebook identical to the one she'd been give
at Brook Hollow to use as a journal. Heart thunderir
like wild hoofbeats, she opened the album. On the fir
page were four sepia-toned pictures. One depicted
young girl with Shirley Temple curls and a frilly dres
The second was a smiling young man in uniform. Th
third showed the same man decades older. The four
featured an old man shot in poor focus.

Under each picture was the word "father" and :
age. The picture of the girl child was captioned *"fathe
age five."* The others portrayed "father" at ages twent
two, forty-five, and seventy-eight respectively.

Turning the page, Thea gasped in horror. There w
a polaroid of Simon Gallatin taken at the opening of tl
gallery show where he and Thea first met. That was al
where she'd first been introduced to Dr. Forman.

Beside the shot was the grisly picture of Simor
corpse taken on the night of the murder. A slash
crimson ink stained the picture. Beneath, the shrir
had written: *"The First."*

The truth was too incredible to absorb. Dr. Forma
had killed Simon. The shrink had committed the mu
der. She set Thea up to take the blame.

All the puzzle pieces tumbled into place. As a do

or, Maxine Forman had access to the kinds of drugs that could induce temporary amnesia. As the medical director of a posh private hospital, she hobnobbed with the sort of powerful people who could provide her with inside information about the personal lives of celebrities like Simon Gallatin.

Had Simon's murder been part of some bizarre symbolic annihilation of Dr. Forman's father? Madame Veruschka's lunatic ramblings reverberated in Thea's mind: *The miserable bastard deserves to die.*

Thea's horror intensified as she turned the page. A candid picture of Brandon Lee Payton was followed by a defiled crime scene photo of the actor's body and the words: *"The Second."* Following were pictures of "Pappy" Alden Gaithwaite, dead and alive.

The third.

Again and again I kill him, but still he refuses to die.

The fourth entry was incomplete. Pasted on the page was a news clipping about a fire in a Bethel home. The attached photo showed a frightened little girl in the arms of a firefighter. The caption identified the child as Cindy Zesch, the same little girl from the Connecticut section cover story in tomorrow's *Times*. The dateline on the story in the album was over a year ago, when the former Zesch home had burned to the ground.

That homicidal lunatic has my daughter!

Thea had to find out where Dr. Forman lived. Opening the journal, she turned to the first entry with trembling fingers.

"The First," it said. And then, *"They say I struck him seven times. . . ."*

Desperately, Thea yanked open the drawers in the file cabinets flanking the supply closet. On the right were nothing but patient files. In the second drawer on the left she spotted a file marked "personal." Flipping through, Thea found a series of bills and other corre-

spondence. Most were addressed to the doctor's offi
here or at Brook Hollow. But toward the rear she foun
something that made her heart stop: a phone bi
directed to the madwoman's home: 300 Cobble Hi
Road—New Canaan.

The elevator was taking forever. Thea ran down th
fire stairs to the car. Desperately, she stomped the g
and twisted the key in the ignition.

Please don't let that lunatic hurt my baby. Please don't
it be too late.

The engine fluttered, then stalled. Cursing, she tri
again. This time, the motor sounded a harsh metall
thunk and died.

No time to lose. I have to get to Gabby.

Lungs burning, Thea raced out of the garage ar
flailed her arm at an approaching set of headlights. Sl
didn't care about what personal risks she might be ta
ing. Nothing mattered but saving her little girl.

CHAPTER FIFTY-TWO

Biederman awoke with a start. Nearly nine o'clock already. Someone had swallowed the afternoon and bitten a major chunk out of the evening.

Damn it.

He'd programmed himself for an hour's nap. Two, maximum. With Buck Delavan angling for Thea's scalp, he couldn't afford to waste half a day like this.

Still groggy, Biederman splashed his face with frigid water and gulped a couple of cups of freeze-dried nerves. Rubbing his eyes, he went to the table to resume his review of the Gallatin records. Maybe the thousandth read would reveal the secret password. He had to keep trying. As he'd done countless times before, he tried to picture the events surrounding the senator's homicide.

Thea is working in her studio. Stuck in some fugue state, she loses track of a few hours. Next thing she knows, she hears her daughter screaming. Racing in, she discovers Gallatin's battered corpse.

Her hands and clothing are smeared with the victim's blood. Her prints are the only ones found on the murder weapon. A hair of hers is embedded in one of the dead man's wounds.

She calls nine-eleven, and the officers summoned to the scene—yours truly included—see no choice but to place the obvious suspect under arrest. The woman offers no resistance, no alibi or excuses. Nothing.

Ransacking his memory, Biederman remembered her: shocked expression, dilated pupils, dead eyes. Something akin to a trance.

So far, Biederman's postmortem digging hadn't accomplished much beyond landing him in a sinkhole. There was Murray Masters's assertion that the killer was far more heavily muscled than Thea. There was the fact that the strand of Thea's hair had fallen out naturally several days before the murder and not in a struggle with Gallatin. And there was the partial lip print and vague tooth impression from the corpse's neck that might link the actual killer to the crime, especially if such a person would be kind enough to step forward and claim credit for the hit.

In other words, he had nothing.

With Delavan breathing down Thea's neck, Biederman still needed to discover who had entered the Harper house that night, lured Simon Gallatin into the den, and bashed him relentlessly with a golf trophy.

Clearly, the killer had been aware that Thea and the senator were an item. The same someone had found the means to dope or hypnotize Thea, then plant her in a handy nearby location so she could be framed for the crime. Plus, the killer had chosen a night when Thea's kid was at a neighbor's house.

Interesting.

It followed that either Simon Gallatin's murderer had known Thea well enough to be familiar with her routines and her daughter's, or the killer had kept an eye on Thea's house and activities long enough to observe the family's habits and use them to plan the hit.

One way or another, Thea herself was the likeliest candidate to hold the missing key. As an artist cued to visual detail, she may have noticed if one of her acquaintances had a dented tooth. Or she might recall seeing a stranger hanging around her neighborhood in the days or weeks before the murder.

Sorry, Mom. No straight A's for your boy genius on this

est. Why the hell didn't I think of questioning the woman in he first place?

Because you wanted to play hero, Danny boy. Be-ause you were so anxious to reel in that lovely fish in he bargain, you forgot that your first obligation was to help get an innocent citizen off the hook.

Biederman dialed Thea's number. He got a busy sig-nal. For the next fifteen minutes, he kept trying. Still busy. Finally, he asked the operator to verify.

"Sorry, sir. That number is not in service at this time."

Odd. Must be trouble on the line.

Whatever it was wouldn't cramp the forward prog-ess of Buck Delavan's lynching party. That could only be accomplished by delivering Gallatin's real killer.

Biederman grabbed the clues he needed to discuss with Thea and headed toward her house.

CHAPTER
FIFTY-THREE

"Where's Mommy?"

"I told you, Gabrielle. Your mother is planning to bring home a very special surprise. That's why she asked me to drive you here and wait for her."

"But what's taking so long?"

"You must be patient, dear. Special surprises can't be rushed."

Gabby didn't mean to whine, but she felt so tired. Her head was a brick, and she had to force her drooping lids to stay open.

"How much longer?"

"Only a little while, Gabrielle. Finish your cocoa now. There's a good girl."

The hot chocolate Dr. Forman had made was delicious. Super sweet with creamy marshmallow froth on top. Gabby leaned forward on the couch and lifted the mug to take another sip. Dumb thing felt so heavy, she had to use both hands and all her strength to bring it to her mouth.

Weird.

Gabby's eyes kept straying out of focus. Dreamily she stared at the blaze Dr. Forman had started in the fireplace. Everything appeared to be split in two. Twin flames danced atop the woodpile. Two hills of smoldering ash lined the hearth. There was a double set of fireplace tools beside a pair of identical grates. Double everything. Opal and Jazzy would love this, Gabby thought. Drunk with exhaustion, she giggled aloud.

The giggles made her hiccough. "Isn't—Mommy—

here yet?" Her tongue was thick, her words stretched long and limp like pulled taffy.

"Relax, Gabrielle. Close your eyes, now."

"But I can't, Dr. Forman. I don't want to miss the surprise."

"You won't miss it, dear. I can promise you that."

Sleep was rolling over her like that monster wave at Jones Beach last summer. Gabby struggled to grope her way to the surface, but an irresistible force kept dragging her under.

So much easier to simply sink beneath the crush of exhaustion. She would see the big surprise soon enough.

CHAPTER FIFTY-FOUR

The man behind the wheel exuded a pungent stew of old sweat, stale tobacco, and beer. As he drove, his rheumy eyes kept drifting in Thea's direction.

"Sure you wouldn't like to stop for a little drink, doll?"

"I told you, this is an emergency. Please *hurry*."

"Come on, now. One little drinkie-poo couldn't hurt." His hand snaked over and squeezed her shoulder.

"Take your hands off me. Stop the damned car! I'm getting out," Thea snapped.

He tugged back his hand as if he'd touched a hot iron. His leer faltered. "Hey, okay. You don't want a friendly drink, no problem. Just cool it and I'll take you where you want to go."

Turning away from him, Thea beat down her terror. She couldn't afford to yield to mindless panic. The only way to retrieve her daughter safely was to read the monster's thoughts.

I'm coming, sweetie. I'm going to get you away from that crazy woman.

She kept seeing the gruesome photo album. Three of the shrink's intended victims were already dead. The fourth, the little girl, had barely escaped serious injury. Swallowing back the bile, Thea knew that Gabby had been chosen as a substitute.

Again and again, I kill him. But still, he refuses to die.

For some insane reason, Dr. Forman was determined to destroy the specter of her father at every stage of his existence. Pappy Gaithwaite had symbolized the shrink's father in old age. Simon Gallatin had been a stand-in for the middle-aged version. Brandon Payton represented Dr. Forman's father as a young man. Lindy Zesch, and now Gabby, were surrogates for the lunatic's father as a little boy.

A little boy whose mother had dressed him as a girl.

It didn't take a Freudian analyst to imagine the possible psychic consequences of that. Maxine Forman's father may have been set on a collision course with sexual deviance. He'd certainly turned out to be an abuser, a pederast preying on his own little girl. Thea's mind flashed to her own father's abuses. Whenever he got her alone, dear Daddy would vent his nasty temper at Thea. Call her ugly names. Threaten to hurt her. But clearly, Hugh Sparks had been an angel compared to Dr. Forman's father.

The things he did to me! The miserable bastard deserves to die.

And now, Father's little princess, grown in his insane image, was insanely determined to pay him back.

The house was dark. Waiting impatiently until the leering driver took off, Thea hurried toward the stately white Colonial. Her heart was a sledgehammer, her breaths sharp and shallow.

Hang on, sweetie. I'm almost there.

Thea listened at the front door. Not a sound from inside. She peered through the living room window.

Nothing.

Hurrying around to the rear of the house, she couldn't see anyone in the kitchen or the family room. She tugged open the powder room window, hoisted herself over the sill, and slipped inside.

Quickly, she confirmed that the ground floor was deserted. No one in the basement either. Padding soundlessly to the second story, she swiftly checked the bedrooms and baths. To be sure, she poked in the closets and climbed the narrow flight to the attic.

No hint of life anywhere.

Nor was there anything to indicate that the doctor had brought Gabby here. No sign of Gabby's jacket or the shrink's coat or purse. When Thea went outside to check, the garage was empty except for a red Harley.

Thea had driven a friend's motorcycle a couple of times back in Idaho. She could use the Harley to get to Gabby and Dr. Forman. But where was she going?

Where can they be? I must find my baby!

Think rationally. Except for Simon, each murderous attack occurred in the victim's own house. Gaithwaite, Payton, the Zesch child.

Home. The lunatic must have taken Gabby home.

The relentless press of time made Thea shiver. Every passing second might be Gabby's last. Even at top speed, it would take her ten or fifteen minutes to get to Linden Street. Frantic, she rushed back into the doctor's house and picked up the phone.

"Amber? It's Thea. Let me speak to your dad."

"My folks went out to a movie, Mrs. Harper. Anything I can do for you?"

However tempted, she couldn't put the teenager at risk. "No. There's nothing." Her voice snagged as she broke the connection.

No answer at Detective Biederman's number. She couldn't rely on the Westport police. She imagined them thinking she'd gone over the edge again. What if they put out an APB and intercepted her before she could get to Gabby?

Her only choice was to rush home. She must get there before that madwoman added her daughter to her list of victims. Heart pounding, she turned the key and kicked down the motor on the Harley. Merciless time was ticking away.

CHAPTER
FIFTY-FIVE

A late-model black Mercedes was parked in Thea's driveway. Biederman imagined her in the company of another big-shot power broker like Simon Gallatin. Deflecting a foolish stab of jealousy, the exiled detective paused at the door and ordered himself to be gracious and charming.

Relief edged out the envy when an attractive blond woman, not some slick suitor, answered the bell.

"Yes?" she said.

"Sorry to barge in like this, but the phone's out of order."

"I know. It was accidentally left off the hook."

"I need to see Thea for a minute."

"She's out. Whom shall I say called?"

"Daniel Biederman."

"The detective?"

"Yes. Do I know you?"

"No. Thea has mentioned your name."

Biederman suppressed a grin. Thea had talked about him. Nice.

"It's important that I see her tonight. Mind if I wait?"

"Actually, I don't expect Thea until quite late, perhaps not before morning. She's on a date, Detective. I'm looking after her daughter."

His good mood evaporated. "I'd like to leave her a note, then." Rummaging through the pockets of his Windbreaker, he found nothing of use. "Can I trouble you for a piece of paper and a pen?"

"Wait here."

She shut the door in his face. Moments later, she returned bearing a note pad and pencil.

"I'm in the midst of putting Gabrielle to bed, Detective. Please be quick about it."

Biederman scrawled a short note asking Thea to call as soon as she got in, regardless of the hour. As he handed the folded paper to the sitter, she forced a stilted smile.

That was when he spotted the dented tooth.

Warning flares erupted in his brain. This woman fit the profile perfectly: muscled arms, pale pink lipstick, tulip-shaped tooth with a line down the middle. She was holding the kid inside. And probably Thea.

Before he could react, she'd closed the door again, shutting him out. Groping for a plan, Biederman strode to the curb, played footsie with the gas pedal in his Toyota, then quickly returned to the house.

This time, the woman talked from behind the security chain.

"What is it now, Detective?" Her voice was still pleasant but guarded.

"Battery must be dead. Can I use your phone?"

"What's wrong with your radio?"

"The battery works that, too. I'll just be a minute."

Grudgingly, she slipped the chain. "Gabrielle has just gone to bed. I'll show you to the studio phone so you don't disturb her."

Following her through the house, Biederman searched for signs of a struggle. A fire crackled in the den. Nothing seemed out of place in the living room. Ditto the kitchen, where the killer retrieved a key that hung on a cuphook near the back door. The little girl and Thea were nowhere to be seen.

He followed the woman out to the studio and watched her unlock the door. He'd take her down as soon as they got inside.

Once the door was open, she stood aside to let him enter first. Biederman took one long stride into the room. Then he quickly wheeled around to level the murdering bitch.

But as he reached out to grab her, she caught his wrist and flipped him. He landed hard on his spine, spewing air like a blown tire.

Startled, Biederman tried to shake off the assault. He had to tame this crazy woman and make sure Thea and the child were okay. Rising, he looked around for the killer, but she had disappeared.

How the hell—?

He was still trying to dope out where she'd gone when a crushing blow caught him from behind.

His bones melted; a fuzzy haze settled over the room. As he crumpled helplessly to the ground, he imagined Thea planting a gentle kiss on the back of his neck.

Halfway down Linden Street, Thea spotted the cars. Forman's Mercedes was in the driveway; at the curb was Detective Biederman's Toyota.

Thank God.

Thea didn't bother to wonder why the detective had stopped by. Weak with relief, she pulled in behind the shrink's car. She was nearing the front door when she heard the commotion from the studio.

There was a man's startled cry. The crash of falling objects. Silence.

Thea sprinted around the house toward the studio. The lights were out. A single silhouette hovered near the window.

It was not the detective.

Fear stalled her for an instant. But the thought of Gabby in the hands of that homicidal madwoman snapped terror's grip.

The key was in the studio door. Thea pushed it open. The detective was splayed on the floor, his head in a spreading pool of blood. Frozen in horror, Thea pictured Simon Gallatin's battered body in her den. She envisioned Simon's crumpled face. His dead eyes.

Then Thea saw the detective's chest rise.

Still alive.

A shadow loomed behind her.

Wheeling quickly around, Thea saw the doctor. Maxine Forman had the trash can poised over her head, ready to bring it down on the unconscious man again. Catching Thea's eye, she paused. Then, slowly, she set the barrel down.

"So you've arrived at last," she rasped. "I was wondering what was keeping you." Her eyes glinted. Her
ace was flushed and tight.

"Where's Gabby?"

Dr. Forman ticked her tongue. "You must stop fret-
ing about that child all the time, Thea. You'll make
er crazy."

"But never as crazy as your father made you."

Dr. Forman looked startled. "Actually, you have it
vrong, Thea. My father didn't steal my sanity. I was
quite capable of recovering from his disgusting sex
games. It was his seed. All the little saplings he plant-
d. Those, I could not abide."

"You're out of your mind."

"Perhaps I am. But who can blame me? I survive his
abuse; I grow up well and competent. A brilliant future
pread before me. I even meet a man. Stephan was
right, giving, the perfect companion."

The woman's eyes were wild, darting crazily like
ight creatures. But her voice was obscenely calm.

"Look. All I want is my daughter. Where is she?"

The shrink's face twisted. "*I* say when the session is
over, Thea. Until I do, you shall be still and listen."

Cautiously, Thea scanned the studio. There had to be
omething she could use as a weapon. The detective was
till unconscious. Thea could see the steady rise and fall
f his chest.

Maxine Forman said: "Daddy was an obstetrician,
ou see. A fertility specialist. Women would come to
im for artificial insemination and in vitro fertilization.
They thought he was using donors, a sperm bank. But
fter his death two years ago, his nurse revealed that
e'd used his own sperm to impregnate all those pa-
ients. Thirty years' worth of patients. Hundreds of off-
pring. My father kept careful records. My husband
Stephan was one of the first children he sired."

In the fray, the trash can lid had slipped off. Turpen
tine fumes wafted out. The shrink was standing besid
the barrel, gesturing wildly, her voice relentlessly an
impassively recounting these horrors. Slowly, The
slipped a hand into her pocket.

Be there. Please!

"That bastard fathered the only man I ever love
When I learned the truth, I had no choice. The rel
tionship was unthinkable. Incestuous. I had to destro
Stephan."

The matchbook from Sole e Luna was still in Thea
pocket. Thank heavens she'd spotted Gabby trying
pick up the matches and taken them away.

"But killing him didn't cleanse the sin. My basta
father soiled my soul. He left me rank and filthy."

Thea's fingertips bent one of the matches. She struc
it against the flinty base. Nothing.

Forman ranted on. "Then a vision came to me. A
angel, pure and innocent, approached me with the an
swer. I was chosen, you see. I was tapped to serve as th
Lord's avenger."

Carefully, avoiding unnecessary noise, Thea struc
the match again. The hot tip seared her fingers. Sh
hurled the flaming missile into the trash bin.

With an explosive whoosh, the turpentine-soake
rags and paper towels burst into shooting spires
flame. The sleeve of the shrink's blouse blossomed wit
fire. The blaze leaped greedily toward her head. Ther
was the stench of charred skin and hair.

Maxine Forman recoiled in horror. Desperately, sh
tried to slap down the rising blaze.

Thea raced to the unconscious detective, knelt besid
him, and shook him by the shoulders. "Get up, Dete
tive."

He stirred, but didn't open his eyes.

"Hurry! We have to get out of here!" she urge

shaking him harder. Dr. Forman dropped to the floor. She was rolling like a storm-tossed boat, trying in vain to douse the flames.

Biederman's eyes fluttered open.

"That's it, Daniel. Get up!" Awkwardly, Thea helped him to his feet, prodding him through the acrid wall of smoke toward the studio door. She was about to follow him outside when a hideous thought stopped her dead.

"Gabby! Are you in here, sweetheart?"

No response.

"Gabby!" Thea heard the terror in her voice.

The flames were spreading. The doctor's furious cries mingled with the crackling roar of the fire which was consuming her. Holding her breath, Thea shoved over the stacked canvases and wrenched open the cabinet doors.

There was no sign of the child.

Oh, dear God, where is my daughter?

Her lungs were aflame; the searing heat raked her skin like cat's claws. Satisfied that Gabby was not in the studio, she bolted.

Gasping, drawing greedy gulps of the sweet air, she slammed the studio door behind her. As she did, the smoke alarm screamed. There was the hissing sound of the sprinkler system. So the lunatic would survive.

The detective was sprawled on the lawn, his face buried in the grass. Leaving him there, Thea ran into the house. She dialed nine-eleven. "Help me," she cried. "Please help me."

"Easy now, ma'am. What do you need? Police, fire, or ambulance?"

"All three."

In a rush, Thea gave the dispatcher the address and phone number and a brief sketch of the circumstances. The man on the line was openly skeptical. Thea

couldn't wait to hear him relay the call over his radic
She slammed down the phone.

She had to find Gabby.

Racing through the ground-floor rooms, she calle
the little girl.

"Gabby? Where are you, sweetie?"

Thea hurried upstairs. Gabby's bedroom door wa
shut.

"Gabby?"

Her heart was thundering. *Please let her be all right*

Holding her breath, Thea turned the knob. Gabb
was laid out on the bed, pale and unmoving.

"Gabby?"

Thea shook the slender body.

No response.

"Gabby, *wake up!*"

The child was limp and weightless.

"You have to be all right," Thea cried. "Please wak
up, sweetie. Please don't take my baby!"

Then, miraculously, she felt a small hand patting he
on the back. Peering up, she saw Gabby's eyelids flut
ter. Tears welled up in Thea's eyes and spilled over. A
long last, the stony dam of her emotions had broken

"Mom? How come you're crying?"

"Oh, sweetie. I'm just so glad you're okay. S
happy."

"And I'm happy you finally came home, Mommy,
the child mumbled drowsily. "I waited and waited fo
you. Now what's the big surprise?"

CHAPTER
FIFTY-SEVEN

He marveled at the mansion. There had to be forty rooms or more. Place probably had fur-lined toilets. Jeweled tubs. Hot and cold running servants. You name it. But did all that make these people happy?

Nowhere close.

Well, he was about to bring a little joy into old lady Gallatin's bitter existence. Frowning ruefully, Max Perry followed the slick-haired butler down the hall to the study.

He knew what he had to do, but that didn't make him like it. Or himself.

The corridor's high, dark walls boasted somber oil renderings of grim Gallatin forebears. An uncanny family resemblance had survived several generations of genetic challenge. Max Perry scowled back at the imperious guises of Great-grandfather Elijah Gallatin and his twin sons: Darwin and Squire.

These people thought they were better than the riffraff, above it all. And if he was their standard of comparison, maybe they were right.

To be fair, it appeared that the arrogant Gallatin attitude was softening. Perry had been pleasantly surprised when he contacted Cassandra Rodbury that morning. The lawyer had invited him to deliver his message in person to Lily Gallatin at the estate. He'd expected the usual anonymous meeting at some deserted outdoor locale. The beach, maybe. Or the eighteenth hole of the municipal course after the final foursome had putted out at dusk. Being asked to the house was a large step in the right direction. But given that he was about to cut bait and bolt, the unaccustomed courtesy didn't count for much.

The butler opened the double doors to the study and motioned him inside. Perry had expected a solitary audience with the old lady and her omnipresent dummy daughter, but her lawyer was waiting as well, not to mention a stranger.

"Sit down, Mr. Perry," Lily Gallatin ordered crisply.

So the old bat knew his name after all. This was the first time she'd deigned to use it. He took the vacant chair in the tapestried Chippendale trio surrounding Lily Gallatin's ornate desk. The mute daughter took her customary place behind her mother.

"Maxwell Perry, meet Brian Delavan," the old woman said in her stony voice.

The stranger's nod was grim. "That's *Buck* Delavan," he corrected. "*Inspector* Buck Delavan. Westport's chief of detectives."

Lily Gallatin's penetrating gaze moved from Perry to the detective and back again. "I wanted both of you here at the same time in order to dispose of this unpleasantness as quickly as possible."

"What unpleasantness?" Delavan asked. "I only did what you hired me to do, Mrs. Gallatin."

"That's incorrect, Inspector. What I engaged you to do was to vindicate my son's murder. I wanted the truth."

"I've got good news for you, then, Mrs. Gallatin," Max Perry chimed in. "I saw Thea Harper last night. She admitted that she remembers the killing now."

Perry knew the alleged confession would be worthless once he beat it out of town. Insupportable hearsay. But it would get the old lady off his case long enough to complete his disappearing act.

"Is that so, Mr. Perry?" she said. Her icy eyes studied him. So did her daughter's.

"Yes. We were talking. I guess her conscience has been bothering her."

Buck Delavan made a sour face.

"Perhaps you'd like to point out the difficulty with Mr. Perry's revelation, Mr. Delavan." Lily Gallatin's wrinkled face was pinched with disdain.

The inspector puffed a breath. "Turns out the Harper woman didn't kill the senator after all. Last night, we got a full confession from the real perp. A shrink named Forman."

"Thea's doctor?" Max Perry remembered the woman from the trial. Starched, stern, too perfect to be fully believable.

And apparently she wasn't.

"Right. The doc confessed to a series of homicides, Senator Gallatin's included. Seems she was trying to murder her dead father. The woman was totally whacko."

"To come to the point, gentlemen. You have both demonstrated an unconscionable willingness to crucify an innocent woman. I instructed you to uncover the facts, and you've both failed miserably."

Her holier-than-thou attitude incensed Max Perry. "All you wanted was Thea Harper's neck, Mrs. Gallatin. That's what you recruited me for."

"Like Inspector Delavan, you are sadly misguided, young man."

"If I was misguided, it was by you and your legal mouthpiece over there," he snapped.

"Are you quite finished?" Lily Gallatin said.

Max Perry didn't bother to answer. They all knew he was finished.

"Inspector Delavan, I plan to discuss your questionable ethics and professional misconduct with my friend Arthur Keenan."

Keenan was Westport's mayor. Delavan's boss and executioner-elect.

"And as for you, Mr. Perry—"

Perry raised his hands in surrender. "Don't bother, Mrs. Gallatin. I know you're planning to turn me over to the feds for that bullshit narcotics charge. Well, the hell with it. After being under your thumb, the federal pen will feel like a vacation."

Lily Gallatin shook her silver head. "Actually, I have no such intentions. If I hadn't known the charges were baseless, I would never have gotten you released or engaged your services in the first place. I did so solely out of admiration for your journalistic talents, Mr. Perry. Had you comported yourself more admirably, I planned to offer you the opportunity to write an authorized biography of my late son."

Perry couldn't believe his ears. All this time, he'd been collecting every possible scrap of information for an unauthorized volume on the Gallatins.

"That's terrific, Mrs. Gallatin. I'd give anything—"

She silenced him with a look. Then she continued. "Unfortunately, by coming here today and spewing those ridiculous lies about Thea Harper, you've changed my mind. Clearly, you are not the sort of person the Gallatin family can trust."

Her mute daughter offered a single nod of agreement. A devilish grin formed on her lips.

"But that's not true, Mrs. Gallatin. I was desperate, that's why I said those things. That's not the way I am. You have to believe me—"

"I don't have to do anything of the sort. Good day, Mr. Perry. Mr. Delavan." Lily Gallatin rose and pressed a buzzer on the wall. The massive emerald on her hand winked with a dead green light. "Frederick will see you both out."

CHAPTER FIFTY-EIGHT

Except for being born, this was the first time Gabby had been a hospital patient. To be honest, she'd always considered hospitals pretty yucky. But this one wasn't so bad.

She'd had one pinchy blood test. Otherwise, she was only here for observation, which meant you had to hang around watching TV while everyone made a big fuss over you.

At mealtime, Mommy brought her favorite foods. Every afternoon, Mrs. Millport visited with the twins and Amber. They came with all sorts of neat stuff to decorate the room.

The kid in the other bed was okay. Her name was Lindy, and she'd been burned in a fire. By now, she only had a couple of bandaged places and a few patches on her arms that looked sunburned. Gabby didn't mind that her roommate was only five and a half. It was sort of fun being older. Gabby got to choose which TV shows they'd watch and decide when it was time to visit the rec room.

On one of their strolls this morning, they'd wandered across a glassed bridge to the other side of the floor. Lindy had been *very* impressed when Gabby spotted Dylan Connable in the lounge and introduced him as a good friend.

Turned out he'd recovered from taking all those pills. Now, he was in the special program Mom had mentioned. After a few months in the hospital, they were going to move him into something called a halfway house. Dylan said he didn't think any of it was going to make a difference. But Gabby noticed he didn't mention death or dead things, not even once.

When the nurse came to kick them out, Dylan promised to come across the glass bridge and visit Gabby in pediatrics. He'd have to make it soon, she told him. First thing tomorrow, she was going home.

CHAPTER FIFTY-NINE

Gabby was erupting with enthusiasm. The child was dressed to kill and full of great expectations. Thea kept her apprehensions to herself. If the day proved disappointing, the child's bubble would be busted soon enough.

The bookstore owner led them through the rows of shelves to the folding table she had set up in the rear. The table was flanked by a blowup of the cover art and two sizeable stacks of the latest great American novel: *Sophie Saves the Day*.

Reviewing the story before submitting it to Pru Whittaker, Thea and Gabby agreed to have Sophie manage her own rescue from the fire. Weird Willy Dillon remained something of a hero in the revised version. He braved the flames to call in the alarm to the fire department. But in the end, it was Sophie herself who doused the conflagration with tubs of melted rocky road and pistachio.

Pru, in her inimitable fashion, had gotten three publishing houses interested in the tale. Thea suspected that the agent had traded on the flurry of publicity surrounding Dr. Forman's arrest and conviction as Connecticut's foremost female serial killer, and the subsequent expressions of regret and apology Thea received from plain folk and luminaries across the country.

But Pru roundly denied the charge. Sophie stood on her own merits, the agent declared.

And now, she would again.

The signing was scheduled to last from 2:00 to 4:00

P.M. Articles publicizing the event had appeared in the
local papers. But despite Gabby's high hopes, Thea
knew that the next couple of hours might prove to be
lonely ones.

How many people would come out in this driving
summer rain to purchase an unknown kid's book by a
team of novice authors? The weather was against them
and so were the odds. Pru, ever the realist, had described the majority of book signings as "deadly." Invite your friends, she'd advised. That way, you're sure
someone will show up.

Which Thea had. And at ten to two, the Millport
clan invaded the place in all their boisterous splendor.
Caro bought five copies of the Sophie book to add to
her already considerable collection. All the kids lined
up for autographs.

"Write 'to my very best friend in the whole world,' "
Opal told Gabby.

"Same for me," Jasmine ordered.

"Wah-wee bes' frien'," Raleigh demanded.

"Dake fen," echoed the baby as he mashed the sodden cookie he'd been munching onto the title page.

Gabby was glowing. "You're all the best," Thea told
them. "Thanks so much for coming to keep us company."

Caro pointed over her shoulder. "Looks like you've
got plenty of company coming, sugar. Come on, kids.
Hurry along so all these other fans can have a turn."

To Gabby's delight, a small queue had formed behind the Millports. By the signing's official start, the
line wound around the horticulture section and spilled
over into arts and crafts. After the initial crush, a steady
stream of people stopped by to purchase the book and
seek the authors' autographs. During a brief lull in the
action, the store manager appeared with a stack of

books that had been preordered over the phone by relatives and neighbors back in Idaho.

Near the four o'clock close, Billie arrived toting an
umbrella and several books she announced she was giving to nieces and nephews. The nurse was in an ebul-
lient mood. After months without a word, Vita
Negrone had finally been located at a private mental
hospital across the New York State border in White
Plains. She'd turned up there on the day she'd wandered
off from Brook Hollow and insisted on being admitted.
Vita had had no trouble at all convincing authorities at
the new place that she was in dire need of their services.

When questioned about the reason for her sudden
departure from Brook Hollow, Vita said she'd been
driven away by the food. "Another meal in that place
would have driven me crazy," she claimed.

Apparently, old Vita wasn't as out of it as people assumed.

The final customer was Daniel Biederman, who had
recently been promoted to chief of detectives.
Biederman had replaced Buck Delavan, who'd agreed to
take a very early retirement.

Thea met Daniel's sheepish smile with a bemused
one of her own.

"Hope I'm not too late to get my signed copies," he
said shyly. His raincoat was drenched; he was dripping
puddles all over the floor.

"I think we can accommodate you, sir. Still raining?"
Thea asked, biting back a laugh.

"Just a drizzle. Would you two ladies happen to be
up for a celebratory ice cream soda at Friendly's?"

The guy was persistent, no question. Over the past
six months, Thea had explained to him countless times
that with her track record, she wasn't ready to even consider a relationship.

But despite her discouragement, he'd hung around,

inveigling himself into Gabby's good graces, making
himself a veritable fixture in their lives.

By now, Thea was accustomed to the big lug. And
she had to admit he was pleasant company. Turned out
they enjoyed the same things: relaxing dinners, con-
certs, old films, long philosophical discussions. Daniel
was reliable, honest, decent, and attractive. And he did
have a terrific sense of humor.

But it was definitely *not* a relationship.

The bookstore owner was closing up. She folded the
signing table and shelved the few remaining books.

"You're welcome to take the posters home if you
like," the woman told Thea.

"Can we really?" Gabby exclaimed. "That's so excellent!"

"I don't know, sweetie. They're awfully big."

"No problem. I'll be glad to carry them for you,"
Biederman volunteered.

"Great, and then we can have that soda at our house
and you can stay for dinner. That's okay, isn't it
Mommy?"

Thea shrugged. "I suppose."

*Anytime you find yourself outdone and outnumbered, best
thing to do is keep still and play along, Checker honey.*

Toting a Sophie poster in each oversized hand,
Biederman walked them out into the soft summer rain.

ABOUT THE AUTHOR

One Last Kiss is Judith Kelman's eighth novel. In addition, she's written articles for major magazines, including *Redboook*, *Glamour*, *Ladies' Home Journal*, and *McCall's*, and for the *New York Times*. Judith Kelman lives in Connecticut with her husband and two sons.